Delores Fossen, a *USA Today* bestselling author, has written over 150 novels, with millions of copies of her books in print worldwide. She's received a Booksellers' Best Award and an *RT* Reviewers' Choice Best Book Award. She was also a finalist for a prestigious *RITA*® Award. You can contact the author through her website at deloresfossen.com

USA Today bestselling author **Barb Han** lives in north Texas with her very own hero-worthy husband, three beautiful children, a spunky golden retriever/standard poodle mix and too many books in her to-read pile. In her downtime, she plays video games and spends much of her time on or around a basketball court. She loves interacting with readers and is grateful for their support. You can reach her at barbhan.com

Discover more at millsandboon.co.uk

MARKED FOR REVENGE

DELORES FOSSEN

TEXAS SCANDAL

BARB HAN

MILLS & BOON

First Published in Great Britain 2023
by Mills & Boon, an imprint of HarperCollins*Publishers* Ltd
1 London Bridge Street, London, SE1 9GF

www.harpercollins.co.uk

HarperCollins*Publishers*
Macken House, 39/40 Mayor Street Upper,
Dublin 1, D01 C9W8, Ireland

Marked for Revenge © 2023 Delores Fossen
Texas Scandal © 2023 Barb Han

ISBN: 978-0-263-30740-5

0923

This book is produced from independently certified FSC™ paper
to ensure responsible forest management.

For more information visit: www.harpercollins.co.uk/green

Printed and Bound in the UK using 100% Renewable Electricity at
CPI Group (UK) Ltd, Croydon, CR0 4YY

MARKED FOR REVENGE

DELORES FOSSEN

Chapter One

Deputy Ava Lawson looked down at the dead woman and saw her own face. Not merely a resemblance.

But literally the image of Ava's own face.

Using a photograph of her printed on thin cloth, the killer had molded it to the dead woman.

Ava couldn't stop the slam of emotion and she had to fight just to be able to breathe. Had to fight to stay steady, too, because this kind of stress wouldn't be good for the baby she was carrying. She was in her fifth month, which meant she wasn't at high risk for a miscarriage but she couldn't take the chance of doing harm to this child.

Even though someone else might want exactly that.

Because if she was the target, then so was her precious baby.

"You okay, Ava?" she heard her boss, Sheriff Theo Sheldon, ask in a murmur. He was standing next to her, taking in the crime scene as she was.

"I'm fine," Ava managed to rasp, both of them knowing it was a lie.

She ran her hand over her stomach and shoved aside the buzzing in her ears. Ava tried to focus on doing her job.

Right now, that job included looking for whatever she could find to get some justice for the dead woman.

And the two other dead women who'd come before this one.

Women who'd all been strangled and left posed in the woods around Silver Creek, Texas, Ava's adopted hometown. A town that relied on its sheriff and deputies to protect it from a killer. Right now, law enforcement was failing at that big-time because women were dying.

Ava swept her gaze around the thick cluster of underbrush and trees. It was spring and everything was in bloom. Wildflowers, trees and the shrubs. It was also still cool enough that she wasn't sweating. Not yet anyway.

Thanks to the spotlights the county CSIs had already set up, she didn't have any trouble taking in the scene despite it being night. Since the site was a good two miles from town, this wasn't exactly on the beaten path, but she could see the drag marks that led from the old ranch trail about ten yards away. If the Silver Creek Sheriff's Office hadn't gotten an *anonymous* 9-1-1 call to tell them the location of the body, the dead woman might never have been found. But, of course, the killer had wanted them to know.

Had wanted *Ava* to know.

He'd wanted her to see that image of herself and get the slam of sick dread that came with the realization she was the reason this was happening. And, worse, that she was no closer to stopping this from happening all over again.

Since the first body had turned up three months earlier, Ava, Theo and the other deputies had put in plenty of extra hours at the office. Plenty. They had pored through every crime scene report of the dead women and followed every lead. Ava had also studied all the files of anyone she'd ever arrested, investigated or confronted. Anyone who had popped up on her radar as conceivably connected to a crime.

Because Silver Creek wasn't that big of a town, the number of files and possible persons of interest wasn't exactly staggering, but she had been a deputy for six years now and, before that, a San Antonio cop for eight. Fourteen years in law enforcement meant she'd had ample opportunity to make enemies and rile people, but so far Ava hadn't been able to connect anyone to what was happening now.

The two other victims had been left with the masks of Ava's face, but there were no other reports of similar crimes in the state. That didn't mean there weren't other murders, though, since the killer could have only started using the masks with these particular victims.

Theo's phone dinged with a text and he muttered some profanity when he read it. "The mayor's heard about the latest murder and he's called in the Texas Rangers."

Ava's head whipped up, her gaze zooming straight to Theo's because she had a bad feeling about this.

"He's called Harley," Theo clarified, showing her the text from the Ranger himself.

Sorry but I've been assigned to your investigation. Will be there soon.

"Good grief," Ava murmured. She didn't need this on top of everything else.

Texas Ranger Harley Ryland. A blast from the past. Both a good and bad one. When she'd been at San Antonio PD, she'd worked with Harley. And had later had a relationship with him, one that had continued as an on-again, off-again kind of deal until five months ago when the off had become permanent.

Things hadn't exactly ended well between them either. Not with Harley being the main reason her scumbag father wasn't in jail. Then, the very day Harley had cleared her dad's name, she'd learned she was pregnant with Harley's child. A child she loved and would raise despite the Texas Ranger being the father. Despite, too, Harley insisting that he would take an active part in parenting the child.

Figuring out how to co-parent with him wouldn't be easy. Ditto for having to work with him again. Along with the tension of being her ex, Harley knew all her past sins and secrets. *All of them.* It was hard to be around someone who had that kind of intimate knowledge about her.

"This is number three," Theo said, drawing her attention back to him—and to the body. "If it's the same guy and not a copycat, we've got a serial killer."

Yes, three was the magic number when it came to earning that particular label. And Ava knew this wasn't a copycat. So did Theo. They hadn't released the specific details of the killer covering the women chin-to-feet with black garbage bags or the cloth photo death masks, and this one appeared to be identical to the other two.

Being careful where she stepped, Ava went closer to watch as the CSI lifted the photo mask from the dead woman's face. Theo cursed again, and Ava knew why. It was because they recognized her.

Monica Howell.

She was a hairdresser at the Sassy Curls Salon just off Main Street. Midthirties, divorced, no kids. But Monica did have parents who lived on a nearby ranch. They were good people and what could be called pillars of the community.

"She wasn't reported missing?" the CSI, Veronica Reyes, asked, looking up at Ava and Theo.

Ava shook her head. If a woman had gone missing anywhere in the tricounty area, the Silver Creek Sheriff's Office would have gotten an alert the moment the report had been filed. That meant Monica's folks, friends and employer hadn't known she'd been taken. That fit, too, with the killer's MO.

The killer didn't keep his victims long. Definitely not long enough to raise any serious red flags about them being missing. From what Theo and she had been able to piece together in the investigation, the other two victims had died less than an hour after they'd last been seen.

"Monica's wearing her work clothes," Theo pointed out when Veronica eased back the black plastic bags from the torso of the body. She was, indeed, since all the salon workers wore powder-blue tops with their names stitched on a breast pocket. "Maybe that means she was grabbed when she was leaving the salon."

"Maybe," Ava agreed, and she mentally went through the handful of businesses in town that had security cameras. None were anywhere near the salon, but that didn't mean the killer's image hadn't been captured.

Obviously, Theo was on the same page as she was. "I'll have the security camera checked from the traffic light on Main Street," Theo said, stepping away no doubt to call whichever deputy was in the office at this hour. "We might get lucky."

Monica certainly hadn't gotten lucky. She'd been brutalized, murdered and then posed here like garbage. Swallowing hard, fighting back the bile rising in her throat, Ava forced herself to steady when she saw the truck pull to a stop behind the CSIs.

Oh, mercy.

What the heck was he doing here? It was Waylon McClintock, the mayor of Silver Creek, and often a thorn in the side of the sheriff's office. Since Waylon was at the crime scene, Ava figured some thorniness was about to start.

Waylon wasn't alone. Ava silently cursed when she spotted the lanky dark-haired man get out of the passenger's side of Waylon's truck.

Harley.

The CSI lights glinted off the Texas Ranger badge pinned to his shirt as he walked toward her. He was all cowboy cop down to the jeans, cream-colored Stetson and cowboy boots. He was even wearing the traditional crisscross double belt holster that some Rangers favored. It made him look like an Old West gunslinger ready to draw down on the bad guys.

"Deputy," Waylon greeted in his usual gruff tone that always seemed to be a mix of rust and gravel. He glanced over at Theo, who was pacing while he talked on the phone.

"Mayor," Ava greeted back, keeping her own tone hard. She shifted her attention to Harley.

Harley's dark brown eyes met hers, and maybe there was an apology in them. Maybe. But, if so, it was brief because he skimmed his gaze over her baby bump. Just a glance before he turned his attention to the body.

"I heard about the murder from the dispatcher," Waylon snarled. "Woulda been nice to have heard it from Theo or you."

"We've been busy," Ava informed him right back. "We came out as soon as we got the call and have been examining the scene. It's Monica Howell," she added. No way to keep the emotion out of her voice, not with this ripping away at her.

Waylon's sigh was long and he squeezed his eyes shut a moment. "Hell, this is gonna bring her mama and daddy to their knees."

It would, indeed, and Theo and she would be making the notification as soon as they finished up here.

"I know I don't need to introduce you to Harley," Waylon added with more than a touch of sarcasm as he tipped his head to Harley. "You can't go wrong with the Texas Rangers, especially since you've found squat so far that'll put a stop to these killings. I want these murders to stop. I want the people of my town to feel safe again."

Waylon seemed to be geared up to add more but he hit the pause button when Theo walked back over to them. Theo nodded a greeting to Harley, who was family to him. Not by blood but in every other way. Theo had been raised by former sheriff Grayson Ryland after Theo's parents had been murdered. Grayson's father, Boone, had adopted Harley and his brothers after marrying their mother.

"You could refuse to work with Harley," Waylon went on, talking to both Theo and Ava now, "but why the hell would you? Let him help you fix this problem before you have to tell somebody else's family that their girl's been murdered by a killer you haven't been able to catch."

The guilt didn't just wash over Ava. It slammed through her. Because Waylon was right about them not having caught the killer. And, worse, Ava was positive she was the link to the killer. Not to Waylon, Theo, or to anybody else involved in this investigation. It was her face on those bodies. She was the connection, and Ava had to believe that, sooner or later, the killer would want to end the game he was playing by coming directly after her.

Waylon's phone rang and, when he stepped aside to take the call, Harley turned to Theo. "This is sort of the devil-you-know kind of a situation," Harley explained. "Waylon has connections, and he arranged for a Ranger to be assigned to this. I figured you'd rather me over someone else."

"I would," Theo assured him, but he glanced at Ava, no doubt to see if she agreed.

Of course, Theo knew about her history with Harley. Plenty of gossip in small towns for folks to know she was carrying Harley's baby. Theo also knew that "history" involved her much-despised father. But Ava wouldn't let that history play into this. Wouldn't let the baby or the old heat between Harley and her play into it either. That's why she nodded to let Theo and Harley know she wasn't going to stonewall when it came to getting any help from this particular Ranger.

Harley nodded as well, and turned his attention back to the dead woman. "Tell me about Monica Howell. I went to school with her, but she was a couple of grades behind me so I didn't really know her. She matches the profiles of the other two victims?"

"Monica was divorced and thirty-four," Theo confirmed, reading from the background info he'd pulled up on his phone. "So, yeah, she fits the profile. Female, single or divorced, no kids, in their thirties."

That was also Ava's profile. Well, almost.

"The first victim, Sandy Russo, had several miscarriages," Ava explained, not looking away when Harley's gaze locked with hers. "The second, Theresa Darnell, also had a miscarriage." She had to pause and gather her breath. "When I talk to Monica's parents, I'll ask them if she'd ever been pregnant."

Ava watched as Harley processed that. Others in town might not know about the piece of her life that didn't fit the MO, but he did. During one of their insomnia-night discussions, she'd told him all about her past.

About the child she'd given up for adoption when she was sixteen.

Even now, twenty years later, Ava felt the pain of that. The shame. The anger that it'd been something her father had forced her to do. But that was an old unhealed wound she didn't have time to soothe right now. One that she couldn't use Harley to help her soothe either. They had to stop this killer because the safety of their child was at stake.

"I'm sorry," she heard Harley say under his breath.

Ava wasn't sure if that was a multipronged apology for the murders or for the baggage she'd always carry for giving up her child.

"Your father talked Waylon into calling the Rangers in on this," Harley added a moment later. "I'm sure your dad would have preferred a Ranger other than me, but he definitely pushed Waylon on this."

Everything inside her went still. Not for long though. The fresh wave of anger punched her as hard as the killer had hit Monica. Her father, State Senator Edgar Lawson, didn't live in Silver Creek. Never had. No, his grand estate was over fifty miles away in an exclusive gated neighborhood in San Antonio. That didn't mean, though, that he wouldn't use his power and influence to try to mess around with her life and career.

"Waylon told you this?" she managed to ask.

Harley shook his head. "I have my own contacts, but I found out your father called Waylon and pushed him to bring in outside *assistance*."

Some people might believe her father had done that to help the Silver Creek Sheriff's Office, to make sure his pregnant daughter didn't end up dead in the woods, but Ava knew that Edgar's motives had nothing to do with love. No. He'd have his own reasons, and she would need to find out what those were.

"Your father might not want any bad publicity from having a string of unsolved murders under your jurisdiction," Harley suggested, obviously reading her expression. "After all, he's up for reelection and the press will definitely point out that you're his daughter."

Yes, it could be something as simple as that, and in Edgar's mind, it was bad enough that his heiress daughter was a career cop. Bad enough that she was unmarried and pregnant and wouldn't play the part of being devoted to him so as to help him keep his seat in the Texas senate. But *bad* would be multiplied many times over when the media continued to point out that the senator's daughter hadn't been able to stop a killer who was terrorizing the town where she was a deputy.

A killer who had to be connected to her since the snake was covering the dead women's faces with her photo.

"We have a problem," she heard Veronica call out. The CSI got up and practically ran away from the body.

"What's wrong?" Theo and Harley asked in unison.

"We need to evacuate the scene and get a bomb squad out here right now," Veronica blurted. "There's a bomb beneath the body."

Chapter Two

When Harley had gone to the latest crime scene, he hadn't expected to be chased out of the area because of a bomb. But that's exactly what'd happened. Ava, he and the rest of the responders had been forced to evacuate and hope like hell that they didn't get killed in an explosion the killer had set up.

Harley had had the additional fear of Ava and the baby being hurt. Thankfully, though, they'd all gotten safely out of there so the bomb squad could be called in to do their job. Then Harley had gotten on with doing his.

For starters, Harley knew he really needed to take a harder look at the area where the killer had dumped this latest body. He also needed to find some evidence and find it fast because he wasn't sure how much time they had before the killer struck again.

Correction—how much time Ava had.

A thought that tightened every muscle in his body.

Because Ava was pregnant, it meant she didn't precisely fit the profile of the other murdered women, but it was obvious the killer had "involved her" by using her face on the masks. Maybe the fact Ava was pregnant didn't play into this sick plan. Or the pregnancy could be at the core of it. It was something he needed to try to work out and fast.

And that's exactly what Harley was trying to do now.

Sipping coffee that was strong and bitter enough to burn a hole in his stomach, Harley sat in the chair next to Ava's desk in the Silver Creek Sheriff's Office and waited for Ava and Theo to return. A wait he wasn't sure how long would last, but he was using the time to study the files on the previous two murders.

Harley practically had the entire building to himself tonight since Waylon thankfully hadn't accompanied him to the sheriff's office. No reason for it. Waylon had already gotten what was no doubt his cheap thrill for the night by reminding Theo, and Ava, that he had plenty of power in town. Not that his power was ever in dispute. He had it. Money, too. And apparently the man had enough allies to keep his butt firmly planted in the mayor's seat.

Harley glanced up when the phone rang and he halfway listened when Deputy Diana Warner took the call. Other than Harley, she was the sole occupant of the building, and was working Dispatch and doing what appeared to be a mountain of paperwork. The other deputies were no doubt out in the field, trying to track down any leads on the killer.

The call seemed to be about some cattle breaking fence and getting on the road, so Harley tuned it out and went back to the files. And to waiting.

After Theo and Ava had been told it could be hours before a bomb squad showed up and cleared the explosive, Ava and Theo had left to drive to Monica's parents to tell them of their daughter's murder. Neither Ava nor Theo had invited him to go along with them, and Harley hadn't pressed. Ava already had enough blows to handle tonight without him adding more, even though he would have liked to get in a question or two with the dead woman's parents. That way, he might be able to figure out why the killer had left explosives under her body.

There'd certainly been no other such devices near the other two dead women, and it was always a flashing red light when a murderer changed his MO. Of course, maybe the killer was still evolving, still creating a signature that some predators had. The MO was a given in a crime, but not every serial killer had a signature.

This one did though.

The facial beatings, posing the bodies, the locations of the dumpsites, drugging the victims. And, of course, the cloth masks. The ones of Ava's face.

Yeah, this killer had a very sick signature.

Harley suspected that seeing those masks was giving Ava some nightmares. But that was just the tip of the iceberg. She was a veteran cop. A good one. And she had to know that, one way or another, this executioner had her in his sights. That twisted at Harley, too, because he doubted the killer would give any consideration to the fact that Ava was pregnant.

In fact, the pregnancy might be a motive for the murders.

No way could he ignore the fact that the murders had started three months ago, right about the time Ava was letting people, including Harley, know she was pregnant. So far, this sick SOB had seemingly gone after women who'd lost babies, and maybe that's what the killer wanted in store for Ava. Harley had to make damn sure that didn't happen.

Because Ava had shared the ultrasound results with him, he knew she was carrying a girl. A daughter. Before Ava had told him she was pregnant, Harley had never actually considered fatherhood, but he was more than considering it now. He wanted his baby girl in his life, wanted to be the best possible father he could be, and that started with keeping Ava and her safe.

He glanced up from his laptop again when the front door opened. Since he was sitting in the open-bay bullpen, Harley had no trouble spotting Ava and Theo as they came in. He also had no trouble spotting just how much of a toll the notification had taken. They looked weary and exhausted.

"I need to call the bomb squad and push for some answers on what the heck is going on," Theo said to him, "but Ava can go ahead and update you on what we do have." He headed into his office.

"How rough was the notification?" Harley asked.

Ava nodded and sank down in her desk chair. "Rough." She squeezed her eyes shut a moment. "I really need to stop this guy."

Yeah, and he figured some of that need was because the crimes were personal in that they were linked to Ava. Unfortunately, Harley had read nothing in the case files to indicate what exactly that link was.

"Monica had a miscarriage when she was married," Ava added a moment later.

"So, that fits with the other victims." He waited until her gaze came back to his and then leaned in and lowered his voice to a whisper. "How many people know you had a child when you were a teenager?"

Her mouth tightened a little. "Only a handful who are still living. You, my father, the baby's father and Duran Davidson."

No need for her to spell out that Duran was her father's close friend along with being his campaign manager. Harley suspected Duran had done all sorts of things for his boss. Maybe even covered up a crime or two.

Ava sighed. "I gave birth to the baby in Dallas under an

alias that my father had set up, but the housekeepers might have overheard something. If there was gossip, though, it didn't get back to me."

It was possible Edgar had paid off the staff to stay quiet. But money didn't always buy silence. After all these years, someone could have spilled Ava's secret.

"How long were you in Dallas before the baby was born?" Harley asked, hoping it would spur her to aim her thoughts in that direction. It wasn't necessarily the right direction though. The murders could be connected to something much more recent in Ava's life, like her pregnancy, but it was ground that needed to be covered.

"Four and a half months," Ava answered. "Before I started showing, my father arranged for me to stay with Duran's grandparents, who owned a ranch outside Dallas. Then he told everyone I was doing a student exchange program in Ireland for six months. The grandparents died years ago, and they would have never gone against my father. They kept quiet about my pregnancy and the baby."

Maybe, but all it would take was one slip of the tongue and people would know the senator had a pregnant teenage daughter. Still, Harley couldn't see how such a slip would come back to the murders. If Ava was the key, and he was positive she was, then there had to be a trigger that'd gotten all of this started.

"How about the baby's father?" Harley pressed, still keeping his voice low so the deputy wouldn't overhear. "Would he have told someone?"

She took a moment, obviously processing that. "It's possible. I haven't seen or heard from him since my father whisked me away in secret to Dallas, but his name is Aaron Walsh." Ava paused again. "After the first murder, I ran a background check on him." She typed in something on her laptop, pulled up a file, and turned the screen so he could read it.

It only took a glance for Harley to see that Aaron Walsh hadn't exactly led a charmed life. Orphaned at a young age and brought up in foster care, he was two years older than Ava, which meant he would have been eighteen when she got pregnant.

During that "too much to drink" confession, Ava had said her father had threatened Aaron with jail time to force her into giving up the baby for adoption. Her father had also used that jail time threat to basically run Aaron out of San Antonio and force the young man's silence. But since the statute of limitations would have played into this at the seven-year point, how had Edgar made sure that Ava's lover would stay quiet?

That was a question he'd ask Edgar, and Harley didn't think the man was going to like having the past tossed in his face.

Harley kept reading from the background check on Aaron. Shortly after Aaron had left San Antonio, he'd done a six-month stint in jail for auto theft. He'd stayed clean behind bars and had gotten an early release. After that, he'd done two more years on parole. And that was it. Nothing else in the background.

"I haven't been able to find anything else on Aaron," Ava explained. "He didn't put in for a legal name change, but it's possible he moved and just started using an alias. Or he could have stolen the identity he's using."

Yeah. Harley mentally played with that for a couple of moments. Maybe the jail time and experience with Ava's father had left Aaron bitter enough to disappear.

Or to kill.

"If it is Aaron who's doing this, why wait twenty years

to start killing?" Harley muttered, hoping that by saying it aloud, a good theory would come to him. But he came up with nothing.

Ava shook her head. "I told Theo about my former boy-friends, including Aaron. I didn't tell him about the baby," she quickly added. "But I briefed Theo on anyone from my past who could play into this." She paused. "Now, I need to tell him that I had a child. Until tonight, I wasn't sure a pregnancy or baby was part of the profile. I mean the others had had miscarriages, but I never did."

Harley picked up on that thread. "You were thinking more along the lines of someone tormenting you because you'd failed to get justice or had gotten justice that was a trigger for the killer to go after you?"

"Yes. And that might still be what this is. I don't want to dismiss it in case the killer is using my face on those masks as some kind of diversion to throw us off his scent." She paused. Probably had to, because all of this was no doubt hitting her hard. "But with the third victim having had a miscarriage, there's a strong possibility that it's connected."

Harley made a sound of agreement but didn't add more because Deputy Diana Warner walked past them, heading to Theo's office with some call memos.

"Any reason you didn't run for sheriff when my uncle Grayson retired?" Harley asked Ava while he glanced around the bullpen. Better to switch to a less personal topic with Diana in hearing range. "You're the most experienced deputy."

"Because I dislike paperwork and politics." Ava shrugged. "Plus, Theo's a lot better as sheriff than I'd ever be."

Harley figured that was true about Theo, who had a way of soothing ruffled feathers while still staying in control of a situation. Theo was born to be a cop, and so was Ava.

Ironic, since she was practically Texas royalty. Four generations of state senators, congressmen, judges, etcetera. Four generations of old money that had added even more money to the family coffers. Harley figured her ancestors were shaking their heads over why she'd want to ditch all of that and pin on a badge.

She opened her mouth to say something else but obviously rethought it when Diana returned from Theo's office and passed by them again. "You'll be staying with your folks at the family ranch?" she asked him instead.

Harley nodded, though the term *family ranch* wasn't an adequate description. It was more of a sprawling estate with an equally sprawling ranch and multiple homes for the three generations of the still-growing Ryland clan. Many of his siblings and cousins lived there.

"Mom's baking and Dad wants us to go fishing," Harley added to the conversation. He probably wouldn't have time for a fishing trip, but he needed to carve out a few hours with his folks. His adoptive dad, Boone, was in his eighties now, so Harley needed to make more of an effort to be with him and his mom.

Theo was finishing up a phone call when he finally came out of his office and made a beeline toward them while slipping his phone into the pocket of his jeans. "The bomb wasn't active. It was the real deal with enough explosives to take out anyone within ten feet of the body, but there was no timer or switch to detonate it."

"So why put it there?" Harley had to ask.

Theo shook his head and, in a weary gesture, he scrubbed his hand over his face. "Maybe just to add another layer of fear."

Maybe. The killer was definitely playing games with them. "The Ranger lab might be able to find out if the bomb has a signature." A long shot, especially considering the killer hadn't used such a device before. Still, he'd either made it himself or gotten it from someone who could have left a signature with other bombs.

"Mind if we go into your office?" Ava asked Theo. "There's something I need to tell you."

Theo stared at her a moment before shifting his gaze to Harley. Then he nodded and motioned for them to follow him. However, they'd only made it a few steps before the front door flew open and the visitors stormed in.

The operative words being *flew* and *stormed*.

Senator Edgar Lawson entered, followed by Duran Davidson, and they brought with them an urgency that seemed to radiate off them in thick, hot waves.

"Ava," Edgar immediately said. There was plenty of concern in his voice, but Harley wasn't sure how genuine it was.

Edgar was one of those people who had a powerful presence just by coming into a room. That was in part because of his size. He was six-foot-four. And, even though he was in his sixties, he still sported the body that had earned him plenty of accolades back in the day when he'd been a college football star. He modeled the good-ol'-boy looks, too, which he no doubt kept fresh with the occasional plastic surgery that made him look a good decade younger.

Duran was a different story and had a presence of a totally different kind. Lanky to the point of being bony, with sharp features and ink-black hair that only emphasized his too-pale skin. His movements were jerky, clumsy and he always seemed to be on the verge of tripping over his own feet. Or apologizing. Harley had discovered the man was good at that. Placating, apologizing, groveling or doing whatever it took to keep his boss in a favorable limelight.

Harley didn't trust either of them one little bit.

And, despite Duran's wimpy demeanor, Harley suspected the man was capable of just about anything. He'd have to be to have stayed this close to Edgar for all this time.

Edgar slid his gaze over them and scowled when his attention landed on Ava's stomach. Publicly, Edgar had played up the fact that he'd soon be a grandfather, but Harley figured the man despised him for getting Ava pregnant. Worse, Edgar couldn't shove Harley out of the picture the way he had Aaron. That almost certainly overrode Edgar's feelings of gratitude over Harley's part in keeping him out of jail. If the man had such feelings, that is. Edgar might have dismissed it as Harley simply doing his job.

"I heard about the latest murder," Edgar said, aiming his comment not at Ava or Theo but at Harley. "And I want to know what the heck you're doing about it. My daughter is obviously in danger."

"Your daughter is a cop who can take care of herself," Ava snarled, and she added a huff to that. "We're in the middle of an investigation, so unless you have pertinent info, you need to leave."

Well, that took care of Edgar's concerned look. His eyes didn't narrow. His jaw didn't go stiff. But Harley detected some anger simmering behind that oily façade.

"As a matter of fact, I do have something," Edgar said, matching his daughter's tone with one that was just a tad too sappy-sweet. He motioned toward Duran, who handed a thick manila envelope to Harley. Or rather, he tried to do that. Harley didn't take it.

Instead, Harley hitched his thumb to Theo. "He's the sheriff and the one in charge of this investigation."

Oh, that didn't set well with Edgar, and Harley added a checkmark on his mental chart of ways to rile the senator. Yeah, it was petty, but Harley didn't like being played, and he was certain that's what Edgar was doing now. And what he'd actually done with the investigation where Harley had been forced to clear the man's name.

Edgar gave Duran a subtle nod, which must have been a green light because he handed Theo the envelope. "Those are copies of the senator's threat files. The more recent ones," he clarified when Theo made a show of looking at the thickness of the envelope.

"I shouldn't have to tell you to keep those private," Edgar interjected. "No need to give mean, ugly people any more attention than they deserve. I just wanted you to have it in case it connects in some way to the murders."

"Why would you think the killer would have any connection to you?" Harley asked.

Edgar opened his mouth, closed it and obviously rethought what he'd been about to say. "I know about the masks the sick bastard puts on the victims. I know it's my daughter's face."

Ava groaned, and Harley muttered some profanity under his breath.

"That info wasn't released to the public," Theo quickly pointed out.

"I'm not the public," Edgar fired back. "If the murders are linked to Ava, then they could be linked to me, linked to something in those files," he added, tipping his head to the envelope. "Somebody might be trying to cause trouble for me and the campaign by creating havoc in the county that Ava has decided to call home."

"Do you have someone specific in mind?" Theo asked. "A political adversary? A riled lover?"

"I don't have a riled lover," Edgar quickly noted, "and my opponent probably wouldn't go to such lengths."

Harley would check on both of those possibilities, but he

already had some info on the "lover" part. When he'd been spearheading the investigation that'd dealt with Edgar possibly being involved in black-market land sales, Harley had had to interview Valerie Chandler, the widowed socialite who'd been Edgar's companion for going on two decades. Edgar had started appearing in public with the woman several years after Ava's mother had been killed in a car accident when Ava had been just eight.

"This is costing Edgar votes," Duran piped in. "With each murder, he's taken a dip in the polls."

Ava groaned and threw her hands up in the air. "Pardon me if I'm more worried about three women being dead more than I am poll rankings."

"I'm worried, too. Worried about you and my grandchild. About me," Edgar admitted. "About the election. Do something to find this killer and stop him," he snarled while he volleyed glances to Harley and Theo. Not to Ava though. He obviously didn't have a lot of faith in his daughter's cop skills.

Theo's phone rang and he muttered, "I have to take this," when he looked at the screen. Tucking the envelope under his arm, he went to his office.

Edgar, and therefore Duran, turned to leave, but Harley stepped in front of them. "When's the last time you heard from Aaron Walsh?" Harley asked, keeping his voice low since Diana was back at the dispatch desk.

Now, Edgar's eyes narrowed and he aimed a strong shot of venom at Ava. "You told him?"

"I did," she readily confirmed, stepping to Harley's side. "Answer the question."

Edgar kept up the steely glare for several snail-crawling moments before he finally snarled, "I haven't seen or spoken to that worthless piece of trash in twenty years. But I have kept tabs on him."

"Tabs?" Harley and Ava questioned in unison.

"I have a PI assigned to keep an eye on him, to make sure he doesn't try to worm his way back into my daughter's life."

Ava exchanged a glance with Harley before she said anything. "So, you know where Aaron is?" she asked her father.

"I did. He was living in Bulverde, using the name Eddie Walker, until about seven months ago. His live-in girlfriend died of an overdose and he disappeared. The PI hasn't been able to find him since, though he's had reports that Aaron is still in the Bulverde area."

Harley huffed. "And you didn't think it was relevant to tell someone this? Bulverde is only a thirty-minute drive from Silver Creek."

"No, it wasn't relevant," Edgar snapped. "That man doesn't have anything to do…" He stopped and obviously clued in to why Aaron's whereabouts would be important.

"We'll want any and all info you have on Aaron Walsh," Ava insisted.

That brought on a fresh glare from her father. "Any and all info that'll remain private."

She shook her head. "I can't guarantee that. If Aaron is a killer, his history with me will have to come out."

It was the truth, but it was fuel to an already hot fire, and Edgar looked ready to explode. Duran must have thought so, too, because he nudged Edgar and tipped his head to Diana, a reminder to his boss that this conversation could be overheard.

The fit of temper stayed in Edgar's eyes, but he did lower his voice and aim his index finger at Harley. "I pushed to get the Rangers brought in on this. I can push to have you removed from this investigation."

Harley looked the man straight in the eye. "Go ahead, push. See where it gets you. I'm on this investigation whether in an official capacity or not. And I won't obstruct justice by concealing evidence that might save lives. It might save your butt in the polls, too," he reminded the man.

Apparently, Edgar decided he couldn't argue with that. Or rather, that he didn't intend to verbally argue anyway. Maybe that was because of Diana's presence or because Theo was making his way back toward them.

"This isn't over," Edgar murmured like a threat as the two men went out with the same speed and intensity as they'd entered.

Harley was about to explain what had caused the pair's hasty exit, but then he looked at Theo's expression. Oh, hell. What now?

"Once the bomb was removed," Theo said, starting that with a heavy sigh, "the CSIs found a note beneath it." He lifted his phone screen for them to see.

Harley repeated that "Oh, hell," but this time it was aloud. Ava didn't say anything. She merely stared at the screen. At the words written on the note.

This is all for you, Mom.

Chapter Three

Ava's throat clamped shut and she couldn't breathe. Couldn't move. Couldn't speak. She just stood there and felt the words stab out at her.

This is all for you, Mom.

"In my office, now," Theo insisted. Not in a demand-for-answers sort of way but rather with mountains of concern. That was probably because she looked ready to drop to the floor.

Harley hooked his arm around her waist to steady her and to get her moving. Good thing, too, since she wasn't sure she could have managed to take a single step on her own.

Oh, God.

Was the child she'd given birth to all those years ago actually responsible for this? Ava's mind wouldn't process the answer.

Theo shut the door once they were in his office and went to the fridge to get her a bottle of water while Harley helped her to a chair. She nearly asked Harley to fill Theo in on what the note meant, but Ava forced herself to steel up. She was a deputy, for heaven's sake, and she could do this. She gulped down some water and looked up at her boss.

"When I was sixteen, I had a baby. A boy," she managed to add, "and I gave him up for adoption."

"Edgar forced her to do that," Harley supplied. "And he also forced her to keep the pregnancy a secret."

Dragging in a long breath, Theo sank down into his chair, putting himself at eye level with her. "That means the child would be nineteen or twenty now?"

"Twenty," she confirmed. Twenty years, two months and four days.

She could have given him the hour had it been necessary.

Ava paused again, drank some more water and continued. "It was a closed, private adoption, but after I became a cop, I managed to get hold of the records." And she hoped Theo didn't ask how she'd managed that. "He was adopted by Megan and Gene Franklin, both teachers, from Kerrville. They got him when he was two days old, and they named him Caleb James."

It was the first time Ava had allowed herself to say his name out loud. Her son's name. Except he wasn't hers. Never had been because she'd never even been allowed to hold him. Per her father's orders, the baby had been whisked away from her only seconds after he'd drawn his first breath.

"I should point out that Caleb probably isn't the actual killer," Harley said. "If he was doing this, why point a huge neon arrow at himself?"

Ava latched onto that like a lifeline. The note was basically a confession—if Caleb was the killer, that is. But if he'd wanted to confess, why not just come to the source? To her. So, this meant someone had set him up, had wanted her to believe that Caleb might be killing because of her.

"You've met Caleb and the Franklins?" Theo asked, drawing her attention back to him.

She shook her head. "No, but I've seen a couple of pictures of them on social media. Not many, but I recall a few years back, they celebrated their thirtieth wedding anniversary. Caleb's a criminal justice major at University of Texas."

That was in Austin, less than an hour from Silver Creek, where the murdered women had been dumped.

That caused Ava to groan. Cops looked at means, motive and opportunity when it came to identifying a criminal. The opportunity could have been there since Caleb lived so close, and the person who'd set him up would know that. Except there was something else. Something Ava didn't want to consider but had to.

That Caleb had used the note as a way to make them believe he was innocent.

A sort of reverse psychology. One that would involve him in the investigation where he might have an easier time getting to her. So he could kill her.

"Is Caleb's bio father in the picture?" Theo pressed.

"Not if he listened to my father's threats, he isn't." Ava didn't bother mincing words that might have painted Edgar in a better light. "His name is Aaron Walsh, but he's apparently been using the name Eddie Walker. My father threatened him with jail time if he didn't disappear, so that's what he did. I just learned my father has had a PI keeping an eye on him. We should have the PI records soon." If not, she'd have a *conversation* with her dad.

"I'll go ahead and order a background check on him and the alias," Theo said, shifting his attention to his laptop. While he typed in the request, Ava gave him Aaron's birthdate and the address where he'd lived when they'd dated.

"If Aaron was run out of town," Theo went on after he'd finished the request, "it's possible he's holding a grudge.

Maybe against Edgar. Maybe against you, too," he added to Ava.

Harley made a sound of agreement. "And according to Edgar, Aaron's girlfriend died of an overdose about a year ago. That could be the trigger that got him to start planning and executing the murders."

The icy chill went through Ava, skin to bone. It was something she should have considered right off—and she probably would have had the note not put an F-5 tornado in her head.

"All right, we'll locate Aaron and bring him in for questioning," Theo continued. "Give me the names of anyone else who knew that you'd had a child."

"Harley and I were going over that when we were in the bullpen," Ava said. "The only living people are my father, Duran, Harley, me and now you. The couple I lived with when I was pregnant have both passed away. So has the doctor who delivered the baby."

"Passed away of natural causes?" Theo asked, obviously latching right onto the possibility of foul play.

"Yes. I checked," Ava assured him. She glanced at Harley. "Because I know my father is capable of pretty much anything and can't be trusted."

Harley didn't wince, didn't dodge her gaze, either, but he had to know she'd just sent a zing his way. "I agree with you," he readily admitted. "But Edgar was set up for those black-market land deals, and I had no choice but to drop the investigation."

Theo turned to Harley. "I remember you mentioning that. It happened…when, about six months ago?"

"Five months," Harley verified. Since Theo knew that Ava was five months pregnant and the baby was Harley's, he could no doubt figure out why Ava and he had split.

And that was something else Ava had yet to consider. Even though it was a bitter pill to swallow, she had to accept that her father had undeniably been innocent and framed, and that meant there was someone out there who wanted to ruin Edgar. Maybe it had escalated into the murders because going after her could be a way to get back at Edgar.

"I can check my father's alibis for the times of the murders," she suggested. "Because if it is someone trying again to set him up, we could use the alibis to establish his innocence. If we make that public, it could stop someone else from being killed."

Of course, that was a long shot, but it was something they needed to at least consider. A big problem, though, would be getting her father to agree to it. He likely wouldn't want it known that he was possibly the reason these murders were happening.

"At my father's insistence, I used an alias when I was pregnant and delivered the baby," Ava continued. "There are medical records under that name Alyssa Monroe. I don't think there's anything in them, though, that could link back to me, but we should take a closer look just in case."

Theo nodded and jotted down the name. "Have you gotten any messages or threats over the years that have to do with the child you gave up?"

"No." She didn't have to search her memory for that particular answer. If someone had contacted her about Caleb or Aaron, she would have remembered.

Another nod from Theo. This time, he leaned back in his chair. "What do you think Caleb would have done if he'd found out he's adopted and you're his birth mother? A birth mother who's now pregnant and intends on keeping her child?"

This time, she had to pause, and then she shook her head.

"I don't have a clue because I don't know him. I don't know his adoptive parents, either, and don't have any idea how they'd react if they knew a senator's daughter had given birth to their son."

But it was definitely something to think about, and Ava had already gotten started on that thinking when her phone dinged. It was a short text from Duran.

"The PI just emailed the sheriff the info on Aaron Walsh," Ava relayed.

Ava immediately showed the text to Harley and Theo, and Theo went to his emails while Harley and she positioned themselves behind him so they could see the laptop screen. When Theo opened the file, she was shocked to see that it was over a thousand pages of reports.

"Well," Theo muttered, "this surveillance has obviously been going on a while."

It had been indeed and had started the same week Aaron had left San Antonio, and Ava. Theo quickly scanned through the years until he got to the most recent ones where Aaron had been living in Bulverde as Eddie Walker.

There was an attached coroner's report of his girlfriend's death that Ava would want to take a look at later but, for now, they focused on the PI's latest attempts to find Aaron. The PI had highlighted the name and phone number of the dead girlfriend's sister, Marnie Dunbar, who also lived in Bulverde, and he had added a note that he was certain Marnie knew Aaron's whereabouts.

Ava checked the time. It was close to midnight, late to be making a call, but she didn't want to wait until morning. Obviously, Theo thought so as well, because he took out his phone, pressed in the number and put the call on speaker. It took four rings, but someone finally answered.

"Yeah?" the woman said, sounding very groggy. No surprise there. She'd probably been asleep.

"I'm Sheriff Theo Sheldon," Theo greeted, "and I'm sorry to bother you. Are you Marnie Dunbar?"

"Yeah," she repeated. "Why are you asking?"

"I'm trying to track down Aaron Walsh, aka Eddie Walker."

There was a groan followed by a huff. "What do you want with him?" Marnie snapped. The grogginess was gone and Ava knew defensiveness when she heard it. What Ava didn't hear was any kind of surprise over Aaron using an alias.

"I just need to talk to him," Theo assured her. "Do you have a contact number, or can you tell me how to reach him?"

"No, I can't—"

"I'm a friend of Aaron's," Ava interrupted because she knew the woman was within a fraction of a second of ending the call. "It's important we talk to him because he could be in danger," she lied.

Well, maybe it was a lie. They didn't know how, or if, Aaron fit into the picture.

"Danger how, why?" The woman was no longer defensive or riled, but she didn't seem overly worried either.

"I'm sorry, but I can't give you the specifics of an active investigation," Ava insisted. "We just need to find him and make sure he's okay."

There was a long silence. "You're really his friend?" she asked.

"I was. I'm Ava Lawson. Maybe you heard him mention me."

"No, I don't think so. How do you know him?"

Ava decided to go with a piece of the truth. "We went to school together. He was my boyfriend."

Another silence. "You're the rich girl he dated."

"Yes," Ava answered after a pause of her own. "He mentioned me?"

"He told Christina—that's my sister—that he'd gotten messed up over some rich girl back in high school. I'm guessing you two had a bad breakup or something?"

"Or something," Ava muttered. It didn't surprise her that Aaron had gotten "messed up" over her. Or more specifically, over their situation of her being pregnant with his child. She had certainly been in the messed-up category, too. "How is Aaron?"

"He's a train wreck right now. Correction, he's been a train wreck since I've known him. In fact, I don't have a whole lot of love for the SOB, and I think Christina would still be alive if she hadn't gotten mixed up with him."

"Oh?" Ava settled for saying, hoping it would spur the woman to continue. It did.

"Yeah, Christina wanted to marry him and start a family."

That caused Ava's breath to stall a little and she braced herself in case Christina was about to admit that Aaron had confessed to her that he had a child. But she didn't.

"My sister just couldn't see the bad in him," Marnie added.

"What kind of bad?" Ava pressed. "Drugs?"

Marnie groaned. Then cursed. "He didn't use drugs, not that I know of. He used my sister. He'd go off drinking with his friends and wouldn't come back for days. When she would get mad, he'd try to put it all on her, telling her if she'd quit nagging him, he wouldn't have to drink." She paused. "But I will say when Christina died, it just about ripped him to pieces. He fell apart at the funeral."

Maybe it'd done enough *ripping* to set Aaron on the path to murder.

"Christina had a drug problem?" Ava asked, hoping to get more insight into what had gone on.

"No." Marnie paused, cursed, then groaned. "Okay, so she used every now and then, but she got a bad batch or something, and it caused her heart to stop. Aaron was at work and didn't find her for hours."

"I'm sorry," Ava said and hoped it didn't sound too abrupt to move on to the next question. "What kind of work does Aaron do these days?"

"He's a mechanic," the woman readily answered. "A decent one from what I hear. When he's sober, he can build just about anything."

Ava wondered if that included a bomb. Yes, she really needed to have a chat with Aaron all right.

"You said Aaron might be in some kind of danger?" Marnie continued a moment later. "Is that because of Christina's death?"

"Maybe," Ava settled for saying. "We're looking into some possibilities. Was anyone arrested for supplying the drugs to your sister?"

"No. We don't know who she bought them from. Aaron asked around, of course, but if he ever got a name, he didn't tell me." She made a grumbling sound. "You don't think the drug dealer is after him, do you?"

Ava went with a safe answer that would hopefully get the woman to cooperate. "Like I said, we're looking into that possibility. Do you have his number so I can talk to him about it?"

Marnie groaned again, and Ava could practically see the woman biting her lip while she mentally debated what to do. "Even though he didn't always treat my sister right, she loved him, and I wouldn't feel right just giving you his number what with you being a cop and all. But I'll call him and let him know you're looking for him. You said your name was Ava Larson?"

"Lawson," Ava corrected. "Take down my number," she added and waited for Marnie to give her the go-ahead to do that before rattling it off. Then, Ava tried to imagine how Aaron would react when he learned she was looking for him. "Tell him it's about what happened when he was eighteen," she added.

Maybe that would stir Aaron's curiosity enough for him to call her. Of course, if he was the killer, he might be waiting for contact like this. Might even welcome it.

"I will," Marnie assured her and paused again. "If he really is in some kind of danger, you intend to make sure he stays safe?"

"We'll try," she said and ended the call. Again, it was a lie because if Aaron was the killer, keeping him safe was the last thing Ava intended. However, she would make sure he was locked up so he couldn't hurt or kill anyone else.

It was hard for her to wrap her mind around the fact that her high school boyfriend, who'd been her first lover, was now a down and broken man. Then again, her father had had a good start on breaking Aaron so maybe that was playing into this. Payback that would strike out at her father and her, and Aaron might consider the other dead women collateral damage.

"I'll record the conversation if Aaron calls me," Ava told Harley and Theo. "In the meantime, maybe we can get someone to Bulverde to press Marnie on his whereabouts."

"The Rangers can handle that," Harley said. "I can get someone from the San Antonio office to go to her place."

"Do it," Theo said with a nod, and he waited for Harley to send a text before he turned back to Ava.

She saw the not-so-subtle shift of emotion in Theo's eyes. There was worry and concern, and Ava knew it was for her.

For what he was about to tell her.

"Get some rest," Theo instructed. "Both of you," he added to Harley. "You'll be staying with Ava tonight?"

Ava was about to nix that, but then it occurred to her that if Aaron or Caleb was behind these murders, then she was definitely in danger. That meant so was the baby. She didn't especially want Harley as an overnight guest, but she also didn't want to take any unnecessary risks. Not having readily available backup would definitely be a risk.

Harley looked at her, no doubt waiting to see if she was going to issue him an invitation to stay with her. She sighed then nodded.

"Good," Theo said. "Get some sleep. Then, first thing in the morning, we'll drive into San Antonio." He looked Ava straight in the eyes. "I want Harley and you with me when I interview your son."

Chapter Four

Harley knew he was on shaky ground by going to Ava's house with her, but, thankfully, she hadn't protested. Well, she hadn't with words anyway, though he could see the disapproval in every inch of her body language.

Hell, he'd disapprove, too, if he were in her shoes. But Ava was a smart cop and she understood the bottom line here.

Their child was in danger.

It didn't matter that Ava and he weren't on the best of terms. Didn't matter, either, that those terms might stay bad. Both of them loved their unborn baby and would do whatever was necessary to keep her safe.

While Ava drove them from the sheriff's office to her house, Harley focused on the list that Duran had sent them. Possible candidates for those wanting to use Ava to get back at Edgar. Harley didn't think the killer's name would be listed there, but since it was a possibility, it had to be checked.

"I might be able to get through that faster than you since it's possible I'm already familiar with some of the names," Ava commented, glancing over at him. Glancing, too, at the road, as Harley was doing. Both of them were keeping watch of their surroundings to make sure they weren't about to be attacked.

"I'll half it with you," Harley offered after he gave it some thought. "Ditto for halving the list we'll no doubt get from the bomb squad once they have a signature of who could have made that bomb."

"Yes," she murmured, and he heard the other emotions snaking beneath that one-word response. That's because she was no doubt thinking of what had been on that note beneath the bomb.

This is all for you, Mom.

Without Ava's picture on the masks, Harley could have reasoned that the killer was going after women he was punishing for something his mother had done or hadn't done. But that mask either meant Ava was the mom figure in this scenario or else that's what the killer wanted them to believe.

That meant...well, anything.

Because if the killer was only using Ava to throw them off his scent, then the murders could be about anything, including any and all connections to anyone in Silver Creek. Or to her father. Or, hell, to anyone else for that matter.

Harley wasn't able to bite back the grumbled profanity over the frustration that they had three dead women and no answers that would get them closer to stopping this sick SOB before he went after someone else.

Ava turned into the driveway of her house and Harley was glad to see the security lights flare on as her vehicle approached. He knew, too, that she had a good security system that would have alerted her had anyone tried to break in. Still, systems could and did fail, so they couldn't let down their guard.

She used the remote on her visor to open the garage door and neither of them got out until the door closed behind them. Neither actually removed their guns from their holsters, but they placed their hands over them.

Ava stepped in first, with Harley right behind her, and they immediately went in to start a search of the place. Harley had been here before so he knew his way around, and he headed for the hall where the bedrooms were located. He searched the guest room, the master and the two bathrooms before he made it to the nursery.

The crib was already in place, giving him a jab of emotion. And worry. Soon, Ava and he would be parents, and he figured some worries would still be there. But he didn't want a serial killer to be on their list of concerns.

After he was sure there were no signs of a break-in or an intruder, Harley made his way back into the main part of the house to join Ava, who was at the sink taking some meds. No, not actual meds, he realized when he saw the bottle, but rather a prenatal vitamin.

Harley certainly hadn't needed another reminder of the baby, but he got a couple what with the vitamin and the chalkboard wall next to the fridge. There were names on it.

Abigail, Rebecca, Gracelyn, Holly, Laine, Isabel, Jemma, Carly.

"I jot down possible baby names as they come to mind," she explained when she followed his eyes. "I'd planned on asking you for input," Ava added.

"Thanks for that," he said. Harley picked up the chalk from the ledge above the board and added two names. Olivia and Charlotte.

Ava nodded her approval and tipped her head to the hall. "You can use the guest room," she said, all business now. She was no doubt making sure he remembered there was a reason he was being sent there and not to her own bed.

She looked at him, and Harley felt the old punch of heat

when their gazes connected. Old but still somehow new and fresh. Apparently, his body had no intentions of letting him forget that Ava had once been his lover, even if he wouldn't be sharing her bed.

"Go ahead and send me my half of the names from Duran," she said, pulling her eyes from his. "I'll look them over before I fall asleep."

Harley frowned because he figured if she was looking over possible candidates for a serial killer, then she wouldn't be getting much sleep. "Let's just both glance through them now. *Glance*," he emphasized. "And then you can get some sleep."

Her silence let him know she was debating that, but Ava finally motioned for him to follow her to her office. She booted up her laptop and opened the file after Harley sent it to her from his phone.

"Hundreds of them," she muttered on a sigh.

Harley had done some sighing as well, and he pointed out the names that Duran or Edgar had highlighted. "Those are the people who tried to set up your father for the black-market land deals that were basically fronts for money laundering."

It was a sore subject, all right. Because it'd been this very investigation that had caused her to break off things with Harley.

Ava's mouth tightened. "You've already investigated these people." It wasn't a question, and there was a chill in her voice to go along with that tightness.

"I have," he confirmed. "I found offshore accounts and false documents to prove they had indeed set him up."

"You found what my father wanted you to find," she muttered. "That doesn't mean he was innocent."

"No," Harley agreed, and then he stared at her until she

made eye contact with him again. "Are you ever going to be able to forgive me for dropping the charges against him?"

"No," Ava snapped, but then she sighed again and waved that off. "I don't want to get into all of this again."

Part of him didn't want to push her on this. Not when she was tired and had been through hell and back over the past couple of hours. But another part of him wanted to give it one last shot at trying to clear the air between them.

"I had a strong gut feeling that Edgar had some kind of connection to those land deals. Maybe connections he wasn't aware of at the start, but when the investigation started, I believe he covered his tracks so all the evidence would point to them." He tapped the names that had been highlighted. "Trust me when I say that I looked for anything and everything that could prove your father's involvement."

She shifted her attention from him and back to the list, but her body language was still defensive and all business. "Could any of the men on that list have committed these murders to get back at my father?"

He sighed, and while he wished they'd been able to dive into the more personal parts of this situation, Ava did have a valid question. "No," he assured her. "They're all in jail and are being monitored closely for any attempts at retaliation."

"*Closely monitored* doesn't mean they couldn't find a way," she quickly pointed out.

Harley made an equally quick sound of agreement. "True, but I don't think they'd do that because I also believe your father might have paid them to take the fall for him. They won't spend that much time in jail, and your father could have made sure they were well compensated for their silence."

That got her attention and Ava's gaze speared right to his. "Is there any proof of that?"

"None," he said.

What he didn't add was that he was still digging, still looking for any connection whatsoever that his gut feeling was right. And that gut feeling was that Edgar was a dangerous criminal. Unfortunately, Harley couldn't see how murdering three women and linking those murders to his daughter would earn him anything.

Unless…

"Just how mad was your father when he found out you were carrying my baby?" Harley asked.

"Mad," she answered while she studied him. He saw the exact moment she realized where Harley was going with this. "You think Edgar's so enraged that he plans to murder me and make it look as if it's a serial killer's doing." She shook her head. "Then, why drag Caleb into it by leaving that Mom note?"

Harley hadn't thought that far into this possible theory, but he instantly made a connection. A bad one. "What if Edgar's worried that the way he handled your teen pregnancy will come to light? He won't come out looking good in the eyes of the voters. After all, he forced his daughter into giving up her child and threatened her boyfriend with jail time."

Her forehead bunched up while she obviously gave that some thought. "It's possible Edgar's worried about that," she finally conceded. "But that would mean something has happened to make him believe that what he did is about to come out."

"Secrets get uncovered all the time," Harley pointed out. Even though it was a stretch for him to believe that Edgar would want his own daughter dead because of an ugly secret being revealed. Then again, Edgar wasn't a loving, devoted father, and he might be willing to go to any lengths to prevent himself from being dragged into a scandal.

"If this is about getting revenge by killing me," Ava said, "or wanting to cover up what he did all those years ago, then Edgar wouldn't want anything to be made public about Caleb."

"True." Harley had to give it some thought as well. "This theory might be out there, but maybe Edgar intends for Caleb to be blamed."

He was about to expand that theory when his phone dinged with a text. Since it was from Theo, Harley figured the sheriff hadn't taken his own advice about getting some rest.

Harley froze when he read the single sentence Theo had sent. Froze and then cursed. "Caleb's adoptive parents were both killed in a car crash seven months ago."

Judging from the way Ava sucked in her breath, she hadn't had a clue. But she certainly knew what it could mean. Losing one's parents was traumatic and it could have triggered some kind of break.

Ava groaned and would have no doubt tried to wrap her mind around that, but her phone rang. Considering how late it was, he figured this wouldn't be good news, and his stomach automatically knotted. He hoped like hell there hadn't been another murder.

"It's Marnie," Ava relayed to him. "I added her info to my contacts because I'd given her my number," she explained while she took the call and put it on speaker.

"Ava Lawson?" the woman immediately asked. There was an urgency in her voice.

"Yes, it's me. Marnie, how can I help you?"

Despite that urgency, Marnie didn't jump to answer. "This might be nothing, but after we talked, I got to thinking about Aaron. About the last time I saw him. It wasn't long after Christina died, and he came over to drop off some of Christina's clothes and personal items that he thought I might want. He was drunk and rambling, so I'm not even sure what he said was important."

"What did he say?" Now, Ava was doling out some of her own urgency.

"Remember, he was rambling," Marnie reminded her, "and he was going on about talking to somebody who was connected to some things that happened to him when he was a teenager. After your call where you told me you were once involved with him, I wondered if Aaron was talking about you."

Harley wanted to jump in with a bunch of questions. Specifically questions that might connect anything Aaron had said to the murders, but he held back because he figured Ava would be able to get more from the woman without him interrupting.

"Did Aaron give you any details about what happened to him?" Ava prompted. "And did he say who the person was and why he was talking to him or her?"

"Sort of. He talked about being scared, that he had to stay quiet about something or that he could be in big trouble. I thought he maybe meant Christina's drug dealer, but Aaron kept going on and on about being a teenager and making a mistake. A mistake he said that'd come back to haunt him because now he was being threatened."

"'Threatened,'" Ava repeated in a murmur. She cleared her throat before she asked, "Did Aaron mention the name of the person who was threatening him?"

Harley automatically moved closer to the phone, wondering if the woman was about to tell them it was Ava's father.

But it wasn't Edgar's name that came out of Marnie's mouth.

"Caleb," Marnie said. "I'm pretty sure that's who Aaron kept going on about. Aaron was really worried that this Caleb was going to do something to hurt him."

Chapter Five

One of the things that Ava missed most with her pregnancy was not being able to have enough coffee to clear her head. And, right now, while Harley was driving them to Austin, she could have used a serious amount of caffeine to do just that.

She'd barely slept, and that was in part due to having Harley just up the hall from her. Also in part because the images of all three of the murder victims had continued to flash in her head like grisly neon signs. But Caleb's name had done some flashing, too, and the thought of him being connected to all of this put ice in her blood.

Mercy, she prayed he was innocent.

Marnie's claim of what she'd heard Aaron say would have to be investigated, of course, and questions about that would be included in the interview that would soon be starting.

According to the call Ava had just gotten from Theo, he was already in Austin since he'd wanted to stop by the local PD there to let them know he was on their turf. The plan was for Theo to then meet Harley and her for the interview. Because there had been concerns that Caleb might flee, Theo hadn't told him that two Silver Creek cops and a Texas Ranger would soon be arriving on his doorstep. But

Caleb was supposedly at his apartment near the campus because the Rangers had set up surveillance on him to make sure he stayed put.

And that he didn't slip off to kill anyone.

"My offer still stands," Harley said, yanking her out of her thoughts. "Theo and I can do this interview, record it, and you can listen to it later."

It was tempting if only so she could avoid the stress this might put on the baby, but Ava had to know the truth. She didn't want to learn that truth from a recording. If the son she'd given up for adoption wanted her dead and was killing in her name, she needed to face him and deal with it.

"Thanks, but I'm doing this," she stated. "And I do mean the thanks," she added so he'd understand that she appreciated it.

Right now, she'd take all the help she could get. She was in danger, which meant so was her baby and anyone around her, and that danger could be connected to her father. Or her son. But Ava was hoping it was neither of them, that this was just the killer's attempts to make it look connected. She hated her father, but if he was indeed the one killing women and targeting her, then it was going to create an emotional nightmare. Still, if Edgar had anything to do with this, she wanted him punished and punished hard.

Harley pulled Ava's car to a stop in front of the Crossroads Apartments. Not upscale but not a dump either. Since it was only a few blocks from campus, she was betting most of the residents were students.

"Have you changed your mind about not telling Caleb who you are?" Harley asked.

She shook her head. "I want to see his reaction to me. If he knows I'm his birth mother, I might see some signs of recognition even if he doesn't volunteer it. If he doesn't know, then that's an indication he's innocent in all of this."

Harley made a sound of agreement and gave her a look that let her know he was worried about her going through this. So was she, but that wouldn't stop her.

Ava took some deep breaths, trying to steel herself up as they got out of the car. She automatically glanced around, looking for any signs of trouble. No trouble, but she spotted Theo already outside the door to Caleb's apartment.

"That's the Ranger who's been watching the place," Harley informed her, tipping his head to the gray Ford Focus on the far side of the parking lot. He waved to the Ranger who then drove away now that he knew Theo had backup. "If we decide to keep eyes on Caleb after we finish, then I can have him come back."

She was hoping that wouldn't be necessary, that with just this interview, they'd be able to eliminate Caleb as a suspect and be absolutely certain he was innocent.

Theo, too, studied Ava's expression when they got closer to him, and he must have been satisfied she could handle whatever was about to happen because he rang the doorbell. Ava had to tamp down another slam of nerves when she heard the footsteps.

"He has a roommate, Jonah Chavez, but he's not home," Theo explained, keeping his voice low. "According to the Ranger, the roommate left about an hour ago."

Good, because Ava thought it would be even harder if this interview played out in front of someone else. Then again, it was possible once Caleb realized they were there to talk to him about a trio of murders, he might want a lawyer present.

The door opened and the young man looked out at them with both surprise and caution in his eyes. Eyes that were a genetic copy of Ava's. That was the first thing she noticed

about him, and she didn't have to look hard to see the resemblance to Aaron, either, with his sandy-blond hair and
square jaw. Aaron had been handsome as a teenager, and
he'd obviously passed those genes along to Caleb.

"Yes?" Caleb said, his attention landing first on Theo.
Then Theo's badge. "Is something wrong? Did something
happen to one of my friends?" Now, there was alarm in the
young man's eyes and he shifted his gaze to Harley. Then
to Ava.

And there she saw it.

The recognition that she wished hadn't been there. Caleb
knew who she was. He knew, and that meant he'd just
zoomed to the top of their suspect list.

"Your friends are all fine as far as we know," Theo said.
"I'm Sheriff Theo Sheldon." He tipped his head toward Harley and her. "This is Texas Ranger Harley Ryland and Deputy Ava Lawson."

"Yes," Caleb muttered, his eyes locked with hers. He
stayed like that, staring at her, until he finally gave his head
a little shake as if to clear it. He stepped back, motioning
for them to come in.

But not before his attention landed on her baby bump.

Ava hated that he immediately turned to move out of the
doorway because it meant she couldn't see his reaction. In
the couple of seconds that it took him to get into the living
area, he could have managed to compose himself. Well,
he could have if he was very good at concealing what was
going on in his head.

They stepped inside, automatically glancing around to
take in the place. Since it was small, there wasn't much
to take in, and even the doors to the two bedrooms were
both open. Ava saw no weapons and, thankfully, no sick

"shrines" to her that would indicate she was the motive for murder.

"Wow," Caleb said, still staring at her. "I didn't expect this. I mean, I thought I might meet you one day, but I always figured it'd be just the two of us. And that I'd be better prepared for it," he added with a nervous chuckle.

Ava found herself latching onto every word. As both a mom and a cop. And she studied his face for signs of resentment or calculation. She didn't see any, but she had to accept that might be because she didn't want to see it. That's why she was thankful Harley and Theo were with her. They would be able to see anything that didn't make it through her mental blinders.

"How did you find out who I am?" Ava asked. She had plenty of questions but decided to go with that one first.

"Oh…" he started but then held up his finger in a wait-a-second gesture.

He went to the adjoining kitchen, which, of course, put them all on alert in case this was a ploy to grab a weapon, but Caleb simply poured himself a glass of water and downed most of it.

"All right," Caleb said, coming back toward them. He repeated those two words as if to steady himself, but there were still plenty of nerves showing when he finally continued.

"After I lost my parents in a car wreck, I was a mess and thought having answers about my bio-parents would help, so I did one of those DNA tests," he explained. "It came back with some genetic cousins. I sorted through them until I saw that many of them were connected to the surname Walsh. I emailed some of them, asking if anyone knew who my bio-parents were, and one cousin said my bio-dad might be Aaron Walsh but that the family had lost touch with him."

Ava felt everything inside her go still. Even with all Edgar's wrangling to keep the pregnancy a secret, Caleb had unraveled the truth with a DNA test and some digging. Again, she had to fight the urge to fire off a bunch of questions. Questions that might alarm Caleb and have him withholding information. Right now, it was best if she just stayed quiet and let him finish.

"No one seemed to know where Aaron Walsh was," he went on. "My roommate's mom is a PI, so as a favor, she looked into finding him. It took more than a month, but she was finally able to track him down. She got his phone number and I called him. When I told him who I was and when I was born, he said yeah, that I was probably his son."

There was no stillness in the reaction Ava had to that. Her heart dropped and her chest tightened. It shouldn't have shocked her that a private investigator could get this kind of info since Edgar's PI had managed it, but still she hadn't expected Aaron to confirm that he was possibly Caleb's father. Not after the threats Edgar had doled out to Aaron.

"Aaron told me if he was actually my bio-dad then you'd be my bio-mom," Caleb explained. "So, that sent me back to the DNA cousins and, sure enough, I found a couple of your distant relatives. None of them took my calls or answered my emails, but I figured that's because I was somewhat of a family secret."

Oh, yes. Edgar had made sure of that, and part of Ava was glad that her father hadn't been able to keep all of it buried. But there were some possible big problems with the truth coming out. For instance, had her father known about any of this and then set a murder plan in motion?

"How long ago did you have that conversation with Aaron?" Harley asked. And Ava knew the reason for the question. Harley was trying to pin down if learning about his bio-parents had been around the time the murders had started.

Caleb didn't even have to pause to give it some thought. "Four months ago. I remember the exact date because it was the five-month anniversary of my parents' deaths."

Oh, mercy. The first murder had happened three months ago, so the timing could fit since the killer would have needed a while to work out the details of the murders. Caleb seemed awfully calm and collected for a serial killer who was now facing three badges, but Ava couldn't use that to dismiss him as a suspect.

"Look," Caleb continued, "my parents were awesome, and they always told me up-front that I was adopted. Because the adoption records were sealed, they didn't know any info about my bios. I just thought it would help with my grief, that's all." His gaze met Ava's. "And I never intended to interfere with your life. Or Aaron's."

He seemed so sincere and, heaven help her, she believed every word he was saying. Later, she'd find out if Harley and Theo did, too.

"What exactly did Aaron tell you about me and him?" Ava asked.

"Not a whole lot, and FYI, I asked him if he wanted to meet me and he said sure, but then he wouldn't come up with a time or a place. I got the idea that he was still dealing with some bad things because of me."

"Not because of you," Ava quickly corrected. No way did she want to put blame for what had happened on Caleb's shoulders. "You know who my father is?" she tacked on.

Caleb gave a slow nod. "Aaron didn't have anything good to say about him."

Ava didn't spell out that was because there wasn't much good to say about Edgar. "I got pregnant with you when

I was sixteen, and my father took many steps to ensure it was kept secret."

Oh, how much to say Ava didn't want to come off sounding as if none of what had happened had been her fault. After all, she hadn't taken proper precautions and had gotten pregnant.

If she'd been stronger, she could have run away, had the baby and kept him. But even then, as a teenager, Ava had known that would have ended up being a tough life for her baby since she'd had no way to support him. Added to that, she'd known her father would have carried through on his threat and made sure Aaron ended up in jail.

Considering what Marnie had told them, maybe Edgar was still trying to make that happen.

"Yeah, Aaron said he didn't see you after you told him you were pregnant, and he figured your dad had hidden you some place. Aaron said he looked for you but couldn't find you."

That was probably true. She had looked for him as well, all the while knowing they could never be together. That had crushed her back then, but considering the kind of man Aaron had become, she figured a relationship wouldn't have worked out between them. Especially with her father doing everything to destroy Aaron.

"Aaron and I wanted to keep you, but we couldn't," Ava settled for saying, and she braced herself, figuring that Caleb would lash out at her for not doing more.

A lashing she would absolutely deserve.

He didn't. His body language tightened some, suggesting he was still trying to come to terms with his feelings about her and what she'd done, but there was no venom or anger.

"You're pregnant," Caleb murmured, his gaze dropping to her stomach.

She nodded and automatically brushed her hand over her stomach, her gaze pinned to Caleb to try to gauge his reaction. "I'm in my fifth month."

It was hard to tell, but she thought that maybe he hadn't known before today. Of course, she hadn't posted about it on social media, and she wasn't in the media's eye enough for them to pick up on it.

Not yet anyway.

If the murders continued and if the bit about the masks leaked, she had no doubts that she would soon be the center of a media firestorm.

Caleb shifted his attention to Harley and Theo, his eyes looking down at their hands, maybe to try to spot a wedding ring. There weren't any, though Theo was engaged to the Silver Creek assistant district attorney, Kim Ryland.

"I'm guessing the three of you didn't come here just to talk about Deputy Lawson being my birth mom," Caleb remarked. "What's wrong? Is Aaron in some kind of trouble?"

Ava shook her head and then shrugged because she had no idea if Aaron truly was in trouble. Maybe he was, but for now she had to focus on the main reason for this visit.

"Three women have been murdered in or around Silver Creek in the past three months," she stated, trying to keep all the emotion out of her voice. She wouldn't mention the masks since that tidbit was being withheld from the public. "The murders seem to be connected to me."

Caleb's shoulders snapped back. "Connected how?" he asked.

"The killer left a note at the last crime scene," Harley answered. "We haven't identified the killer, but we know he's somehow linked to Deputy Lawson and that he could be killing to get back at her in some way."

Caleb shook his head as if puzzled by that, and then his

Marked for Revenge

eyes went wide. "You think I killed somebody. I didn't," he quickly added. He staggered back a step, his pleading gaze going to Ava. "You have to believe me. I wouldn't kill anybody."

"Are you angry about her giving you up for adoption?" Harley pressed.

"No." His reply was fast and loud. "I mean, I guess I wondered why she didn't want to keep me, but then Aaron told me they were just teenagers, so I understood. And, hell, even if I was angry, I still wouldn't kill anyone."

"I'm going to go ahead and Mirandize you." Theo spoke up, causing the color to drain from Caleb's face. "It's for your protection, so you know your rights," he added.

Caleb didn't make a sound while Theo gave him the Miranda warning, but he did sink down onto the sofa and put his face in his hands for a moment.

"Do you want a lawyer present?" Theo asked him once he'd finished.

Caleb looked at her, maybe trying to decide if he could trust her not to allow him to be railroaded. He must have decided he could because he shook his head. "I've done nothing wrong, so go ahead and ask me whatever it is you came here for."

Theo took out a piece of paper and handed it to Caleb. "Where were you on those dates and at those hours?"

Caleb dragged in some quick breaths, but then he seemed to steady himself when he actually looked at the paper. "Yes. For this one anyway." He tapped the first date. "I was at a weekend seminar in Dallas. I didn't post about it on social media because my roommate was with me for that, and I didn't want to let anyone know the apartment would be empty."

Theo nodded and handed Caleb a small notepad he took

from his pocket. "Jot down the name of the seminar and the person in charge of it. What about the other two dates?" Theo prompted after Caleb had finished writing.

Caleb took out his phone and pulled up his calendar. Some of the color came back to his cheeks. "I was with someone on the third date." He looked up at Theo. "I'll give you her name and contact info, but when you talk to her, don't make it sound like I'm some kind of killer. I'm not, and I really like her. I don't want this to screw things up between us."

"I won't volunteer any details, and I'll make it seem routine. I've found if I throw in the words *background check*, most people just accept that."

Caleb sighed in a way that could be interpreted that he hoped it was true and then shook his head. "I don't have anything on my calendar for this second one. It was right before a big exam, and I was here studying. My roommate spent that night at his folks since it was some kind of family deal. Does this mean you'll arrest me?"

"No," Theo informed him. "I'll look into the other two alibis, and if they check out, then I can ask around and see if anyone saw you on the other night in question." He paused a heartbeat. "Ever had any experience with explosives?"

Again, Caleb's eyes widened. "No. Well, nothing other than cherry bombs on the Fourth of July, but that doesn't count. Right?" he questioned, his demeanor more than a little shaky.

"It doesn't count," Theo assured him. "But I will ask around and find out if you've been lying to me."

"I haven't been," Caleb quickly insisted and then shifted his attention back to Ava. "How are the murders connected to you? Are you in danger?"

No way could Ava spill any other details about the killings, but she could answer the second part. Well, sort of answer it anyway. "Maybe I'm in danger. Can you think of anyone who'd want to set you up so we'd think you had a part in the murders?"

"No." Again, his answer was quick and his face was a textbook picture of shock. He slowly got to his feet. "No," he repeated. "I mean there are some people who might not like me, but there's not enough hate to kill."

As a cop, Ava knew it didn't always take a lot of hate. Murders happened with all levels of heat, and these particular murders felt cold to her. Calculated and organized. Certainly, they hadn't been done in the heat of anger.

Theo tipped his head to the notepad Caleb was still holding. "Write down the names of those who don't like you. Include any you might have broken up with or rejected in some kind of way."

This was standard procedure but, like Ava, Theo knew it probably wouldn't help them come up with the names of suspects. Besides, they already had names.

Her father, Duran and Aaron.

And the next step would be to question all three of them, along with pressing her father and Duran to find out if one of them was still threatening Aaron.

Caleb handed Theo the notepad after he was finished, and Theo looked it over. The sheriff was no doubt doing a mental comparison to the handwriting on the note that'd been left at the last crime scene. Ava had a look, too, but she couldn't see a resemblance. Still, Theo would have it analyzed.

"I really don't want to mess up anything in your life," Caleb said, looking at her now. "But I'm glad I got to meet you." He opened his mouth, but he must have changed his mind as to whatever he'd been about to say because he shook his head and waved it off.

"I'm glad I got to meet you, too," she said once she managed to clear the lump in her throat.

Their gazes stayed connected with the silence hanging between them, and then Caleb looked away. "Am I in danger?" he asked, not aiming that at anyone in particular. "I mean, if this killer is trying to set me up, maybe he'll come after me."

No way could any of them dismiss the possibility, and hearing it spelled out tightened her chest so much that it was hard for her to breathe. She was ready to offer private protection, a bodyguard, but Harley spoke first.

"I'll have the Texas Rangers keep an eye on you, and you'll need to take some precautions. For instance, don't go anywhere alone at night and be aware of your surroundings. If you see or sense anyone watching or following you, call me, the sheriff or Deputy Lawson."

Harley handed Caleb a business card with his contact info, and Ava and Theo did the same.

"Thanks," Caleb muttered.

Ava could tell he was scared and, along with tightening her chest even more, it riled her to the core that someone was doing this to him.

To her son.

Yes, she allowed the thought in her head. Someone was playing sick games with her son and her, and she had to figure out a way to make it stop. Even if this was the one and only time she got to see the child she'd delivered all those years ago, she wanted him safe.

And she loved him.

That was the other emotion that came through loud and

clear. Maybe it was some kind of primal DNA connection, a survival of the species thing, but she loved him.

"Call us if you think of anything else," Ava reminded Caleb, hoping that was an invitation for him to contact her. That contact probably wouldn't be easy, but part of her wanted it more than her next breath.

Rather than risk saying anything she shouldn't, Ava turned to go to the door. Theo and Harley were right behind her.

"Thanks for your cooperation," Theo told Caleb. "One of us will be in touch with you soon."

They stepped outside and Harley immediately took out his phone. "I'll get the Ranger back out here. We can wait in the car until he shows."

"Good," Theo confirmed. "I'll get started on checking these alibis as soon as I'm back in Silver Creek." With that, Theo headed to his cruiser and Harley and Ava went toward her car.

They didn't get far.

Gunfire cracked through the air.

Chapter Six

Harley reacted out of training and instinct when he heard the gunshot. He hooked his arm around Ava and pulled her to the ground, having her land on top of him so the fall wouldn't be so jarring.

He instantly thought of their baby. Of the child Ava would want him to protect at all costs, and even though she was a cop, he had to make sure she was all right.

Before he could move in front of Ava to shield her, there was the sound of another gunshot. This bullet slammed into the vehicle they were using for cover.

Terrified that the shot had ricocheted and hit Ava, he glanced back at her. She wasn't bleeding, thank God, and while she had her gun drawn, she also had her arm over her stomach. Protecting the baby even though all hell was breaking loose around them.

"Theo," Ava blurted. "Is he okay?"

Harley couldn't see him without lifting his head, and at the moment that wouldn't be a good idea. However, he hoped like the devil that the sheriff had managed to either get inside his cruiser or was close enough he wouldn't be out in the open and an easy target.

A third shot came, slamming into the car's windshield,

and it told Harley loads. The shooter was positioned across the street, probably on the roof of the two-story apartment building that faced Caleb's door. The shooter also didn't have the best aim or he would have already succeeded in hitting them.

Not exactly a comforting thought.

Ditto for the realization that either Ava or he was the target since so far all the shots had come directly at them. But Harley could be certain of something else. Caleb wasn't the shooter. No way could he have gotten out of his apartment and across the street in the couple of minutes since they'd left him.

"Stay down," he heard Theo shout.

Just as there was another round of gunfire. Maybe folks would listen because this was a situation where there could be some collateral damage.

"I've called the Austin cops," someone shouted.

Caleb.

Because Ava's left arm was against his back, Harley felt her tense, and she muttered some profanity. "Caleb, stay down!" she called out to him.

She didn't add anything else. Didn't have to. Harley had seen the emotion in her eyes as she'd looked at him when they'd been in his apartment. Even if she didn't want to have deep feelings of love for her son, she did. It was already there, and love could be a bad distraction. Harley had firsthand knowledge of that because he loved his unborn child, and here this SOB shooter was putting her in danger.

Harley adjusted his position just a little so he could get a better look at the building across the street. He couldn't see the shooter or the barrel of a rifle—the weapon the guy must be using to get this kind of range. Harley also couldn't see any side stairs, thus he wouldn't be able to get a glimpse of the shooter if he tried to come down from the roof. It was possible there were stairs at the back, but since it was only two floors, he could have used whatever fire escape was available.

In the distance, he heard the wail of the sirens. It wouldn't be long before the local cops arrived. Thank God. Every second Ava was out here was a second that he could lose her and the baby.

Harley braced himself for more shots. And, even though he probably wouldn't be able to return fire in the middle of the city, he wanted to have his gun ready in case this snake threw all caution to the wind and came down those steps firing on all cylinders.

But Harley doubted that was the plan.

No, if this was their killer, it didn't fit with his MO. He was a snatch-and-grab kind of attacker. One who liked to play sick mind games with Ava. So, maybe that's what this was all about. It could explain why the shots had missed them. If so, the killer was no doubt already hurrying for cover to plan his next move.

Harley glanced in the direction of a cruiser as it stopped just up the street. The cops inside were likely checking to see if this was a scenario with active fire. Harley figured Theo was in contact with them about just that, and they were working out how to respond.

Some movement caught Harley's eye. Not on the stairs or the roof but at the right side of the building where the shots had originated. It was a tall, lanky man with sandy-blond hair, and while he didn't appear to be armed, he was looking in their direction.

"You see him?" Ava muttered, motioning just as the man took off running. He wasn't coming toward them but away from the apartment where the shots had been fired.

Harley nodded and kept his gaze pinned to him. At least he did until he heard Ava gasp. Harley snapped his attention toward her, praying that she hadn't just realized she'd been shot. But she wasn't looking at any part of her body. Her focus, too, was on the man.

"I know him," she said, her breath rushing out with her words. "That's Aaron Walsh."

WHILE THE EMT checked her blood pressure, Ava tried to level her breathing and settle her nerves. Hard to do, considering that someone had just tried to kill Harley and her. But she had to at least try to calm down for the sake of the baby. And so she could have a clear enough head to help the Austin cops in any way.

They had to find Aaron.

Ava was certain that had been Aaron fleeing the scene and, thankfully, the cops had been able to respond by going after him in pursuit. A pursuit still underway while Harley and she were at police headquarters. Theo had whisked them there in his bullet-resistant cruiser since it was the station nearest the shooting and, after they'd all given brief statements, the sheriff had left to assist in the search for Aaron.

Before Theo had done that, though, he'd insisted Ava stay put and be checked out by the EMTs who were already en route to do the exam at the police station. Ava hadn't refused. Despite her not having any visible injuries, she needed the baby checked, and Harley had done more insisting by letting her know that he'd be staying with her. Maybe in part to make sure she remained in place, but she also knew he was as worried about their daughter as she was.

Caleb was okay, and that helped big-time with her raw nerves. Because Caleb had had her phone number, he'd texted her several times to ask how she was doing and to let her know that he hadn't been hurt. In fact, there'd been no reported injuries, which was somewhat of a miracle, considering multiple shots had been fired into a heavily populated area.

Ava's phone dinged again with another text, but this time it wasn't from Caleb. It was from her father, so she ignored it. She'd already declined two calls from him so it was obvious he was trying to find another way to get her to communicate. Since Edgar worked in Austin when the senate was in session, Ava wouldn't put it past either of the men to try to find her location and come see her. After all, it wouldn't do for the senator not to personally respond to an attack on his daughter.

"Are you cramping or having any contractions?" the EMT asked, yanking Ava's attention back to the exam. According to her name tag, she was Lisa Mendoza.

Ava shook her head.

"What about spotting?" the EMT pressed, prompting Ava to shake her head again. "And has the baby moved since the incident?"

"Yes," Ava verified. "She's moving now."

"Good," the EMT said. "I need you to lift your top so I can listen to the baby's heartbeat with this fetal Doppler." She took the device from the medical supply bag.

Ava was wearing a loose shirt to cover her bump, but she hesitated when she started to lift it. It was foolish, of course, since Harley had seen her naked. Ditto for her seeing him naked as well. However, it occurred to her that he'd yet to see her baby bump. He had gone with her to some of her appointments, but he'd always looked away whenever it required her to bare any part of her body.

That's what Harley did now, too.

"It's okay," Ava told him. Why, she didn't know, but after

what they'd just been through, it seemed ridiculous that he wouldn't be able to see that particular part of her. Especially since he was clearly waiting on pins and needles to make sure the baby was okay.

"Ranger Ryland is the baby's father," Ava explained to the EMT when the woman hesitated.

Ava lifted her top and pulled down the waist of her maternity jeans, and the EMT got the wand in place. "How far along are you?" she asked, and she kept her attention on the Doppler monitor she was holding in her left hand.

"Twenty weeks. Halfway there," she added in a murmur though she was certain Harley was already aware of that.

Moments later, the EMT smiled. "The baby's heartbeat is strong." She continued to move the wand around. "And steady." She showed the monitor to both of them. The average was a hundred and forty beats per minute, which Ava knew was normal.

Some of the tightness in Ava's chest finally eased. Thank heavens her baby was all right.

"Everything looks good," the EMT said, packing her things away. "I'd advise you to go ahead and make an appointment for a check with your regular OB."

Ava nodded because she'd expected that. Obviously, Harley hadn't because that put some fresh alarm on his face.

"It's routine," Ava assured him.

The EMT made a sound of agreement and stood. "Anytime the mother has experienced any kind of trauma, we advise her to speak with her doctor. You're sure you don't want me to give you a quick checkup?" she tacked onto that, glancing at Harley.

He'd declined the EMT's first offer and he nixed the idea again. "I'm not hurt."

Ava doubted that was true. There was blood on the knee

of his jeans. He'd likely scraped it when he'd gotten her behind the cover of that car. Later, she'd remind him to at least
check it himself and make sure it didn't need a bandage.

"Thank you," Ava muttered to him after the EMT left
them in the office that one of the lieutenants, Scott O'Malley,
had allowed them to use.

"For what?" he asked.

"For getting me and the baby out of the line of fire."

He shrugged, but there was nothing casual about the
gesture. No. This had hit him as hard as it'd hit her, which
meant they'd both be dealing with it for a long time. Worse,
it might not be over.

She stood so she could give her jeans an adjustment, and
Harley turned to her just as she looked up at him. Their
gazes connected. Held. And they both muttered some profanity. No need for her to question why he was cursing. He
didn't want this heat any more than she did. Because the
timing sucked. Now wasn't the time to try to work out any
personal stuff between them. Not when they had to focus
on stopping a killer.

"Why do you think the killer came after us like this?"
she asked. "Why break his MO?" And then she threw in a
possible answer. "Is it because he thought Caleb might be
able to tell us something that would ID him?"

Ava watched Harley's expression, looking for any signs
that he was going to say that Caleb did this to throw him off
his scent. But Harley probably wouldn't go there. If Caleb
was indeed the killer and wanted to cover his tracks, he
wouldn't have left the Mom note with the third body.

"Possibly," Harley said a moment later. "Or it could have
been a warning. Keep coming after him, and we'll pay and
pay hard."

"That could definitely be part of it," she admitted. "But

the bodies had been staged as a taunt to me. The killer wants me involved in this investigation."

Harley looked at her again. "You think I was the target? That the gunshots were a warning for me to back off. FYI, I won't," he insisted.

There'd been no need for him to say that last part, and if the killer knew Harley, he'd be aware of that as well. "This shooting will make the news," she spelled out a moment later. "No way to keep this under wraps, and it'll come out that the sheriff of Silver Creek, his deputy and a Texas Ranger were here to investigate a serial killer."

As if on cue, her phone dinged with yet another text from her father. Ava ignored it, but she couldn't ignore the knock at the door. She groaned because she figured her father had certainly found her, but when Harley answered it, she saw it was Theo.

Theo's attention went straight to her. "I just saw the EMT and she said she'd given you a checkup. I wasn't sure if you'd be dressed or not."

"It was just a heartbeat check for the baby. Everything is fine," Ava explained, and she immediately shifted gears. "Please tell me the Austin cops have found Aaron."

"They didn't have to," Theo informed her. "Because Aaron just showed up here."

Of all the things Ava thought he might say, that hadn't been one of them. "He's turning himself in? Has he confessed?" She would have added even more questions had Theo not held up his hand to stop her.

"No confession. He claims he's the victim, that someone is trying to set him up so it looks as if he tried to kill you. He says he's here to set the record straight."

Ava had to take a couple of moments to process that. "Does Aaron know who I am?"

Theo nodded. "He mentioned you by name."

"I want to talk to him," she insisted.

"Me, too," Harley piped in.

"Figured you would, and Lieutenant O'Malley is going to give you a few minutes with him." Theo motioned for Harley and her to follow him. "Aaron's been Mirandized, so he might just clam up and wait for a lawyer. If that happens, then the lieutenant doesn't want us pressing Aaron on anything."

Ava understood because that kind of pressure could hurt with a conviction. "Is there enough to arrest Aaron?" she asked as they walked down a long corridor lined with interview rooms.

Theo stopped outside one of the doors and shook his head. "Aaron consented to a gunshot residue test, and it came back negative."

That didn't mean the man hadn't recently fired a gun, especially if he'd fired a rifle, but since he'd agreed to the test, it likely meant he knew he was going to be clean.

"Can any witnesses put Aaron on the roof of that building where the shots were fired?" Harley asked, keeping his voice low.

"Not so far, and Aaron told Lieutenant O'Malley he was in the area so he could visit Caleb. He'd parked up the street and claims he was walking to Caleb's apartment when the shots started. The Austin cops found his car and verified that it would have been the nearest parking since all the visitor spots were filled for the parking lot at Caleb's building."

Ava groaned because that was a plausible explanation. Not necessarily a truthful one but being in the vicinity of a shooting wasn't enough to arrest the man. If Aaron was the killer, she could only hope he'd say something incriminating that could be used to hold him.

"Marnie said Aaron had told her that Caleb had threatened him," Ava reminded them. "It's possible Marnie got it wrong, but if Aaron came here to try to silence Caleb, he might have planned on shooting him."

Harley made a sound of agreement but then shook his head. "Caleb came outside his apartment after the shots started, but the gunman still continued firing at us."

True. That was possibly some kind of ploy. Ava couldn't wrap her mind around it just yet, but she intended to give it plenty of thought.

"I'm going to insult you by asking you if you're sure you're up to talking with Aaron," Theo told her. "You could just watch from observation if you want."

Ava wasn't insulted. Okay, maybe she was a little. "I'm a cop. If I can't be objective, I'll just keep quiet and let Harley and you do the questioning."

Theo nodded in approval, opened the door and they went in.

Aaron wasn't seated at the lone table in the room. He was pacing, and he came to an abrupt stop, his eyes spearing hers.

"Ava," he said, looking her over, his attention stopping only briefly when he noticed her baby bump.

"Aaron," she *greeted* back.

The past twenty years hadn't been kind to the man. Even though he wasn't yet forty, there was plenty of gray in his sandy-blond hair, and his thin almost gaunt face was lined with wrinkles.

As she'd done with Caleb, she looked for any hatred or venom aimed at her, but she didn't see it. Maybe because Aaron was good at keeping it concealed. Or maybe because it wasn't there. Still, he was a suspect, and even though they'd once been in love, Ava had no intentions of letting the past sway her opinion of him.

Especially since the past might be at the root of the murders.

"You look good, Ava," Aaron commented. "And you got that badge you always wanted." He shifted his attention to Harley, who was standing side by side with her. "Is this your husband?"

"No," she replied and kept it at that.

Even though Aaron didn't add more to his question, she could see that he sensed Harley and she were together, and Aaron didn't seem ready to say anything snarky. Such as, *Are you going to keep this baby after you gave up ours?* Nope, no snark. But he shook his head the way a person did when they couldn't believe something was happening to them.

"Your daddy would pitch a fit if he found out we're here together in the same room," Aaron commented.

Edgar would indeed, but Ava didn't confirm that. "You've been in touch with my father?"

"No." His answer was firm and fast. "Last time I saw him, he said he'd have my butt thrown in jail if I didn't get out of town." He paused a heartbeat. "The last time I saw you, you were pregnant then, too," Aaron remarked. While it seemed an odd thing to say, Ava thought he might have been going for some levity because he gave a small smile.

Since there was nothing to smile about, Ava launched right into what she wanted to ask him. "Did you fire shots at me about an hour ago?"

Aaron groaned and then scrubbed his hand over his face. "Hell, no." He looked at both Theo and Harley—specifically at their badges—and repeated his denial. "Like I told the other cops, I was there to see Caleb." His attention went back to Ava. "Did you see him?"

She took her time but finally nodded.

Aaron smiled again. "Did he look like us? What did he say? I've talked to him on the phone, but I've never met him."

Ava ignored that and went with another question. "Why did you come to Austin to visit him today?"

Aaron wasn't so quick to answer this time. "Because of you. Marnie called me and said you were looking for me. I figured you wanted to talk about Caleb, so I came to Austin to introduce myself and let him know you might be in touch with him." He paused again. "All right, I just wanted him to hear my side of the story about what happened. I would have never given him up for adoption if I'd had a way of keeping him."

She considered not only his words but his tone. What she didn't hear was any of the concern Marnie had mentioned about Aaron being worried that Caleb might try to hurt him.

"And you thought I had a way of keeping him, gave him up anyway and that I might try to put some of that blame on you?" she asked.

"Maybe," Aaron conceded.

So, there was some anger for her, but Ava couldn't tell if it was enough for him to kill. "Was Caleb threatening you in any way?"

Aaron pulled back his shoulders. "Did he tell you that?" he demanded.

"Did Caleb threaten you in any way?" Harley repeated.

Aaron glared at him, but it seemed to Ava that he quickly tried to rein that in. He had to know he was under suspicion, and since he had a police record, he also knew it was best not to clash with a Texas Ranger.

"No, Caleb didn't threaten me," Aaron finally answered. "And I want to know what made you think he had."

Ava lifted her shoulder. No way would she spill what Marnie had told her, but Aaron might soon be able to figure it out since he'd already mentioned he'd spoken with Marnie. Ava also gave Theo a subtle gesture so he could proceed with the things he needed to get out of the way.

Theo took out his notepad and turned it to a fresh page, one with only the dates of the murders and not any of Caleb's notes. "Do you have solid alibis for those nights?" Theo asked.

Aaron looked over the list and his eyes registered the shock when he turned not to Theo but to Ava. "I know how this works. There were crimes committed on those dates—"

"Murders," Theo interrupted.

"'Murders'?" Aaron repeated, his gaze sweeping over all of them. "You think I killed somebody?"

"I'd like to know if you have alibis for those nights," Theo stated.

That obviously rattled Aaron. He shook his head, muttered some raw profanity under his breath and took the notepad. Because Ava was watching him, some of the color drained from his face.

"I was at Marnie's on these dates," Aaron finally said.

"You can recall where you were two and three months ago?" Ava asked, and she didn't bother to take the skepticism out of her voice. Most people had to consult a calendar to recall such things.

Aaron's eyes narrowed. "I remember because the first date was the four-month anniversary of Christina's death, and Marnie and I were both having a hard time. The second one was Christina's birthday. Last night, I was at Marnie's to pick up some pictures that Marnie thought I'd want."

"Did you stay the entire nights with Marnie?" Harley asked.

"Yeah, I would have been drinking," Aaron muttered while he looked at the dates on the notepad again. "It wasn't safe to drive so I crashed in her guest room."

That meant Aaron had been at Marnie's when Ava had been talking to the woman on the phone. Well, maybe he had, if Aaron was telling the truth.

"Let me check and see if Marnie will verify that," Theo said, stepping outside the interview room to make the call.

"I didn't kill anybody," Aaron repeated to Harley and her. "I know it looks bad because I was in Austin during this shooting, but if I'd wanted you dead, I would have gone after you a long time ago."

That put some ice in her blood and, while that seemed to be logical on the surface, there was another factor here. Christina's death. It could have triggered Aaron to want to do something to get back at the world. Or, more specifically, to get back at her for the old wrongs that had been done to him. Yes, those wrongs had been her father's doing, but maybe punishing and ultimately killing her was the way for Aaron to get back at Edgar.

"Have you told anyone about me having your baby when I was a teenager?" Ava asked.

"Christina knew," he readily admitted. He paused, his mouth suddenly a little unsteady. "She was sorry that I hadn't been able to raise my son, so she wanted to have a baby. I thought maybe that would be a good thing, and I told her if she stayed clean for six months, we'd try." He shook his head and groaned. "According to the medical examiner, Christina was about four weeks pregnant when she died."

Oh, mercy. Hearing that could have definitely been a trigger for Aaron.

"I'm sorry," Ava told him, and she meant it.

She couldn't imagine losing the baby she was carrying. Couldn't imagine having something bad happen to Caleb. But someone obviously wanted bad things for him because they'd tried to set him up by leaving that note with the bomb.

"Were you aware that my father had a PI following you?" Ava asked. Again, she studied his response to see how much alarm that would cause Aaron.

It caused him plenty.

"When?" Aaron demanded.

"Recently," she supplied. She didn't add that the PI hadn't been on Aaron during the murders, and she recalled Duran explaining that was because the investigator hadn't been able to find him. Ironic since Aaron was claiming to have been at Marnie's on three separate occasions. So, either her father's PI had simply missed spotting Aaron on those dates or someone was lying.

Aaron muttered some profanity. "I don't have to ask why your SOB of a father would do that," he snarled. "He's worried I'll rat him out. And I've thought about doing just that over the years. Trust me, I've thought of doing a lot of things—"

His tirade came to a quick stop, and Ava wished it hadn't because it had seemed as if Aaron had been on the verge of spilling something. She didn't get a chance to press him on it, either, because Theo came back into the room and immediately speared Aaron with his cop's glare.

"I just talked to Marnie," Theo stated, "and she said she's not sure if those are the dates you stayed over at her house. In other words, she can't confirm your alibis."

Ava got a jolt of the firestorm of emotions that raced through her. If Aaron had lied about being at Marnie's, then he could have also lied about why he was here in Austin.

And it soared him to the top of their suspect list.

Aaron cursed again, but this time it wasn't muttered. It was raw and vicious. "Marnie." He spat her name out like a continuation of the profanity. "She's lying. She has to remember I was over at her place for Christina's birthday and the anniversary of her death. Hell, Marnie invited me over there for those dates."

Theo lifted his shoulder and the gesture conveyed he wasn't the least bit convinced with Aaron's denial. "Why would Marnie lie about something like that?" he asked.

"Because she hates my guts, that's why," Aaron insisted. "Marnie's always thought I should have done more to help her sister stay off drugs. I tried my damnedest to do that, but Christina just couldn't quit. Marnie never got that, and she blamed me when Christina died."

Ava worked that explanation through her mind and immediately saw a flaw in Aaron's logic. "If Marnie hates you, then why would she have allowed you to come to her house, much less stay there, as you've claimed."

Oh, if looks could kill, Aaron would have blasted her to smithereens. "*Claimed*," he snapped. "You think I'm guilty. You think I murdered those women. Well, I didn't."

Ava was ready to pepper him with a few more questions. Ready to try to hit Aaron's hot buttons to get him to blurt out something that might end up incriminating him. She hadn't remembered Aaron having much of a temper when they'd been teenagers, but considering the life he'd led, it could have turned him bitter, and bitterness often manifested itself as rage.

"You want to know who's capable of these murders?" Aaron asked before she could continue. He didn't wait for any of them to respond. "Marnie, that's who. You're looking for a killer? Well, look straight in Marnie's direction."

Chapter Seven

Harley pulled Ava's car to a stop in front of her house and waited for her to open the garage. After she had, they went through the same security precautions they'd taken the night before. Searching her house again with weapons drawn had to be another jolting reminder of just how dangerous her life had become.

And exhausting.

Harley had seen the signs of fatigue from the spent adrenaline and the lack of sleep the night before. That's why he'd hoped she would nap on the drive back to Silver Creek, but she'd instead spent the time on her phone, trying to get updates on the Austin PD investigation. Specifically, trying to learn if the cops there could dig up enough to arrest Aaron for either the shooting or the murders.

Harley wasn't betting on either.

Simply put, there was no evidence to link Aaron to the crimes, and even with Marnie unable or unwilling to confirm his alibis, the cops would need to find some kind of smoking gun, maybe a literal one, to get any charges to stick.

During the drive, Theo had used his hands-free to try to get some updates of his own, but he wasn't having any better luck than Ava was. He'd had a fellow Ranger dig into Marnie's background, to see if she was the kind of woman who would lie about Aaron's alibis. Or if she was a woman who could really kill, but the only indication of that was Marnie's devotion to her sister.

Maybe extreme devotion.

That info had come up when Harley had questioned the Bulverde cop, Sergeant Gideon Gonzales, who'd been in charge of the investigation into Christina's death. According to Gonzales, Marnie had been beyond distraught over her sister's death. Marnie had been hysterical and sobbing in the first interviews he'd done with her, and then when he'd gone out to her house to tell her that Christina's death had been ruled an accidental overdose, Marnie had demanded that he arrest someone, that her sister's death wouldn't go unpunished.

Wouldn't go unpunished was something that definitely stuck in Harley's head, and it made him wonder if Aaron was right about the woman being capable of committing three murders. Especially if those murders got pinned on Aaron, the man Marnie might blame for losing her beloved sister.

"This part of the house is clear," Ava called out to him.

Like before, she'd taken the main living area, and since the bedrooms were clear as well, Harley made his way back to her. His main objective was to get her something to eat and then try to talk her into resting, but Ava had already poured herself a large glass of milk.

"There's sandwich stuff in the fridge," she offered.

He took her up on that, grabbing the items to make not one but two sandwiches so that Ava could eat as well. It was impossible to make himself stop worrying about her and the baby, though he doubted Ava wanted any TLC from him.

But Harley rethought that when she turned to him.

Their gazes met and he saw not only the fatigue but something else. Something he couldn't quite decipher until she spelled it out for him.

"Thank you for being here," she said. "I know we have our differences, but I really don't want to be alone in the house right now."

Yeah, he got that. Even though she was a good cop, she was still a mother-to-be, and that played into this. She could lay down her life for the badge, it was something good cops did, but she hated the risk to their child.

Harley was right there on the same page with her.

He set aside the sandwich stuff, went to her and took hold of her shoulders. He'd hoped to come up with just the right thing to say to ease some of the tension he could feel in her muscles. But her breath broke and Ava went into his arms as if she belonged there.

There'd been a time not that long ago when she would have hugged him, and more, but he could tell this particular embrace was costing her. Because this wasn't out of lust, wasn't the start of some hot foreplay that would lead them straight to bed. This was her leaning on him, and part of her would see that as a weakness.

It wasn't.

Because part of him was leaning on her, too. He needed this; the contact that gave him assurance that the baby and she were alive. Now it was up to both of them to make sure things stayed that way.

Harley didn't dare speak for fear it would cause her to move away from him. He just held her and hoped it would give her as much comfort as it was giving him.

Unfortunately, having her body pressed against his was also giving him some flashbacks of the times they'd had sex.

Definitely not images he wanted in his head right now, but no matter how much he tried to fight them off, they came anyway. Still, he didn't move other than to try to give her a reassuring rub on her back.

After several long moments, Ava finally leaned away from him. Not far though. Their bodies were still touching when she looked at him.

"It's wrong for me to lean on you like this," she said, sighing. And she broke the contact for real then by stepping away.

"It's not wrong," he assured her. "You've had a really bad day. Added to that, you met your son and had to interview your ex. I think that means you've earned all the leaning you want."

The corner of her mouth lifted in the briefest of smiles, but she didn't move back toward him. Instead, she picked up her glass of milk and continued to drink. That's when he noticed her hands were trembling a little. It was barely any movement, but for Ava, it might as well have been an earthquake of a reaction.

Hell.

All of this was tearing her apart. Harley would have gone to her to try to do something about that, but her phone rang.

She groaned when she looked at the screen. "It's my father."

Great. Just what she didn't need on top of everything else. "You want me to talk to him?" Harley offered. Verbally blasting Edgar might help burn off some of this restless energy he'd gotten from the hug.

"No, but thanks," she answered. Ava took the call and put it on speaker.

"I've been in committee meetings all day, and I get out to

learn that someone tried to kill my daughter," Edgar immediately snarled. "Any reason I didn't hear about it from you?"

"I've been busy," she informed him. In contrast to Edgar's fiery tone, hers was low level. Probably because she was too tired to work up a snit as her father had.

"Too busy to let me know about an attack," Edgar countered. "Too busy to give me a heads-up? I had to learn about the shooting from a reporter."

So, the press had picked up on that. Harley fired off a text to let Theo know that Silver Creek might soon be getting a share of reporters out looking for a story about the senator's cop daughter. Theo wouldn't give them that story, but at least he'd be prepared before the first one showed up.

"Yes, too busy," Ava confirmed. "I had to give my statement to the Austin PD and then I got tied up with the investigation."

She didn't add more. Nothing about Caleb or Aaron. She was no doubt waiting to see how much her father knew about all of this.

Or to maybe learn if Edgar had been involved in some way.

Edgar, however, stayed quiet for several long moments, maybe because he'd been hoping Ava would be the one to do the spilling. It must have occurred to him, though, that wasn't going to happen because the man finally huffed.

"I have contacts in Austin PD, so I know you met with Aaron Walsh," Edgar finally said. "And I know where you were when those shots were fired at you. Did Aaron try to kill you, or did he put his spawn up to doing it?"

Oh, that was so not the right thing to say, and Harley saw the anger whip through Ava's eyes. "My son's name is Caleb. If you use that disgusting term again, I'm hanging up. Now, tell me what the heck it is you want so I can end this conversation and eat."

Maybe Edgar was weighing his options because he went quiet again. "All right, I'll tell you what I want." Obviously, his brief silence hadn't toned down his own anger, because he then used the mean-as-a-snake tone that suited him so well. "I want you and your fellow cops to be more discreet when dragging me into this investigation. I had nothing to do with those shots being fired, nothing to do with the murders."

Ava's forehead bunched up. "What do you mean dragging you into this investigation? Are you doing general griping about that, or is there something specific?"

"Something specific," he snapped. "The sheriff you work for called Valerie Chandler and my campaign manager so he could verify that I had alibis for the dates of the murder. He wanted alibis from me." Edgar's voice rose on that last bit, said in a way that he felt he was above the law for such things.

He wasn't.

And Harley decided to let him know that.

"Senator, your daughter could have been killed today," Harley spoke up. "I'd think you'd want to do anything and everything possible to make sure her attacker is caught. That means providing pesky info to law enforcement so they can do their jobs. That also means the cops interviewing your longtime social companion, Valerie Chandler, so you can be ruled out as a potential suspect in three murders."

"Harley," Edgar grumbled, stretching out his name. "Of course, you'd be with my daughter. Why the hell didn't you stop shots from being fired at her?"

Ava huffed and moved as if to end the call, but Harley waved her off. Edgar was riled, and they might get something out of all this ranting.

"Harley put himself in between me and the shooter," Ava informed her father. "Unfortunately, Harley doesn't have wings or a superhero power, so he couldn't fly to the top of the building and dissolve the shooter with his laser vision."

"He shouldn't have put you in the position where you could have been shot in the first place," Edgar fired back. "If you hadn't insisted on seeing…that young man, you wouldn't have been such an easy target."

Well, at least Edgar had refrained from using the *spawn* word again, but Harley couldn't tell if the man's anger was because he was genuinely worried about Ava's safety or because of the bad publicity this might generate. Maybe it was some of both, but considering this was Edgar, the publicity was definitely a big factor.

"Why did you go see that young man anyway?" Edgar pressed a moment later.

"I figured your sources would have told you that," Ava countered.

"Is it because he's a suspect in the murders?" Her father threw it out there.

Ava dragged in a long breath. The weariness was coming back in her expression, and Harley so wished he hadn't stopped her from hanging up on this dirtbag father of hers.

"We questioned him," Ava said. "And he's not a suspect. That's because he fully cooperated with the police and didn't whine to me that he was being treated unfairly. Ironic, since he of all people could have claimed mistreatment at his bio-mother being forced to give him up or else see his bio-father arrested."

"That wasn't mistreatment," Edgar stormed. "It was the right thing to do. I was trying to save you, and look what you did. You ended up throwing your life away by pinning on that badge and bedding a damn Texas Ranger—"

Ava hit End Call, and Harley could see the visible effort she had to make to steady herself. She didn't get long to do that, though, because within seconds, her phone rang again.

"I'm going to block him," she muttered, but when she looked at the screen, a different kind of tension crossed her face. "It's Theo. Is everything all right?" she immediately asked. She put this call on speaker, too.

"No one else has been shot at or murdered," Theo let her know. "I'm just calling to give you a heads-up that your father might be getting in touch with you."

Ava frowned. "I just got off the phone with him."

"Ah. Well, he was fast. I'll bet he was mad because I talked to Valerie Chandler and Duran."

"Bingo," Ava verified. "Please tell me there's some inconsistencies you can use to open an investigation on one of them."

"Nothing on Edgar. His alibis checked out. Apparently, Valerie spends a lot of nights at his place, and she was there all three of the nights of the murders. Her driver dropped her off and picked her up the following mornings, and he confirmed that she was at that location."

"Is it possible Edgar left when she was asleep?" Harley asked.

"Possible but not likely. Valerie claims to be a light sleeper and insists she would have known if Edgar had left the bed. Also, once I pressed Edgar, he said he'd provide me with security footage to prove he arrived at and didn't leave the premises on the nights of the murders. Oh, and of course, he demanded I keep the footage private or he'd sue me."

Yep, that sounded like Edgar. It also sounded as if his alibis were fairly solid. Considering that Caleb's had checked out, too, both men had moved way down on their suspect list. However, there was one person directly connected to Edgar who was still firmly a suspect.

"What about Duran's alibis?" Harley asked.

"His aren't nearly as airtight as Edgar's," Theo explained. "In fact, he doesn't have one for two of the nights. Claimed he was home alone and, unlike Edgar, he doesn't have any security footage that might substantiate that. For one of the other nights, the last one, Duran was on the phone with a colleague who will confirm he had a lengthy conversation with Duran."

"Duran could have been on the phone while he was in Silver Creek," Ava quickly pointed out.

"Yep, and that's why I've asked Duran to voluntarily give me his phone records. He said he needed to consult with his attorney first."

That sounded like a possible red flag. Possible. But there were also people who didn't automatically cooperate with law enforcement even if that cooperation would help clear their name and catch a killer.

"If I don't have Duran's phone records by tomorrow," Theo went on, "I'll press to get a warrant. That won't be easy," he added. "Because I'm sure Duran has contacts in high places."

True, but he wasn't a senator, and Edgar could possibly be persuaded to press Duran to cough up the records. *Might*. Edgar and Duran were close, but since Edgar had had his privacy violated, he might insist his campaign manager do the same. Edgar might especially go for that if it gave him some good press to prove he was cooperating with the investigation.

"I just got an update from Austin PD on the shooting," Theo advised. "There was no rifle on the building. Nor was one found in the general area. There are no witnesses who can put Aaron on that roof."

That didn't mean, though, that Aaron hadn't been there and fired those shots. "How'd the shooter get up on that building?" Ava asked.

"Probably used the fire escape. Unless he was up there all night, it means he went up in broad daylight, but the back of the building doesn't have any visibility from any of the streets that crisscross that area."

Still, that was a gutsy move. Unless the shooter blended in so well that no one would have been suspicious. With Caleb ruled out, Harley went with another possibility.

"The shooter could have been a hired gun," Harley interjected, throwing it out there. "If so, then he was hired to purposely miss us because he would have had a clean enough shot of Ava, you or me when we left Caleb's apartment."

Both Ava and Theo made a sound of agreement. "The motive could have been just to terrorize me," Ava added. "Or to make us believe it was connected to Caleb. Even though Caleb couldn't have fired the shots, the shooter might have wanted us to believe he was trying to silence us for something Caleb might have told us."

Yes, and that took them back to Aaron. "Is there anything Caleb could have said that would have incriminated Aaron in some way? Or," Harley tacked onto that, "incriminated any of our suspects?"

Ava clearly didn't know because she shook her head. "Nothing I can think of," she conceded, spelling it out. "But I might not be the best judge of that."

She didn't spell out that it was hard to be objective about her own son, but Theo picked up on it.

"How are you dealing with all of this?" Theo came out and asked.

She paused a long time. "I'm not sure. What I'm feeling for him is getting mixed up with the attack and the murders. I considered asking him to come and stay here so I can better protect him, but since I'm the target, that would be like putting him straight in a path of danger."

Harley couldn't argue with that. Apparently, neither could Theo.

"The Rangers are keeping an eye on Caleb," Harley reminded her. And, while that wasn't a foolproof plan, the alternative was sending Caleb to a safe house. That might still happen if there was even a hint of an attack aimed at him.

"And I'm keeping in regular contact with both the Rangers and Austin PD," Theo assured her. "One more thing. I called Marnie on the drive back to Silver Creek, and I'm having her come in for an interview tomorrow."

"She agreed to come here?" Harley asked.

"I didn't give her much of a choice. I said there were some inconsistencies in what she reported to Ava and you, and that I needed her to clarify it face to face. Aaron might have just been tossing around accusations about Marnie to try to get himself out of hot water, but I still want to hear what the woman has to say. If she truly does hate Aaron, he could be right about her trying to set him up for the murders."

Harley tried to work that out in his mind. He'd read Marnie's bio and knew she'd once taught martial arts, so it was possible she would have been strong enough to abduct and kill three women. Strong enough to pose them, too. But for Marnie to set something like this in motion, it meant she's known all about Aaron and Ava having a child together. Maybe that was something Aaron had revealed during one of his self-confessed drunken talks with the woman. Or, if he'd told Christina, she could have passed along the info to her sister.

"Marnie is coming in at nine tomorrow morning, and I told her she was more than welcome to bring a lawyer with her," Theo added. "I'd like you both in the interview room."

"We'll be there," Ava assured him as Theo ended the call.

Ava's sigh was long and weary, and she continued to stare at the phone for several more seconds. "Whoever's behind the murders and the attack today...why didn't he or she just directly come after me since I'm almost certainly the intended target?"

Harley had already given this plenty of thought and he kept going back to one point. "Maybe the killer is waiting for you to have the baby. After all, none of the other three victims were pregnant."

That didn't help the weariness in her eyes. "So, four more months of murders and then me. If that's true, I guess I should be thankful that the serial killer doesn't want to harm our baby."

The "our" caused his stomach to jitter because it made them sound like a unit—which they were. For parenting anyway. Harley was hoping that was a start. Even if Ava and he were never lovers again, he wanted her to at least be in the same room with him without tensing up.

"Duran, Aaron and Marnie," she muttered, obviously leaving that "our" behind. "There's also the possibility my father could have hired someone." Ava stopped, shook her head, obviously rethinking that. "No, he wouldn't have needed to hire anyone. Not when Duran will do anything and everything for him."

"Good point. And, rather than risk anyone finding out what was happening, Duran could have done the murders himself."

Even though he'd been in law enforcement for well over a decade, it was still hard for Harley to wrap his mind around calculated murder. Especially murders like these that were meant to send a message and not because the actual victims had given the killer cause to murder them.

Ava stayed quiet a moment, but Harley could see the tightness creep back into her body. "Edgar told me that he struck a deal with you."

She couldn't have shocked Harley more if she'd slapped him. "What?" he demanded, his shoulders snapping back.

Ava took another moment and she pinned her cop's eyes to him. "My father's exact words were *I struck a deal with that bedmate Ranger of yours.* He said there'd be no charges against him and that his name would be cleared within the hour. And his name was indeed cleared."

Harley was shaking his head before she even finished. "I made no such deal, not with him or anyone else I've ever investigated. That's not how I work, and you know it."

"He had me listen to a recording of a conversation between the two of you. In it, you said he'd be cleared, that you'd make sure of it." She stopped, cursed. "He could have doctored the recording."

"Damn right he could have, or taken it out of context." Harley groaned and wanted to join Ava in that cursing. "Is that why you split with me?"

"It played a part in it," she admitted. "But so did the pregnancy itself. I figured if we were together, you'd feel obligated to do something. Like propose or suggest we move in together for the sake of the baby. I didn't want that."

He opened his mouth to say that wouldn't have happened, but Harley had to admit that, yes, it would have. He would have certainly offered marriage, and while he'd had deep feelings for Ava, she would have known the proposal had only come because she was pregnant. No way would she have accepted, so it'd just been easier for him to keep her at arm's length.

"Edgar told you that lie to put a wedge between us," Harley spelled out. He would have pressed for a heart-to-heart that he thought they should have now, but her phone rang again.

It wasn't Theo's or her dad's name on the screen this time. It was Candice Barlow, Ava's nearest neighbor.

"She probably heard about the shooting and wants to make sure I'm okay," Ava muttered, answering the call on speaker.

"Ava," the woman immediately said, and Harley had no trouble hearing the distress in her voice. "I was just looking out my kitchen window and I think—" She broke off and a hoarse sob tore from her mouth. "Oh, God. Ava, I think there's a body on your back porch."

Chapter Eight

A body.

Ava had thought this day couldn't possibly get any worse, but she'd obviously been wrong.

"I think it might be a woman's body," Candice continued. "I didn't want to get any closer to see for sure—"

"Stay inside your house," Ava instructed. "I'll check it out."

"Not alone, dear. Please not alone. I can call the sheriff," her neighbor offered.

"I'm not alone. Harley Ryland is with me." No need for Ava to explain that Harley was a Texas Ranger. In a small town like Silver Creek, everyone already knew that. "Just stay inside," she repeated, ending the call.

And drawing her gun.

Harley had already drawn his, and stooping low so his head wouldn't be an easy target from her kitchen window, he went closer so he could look. Then he cursed.

"Not a body," Harley assured her. "It's just a mannequin head, like the ones that people put wigs on. There's a garbage bag, but it doesn't appear to have anything in it." He paused a heartbeat. "It has a mask of your face."

That knocked some of the air out of her. So, this had been

left by the killer or at least by someone who had unreported details of the case. A sick prank, and it meant the killer had been right here, right at her home.

"Don't go out there," Ava muttered.

No need for her to spell out this could be a trap to lure them outside to be gunned down. Even though she, technically, lived in town, there was a heavily wooded greenbelt area behind her house that separated the residential area from the park, which had a lot of trees and trails. The killer could be waiting out there, hiding in those trees.

"I'm calling Theo," Harley let her know, keeping his attention on the backyard while he did that.

Staying to the side, Ava went to the window and had a look for herself. At first glance, it definitely did appear to be a body, and it would have especially seemed that way from Candice's house. But Ava immediately saw the white Styrofoam neck, the only part that was visible what with the garbage bag and the mask.

The mask was identical to the other three.

Oh, yes, that knocked more of the air from her lungs. She'd considered that it would have been risky for someone to haul a body from those woods to her porch, but it wouldn't have been that hard to bring in just the head, garbage bag and mask.

"Theo's on his way," Harley relayed to her. "And he'll contact the CSIs."

Her mind hadn't gone there yet; that soon a team of CSIs would be combing the area. Maybe looking inside, too, even though she'd gotten no alerts of a break-in. Still, Theo would want to be thorough.

"I'm not going to ask if you're okay because I know you're not," Harley said. "But will you at least consider sitting down. You've gone pale."

Pale and a little sick to her stomach, but she knew sitting wasn't going to help with the symptoms. She was a cop and had a job to do even if right now that job was simply giving a visual assessment of the area while she waited for the sheriff to show up.

"When I got back from the murder scene in the wee hours of the morning, I didn't check the back porch," she admitted.

"Neither did I. And I didn't even glance out there when we got back today."

"Same," Ava confirmed. "I glanced out the window when I was drinking some milk and taking my vitamin, but I didn't look down at the porch. That means, the head could have been put there at any time during the past twenty-four hours."

She could have slept while it was out there. A thought that sickened her even more. Even though it wasn't a human head, it still represented what this sick snake intended to do to her and any others on the hit list. He wanted to make them lifeless things.

And that sent a shot of pure raw anger through her.

Ava wanted to do something to stop this, and she nearly started calling neighbors to ask if they'd seen absolutely anything. But it would be a waste of time. If anyone in the neighborhood had seen anything suspicious, they would have already let her know. That probably meant the killer had put the head there when it'd been dark. Heck, maybe even after Ava had been called out to the crime scene for the third murder.

"I can take you to my house on the ranch," Harley offered.

It was tempting and, while the ranch was secure, it wasn't impenetrable. A shooter could still get to them. Plus, Ava wasn't sure running and hiding was the way to go here. In fact, drawing out the killer might be the fastest way to stop him from going after someone else.

"No," she answered, "I think it's best if we stay here. Notice that I said *we* because I know there's no way you'd leave me."

"You got that right." He glanced at her, frowning. "You're thinking of trying to use yourself as some kind of bait. You're not," he added, and there was plenty of insistence in his tone.

"I don't want another murder on my conscience," she muttered.

"It's not on your conscience. It's on the person who's doing these killings."

Harley moved closer to her and, even though he was still keeping watch, he also ran his hand down the length of her arm. For such a small gesture, it was plenty comforting.

Ava nearly broke then. She nearly gave into the despair of not being able to stop the monster who was killing and tormenting. She nearly allowed herself just to lean on Harley and let him give her all the comforting gestures in his arsenal. Since he'd once been her lover, she knew that arsenal was plenty full.

But she held back.

For one thing, if she broke, she wasn't sure she could piece herself back together any time soon. Not even with Harley's help. Added to that, she heard the vehicle pull into her driveway and knew that Theo had arrived. A moment later, she got a text confirming that.

I'll have a look around. You and Harley stay put but be ready to give me backup if needed.

Will do, she texted back.

Harley took Theo's instructions to the max by going to the back door. He opened it just a few inches, which gave him a better view of the yard and the woods. It also meant he was now in a position to fire if it became necessary.

Ava stayed at the window so she'd be able to cover the yard and woods from a different angle. She tried to pick through the trees and underbrush, but it was thick, and indeed possible that someone was out there watching and waiting.

There were the sounds of more vehicles arriving, and Ava soon spotted Deputy Jesse Ryland join Theo to observe the scene. Like Theo, Jesse was a good cop, and she was hoping they'd spot something they could use to crack this investigation and ID the killer.

Two more deputies arrived, Nelline Rucker and Cruz Molina, and Theo sent them to search the woods. Ava watched. Watched, too, as Jesse took some pictures of the fake head and then leaned in for a closer examination.

"There's a piece of paper sticking out from beneath the side of the trash bag," Jesse called out, and he looked through the kitchen window to meet her gaze. "It's a note, and it just says *Soon*."

So, another taunt. Once again, Ava was glad she hadn't fallen apart, because she needed her anger right now. That would keep her going.

She heard yet another vehicle approach the house and figured it was the CSIs. But Ava rethought that when she saw Theo peer around the side of the house and curse.

"It's Duran," Theo relayed to her. "Any idea what he wants?"

"No," Ava said, going closer to the open door so Theo would be able to hear him. "He's never been to my house, and he didn't call ahead. My father probably sent him." Why Edgar would do that, Ava didn't know.

"You want me to get rid of him?" Theo asked her.

"No, I'll talk to him. Are there any signs of a shooter out there?"

"Not so far." Theo glanced at the two deputies who were looking through the wooded area before he pinned his gaze to Ava's. "Just remember that Duran is a suspect. Frisk him before you let him in the house. He probably won't like that, but I'd rather have you in the 'better safe than sorry' mode."

So would she, and that's why Ava gave Theo a quick nod—just as there was a knock at the front door. Harley was right by her side, of course, when she answered it, and he didn't allow Duran to get out a single word before he pulled the man inside and checked him for weapons.

Duran was clearly surprised because he made a strangled sound of protest. "Really? Is this necessary?"

"It is," Harley assured him without missing a beat. He extracted a snub-nosed .38 from a concealed holster inside Duran's jacket and held it up. "You'd better have a license to carry concealed," he informed him.

"I do." There was plenty of indignation and anger in Duran's body language, but he didn't reach out to try to snatch back the gun. "What's going on? Why are those police cars here, and why would you have to disarm me when I just came here to talk to you?" He aimed those questions at Ava.

She debated how much to tell him but decided to go with full disclosure so she could observe his reaction. "Someone—a coward, no doubt—left a dummy's head on my porch. A coward because he wasn't man enough to confront me head-on."

Harley shot her a warning glance, obviously reminding her that he didn't want her to make herself bait. She was sort of doing that by trying to goad Duran, but the man didn't react with temper.

"You mean like a sick prank?" Duran asked.

"Exactly like a sick prank," she verified. "He was probably hoping it'd send me into an emotional tailspin so I'd do something foolish."

Ava wouldn't mention that the emotional tailspin likely would have happened had Harley not been there to anchor her.

Duran muttered something under his breath she didn't catch and shook his head as if disgusted. She reminded herself that his reaction could be faked. After all, Duran probably had to conceal a lot of what he was thinking when he was on the campaign trail with her father.

Duran glanced out the window as the CSI van arrived and he shook his head again. "What can I do to help?" he asked.

She was betting he'd had to offer that a lot, too, but Ava figured he wasn't going to like how she was about to take him up on that offer.

"You can help by truthfully answering some questions," she spelled out for him.

Duran didn't look especially offended. "Questions about what?"

"Everything," she supplied, and since this could take a while, and Ava didn't especially want to be standing in front of any windows, she motioned for them to have a seat in the living area. "Start with anything and everything you haven't told me about Aaron and Caleb, and then move on to any knowledge whatsoever you have about the murders or the shooting today in Austin."

Duran dragged in a long breath and she could see the calculation in his eyes. Oh, what to say and what to keep to himself.

"I'll arrest you for obstruction of justice if you withhold anything about this investigation," Harley threatened. "And, FYI, this is a broad investigation, and it includes anything that's happened to Ava or Aaron for the past twenty years. If you've been keeping secrets, spill them now."

Ava couldn't have said it better herself, and she matched Harley's hard stare with one of her own.

Duran volleyed glances at both of them before he sighed.

"I don't have any details about Ava's pregnancy that you don't already know," Duran started. "Edgar was furious when he found out she was pregnant, and he did tell Aaron he'd be arrested if he didn't leave town and never contact Ava again. By the way, even if that was criminally wrong, the statute of limitations has long passed. There's absolutely no reason for anyone else to know about it."

"I'll determine that," Ava said, and she made a keep-going motion with her hand.

Duran sighed again, but he did, indeed, keep going. "Edgar asked me to keep an eye on Aaron to make sure he stayed away, so I'm the one who hired the private investigators. One to monitor Aaron's whereabouts. Another to keep an eye on you."

Ava knew she shouldn't have been surprised about that last part, but it was a bit of a shock to hear it confirmed. "How long did you keep PIs on me?" She wanted to know.

"Until you went to the police academy. I figured you'd notice someone following you around, and I didn't want it to lead to a potentially embarrassing situation for your father."

There was a definite creep factor in having her under surveillance for all those years, but the PIs wouldn't have seen anything worth reporting back to Duran or her father. After she'd given up Caleb for adoption, she'd followed the straight and narrow. No boyfriends, no parties, no social stuff whatsoever. Ava had focused on her studies so she could become a cop. It had become an obsession, probably because she'd wanted to right wrongs. She could thank her father for that particular legacy.

"I want the names of the PIs," Ava ordered.

Duran reluctantly nodded. "The one who was on you died a few years ago. Pancreatic cancer. His name was Don Stewart. The one on Aaron is Darcel Harrison. He's good," Duran added. "He's been on Aaron all these years with calls and cursory checks to make sure he's staying away from you."

Harley fired off a text, no doubt to one of his fellow Rangers so they could do a background check on the PIs. Harrison would also have to be interviewed.

"Did the PI actually lose touch with Aaron after Christina's death?" Ava came out and asked.

"Yes," Duran readily answered. "For a while, anyway. Aaron lost his job and moved from his apartment, but he resurfaced a couple of months later."

"Resurfaced at Marnie's?" Ava pressed, hoping that the PI had been on Aaron when he'd visited the woman.

"No. You're wanting to know if I had Marnie's house under surveillance during the dates of the murders? I didn't," Duran supplied before Ava could confirm that was absolutely what she wanted. "I have no idea of either Marnie's or Aaron's whereabouts for those dates."

Duran stopped, but Ava could tell there was something else he was holding back. "Spill it," she ordered.

The man looked at Harley. "I'm about to tell you both something...sensitive. Something that we must keep among just the three of us."

"No," Harley said without hesitation. "If what you're withholding can catch a killer, it won't be kept hush-hush."

He leaned in closer, violating the man's personal space. "Now, talk."

Duran swallowed hard and paused a long time. "Aaron has been trying to blackmail Edgar for months now. Edgar doesn't know," he quickly added. "I took the initial call from Aaron, and I'm the one who's been dealing with him."

Ava was certain the look she gave Duran was loaded with skepticism. "Someone was trying to blackmail my father, and you didn't let him know? Why would you keep something like that from him?"

"Because I didn't want Edgar to be involved in something that could be potentially construed as unsavory, possibly even criminal. Aaron demanded hush money, and I reasoned with him that he didn't have a shred of proof that Edgar had had any part in what happened twenty years ago. Aaron said he'd go to the press, and that they'd believe him. I assured him that they wouldn't, that it'd be his word against a sitting state senator."

She could see it possibly happening that way. Possibly. But she was almost positive Edgar knew. Then again, if he had, and Aaron had continued to push the idea of spilling the truth, Aaron might have had some kind of fatal "accident" to get him completely out of the picture.

"You said Aaron had been trying to blackmail Edgar for months," Harley restated. "How long exactly? And how much have you paid him?"

Duran's mouth tightened. "Seven months." He paused again. "I gave Aaron a one-time payment of ten thousand dollars. I emphasized that was all he was going to get."

Ava zoomed right in on the seven months. "Did Aaron make the contact before or after his girlfriend's death?"

"Right before. In fact, I had the PI deliver the money in cash, and that night his girlfriend died."

Oh, mercy. That was either a horrible coincidence or else Aaron had given Christina the money to get the drugs that had killed her.

"And Aaron hasn't contacted you since about getting another round of cash?" Harley asked.

"He did," Duran admitted. "But I informed him if he pressed the matter, that I'd tell everyone he was responsible for his girlfriend's death. I believe he's worried how Marnie would react to that."

"Should Aaron be worried about Marnie?" Ava asked.

Duran's mouth tightened again. "Yes, I think he should. I've had a background check done on the woman, and Marnie practically raised her after their folks died. She was fiercely protective of Christina. She already despises Aaron, so news like this wouldn't sit well with her."

"'Protective,'" Ava repeated in a mutter. "Protective enough that Marnie would kill and try to set up Aaron?"

Duran paused again. "Possibly. But I think a stronger scenario here would be that Aaron is committing the murders with the plan to try to set up Edgar." His eyes met hers. "And Aaron could want to punish Edgar by killing you. That's why I'm begging you to take precautions, Ava. Despite your differences with your father, he loves you and doesn't want you hurt."

Ava could have debated whether or not her father was even capable of love, but Aaron might believe he was. If so, that was a fairly strong motive for murder, and Aaron might be savoring the notion of Edgar sitting on death row to pay for crimes he hadn't committed.

"May I get back my gun before I leave?" Duran asked, standing.

Harley thought about it a long time while he kept his steely stare aimed at him. He finally nodded, but he didn't hand Duran the gun until the man was out the door and on the porch.

"Duran is staying on our suspect list," Harley insisted the moment he shut the door and locked it.

He'd taken the words right out of her mouth. "I agree, because Duran could be killing with the plan to set up Aaron. If I'm dead, too, then there's no one to verify Aaron's claims of what my father did twenty years ago."

It sickened her to think that the man who'd just sat and chatted with her would want her dead, but keeping his boss out of trouble was Duran's specialty. In this case, Duran might have seen this as a perfect solution to tying up a lot of potential problems.

Her phone rang and her stomach jumped when she saw Caleb's name on the screen. She prayed he wasn't calling to tell her he'd been attacked, and she nearly fumbled her phone because she tried to answer it so fast.

"Are you okay?" she blurted out, putting the call on speaker so Harley could hear.

"I was going to ask you the same thing," Caleb answered. "Someone emailed me a picture. It looks like a mannequin's head, but it's got your face on it. I'm guessing it's some kind of mask, but it's definitely a picture of you on the mask."

Oh, mercy. Ava had hoped that Caleb wouldn't be pulled into the sick details of this. "When did you get the picture?" she asked, forcing herself to be the cop and not the mom.

"About ten minutes ago. Should I report it to the Austin police?"

"No, I'll take care of that." Or rather, Harley would, she realized, when he stepped aside to get that started. "Austin PD will send someone out to look at the email," she informed Caleb.

Though Ava was betting the killer probably wouldn't

have used a server that could be traced back to him or her, they might get lucky.

"I'm sorry this happened to you," she said. "I'm sorry… for a lot of things," Ava settled for saying.

"I'm sorry for you, too." Caleb muttered some profanity. "Are you safe where you are? I mean, this killer can't get to you, can he?"

His concern touched her and she started to lose the battle she'd been having with her nerves. Her eyes watered, the tears threatening to spill.

"I'm taking precautions," she told him, giving him the best assurance she could. "You're doing the same?"

"I am. I'm taking my classes online for a few days, just until this is over. Stay safe," he added before he muttered a goodbye and ended the call.

Harley finished up his call, too, and made his way back to her. He must have seen she was on shaky ground because he immediately pulled her into his arms.

"Lieutenant O'Malley is sending an officer to Caleb's place right now," he murmured directly against her ear.

She felt the warmth from his breath, the gentle way he was holding her, and she welcomed every bit of it. And wanted more. For just a few seconds, she wanted not to be able to feel all these horrible emotions. Emotions that a killer had her son in his sights.

Ava turned and kissed him.

This was wrong. She knew it was. But didn't care. Apparently, neither did Harley because a deep sound rumbled in his throat. A sound of instant need and heat, and he returned the kiss. Not with a fiery, urgent need, but with a gentleness.

He tasted good, just as she remembered, and that savor sent an instant ache for him through her body. She automatically slid her arms around him, drawing him closer. And closer. Until they were body to body and mouth to mouth. Until Harley deepened the kiss and shot the heat and need straight through the roof.

It was that intense, clawing need that caused her to pull back. Her breath was gusting when she tore her mouth from his, and the shocking realization of what she'd just done made her want to be filled with regret.

But she wasn't.

No regret. Only the need. And that's why she'd had to pull away from him.

"I can't fall for you again," she said. "I just can't."

Because it could lead to more than just a broken heart. This time it could be the fatal distraction that got her and her baby killed.

Chapter Nine

Harley worked on the ever-growing paperwork at Ava's kitchen table while he waited for her to make a morning appearance. He could hear her in the shower, so he knew it wouldn't be long before she joined him, hopefully for breakfast and then they could leave to go to the sheriff's office for Marnie's interview.

For now, Harley welcomed the quiet moments so he could try to give himself a serious attitude adjustment. Hard to do, though, with Ava's words constantly repeating in his head.

I can't fall for you again.

That hadn't exactly been what he'd hoped to hear after the scalding kiss they'd shared. Not with the need for her skyrocketing. But he totally got where she was coming from. This was the absolute worst time for either of them to be distracted with things such as heat, need and kissing. It was there though.

Mercy, was it.

Harley knew he would have to stomp all of that down and focus on catching a killer. That was the only way to ensure Ava and their daughter were safe. Once they had this SOB behind bars and dealt with the aftermath, then maybe he could start trying to convince Ava to give that *falling for him again* a chance.

For now, he just had to work and make sure he was doing everything possible to keep her safe. Thankfully, plenty of people were doing that as well. Theo and some of the other deputies were working round-the-clock, and the CSIs had searched through every inch of Ava's yard and the woods. The plan was for the CSI team to return today to undertake a check inside her house while Ava and he were at the sheriff's office. Harley didn't expect them to find anything useful, but it was one of those things that needed to be done.

Harley had higher hopes in the usefulness department with the reports that had come in from the PI, Darcel Harrison. There were twenty years' worth, so it would take a while to go through them all. But on Duran's okay, Darcel had sent the complete file to the Rangers and copied Theo. Theo didn't have the manpower to assign someone to pore through them, but there were techs in the Ranger crime lab making the reports a high priority. After all, it could lead to catching a serial killer.

An email that popped into his in-box got his attention off Ava and back on the investigation. It was a report from Austin PD to let him know the photo sent to Caleb had been examined and that there was no traceable info on it. That's what Harley had expected, but it was still a disappointment.

That photo taunt had been plenty gutsy, and sometimes killers made mistakes when they took risks like that. Apparently, though, this killer had been smart enough to use a temporary email account and had then bounced it around servers to make it impossible to track.

Since Ava and Theo had been copied on the report, Harley figured that's what Ava was reading when she finally made her way into the kitchen. She looked up from her phone at him, their eyes locking for a couple of seconds. She didn't come out and say anything about the kiss, about why it shouldn't have happened, but he knew her well enough to know that was what she was thinking.

"You saw that the emailed photo can't be traced," she said, tipping her head to his laptop.

He nodded. "It's a dead end, but I spoke to Lieutenant O'Malley a little while ago, and we might get something new on the surveillance footage from the shooting. He's having the feed collected from any and all cameras for the surrounding block. It'll take some time, but he thinks we might be able to see someone coming or going from the scene."

Ava didn't look especially hopeful that anything would come from that, and she was probably right. Still, something eventually had to hit. It just had to. Because Harley refused to believe there was absolutely no evidence out there that wouldn't help them ID this killer.

"Did you read the report from the crime lab on the mannequin head?" he asked, already knowing the answer.

The report had come in an hour ago, and since Ava was checking for such things as often as he was, she would have already seen it. Heck, she'd likely studied it, combing for any details. But even with the combing, there just wasn't anything in it they could use. Not from this initial info anyway.

"Yes," she verified. "There's no way to trace the garbage bag, but locating the source of the mannequin head is possible."

That was it in a nutshell. What she didn't add was that finding the source for the mannequin head was a long shot, especially since the killer could have bought it online or paid cash for it at a store.

Ava looked at him again as if she might say something of a personal nature, but her phone rang and the moment was lost. Her attention snapped to the screen and he could tell from her soft groan that this wasn't a call she wanted to take.

"It's my father," she explained. On a heavy sigh, she answered and put it on speaker. "I'm busy," she greeted, her voice snapping. That wasn't exactly a lie. They did have to leave soon for the sheriff's office for the interview with Marnie.

"So am I," her father snapped right back. "And that's why I'll make this quick. I understand Duran paid you a visit yesterday. What did he want?"

Her eyebrow lifted when her gaze met Harley's and, setting her phone down on the counter, she went to pour herself a glass of milk. "Are you saying your trusted friend and campaign manager didn't tell you why he was here?"

"He said he was checking on you," Edgar quickly fired back. "He claims you had questions about the PI I had on that scumbag who got you pregnant when you were a kid. Is that true?"

Harley didn't miss the word *claims*. So, maybe Edgar wasn't feeling a whole lot of trustworthiness for Duran.

"I'm sure Duran can tell you all about what Harley and I discussed with him," Ava replied.

"Harley," Edgar grumbled, using the same tone as he had with the scumbag referral to Aaron. "Of course, he listened in on the discussion."

"Of course," Harley interjected to let Edgar know he was listening now as well. Yeah, it was a petty dig, but Harley didn't mind resorting to pettiness where Edgar was concerned. "You tried to put a wedge between Ava and me by lying to her, by telling her I'd cut you a deal in the investigation I was running on you."

There was silence. For a long time. "You didn't charge me

with anything," Edgar finally said, obviously going for some pettiness of his own. He wasn't going to own up to the lie.

And that's why Harley pushed harder.

"How do you think Ava reacted when she found out you'd lied to her?" Harley threw it out there. "How do you think my boss will react when I announce that you smeared my name for your own gain? And that gain was to make sure your daughter and I didn't end up together."

More silence, followed by a whole string of cursing. "I didn't call my daughter to be threatened by you—"

"It's not a threat. It's a guarantee," Harley assured him. "Either tell Ava the truth right now, that there was no deal cut, or I'll file a formal complaint for your allegations about me."

Even though Harley couldn't see the man's face, he knew Edgar was seething. Ava was actually smiling while she drank her milk. Apparently, she was enjoying the pettiness, too, but underneath the enjoyment and smiles, Harley knew that Edgar's lie had done a lot of damage. It was likely the reason Ava and he weren't together right now.

"Ava misunderstood me," Edgar insisted several moments later. "I said I'd gotten a good deal what with the charges being dropped. I didn't mean for her to infer that you'd pulled strings or covered up anything. What you did was the only thing you could have done by dropping those charges because I was innocent. And now back to the reason for this call," he quickly tacked on. "Is Duran keeping something from me?"

Ava sighed. Her smile had vanished, and now there was plenty of anger in her eyes. "Ask him for yourself," she snarled for a split second before she ended the call.

She stood there a moment, probably waiting for Edgar to call back so she could decline it, but when that didn't happen, Ava's expression changed. Some of the anger vanished and in its place came the kind of look a cop got when they were trying to figure out if a suspect was telling the truth.

"Well, at least he admitted that he'd lied to me about there being a deal," she muttered. "But I think he called because this was a way of covering his butt."

"I agree." Harley couldn't say it fast enough. Edgar was a schemer, and this chat and concern about Duran could have all been a ploy. "This way, if anything leaks about Aaron, Edgar could be planning to come back with the response that he was out of the loop on that, that it was all Duran's doing." He paused and did some more thinking. "Would Duran just go along with this by taking the fall for his boss?"

"Yes," she said without hesitation. "Of course, Edgar would do everything within his power to stop Duran from being charged with anything criminal, but he would absolutely let Duran take the blame for anything that could end up reflecting badly on him."

That's the way Harley saw it, too, and it meant if it came to light about Aaron being threatened and run out of town, then Duran would likely say it'd been his doing and Edgar had had no knowledge of it.

"Did Edgar ever directly threaten Aaron back when he found out you were pregnant?" Harley asked.

She thought about that and finally shook her head. "I assumed he had, but maybe Duran is the one who delivered the message from Edgar. Of course, my father told me he'd have Aaron arrested if I didn't give up the baby. I'm sure he'd deny that, though, and he'd claim it was another misunderstanding."

True, but it would still cause some bad PR problems for the senator if all of this came out. And it would. Harley couldn't see another way around it.

"Now that Austin PD is involved with the investigation, someone will likely spill about Caleb's connection to you," Harley said. "Are you prepared for the fallout?" Because there was no way to keep it out of the media.

Again, she didn't jump to answer, and she looked directly at him before she spoke. "What if I get Caleb's permission to go ahead and leak it?" she suggested. "How do you think the killer would react to that?"

Harley blew out a long breath after he played around with some possibilities. "If the killer is Aaron, it'd likely piss him off since his plan would probably be to set up Edgar or even Duran for the murders, and he hasn't fully set that in motion."

Ava made a sound of agreement. "And, if Duran is the killer, he also hasn't had the time to set up Aaron, if that's what he has in mind." She paused. "If the killer is Marnie, then leaking this might suit her just fine because this would make Aaron the most obvious suspect."

"True," he admitted, trying to figure out the best way to word what he had to say next. "Whoever's doing these murders could be a sociopath or have some other extreme instability. You know both Aaron and Duran. Has either of them ever showed any signs that would make you believe instability could be playing into these murders?"

"I've considered it," she admitted. "Duran, yes. He has such an extreme devotion to my father that he could have crossed some very big, very dangerous lines. *Could have*," Ava emphasized. "As for Aaron, I really can't say. He had that bad-boy thing in high school, a recklessness. In hindsight, I think I was attracted to him because he was the opposite of the boys my father was pressuring me to date."

So, a rebellion of sorts. Harley wasn't jealous of Aaron. Well, probably not anyway. Ava and he weren't kids, and each of them had a past. He just didn't like the idea of thinking of Ava with another man.

So, yeah, jealousy.

"What about Marnie?" she asked. "We've only had that short conversation on the phone with her, but have you read anything in her background to indicate she could be unstable enough kill in order to get revenge?"

"Nothing so far, but if she was as devoted to her sister as Duran and Aaron have said, then Christina's death could have tipped her over the edge." Still, there might be something he hadn't uncovered yet.

At the mention of the woman's name, Harley checked the time. "We should be getting to the sheriff's office. Theo had a cruiser dropped off right before you got in the shower, and I had it parked in your garage."

That would minimize the time Ava was outside, and therefore be a harder target for a sniper. The cruiser didn't guarantee Ava's safety, but it was one of those precautions he intended to take. Another was making sure he was near her at all times. If the killer could get to her back porch, then whoever it was could smash a window and come after her in the house.

Ava took a breakfast bar and a thermos of milk with her as they made their way to the cruiser.

Harley kept watch all around them as he pulled out of her driveway. It was broad daylight, which helped with the visibility, but since the last attack had also happened during the day, that didn't give them any level of comfort.

As Theo and he had worked out, Harley made the short drive to the sheriff's office and parked in the covered lot directly outside the door to Theo's office. It was mere steps away, but each one of them seemed to take an eternity. Harley definitely breathed a little easier once he had Ava inside.

The breathing easier hadn't lasted though.

That was because he immediately spotted one of their suspects. Harley had seen Marnie's DMV photo, so he instantly recognized her face. She was tall and had an athletic build. Some people dressed up for an interview with the cops, but not Marnie. She was wearing capris workout pants, running shoes and a loose top. She had her hair pulled back in a tight ponytail.

"What inconsistencies?" the woman demanded the moment she saw Ava and him.

Since she didn't ask who they were, Marnie must have seen photos of them, too. It wouldn't have been hard for her to find because of Ava's background and some of Harley's high-profile cases.

It took Harley a moment to recall that Theo had insisted Marnie come in for a face-to-face interview because there'd been some *inconsistencies* in what she'd said to Ava and him. And there had been. Aaron had accused Marnie of trying to set him up for the murders.

"This way," Theo said, coming out of his office and motioning for all of them to follow him.

He didn't address Marnie's question while they made their way to an interview room.

Once inside, Theo Mirandized her, causing Marnie to gasp. "Are you arresting me?" she snapped, aiming the question at Theo.

"No. This interview is to put your statement on record. I read you your rights for your own protection, so I could remind you again that you can have a lawyer present."

"So you said when you called," Marnie muttered. Her chin came up and she looked Theo straight in the eyes when she dropped down into one of the chairs. "Well, I have nothing to hide, so ask whatever you want."

Theo, Ava and he sat as well, and Theo slid a piece of paper toward Marnie. "Look at those dates and tell me if Aaron Walsh was with you on those nights."

Marnie picked up the paper, looked at it. "I've already said I'm not sure if he was there or not. Maybe."

"Aaron claims you invited him over on those dates," Ava explained.

"I could have, in a general sort of way. You know, like drop over whenever and pick up that photo you always liked of Christina." She stopped and huffed. "Look, this isn't a big deal. I despise Aaron, but if I could say with absolute certainty that he was at my house, I would because that would give him an alibi. That's what you want, right? To make sure he has an alibi."

"Do you have alibis for those nights?" Theo asked, turning the tables on her.

Marnie gave him one sharp glare before she shook her head. "If Aaron was there, then he's my alibi, but since I can't confirm it, then I guess I don't have any. Why would I need them? I can't possibly be a suspect in the murders."

None of them confirmed that. Because she was.

"You also told us that Aaron was worried about Caleb trying to harm him," Harley threw out there a moment later. "Aaron says that's not true."

"Well, duh." Marnie dismissed that with the wave of her hand. "He said it when he was drunk and rambling. He doesn't remember a lot of things." She paused, her jaw tightening. "Like the name of the person who sold my sister the drugs that killed her."

"You think Aaron knows that?" Ava asked.

"Damn straight, I do." Marnie leaned in, her face tight with anger now. "And I also believe Aaron paid for those drugs. Instead of using the money to get her counseling help, he fed her addiction."

That meshed with what Duran had told them about the timing of the payoff he'd given Aaron. Still, Harley had searched for any connections that Aaron might have known drug dealers and he hadn't come up with anything solid.

Harley went with a different angle. He took the paper and wrote down the names of the three murdered women. "Do you know any of them?" he asked.

Marnie looked at the list and glanced up at him. Their gazes met for just a second before she looked away. "I knew the second one, Theresa Darnell. I read about her murder."

Interesting. As far as Harley knew, this was the first time one of the suspects admitted to knowing one of the victims.

"How'd you know her?" Harley pressed.

Marnie groaned and her mouth stayed tight a moment. "Aaron." She practically spat his name out. "My sister and Aaron had a lot of splits in their stormy relationship, and during one of those splits, he started seeing Theresa. I don't know how they met, so you'd have to ask him about that. Anyway, when Aaron and Christina got back together, Theresa showed up at my place looking for Aaron, and she made a big scene. I had to threaten to have her arrested before she'd leave."

Ava shook her head. "There's no police report about this."

"No, because I didn't file one. Theresa and I had words, that's all. She was looking to confront Christina for stealing her man. A man Theresa had had for a week or two, I might point out." She added an eye roll to that.

Since Aaron almost certainly knew that Theresa's name had been one of the murdered women, Harley had to wonder why the man hadn't just volunteered that info. Because he hadn't, it made Aaron look downright guilty.

"Since you seem to be digging for anything that could put me in a bad light," Marnie went on, "you'll probably find out that one of my old boyfriends, Paul Harmon, was in a militia. One of those groups that plays soldier and stockpiles guns. When I started seeing him, I didn't know about this, and as soon as I learned of it, I broke it off."

Harley jumped right on that. "What militia and when was this?"

Marnie sighed in a way that let him know she'd been hoping they would just drop the subject with the info she'd already provided to them. "About two years ago, and I'm not sure if the group had a name or not. If they did, Paul never mentioned it to me. The only reason I'm telling you about him is because I don't want you to use that relationship to claim I have criminal ties to someone who could murder women or shoot at cops."

Maybe, but another reason could be that Marnie figured her association with this militia member would come up in a deep background check and she was hoping to make it seem unimportant. Unfortunately, some militia groups had members with expertise in explosives, so her connection was more important than she realized.

Harley looked at Theo and tipped his head to the door, silently asking if he should step out and go ahead to try to find out more about Paul Harmon. Theo gave him a nod.

"Excuse me a second," Harley said, and he went next door into the observation room so he could use the laptop there.

Harley could see and hear Theo and Ava continue the interview with Marnie, and Ava was pressing the woman to find out if she'd ever had any contact with the other two victims.

He continued to listen, but Harley started the search for Paul Harmon. There were several men with that name living in central Texas, but it didn't take Harley long to zoom in on the one who was a known member of the Brotherhood militia, a paramilitary group who dabbled in all sorts of illegal things, including gun running.

Harley couldn't immediately see that Paul Harmon had had any kind of explosives training, but that wasn't usually something that popped up in a background search, unless the guy had been arrested for explosive-related crimes. He hadn't been, which meant he needed to do some more digging. Not just into Paul but also the militia itself to make sure one of their members hadn't assisted the killer with making that bomb.

Figuring he'd gotten all he could from the cursory background check, Harley stood to go back into the interview room, but before he could leave, his phone dinged with a text from Lieutenant O'Malley at Austin PD.

The techs went through all the collected feed from the security cameras, and you need to see this particular still frame. This camera was one block from the building where the shots originated and was recorded six-and-a-half minutes from the time the last shot was fired.

Harley tapped on the image to enlarge it, figuring it would be a clearer image of Aaron. It wasn't. But Harley had no trouble whatsoever recognizing the person who'd been captured in the photo.

Hell.

It was Duran.

Chapter Ten

Duran.

Ava's mind was whirling with everything Harley, Theo and she had learned this morning. Marnie's admission that she knew one of the victims. That Aaron had as well. And that Marnie had a connection to someone who could have made that explosive device. But the bit of info that was flashing in her head like a neon sign was that Duran had been within a block of the shooting.

While Harley and she sat in the interview room they'd converted to a makeshift office, eating the lunch that'd been sent over from the diner, she again studied the image that Austin PD had managed to get for them. It was Duran all right. Not wearing his usual suit, either, but rather dressed in dark jeans and a T-shirt.

In the shot, Duran was looking over his shoulder, in the direction from where the shots had been fired. It was hard to tell from the grainy photo, but the man's face was tense, and he wasn't walking but rather running. That speed was the reason he had quickly moved out of surveillance range and another camera hadn't been able to pick him up.

What Duran hadn't had with him was a rifle, but it was possible he'd used his handgun. That would have explained the missed shots since the roof of the building had been at least fifty yards away. An expert marksman could have possibly made the shots, but Ava couldn't find any proof that Duran would qualify as an expert.

Still, the image had been enough for Austin PD to get a warrant to have the gun taken into custody and checked to see if it'd been recently fired. If it had been, and if Duran didn't have a credible reason for being in that specific area at that time, then he could be arrested.

"And what fun would that be for Austin PD," Ava muttered, causing Harley to glance up from his laptop and look at her. Like her, he was using the lunch break to continue to dig into the various threads of the investigation.

"You're talking about Duran?" he asked, obviously noticing that she was still studying the photo from the security cam.

"Yes," she confirmed. "Lieutenant O'Malley will have probably already sent someone to Duran's to retrieve the gun and question him. I suspect, first chance he gets, he'll be calling me to vent about being harassed."

"Then he can claim more harassment when Theo questions him," Harley concluded.

Duran would, certainly, but that wouldn't stop Theo from questioning the man once Austin PD was done with him. If Duran was tied to the shooting, that was Austin's jurisdiction, but anything to do with the murders would need to go through Theo.

"You should try to eat before your father shows," Harley reminded her.

True, because while Duran was in Austin being questioned, her father and Aaron would be coming to Silver Creek. Not at the same time. Sometimes, a heated verbal altercation could lead to a person saying incriminating things, but in her father and Aaron's case, the encounter could get very ugly and cause both men to lawyer up. For this phase of questioning, Theo wanted cooperation to be able to get the info to help them with those threads.

Ava took a bite of her chef's salad and checked the time. Her father was due to arrive in a half hour, but if he was angry enough, he might already be on his way. Aaron wasn't scheduled for another two hours, which would end up making this a tiring day. Then again, it'd already been tiring what with Marnie's interview and learning about Duran being spotted on the security cam.

"I got something," Harley announced, moving his burger aside so he could turn his laptop in her direction.

She immediately saw Paul Harmon's name along with the known members of the militia. Not a huge group, but there were at least a dozen of them.

"I did a cross-match of employers," Harley explained as he tapped one of the names about halfway down the list. "And Aaron worked with this guy, Lionel Henderson, at Tip Top Repairs. Aaron quit working there right before Christina's death. Around the time Duran gave him that big chunk of money. But Lionel is still employed there."

"Does he have a record?" Ava wanted to know.

"A juvie one for stealing a car. He apparently straightened up and joined the army."

She latched right onto that. "Please tell me he had explosives or demolition training."

"Bingo. He was an explosives ordnance disposal specialist. He spent six years in uniform and, from what I can tell, he got out and came back home because his mom had cancer. She died, and he joined the militia about a month later."

So, maybe his grief had driven him to be with the wrong

people. Or it could be the members of the militia were former friends.

"There are no social media posts with Lionel Henderson and Aaron, but when Aaron comes in, I'll be asking him about his former coworker."

It was definitely a connection that needed to be explored. In fact, "connections" was the theme of the new threads in this investigation.

"I wonder if Lionel Henderson ever crossed paths with any of the murdered women," Ava mused aloud. "I mean what if the murders aren't just focused on me? What if these three women got on the killer's radar because of some interaction or altercation they'd had with someone helping the killer? Someone like Paul Harmon or Lionel Henderson?"

Harley stayed quiet a moment, obviously giving that some thought. "The accomplice got to tie up some loose ends either for himself or for his boss, the killer?"

Ava nodded. "It could be a long shot, but it might apply. *Might*," she emphasized. "Because if Marnie had a run-in with Theresa, then Aaron likely could have, too. Maybe even Duran, since this would have been the time that he had a PI on Aaron. Something could have possibly happened between Duran and her to make Theresa stand out as a potential victim."

She stopped, sighed and then groaned in frustration, waving off what she'd just said. "Or maybe the killer hadn't even put that much thought into it," Ava amended. "Maybe the only criteria he or she had was the victims were substitutes for me."

Harley stood, sighing as well, and he went to her. She was seated, but he put his hands on the arms of her chair and leaned in, looking her straight in the eyes. "We're going to catch the person responsible. We're going to stop them."

Ava so wanted to believe that. She wanted to hang on to every reassuring word Harley was doling out. Actually, she wanted to hang on to Harley himself. There must have been something in her eyes to convey that because the corner of his mouth lifted into the slightest and briefest of smiles. Then he must have remembered that part about this heat being a really bad distraction because the smile vanished.

Harley didn't move though.

He stood there, looming over her and sending off scorching vibes that heated up every inch of her. She might have leaned in and kissed him had there not been a quick knock before the door opened. Harley moved away from her as if they'd just been caught doing something wrong—which, in a way, they had.

Former sheriff Grayson Ryland was in the doorway, and even though he was now retired, he obviously still had his cop's instincts because he swept glances over both of them and asked, "Am I interrupting something?"

Ava immediately shook her head and stood. "Harley and I were just…" She stopped trying to fill in the blank with something that would only be a half-truth or an outright lie. This was Grayson, her mentor, and the man who'd been her boss for years before Theo had taken over. Grayson would see right through a lie.

"I'm frustrated and angry," Ava amended. "This snake is killing because of me, and every new piece of info only seems to complicate the investigation, not solve anything."

Grayson nodded and kept his usual unflappable expression. "You know those pieces are eventually going to come together, and you'll just keep working it until they do."

She had to cling to the hope that the "coming together" would happen, and hearing the words from Grayson made it seem like a sure thing. Theo was a darn good boss, and she had total respect for him, but Grayson was and always would be a cornerstone of the Silver Creek sheriff's office, and the new generation of Rylands were following in his footsteps. Theo was his adopted son and Harley was his adopted kid brother.

Grayson shifted his attention to Harley. "Dad and your mom wanted me to check on you." Now Grayson smiled a little when Harley sighed and blew out a long, weary breath. "It doesn't matter how old you are, they'll still worry. You'll understand that better when your daughter is born."

Harley nodded in a way that made her think he already understood it. "I'll call them later and let them know I'm all right."

Grayson nodded as well, and looked at Ava. "Dad also wanted me to extend an invitation for you to stay at the ranch. He heard about what was left on your back porch, and he's worried about you."

Ava hadn't been able to dismiss that taunt, prank or whatever the heck it'd been, but she wasn't ready to surrender yet by leaving her home. She only hoped that wouldn't turn out to be a decision she regretted, especially since part of the reason she wanted to stay put was so the killer would eventually show himself. Or herself. That wouldn't happen if she was tucked away on the Silver Creek Ranch.

"Please tell your dad thank-you," she settled for saying. "I'll consider it."

She didn't add more because her phone rang. "It's Duran," she said when she saw the name on the screen.

Grayson muttered a quick goodbye and good luck, and he stepped back so he could close the door. Ava took the call on speaker.

"The cops just showed up at my door and are demanding my guns," Duran immediately said. "Did you put them up to this?"

"No, but it's a great idea since we now know you were in the vicinity of the shooting in Austin and could have been the one to fire those shots at Harley and me. Did you try to kill us?" Ava came out and asked.

"Of course not," Duran insisted, but Ava had no idea whether or not he was telling the truth. If he was lying, maybe the Austin cops would be able to trip him up and ultimately get a confession.

"Then why were you there during the shooting?" Harley pressed. He didn't add more, maybe waiting to see if Duran was going to deny it.

He didn't.

Duran groaned. "I was in Austin because I was following Aaron. I got a heads-up from the PI, Darcel Harrison, that Aaron intended to make a trip to Austin to see Caleb. I knew you were heading there to interview the young man, and I wanted to be on hand in case things turned ugly."

The whole explanation sounded rehearsed, which it no doubt had been. She didn't press him on how the PI had found out about Aaron going to Austin, but she wouldn't put it past Duran to have managed to plant eavesdropping devices in Aaron's residence.

"Look, I'm giving the cops my guns so they can test them or whatever," Duran went on, "and you'll soon have proof that none of them has been recently fired. I didn't shoot at Harley and you. I didn't try to kill you."

Ava heard the confidence in the man's voice about the firearms and silently groaned. Because, of course, if Duran was the shooter, he would have already gotten rid of the weapon. And that meant there was little chance of them finding it.

"I didn't actually reach the apartment building where Harley and you were," Duran added a moment later. "I was walking there from the car park, and when I heard the shots, I stayed put for a while. Then I turned and ran back to my car after I heard the police sirens. I figured I wouldn't be able to help if I arrived on scene."

He'd no doubt rehearsed that part, too. All very pat. And, worse, it might all be very true. Ava had wanted to hear something, anything, that would clue her in that Duran had been there to kill her, but she hadn't.

Not yet anyway.

"Tell me about Theresa Darnell." Ava threw the name out there.

Duran didn't jump in with a quick answer, but she thought she heard him mutter something under his breath. Profanity maybe. "I'm guessing you found out she was once involved with Aaron."

"Yes, and I'm wondering why you didn't mention it to me sooner," Ava snapped. "The woman was murdered, and you didn't think I'd want to know that she'd had a connection to Aaron. And to you," she tacked on.

"Wait a minute," he protested. "I didn't have a connection with her. I simply read about her in a report that the PI sent me."

Ava went with a theory that was starting to form. "If you thought that Aaron had spilled anything to Theresa about Caleb or what Edgar and you did, you might have been worried that she'd be angry enough to tell someone. Someone who'd be willing to make sure it hit the media."

"That didn't happen." Duran sounded adamant about that. Again, though, Ava wasn't sure if this was part of the façade that he was so very good at creating. "Yes, I had the PI keep an eye on her for a while. And, no, he didn't see who killed her. He just listened in case she started making waves to get back at Aaron. She didn't, so end of story."

Maybe, but Ava would keep digging, and there might be something in the PI's report about it.

"How about Monica Howell and Sandy Russo?" she continued, giving him the names of the other two murdered women. "Do you have a connection of any kind to either of them?"

His silence let her know that she'd hit pay dirt. "I don't have a personal connection, no. But Sandy Russo and Theresa, they knew each other. Apparently, they went to the same school, and the PI reported they'd had dinner together shortly after Theresa and Aaron's breakup."

Ava had to get her teeth unclenched before she could speak. "Again, you didn't think this was pertinent information in a murder investigation. I should have you charged with obstruction of justice."

"I didn't know any of this was important," Duran fired back. "Aaron's come in contact with a whole lot of people over the past twenty years, and I never met these women. They were merely names mentioned in a report that I would have skimmed."

The skimming was possibly true since Duran would have been looking for any red flags on Aaron, but that didn't mean the man hadn't used the connections to select his victims. After all, Duran could have reasoned that Aaron could have told Theresa about Aaron, and then Monica could have passed along the info to Sandy since the two women were friends.

"You're sure there's nothing in the PI reports about Monica Howell?" Harley asked Duran.

"Not that I can recall." Duran paused. "But I'll check."

"Do that. And, my advice if you find a connection, come clean, because right now, all this secrecy could land your butt in jail," Harley warned him.

"Where's Ava?" She heard someone call out.

She groaned because it was her father. "Edgar's here," she relayed to Duran.

"He's worried about you," Duran quickly supplied. "Tell him I'll call him as soon as I've finished the interview."

With that, Duran ended the call, and when her father called out her name again, she opened the interview room door and spotted Theo escorting Edgar toward her. Neither man looked pleased, but since Theo got a call, he handed Edgar off to her and stepped aside so he could answer his phone.

Edgar marched right into the interview room and slammed the door behind him. One look at him and Ava knew he was spitting mad, and it didn't take him long to jump right into the reason for that anger.

"Did you pressure the Austin cops into taking Duran into custody?" Edgar fired the question at them. "Do you have any idea what kind of publicity that's going to generate?"

So, no worry that his longtime friend could have tried his hand at attempted murder. No worry about her. But, yes, bad publicity would get Edgar revving.

"Consider this: Duran was in Austin at the time of the shooting," Harley explained before Ava could gear up to return verbal fire. "And not just in Austin but in the vicinity of the shooting. He could have been the one who tried to kill Ava. Was he firing those shots for you or because he was trying to cover up something he'd done?"

Judging from the way Edgar's shoulders snapped back,

he hadn't been expecting that. "What the heck are you talking about?"

"Surveillance footage captured an image of Duran less than a block from the shooting," Ava provided. "And before you claim it's some kind of mistake, we just spoke to Duran and he admitted he was there."

"Why?" Edgar spat out.

"Because he got a report that Aaron was planning on seeing Caleb," Ava informed him.

She left it at that, letting Edgar fill in the blanks with possible answers, but Ava was going with the obvious on this. If Duran was telling the truth and hadn't attacked Harley and her, then he'd likely gone there to make sure Aaron and Caleb weren't about to expose Edgar and him for what they'd done twenty years earlier.

Edgar groaned and squeezed his eyes shut a moment. "Duran wouldn't shoot at you to stop a meeting like that. He would have found another way to handle it if there was any fallout from it."

Rather than come out and say she wasn't convinced of that at all, she gave him a flat look and went with the topic she'd just discussed with Duran. "Monica Howell, Theresa Darnell and Sandy Russo. If you've have any kind of contact, even of the second-hand variety, with any of those women, you need to tell us now. We're digging, and if we find out you've lied, the bad publicity will be the least of your worries."

Edgar cursed. "Those are the dead women, and I didn't know any of them." He seemed to be gearing up for a tirade, but he stopped and studied her. "Duran knew these women?"

"Two of them," she confirmed, causing Edgar to curse again.

Groaning, her father shook his head as if in disappointment or maybe disgust. "I didn't know. Now, you probably don't believe that, but it's the truth."

"Did you know about Duran paying Aaron blackmail money as recently as seven months ago?" Harley asked.

Edgar whipped his attention in Harley's direction, and either her father was putting on a good act or he truly hadn't known. "No," he said, his jaw muscles tightening and flexing. "But paying someone off doesn't mean Duran killed anyone. Hell, if he'd wanted someone dead, he would have gone after Aaron."

Both Harley and she stared at Edgar, giving him some time to let that sink in. Maybe Duran hadn't taken the direct approach of going after Aaron.

"If Duran could set up Aaron for the murders," Harley spelled out, "Aaron would not have only gone to prison, he would have been totally discredited if he tried to tell anyone what had happened to him twenty years ago." He glanced at Ava. "And, if Ava isn't around to verify what Aaron says, then Duran, or the killer, could spin the truth any way he or she wants it spun."

Edgar stayed quiet for a long time and he finally shook his head again. "No, I won't believe Duran's behind this because that would mean he tried to kill you. He wouldn't have done that."

"The shooter missed," Harley reminded him.

More silence, but she saw the anger erupt in Edgar's eyes. "Duran didn't do this," he snarled, enunciating each word before he turned and threw open the door.

Her father took one step out into the hall, just one, before he smacked right into someone.

Caleb.

Chapter Eleven

Harley wasn't sure who was more shocked at the impromptu meeting. Ava, Caleb or Edgar. At the moment, he thought it might be a tie.

Figuring that Edgar might say something that would ignite a fierce backlash from Ava, Harley moved toward Caleb. Not that Harley would mind Ava doling out a verbal blast to her slimy father, but he didn't want Caleb caught up in any fallout. Neither would Ava, and she would end up regretting anything that could hurt Caleb.

"Caleb," Harley greeted, putting his hand on his shoulder to get him moving closer to Ava and him.

Caleb glanced at Ava. Then Edgar. Caleb definitely knew who the man was and, judging from the lack of friendly greeting in his expression, he was wary of his bio-grandfather.

Edgar stayed put in the hall, staring at Caleb as if his gaze had been pinned to him. Harley didn't see venom, just the shock. And maybe something else. Not love or affection but perhaps some kind of reckoning that he was face-to-face with his daughter's child. A child he'd forced Ava to give up.

"Uh, Senator Lawson," Caleb said by way of greeting before he looked at Ava. "Sorry about just showing up like this, but do you have a minute so we can talk? You, too," he added to Harley.

That caused Harley's gut to tighten. He hoped like the devil that someone hadn't tried to hurt Caleb. Ava was going through enough right now without her firstborn being in danger.

"Of course," she said. And there was definitely love and affection in her eyes. Also some worry. She glanced at her father. "Could you please shut the door on your way out?"

Edgar didn't dole out one of his classic glares. He cleared his throat and directed his comments to Caleb. "I hope you know everything that happened when you were born was in your best interest."

Harley couldn't stop himself from groaning, and he thought maybe Ava would return some not-so-friendly fire. She didn't, though, and neither did Caleb. The young man simply walked over to Edgar.

"Excuse us, please," he said. "It's important that I speak to Deputy Lawson and Ranger Ryland." Then Caleb eased the door shut in Edgar's face.

Again, Harley didn't know who was more surprised by that, and he half expected for Edgar to throw open the door and start bellowing about what he perceived to be an insult.

He didn't.

Maybe because the senator had won that surprise award this round and was too stunned to be his usual jackass self. Either that or he'd been crushed by the gesture. Harley doubted it was the latter, but it couldn't have felt good to be rejected by his grandson even if it was a grandchild Edgar hadn't wanted anywhere in his life.

Caleb turned back to Ava and his expression was filled with worry when he took out his phone and handed it to her. "Someone emailed those to me about an hour ago," he explained.

With plenty of worry flooding her own expression, Ava took the phone, and Harley went to her side to see the blank email. Well, blank for words anyway. But there were three attachments and, before Ava clicked on them, Harley knew what she was going to see.

The three murdered women.

In each of them, the posed women had garbage bags covering their bodies and were wearing the masks of Ava's face.

"That's you," Caleb said, his voice trembling. "Your face, just like the one on the mannequin someone left for you."

She nodded, passed the phone to Harley, and she looked directly at Caleb. "I'm sorry someone sent you these. It must have been a shock to open them and see the bodies."

"It was a shock to see your face on the bodies," Caleb clarified. He groaned and shook his head. "This isn't a mannequin. These women are real. Were real," he amended. "And the killer put your face on them when he killed them."

Ava stayed calm and led him to one of the chairs. When Caleb didn't sit, she did, and that prompted him to take the chair next to her. Harley intended to hear anything else Caleb had to say, but he was also taking a closer look at the photos, looking for anything that could lead them to the person who'd done this. Harley also sent Theo, Ava and himself copies of the photos, and he wanted the lab to take a hard look at them as well.

"Are the Rangers still watching your place to make sure you're okay?" she asked Caleb.

He nodded. "I told the one on duty that I needed to come here and talk to you, and he gave me a ride. He's waiting out front."

"Good. Because I don't want you going anywhere alone, not until we catch the person responsible."

"You're taking precautions, right?" Caleb asked but didn't wait for an answer. He looked up at Harley. "You're making sure she stays safe?"

"I'm trying," he assured Caleb, and Harley dragged a chair over so he could sit across from them. "Ava's a cop, so it's a fine line between protecting her and not trusting her cop skills. She's very good at what she does," he tacked onto that, hoping it would make Caleb worry less than he obviously was. But maybe reassuring him about her safety wasn't possible.

Caleb nodded as if trying to process what he'd been told. "Is the senator involved in any of this?" He tipped his head to his phone as Harley handed it back to him.

"He's personally alibied for the nights of the murders," Harley explained. "And, even though he's not one of my favorite people, I don't believe he'd actually try to hurt Ava."

Caleb studied his expression and, after a few moments, seemed to accept what Harley had just said. "But the killer could be someone trying to get back at the senator by going after his daughter and her baby?"

Bingo. Hopefully, the killer wouldn't go after both of Edgar's grandchildren and would leave Caleb out of this.

"I guess you think I should have just handled this over the phone," Caleb said a moment later. "I mean instead of coming to Silver Creek—"

"It's okay," Ava interrupted. "It's good to see you." She dragged in a long breath. "Even if I would have felt better if you'd just stayed put, where you'd be safe. I want you *safe*, Caleb," she emphasized in a murmur.

The emotion practically flew off those words, and Harley

could see it in every bit of her expression. She was hurting with worry for the son she hadn't been able to keep.

Caleb held Ava's gaze for several moments and then glanced at her stomach. "Do you know if you're having a boy or a girl?"

"A girl," she said, smiling just a little.

Caleb smiled, too. "I hope you don't take this the wrong way, but I always wanted a sibling. A little late, I know," he added with a nervous chuckle. "When she's old enough, will you tell her who I am?"

"I will," Ava assured him.

Caleb nodded, as if pleased with that, and he stood. "I'd better be getting back to Austin, and I'll stay put. Promise."

Ava walked to the door with him. "Uh, when this investigation is over, maybe we can have lunch or something?" she suggested.

This time the smile made it to his eyes and he nodded. "Good. I'd like that."

He muttered a goodbye, but the moment Caleb opened the door, Harley heard a familiar voice. Not Edgar this time. But rather Aaron.

Apparently, this was going to be the day for awkward encounters, and Harley went out into the hall in case things turned bad. Aaron was indeed coming up the hall, and Theo was with him, no doubt taking the man to an interview room.

Aaron froze, his gaze zooming straight to Caleb's, and Harley could tell that he recognized his bio-son. Of course he did. In this day of social media, Aaron had likely seen many photos of the young man, and Harley recalled Aaron mentioning that Caleb and he had spoken on the phone after Caleb had learned of their DNA connection.

"Caleb," Aaron said on a rise of breath.

Caleb nodded but certainly didn't dole out any of the warmth that he had to Ava. Maybe because Caleb had picked up on the clues that Aaron was a suspect in not only the shooting but also the murders.

Aaron continued to look at Caleb for several moments before his gaze fired to Harley's, then to Ava's when she also stepped into the hall.

"You'd better not be interrogating Caleb," Aaron snapped.

"We're not," Ava assured him. "Caleb just came by to talk."

Aaron didn't seem the least bit convinced of that, but Theo didn't give him a chance to press for any other info.

"In here," Theo ordered, opening the door of the interview room across the hall.

Aaron kept his gaze fastened to Caleb. "Will you be around for a while? If so, maybe we can talk when I'm done."

Caleb shook his head. "I was just leaving." He paused. "I'll call you soon." He repeated his goodbye and started walking toward the front of the building.

"I'll have the Ranger who drove Caleb here text me when Caleb's safely back at his apartment," Harley whispered to Ava, hoping that would ease some of the worry she was no doubt feeling about Caleb being out and about.

"Go in and wait," Theo told Aaron.

Aaron did, after he watched Caleb until he was out of sight. Then, on a heavy sigh, he turned to Ava. "Don't you dare try to turn him against me," Aaron warned her.

Now that was the voice of a man who could kill, but Ava didn't take the bait and verbally strike back at him. She just waited until Theo had Aaron inside the interview room. Then Theo shut the door and turned toward Ava.

"Are you okay?" Theo asked her.

She nodded. "Someone sent Caleb photos of the murdered women."

"Yeah. I was looking at the text Harley forwarded to me when Aaron came in for his interview. You'll send them to the Ranger lab?" Theo directed that question at Harley.

"I will," Harley verified. "What about the summary of the reports from the PI? Did you get those yet?"

"I did, and I just got an email update about five minutes ago. You were copied on it, so it'll be in your in-box."

"They found something?" Ava asked, sounding plenty hopeful.

"Something that doesn't look good for Aaron," Theo verified. "The PI was watching Aaron's place the night Christina died. She wasn't out partying or visiting friends. She was at the apartment she shared with Aaron. He was the only person who came and went during the hours leading up to her death."

Oh, yeah. That definitely didn't look good for Aaron. "Too bad the PI didn't spot Aaron actually buying drugs," Harley commented.

Theo made a sound of agreement. "On that particular night, the PI didn't start surveillance until Aaron arrived home. Still, I'll be able to use this to put some pressure on Aaron. If he admits to buying Christina the drugs that killed her, then that might cause him to break and admit to other things."

If so, then Theo might be able to make an arrest today, and even if that arrest wasn't for the murders, it would put one of their prime suspects behind bars where he wouldn't be able to come after Ava or anyone else.

"One more thing," Theo went on. "I'm trying to get the militia member, Lionel Henderson, in for an interview to find out about his explosives training and to ask him about his possible relationships with Marnie, Aaron and any of our victims. So far, though, he hasn't returned any of my calls and he wasn't home when I sent someone out to his place. His boss says he hasn't showed up for work in the past two days."

Ava groaned softly. "He could be on the run."

That'd be Harley's guess. If Lionel had gotten word that both Marnie and Aaron had been brought in for questioning, then he might have figured it was time to disappear rather than face law enforcement with questions about his training with explosives. It was entirely possible Lionel had had nothing to do with the murders directly, but he'd almost certainly be able to tell them who'd hired him.

"Considering Aaron's mood, why don't Harley and you observe the first part of the interview?" Theo suggested. "If you see something in his body language, or if he says something that I'm not picking up on, then you can come in and let me know."

That arrangement suited Harley just fine, and it would give Ava a chance to catch her breath. Theo would ask the necessary questions and it was likely he'd be able to get a lot more out of Aaron than Ava would. Considering the brief encounter Aaron had had with Ava in the hall, Caleb and their past would be playing into this.

Harley didn't ask Ava if she was okay when they went into the interview room, but he did touch her arm and rub it lightly. Just enough to let her know he was there. She winced a little, causing him to yank back his hand. Then her own hand went to her stomach.

"That was the strongest movement she's ever had," Ava muttered. "I've felt flutters before, but this felt like she turned over or something."

That sent a whole lot of alarm through him. "Is that normal? Is the baby all right?"

"It's normal," she assured him. "I don't think you'll be able to feel it yet."

Still, she took his hand and pressed it to her stomach. He didn't feel anything. Well, nothing physical anyway, but touching Ava this way definitely had to break down some personal barriers for her.

"Sorry," Ava added. "She's still now."

There might have been an awkward silence if there'd actually been a chance for that, but just as Harley drew back his hand, Theo started the interview on the other side of the observation glass.

Theo recited the Miranda warning to Aaron again and jumped right into a key question.

"Why didn't you volunteer that you'd had a relationship with Theresa Darnell?" Theo demanded.

Clearly, Aaron hadn't been expecting that because he opened his mouth, closed it and then cursed. "Marnie told you. Of course she did. She wants to get back at me any way she can."

Theo stared at him. "Answer the question."

Aaron huffed. "I didn't tell you because I thought it would look bad that I'd been involved with her."

"It does look bad," Theo verified. "And it looks especially bad when you've been questioned by law enforcement and you didn't come clean. Did you kill her?" Theo added without so much as a pause.

"No," Aaron howled. "Of course not. I haven't killed anybody. Theresa and I hung out for a while, that's all, and when Christina and I got back together, Theresa didn't like it much. She had words with Marnie when she went looking for me."

Theo continued to level that lethal cop's stare on Aaron. "How about Sandy Russo? Did you know her, too?"

"No." Aaron spewed off another round of profanity.

"Well, Theresa and she were friends," Theo said, maybe stretching the truth there. The women knew each other, but Harley wasn't sure they'd been actual friends. Still, a cop was allowed to outright lie during an interview. "Did both women rile you enough to make them targets?"

Aaron stood so fast that the chair he'd been sitting in went flying back. "That's it. I want a lawyer."

Theo nodded, tucked his small notepad back into his pocket. "Call one and we'll resume this interview." He started for the door then stopped. "Oh, and when your lawyer arrives, I'll be questioning you about some info I recently learned. Info that you're the one who supplied Christina the drugs that killed her. Mention that to your lawyer, why don't you?"

Aaron did more cursing, but the moment Theo was out of the room, the man began to pace as well. Clearly agitated, Aaron took out his phone and made a call. Since it was likely to a lawyer, Harley turned off the sound in the observation room.

A moment later, Theo opened the door and peered in at them. "I figured I could push at least another button or two before he lawyered up."

"Good idea," Harley assured him, and then he spoke aloud what they were all thinking. "You don't have enough to hold Aaron."

Theo made a quick sound of agreement. "Not unless we can get something on the drug purchase."

"Then that's where I'll start digging," Ava assured him.

Theo stepped back as if to let her get started on that, but his phone rang. He tensed when he glanced at the screen and then answered it. Seconds later, the sickening dread washed over Theo's face.

"We're on our way," Theo said to the caller and he hung up. "That was the 9-1-1 dispatcher. There's been another murder."

Chapter Twelve

As Theo, Harley and she drove toward the latest crime scene, Ava tried to force herself to stay composed. Hard to do, though, with the emotions whipping through her. It was next to impossible since those emotions were mixed with the adrenaline roller coaster that she'd been on for weeks now, the pregnancy hormones and the sickening dread of another murder.

Mercy, another dead woman.

Well, maybe it was. It could be another mannequin, but the witness had been certain it was a body.

That was all Theo, Harley and she knew at this point. The teenage witness who'd been at the creek to take a swim had seen the body of a woman lying on the creek bank and had called 9-1-1. Other than the location and that it appeared the woman had a trash bag on her, the dispatcher hadn't been able to get much else out of him because the boy was in shock.

Like Theo and Harley, Ava kept watch around them as Theo drove away from town and toward the creek that had given the town its name. The creek coiled through the surrounding area ranches and was accessible by road at three different points. This location would be the most remote of the three since there were no houses nearby. That was no doubt why the killer had chosen it for a body dump.

"I'd rather you wait in the cruiser," Theo said to her when he pulled to a stop on the narrow road near the bridge.

She glanced over at Harley who was in the backseat, and Ava knew he wanted the same thing. For her to remain in the relative safety of the cruiser. It was tempting to do just that.

It was also impossible.

She was a cop, and she was the cause of the murders. Yes, she would take precautions and had done so by wearing a Kevlar vest, but no precaution would completely ensure her safety. It was the same for Theo and Harley.

"I'll be careful," was all she said.

Ava ignored Harley's heavy sigh and looked around to begin her assessment of the crime scene.

Other than the remote location, she could see why the killer had chosen this spot for a body dump. There was no steep incline leading down to the creek. The killer could have stopped near where they were now and dragged or carried the body to the creek bank.

Posing wouldn't have taken long, less than a minute if the garbage bag and mask had already been in place. A quick in-and-out where he or she obviously hadn't been spotted or someone would have reported it.

Ava saw a lanky teenage boy in shorts and a tee, sitting on the bridge railing. The witness, no doubt, and he was visibly shaken. His bike was lying on its side near him, and he had turned himself away from the creek. He had his arms folded over his chest and was crying. Ava didn't know his name, but she knew the boy's parents, David and Melanie Buckner, who owned a ranch just up the road. Since the couple both worked in town, they'd no doubt be here soon.

Theo sighed, too, at Ava's insistence that she not stay

put, and he opened his door just as a second cruiser came to a stop behind them. Deputies Jesse Ryland and Nelline Rucker got out, immediately heading for Theo's cruiser. Both Harley and Ava stepped out.

"You know the boy?" Theo asked Jesse. He took a pair of evidence gloves from the cruiser but left the door open. No doubt so they could dive back in if necessary. Ava and Harley did the same.

Jesse nodded. "Eli Buckner. His folks bought a horse from me for his fourteenth birthday. You want me to see to him?"

"Yeah," Theo verified. "Get him into your cruiser so if there's any evidence on the bridge, it won't be stepped on when his folks get here. Also, I want him away from any potential trouble." He turned to Nelline. "Wait here and keep watch to make sure we're not about to be ambushed."

Even though Nelline was a veteran cop, that put a whole lot of concern in her eyes, and she automatically moved her hand to the butt of her weapon. "You want me to go ahead and call the CSIs and medical examiner?" she asked.

Theo shook his head. "I want to verify that it is indeed a body before we get all of that rolling. Still, try to preserve the scene as best you can." He motioned for Harley and Ava to follow him.

All three kept watch around them, but they also checked the ground for any signs of what had happened here. There were no actual drag marks as there had been at the scene of the last murder, but the ground appeared to have been trampled in spots. They avoided those spots, just in case the CSIs could recover shoe prints, and made their way to the creek bank.

Normally, this was a serene location with the sound of the water rushing over the rocks, the spring breeze gently stirring the leaves on the trees and the wildflowers dotting the landscape. But there was nothing serene about the woman lying just ahead. One look at her and Ava knew this wasn't a hoax.

This was indeed another murder.

The woman's body was posed exactly as the others and had the mask of Ava's face. Even though this was the fourth time Ava had seen the mask on a victim, it still gave her that overwhelming crush of grief and guilt.

Ava drew her gun and whirled around when a dark blue truck came screeching to a halt behind the cruisers. But it wasn't the killer. It was Eli's parents, and they both immediately barreled out of the vehicle and started running toward their son as Jesse was leading the boy to the cruiser.

She didn't put her gun back in the holster. Ava kept a two-handed grip on it, pointing it down but knowing it'd be ready, and they approached the body.

The dead woman's hair was the same color as Ava's. That was about the only part of her they could see what with the mask and the garbage bag. Theo gloved up while Harley took some photos of the body, and then, using extreme caution so as to touch as little as possible, Theo lifted the corner of the mask.

"I know her," Ava blurted out. Her voice was strained because of the fresh slam of adrenaline, but even with the shock of seeing that face, she knew this was not the killer's usual MO. "She's an investigative reporter, Lacey George. She works for one of the San Antonio newspapers."

All the other victims had lived closer to Silver Creek, and none had been from a large city. Ava had no idea if Lacey fit the profile of the other victims by having or losing a child, but she was well aware of the woman's connection to at least one of their suspects.

"Years ago, Lacey had some run-ins with my father about his policies," Ava added. "Which means she had run-ins with Duran."

And that obvious connection had her mentally stopping to consider what this might mean.

Duran likely wouldn't have murdered someone with such an immediate link to him unless this was some kind of reverse psychology. If so, then he might have thought he could eliminate someone who'd been a pain to Edgar and him while pushing his agenda to torment her. Maybe with the end game to kill her or drive her mad.

Theo eased the mask back in place and took out his phone to call in the CSIs and the medical examiner. Harley took out his phone as well, and a moment later, Ava realized that was so he could run a background check on the dead woman.

While they did that, Ava glanced around, first looking for any signs of explosives or someone who might be lurking and ready to attack them. She didn't see either of those things. However, since the body was close to water, she stepped around Harley and looked down at the soft, damp dirt on the narrow bank.

"Maybe a shoe print," she pointed out when she saw the indentation.

Theo and Harley continued their phone conversations, but both of them leaned in to have a closer look. "Nelline," Theo called out to the deputy. "I need an evidence marker down here and steer away from the section of the grass that's been trampled. Follow in our footsteps."

The marker was a flag that would alert anyone to the possible evidence and prevent someone from stepping onto it and destroying it. If they got lucky, there might be enough of an impression for the CSIs to determine the shoe size and type of footwear, and that could maybe help them narrow down their suspects.

While Nelline hurried to Theo with the marker, Ava continued to look around, moving slowly and cautiously, scanning the ground for anything.

"Lacey George," Harley said, obviously relaying what he'd just learned about their dead woman. "She's thirty-six, an investigative reporter for Fulbright Media. Divorced. She has a son who's fourteen, but her ex has full custody of the child."

So that was a deviation, too, of sorts. "Had she been reported missing?" Ava asked.

"Only about a half hour ago. That's why we haven't gotten the alert yet. She lives alone, and her boss reported her as missing when she didn't show up for work and he couldn't contact her. He hadn't seen her since she'd left her office the previous afternoon."

That was a large gap of time, more than twenty-four hours, and it meant any of their suspects could have taken Lacey, killed her and posed her here. The posing likely would have happened at night, but none of their suspects had been in custody or in interviews then.

"Since she's a reporter, the killer could have lured her out with the possibility of a story," Ava commented.

That kept all of their suspects in the running. An investigative reporter likely would have met any of the three if promised juicy details about the murders.

"I requested a thorough background check on her," Harley explained, putting away his phone. "The Rangers will try to pin down anyone who might have seen her so we can figure out how and where she was taken."

So far, knowing those things hadn't helped them catch this killer, Ava had to hang on to the hope that this time it would be different. This time, there had to be an eyewitness or some surveillance camera footage. That footage had been a long shot with the women taken in or around Silver Creek, but a city the size of San Antonio had plenty of operating cameras.

"Take a quick look around, and then we'll head back to the cruiser," Theo instructed while he started snapping some photos as well.

Ava didn't balk at having to leave the scene. Now that they had verified there was a body and had gotten a preliminary ID, there wasn't much more they could do other than secure the scene and wait for the CSI team to arrive.

Harley moved closer to the creek, peering down into the water, maybe looking to see if anything had inadvertently been dropped in there. It was another of those things that needed to be checked. If something was there, it'd need to be secured in case the water swept it away before the CSIs could retrieve it.

Ava scanned the trees that were on the bank just upstream. One of the bigger oaks had a rope swing tied to it, and the underbrush around it had been tamped down. She didn't think that was a recent occurrence though. It looked like that specific spot got plenty of use.

The area to the right of the rope swing, though, was congested with trees of varying sizes, weeds and vines. The trees were thicker here, so not much of the sunlight was making its way through, but she still saw something that caught her eye.

Something that had Ava's stomach dropping to her knees.

Because there was something on the ground that didn't look as if it was part of the natural landscape. It looked more like green camos.

"I think there's another body," she said, motioning to

some underbrush about ten yards away from where she was standing.

She took one step closer to get a better look and she felt something brush over the top of her boot. Harley must have seen or heard something because he practically lunged at her. He turned her, sheltering her body with his just as he'd done when the shots had been fired at them. But this was no shot. No.

It was an explosion.

HARLEY HAD SEEN the glint of the thin wire that had nearly been concealed with leaves, and he knew instantly what it was. A trip wire no doubt connected to an explosive device.

He didn't have time to shout. Didn't have time to do much of anything except grab Ava and pull her to the ground, all the while praying that would be enough to save her and the baby.

The blast was deafening, and it shot out debris, pelting his back and legs. Harley felt the sting of the impact but not actual pain. Thank God. Maybe it was the same for Ava.

He waited long gut-wrenching moments to make sure there wasn't a second blast, and when there wasn't, he lifted himself off Ava enough to check her. She was a little pale and definitely shaken up, but he couldn't see any visible injuries. That was one prayer answered, but Harley knew they weren't out of danger just yet.

"Are you okay?" he asked just as Theo called out the same question to them. The sheriff, having hit the ground, too, was only a few feet away from the dead woman.

"I'm not hurt," Ava assured both of them. "I didn't land on my stomach. Harley cushioned the blow."

When he replayed those nightmarish moments in his head, and he would do just that, he'd wish he had gotten to her before she'd tripped the wire. That might have saved her the terror of the blast along with not destroying the hell out of their crime scene. Right now, it was littered with leaves and bits of shrubs and tree bark that had gone flying during the impact.

On the road, Harley could hear the flurry of activity. Both Jesse and Nelline had obviously gotten out of the cruiser, but he was hoping their witness and his parents hadn't remained on scene. No need for them to see any of this, not when they were already going to have to deal with enough.

"Do you see any other trip wires or devices?" Theo called out to no one in particular. He was certainly checking the ground for both items.

"No," Jesse answered. "There appears to be a body though."

"Yes," Ava verified. "That's where I was heading when I triggered a bomb." She groaned and Harley could hear the dread and apology in that simple sound.

"Not your fault," Harley reminded her. "This is the sick SOB's doing."

"There might be something by Harley's right foot," Nelline shouted. He glanced up to see the deputy surveilling the area with binoculars. Then Harley looked at his boot.

And he cursed.

Because, undeniably, there was a thin silver wire there. Just inches from him, and he didn't know where either end of it was. If he moved, he could set it off.

"The bomb squad's on the way," Jesse relayed a moment later. "No one move. I'll get another pair of binoculars and see if I can figure out a safe path to get you out of there."

This definitely wasn't an ideal situation, but it was a best-case scenario for the killer. Theo, Ava and he were pinned down, unable to move. Heck, even lifting their weapons to defend themselves could get them all killed. Yeah, definitely not ideal. Because at this moment, the killer could be getting in position to gun them down.

Beneath him, he could feel Ava's body. Her muscles were tight and knotted, and she was clearly trying to steady her breathing. Hard to do, though, when they were facing death. Harley knew she wasn't nearly as worried for herself as she was for the baby, and he cursed the killer for putting their child in this kind of danger.

"I see another wire," Nelline called out. "It's on the creek bank by the tree with the tire swing."

That'd been the exact spot Harley had been heading when he'd caught a glimpse of the wire from the corner of his eye. If he'd gone there, he could have ended up blowing them all to smithereens since he'd had no idea how powerful the explosives were. He doubted, though, that there were decoys. No. The killer likely intended for this to be their final resting place. It wouldn't fit with his MO, but it could be the big finale to the four murders that had already been committed.

Correction: five murders.

Because that body in the woods had to be connected to what was happening now. Maybe another dead woman meant to lure one of them into the wooded area where they'd trip a wire.

"There's another wire," Jesse let them know. "Theo, you might not be able to see it, but it's by the rock at the top of your head. It seems to lead to the—" He stopped and cursed. "The bridge. I'll move the cruiser with Eli and his folks."

Yes, and it was more than a precaution since the blast could not only reach the cruiser, it could end up hurting or killing those inside.

"Nelline," Theo called out again. "Make sure we don't have any snipers trying to get into position to shoot us."

Ava didn't react to that. No doubt because it had already occurred to her that they were basically sitting ducks.

Harley hated not being able to stop anything bad from happening to her. He hated this smothering sense of dread that was pulsing through him. But he forced his heartbeat to calm some so he could stop it from throbbing in his ears. He needed to be able to hear in case someone was trying to sneak up on them.

The air felt so still that it seemed to be holding its breath, waiting. Bracing. Theo's body was doing the same, and he figured Ava was having a similar reaction. Along with cursing the monster who'd put them in this position so they weren't able to keep their child safe.

"There's a timer," Nelline shouted. "Oh, God. It's on the one by the tire swing. Theo, it's ticking down."

"How much time?" Theo asked.

"One minute and thirty seconds," Nelline answered, her voice strained to the hilt.

Harley didn't waste his breath on the profanity that he wanted to snarl. It wouldn't help. Right now, he had to focus, to figure out the lowest level of risk to get Ava out of there.

He lifted his head, glancing around them. "Other than the wire by my boot, are there any others near Ava and me?" Harley asked.

Precious seconds crawled by while he waited for Jesse and Nelline to check the area. Seconds that he could practically see ticking off on that damn timer.

"I can't see any," Nelline finally answered.

Not exactly a resounding no, but he couldn't expect the deputies to be able to see through them and the debris to locate trigger wires.

"Check the ground that leads from here to the road," Harley instructed the deputies.

He was almost positive he could retrace the route Ava, Theo and he had taken to get from the cruiser to the body, and they hadn't set off any devices on the walk down. Still, that could have been pure luck, and a fraction of an inch could be the difference between living and dying.

While that ate up even more seconds with the deputies checking, Harley helped Ava to her feet. They both stayed low, both searching the area around them. Across from them, Theo was doing the same thing.

"I can't see anything," Nelline finally said. "You need to move now. There's less than a minute left on the timer."

That revved up his heartbeat even higher and Harley took hold of Ava's arm with his left hand while he tried to keep his gun ready in his right. A thousand thoughts went through his head. Bad thoughts. Thoughts of how he wished he had done a whole lot of things differently so Ava and his baby wouldn't be here right now.

Ava fired glances all around them as she moved. Fast. He was thankful she was in such good shape because even though she had to be terrified for the baby, she moved like the cop that she was. Fast and steady. Keeping watch of every step they took to make sure it wasn't their last.

It seemed to take a lifetime or two to reach the road, and the moment their feet were on the pavement, they hurried to the open doors of the cruiser.

Behind them, the woods exploded in a fireball.

Chapter Thirteen

While Harley drove toward her house, Ava tried to force her body to level out even though that was impossible. Not with the vivid memories of lying on that ground, knowing that every breath she took could be her last.

In those moments, she'd gone through an emotional gambit of cursing herself for being there. Cursing the killer for putting them all in danger and for murdering a woman for the sole purpose of trying to lure them to their deaths. But Ava had also prayed that her baby would come out of this unscathed.

That prayer had been answered.

After everyone had gotten clear of the explosions, Theo and Harley had driven her straight to the hospital to make sure the baby was okay. She was. So were Theo, Harley, her and everyone else who'd been near the series of blasts. That was somewhat of a miracle and probably not at all what the killer had intended. He or she had likely planned on multiple deaths to add to the two that had already been on scene.

No one had been able to get close enough to the body in the shrubs to determine who he or she was, but that was yet another thing that'd need to be checked. An ID could give them yet another clue about the killer.

Now that Harley had dropped Theo off at the sheriff's office so he could assemble the team needed to investigate the blast site and interview the teenager who'd found the first body, Harley and she would soon be at her place. It'd been where Theo had ordered her to go and get some rest.

Of course, rest was impossible, what with her mind racing and every nerve in her body on edge. Still, she hadn't had the fight in her to try to convince him to let her stay and help.

Harley hadn't pushed her either way. In fact, he was mostly silent, doling out a few worried looks, but he hadn't mentioned that, because of her pregnancy she should be on desk duty and not out in the field. He hadn't blamed her for anything that'd happened.

But Ava was blaming herself.

"If I'd just dug harder after the first murder, we might have caught the killer by now," she muttered and instantly regretted that had come out of her mouth. "I didn't narrow down the suspects until Monica's death, and by then it was too late."

Harley shot her one of those flat looks as he pulled into the garage at her house. "You did everything you could have done. Theo and the other deputies, too. Even the mayor called me in to help. Yeah, he did it because he was trying to cut back on the bad publicity, but he assisted with covering all the bases by getting Theo and you the extra help you needed so we stood the best chance possible of catching this SOB."

So, she'd gotten a lecture after all, though not the one about her being out in the field. And every word he'd said was true. Still, the truth hadn't helped any of the victims, and so far, it hadn't helped anyone else who was in this killer's path.

As they'd done previously, Harley and she checked the house and, once they were sure it was clear, Ava immediately excused herself to go take a shower. She needed a moment to gather herself, and resting was out. Instead, Ava was hoping a warm shower would clear her head enough so she could get on her laptop and help with the investigation in any way she could.

With a crime scene in disarray, it would take the CSIs days to process it, and they wouldn't even be let into the area until the bomb squad had done its thing. They'd need to make sure there weren't other devices and collect the pieces of the explosives so they could be sent to the crime lab. The entire process could take a lot longer than they had. The killer was clearly escalating, and there was no telling where he'd strike next or what he would do.

After she stepped from the shower, she groaned softly when she caught a glimpse of herself in the mirror. She looked as if she'd been through the wringer—which she had. But since she didn't want to cause Harley to worry any more than he already was, she combed her wet hair, put on a pair of loose pajamas and tried to look as composed as she possibly could when she went back into the kitchen.

She instantly smelled the chicken noodle soup and saw that Harley had been busy while she'd showered. He'd fixed the soup, a couple of grilled cheese sandwiches and had poured two glasses of juice and another of milk.

Ava had to smile. "You're taking care of me."

"Trying to," he said, returning the smile. A smile that didn't make it to his eyes because of the worry she'd known would be there.

"Any word from Theo yet?" she asked while she drank some of the juice.

"Yeah. He texted a couple of minutes ago to let us know

that he'd just received a report that Lionel Henderson, the explosives expert we've been looking for, has been reported missing."

"For how long?" she asked.

"No one has seen him since yesterday morning. The Rangers pinged his phone, and it's apparently on the side of the road less than a quarter of a mile from the area of the creek where the explosives went off." He paused a heartbeat. "The other body in the woods was probably his."

She knew it couldn't be a coincidence that the explosives expert had ended up that close to the crime scene for their latest victim. A crime scene where there'd been multiple explosives. Ava had to guess that Lionel had assisted the killer, and then the killer had considered him too much of a liability to continue breathing.

"Five dead bodies," she muttered. "Maybe more."

"Yeah," he agreed.

Ava set down her juice and looked at him. "Just let me say this. I'm sorry. Sorry for believing you'd cut a deal for my father. Sorry that I've put you in the middle of this. The killer wouldn't have come after you had—"

She stopped, had to, because he went to her, pulled her into his arms and kissed her. Not a reassuring peck either. A full-blown kiss with his mouth pressing hard against hers. There was a lot of emotion.

A lot of heat as well.

But Ava figured this kiss wasn't about heat. Harley had probably used it to shut down something he hadn't wanted her to say. And it was working. Working, too, because of that heat it was churning out. Hard to keep thinking about killers and such when Harley's mouth triggered a whole other set of emotions in her.

She felt some of the tension drain from her body and everything inside her went a little slack. An amazing feeling considering that, just moments earlier, every nerve in her body had been firing on all cylinders. The nerves were still firing but in a whole different way. One that reminded her that, despite everything, she was still hotly attracted to this man who'd once been her lover.

Harley finally pulled back and she instantly felt the loss of the heat. A small sound of protest left her mouth before she could stop it.

"I'm not going to apologize for that," he drawled.

"Good." Because she didn't want an apology. Ava wanted another kiss, so that's what she got.

She took hold of Harley's arm. Tugging him back to her and pressing herself against him, she kissed him. Yes, it skyrocketed the heat, but she no longer felt on the verge of falling apart.

The kiss was way too hard and hungry for something meant to comfort, and every inch of her responded. She'd done this with Harley before, kissed him until her legs had gone weak, and her body seemed to know what was coming. And what was coming was more.

Well, if she didn't stop it, that is.

Ava didn't want to stop it. Not yet anyway. Maybe not ever. She just took and took, deepening the kiss until she got the full taste of him.

Her body recalled that taste, too, and the feel of Harley's hand when he skimmed it down her back, urging her to move even closer to him. She did. Until her breasts were pressed against the hard muscles in his chest. That upped the heat even more, and she responded by taking hold of his jaw so she could do with his mouth exactly what she pleased.

A husky sound of arousal came from deep within his throat and he apparently was after some pleasing, too, because while he kissed her senseless, his skimming hand went lower and lower. He cupped her butt, pressing her so that she was right against his erection.

Ava upped the ante, too, and she lowered her mouth to his neck, trailing her tongue from the base of his ear to his throat. He groaned, cursed her and then stepped back.

His breath was gusting now. So was hers. And the heat was there in his eyes as he stared at her. She could sense his arousal in every part of her. But she could sense his hesitation, too, and, for one horrible moment, she thought he might say that this had to stop, that the timing was all wrong.

And it was.

But that didn't mean they had to stop. It didn't mean they had to try to work out what this might mean. Not right now anyway. Later, there'd be a price to pay for her seeking comfort in Harley's arms, but "not right now" seemed an eternity away.

Ava kissed him again and had no plans to stop.

HARLEY HAD GOTTEN so caught up in the heat of Ava's kiss that he'd forgotten one big important point.

That Ava was pregnant.

But he sure as heck remembered it when he felt things start to escalate. A big-time escalation since she was adding some touching to the kisses. Her hand was wandering down the front of his shirt and heading to his jeans.

That was the trouble with them being former lovers. The heat spiked a whole lot sooner than if they'd just been making out for the first time. And his body was pressuring him to keep spiking the heat, to keep letting her hand move to his jeans while he moved them both to the bedroom.

However, the pregnancy could be a game changer.

It wasn't easy, but he pulled back to meet her eyes and

hoped he had enough air in his lungs to speak. Man, she was beautiful. Always had been. But now her face was flushed with arousal and her eyes were filled with hunger for him. He was sure that same hunger for her was in his eyes, too, but he needed to get some things straight.

"I figure it's okay for a pregnant woman to have sex," he threw out there. "If not, there'd be a lot of frustrated people in the world. But I need to make sure you're okay with it."

She blinked as if she, too, had just remembered the baby, despite the baby bump pressing between them right now. Ava paused, but he wasn't sure if that was because she was considering what he'd said or if, like him, she was just trying to gather her breath.

It was the latter.

Ava confirmed that when she muttered, "I'm sure," a split second before she slid her hand around the back of his neck and pulled him to her.

The heat was instant, returning with a vengeance that upped the need even more. Something Harley hadn't thought possible since he was already burning for her.

He slid his arms around her, returning the kiss while she backed him in the direction of the bedroom. This was definitely familiar ground. When they'd been lovers, they'd made this trek, often discarding clothes along the way because they hadn't been able to wait to get their hands on each other.

That happened now, too.

The hunger and need were there, already clawing away at them, and it didn't surprise him when Ava paused the kissing only long enough to unbutton his shirt and rid him of it and his holster. Harley caught onto that, hooking it around his arm because even with all this intense heat, he knew he needed to keep his weapon nearby.

She immediately went after his chest, landing some well-placed kisses there that ate away at what little self-control he had. Harley had to battle not to pull her to the floor then and there.

Thankfully, her pajama top was loose and silky, and he managed to get it off her as well. Then, he eased her against the wall, anchoring her there while he shoved down the cups of her bra and kissed her nipples. She made the exact sound he wanted to hear. A silky moan.

Her body went a little slack for a moment as she gave in to the pleasure of him kissing her. But only a moment. Before her own leash on her self-control stopped, and she got them moving again.

Into the bedroom.

And toward the bed.

She took his mouth while she fumbled with his belt buckle. Ava kept brushing her fingers against his erection, causing his body to start begging for release. Since that couldn't happen, not yet anyway, he took matters into his own hands. He yanked off his belt and worked his way out of his boots, jeans and boxers before he put down his holster and gun. Then, he tackled getting Ava's pajama bottoms off. They were as loose as her top and practically slid from her body.

That's when Harley got an eyeful.

Her breasts were full, rising high against her bra that he'd shoved down. As always, her body was perfect. Yeah, especially with the baby bump.

He took a moment to lean down and kiss her stomach. Then he trailed a few kisses lower to the front of her panties. Her breath caught again. She made that silky sound of pleasure and caught onto his hair to anchor herself.

Even though his body was urging him to take her now,

he still continued the kisses, letting the pleasure of it roll right through both of them.

"Now," she insisted when she obviously could take no more.

She pushed him back onto the bed, following on top of him, and she gave him a deep, long kiss while she got rid of her panties.

The curtains were closed, and they hadn't turned on the lights, but there was enough illumination coming from the open bathroom door that he had no trouble seeing her.

Watching her as she straddled him.

Going at a slow, almost torturous pace, she took him inside her. Inch by inch. And she kept her eyes closed until she had all of him. Then she opened them and met his gaze.

Amazing.

And he didn't think he felt that way about her simply because of the sex. No. He'd never felt this much intensity with anyone as he had with Ava.

She began to move, starting the strokes that immediately caused the heat and pleasure to spike. He latched onto her hips, not that she needed help but just so he could touch her, so he could experience the way she felt beneath his hands.

The strokes got faster. Harder. Deeper. Until everything began to pinpoint to fulfilling this clawing need that would not be denied. Until he felt the climax ripple through her.

And only then did Harley let go.

Chapter Fourteen

Ava woke with a jolt and it took her a moment to realize she wasn't alone. That Harley was holding her.

And he was naked.

She was naked as well, and it took her another moment to realize this wasn't some dream from the past. It was the real deal. A hot, naked cowboy. Hot, amazing sex, and it'd obviously worn her out enough that she was able to fall asleep. That was somewhat of a miracle, considering the events of the past few days.

He wasn't asleep though. She looked over at him to see that he was not only wide awake but that he was still taking care of her. He'd draped the quilt over her, had her snuggled in his arms, and was almost certainly keeping watch. Guarding her. He'd moved his holster and gun to the nightstand where it'd be in easy reach.

That was a jolting reminder of the danger.

And that led to reminders of what had happened between them.

Ava didn't groan, but she knew this was the time of reckoning. Now that her body was sated and the pleasure buzz was fading, she needed to deal with what this all meant. Quickly deal with it and then get back to work.

"How long have I been asleep?" she asked.

"About an hour. Not long enough." He leaned in and kissed her, igniting the pleasure buzz again and making her want to sink right back into him. She absolutely couldn't do that though.

"I have to find my phone and check for updates from Theo," she insisted. Her phone hadn't rung or dinged with a text, Ava was certain she would have heard that, but it was possible Theo or someone else had sent an important email.

Harley reached over onto the side of the bed and produced her phone. His, too. "I've been checking," he assured her. "Nothing's come in."

She glanced at the time on her phone and did groan now. It was already past 6:00 p.m., and while she'd clearly needed the rest, that would no doubt mess up any chance of her getting a good night's sleep. Then again, the killer had already ruined that possibility. She hadn't slept well since the murders had started.

"It'll be dark soon," Harley pointed out. "The bomb squad will still be on scene but will have to shut down for the night. It might be morning before anyone can get to the body to verify that it's Lionel Henderson."

Ava had suspected as much. "But they're sure it's a body?" she asked. "I mean, there's no chance the person was just unconscious? Or another mannequin?"

"No chance," Harley verified. "When I spoke to Theo earlier, while you were in the shower, he said he'd gotten an initial report that there'd been massive damage in the spot where the body had been."

In other words, if the person had been alive, he would have died in the blasts. She doubted, though, that the killer would have left the explosives expert alive and waiting to be blown up. No. The killer couldn't have risked Lionel being able to tell them anything about who'd hired him.

"Are you okay?" he asked.

She was pretty sure that not-so-simple question involved both her and the baby. "We're fine," she assured him, not addressing the other part of that simple question. The part about how she was dealing emotionally with what had just happened between them.

"Good," he said, obviously willing to accept her answer. He brushed a soft kiss on her mouth that still managed to pack a lot of heat. "We'll talk once things have settled down."

That was about the best offer he could have made. Harley wasn't going to pressure her into trying to figure out what any of this meant, which also meant they were on the same mental page. Then again, the danger had a way of putting everything else on hold.

After yet another of those heat-packing kisses, he caused her to mentally groan when he moved away and sat up. "You should probably eat something, and I need to grab a shower. After that, we could keep going through the PI reports to see if there's anything in them to link us to the killer."

It was another good offer, and Ava knew he was right about her needing to eat. Just because they had a killer to catch, it didn't mean she could neglect anything to do with the baby.

She got the cheap thrill of seeing a naked Harley head to the shower. Mercy, the man was built, and just seeing him fired up more than it should.

"Eat and work," she muttered, reminding her body that it had already had all it was going to get of Harley tonight.

While Harley showered, Ava dressed and, bringing both her phone and gun with her, she made her way into the kitchen. She checked out the windows, looking for any signs of trouble, but both her front and back yards were empty. Added to that, two of her neighbors who'd been out walking their dogs had stopped to chat on the sidewalk just across the street. Since everyone in Silver Creek knew about the murders, one of them would have alerted her had they seen anything suspicious.

Well, they would if they actually saw it.

She thought of the mannequin's head that the killer had managed to put on her back porch. Way too close for comfort, but it was still light out right now, so that added a small level of safety. However, as Harley had pointed out, it'd be dark soon and the killer might make his next move. That was the reason Ava moved away from the window.

The soup and grilled cheese that Harley had made were now stone-cold, but since she didn't want to cook anything else, she heated them up, poured herself another glass of milk and carried her plate to the table so she could boot up her laptop. She hadn't even managed to open the file on the PI reports when Harley came in.

Dressed, and with his hair damp from his shower, he looked far better than any man should. And her expression must have let him know exactly what she was thinking because the corner of his mouth lifted in a smile.

"You have that same effect on me," Harley assured her in that hot drawl that caused her body to go all warm again. She was fighting the urge to get up and kiss him when his phone rang.

His smile faded and Harley tensed as he glanced at the screen. "It's Quentin Dalton, the Ranger who's watching Caleb."

Ava practically rocketed to her feet, and the alarm shot through her. Oh, God. Had something happened to Caleb?

She didn't have to ask Harley to put the call on speaker. He did, and she immediately heard the Ranger's voice pour through the room. It was a voice she recognized because she recalled meeting Quentin a time or two when Harley and she had still been together.

"Caleb hasn't been hurt or anything like that," Quentin immediately said, no doubt to give them some reassurance, but Ava wasn't reassured of anything. Just the fact the Ranger had called meant there was a problem of some kind.

"What happened?" Harley asked, taking the words right out of her mouth.

"Caleb got spooked, and he wants to see Ava and you. I'm driving him to your place now."

"What?" Ava couldn't say fast enough. "Why? What happened?"

"Someone hacked his social media accounts and posted pictures of the dead women." Quentin's response was equally fast.

"There was a warning from the hacker that you were next," Caleb added. His voice was a tangle of nerves. "That the killer was coming for you tonight."

"Hell," Harley grumbled. "You've reported it?" he asked Quentin.

"Oh, yeah, and the lab folks will be looking into the hacking. I told Caleb that, but I couldn't talk him out of coming to see you."

"He couldn't," she heard Caleb verify. "I just didn't want to be in that apartment when I knew what the killer had planned. God, he put your face on those women he killed. He said he was going to kill you *tonight*," Caleb emphasized. "I couldn't just sit still and do nothing."

Ava wanted to demand that Caleb go back to his apartment. Because she knew full well the hacking could have been meant to get Caleb to do exactly this. Leave the relative safety of his apartment and go out on the road where the killer would have an easier time getting to him.

A killer who would use her son to hurt her in the worst possible way.

"Where are you right now?" Harley asked, sounding calm, but Ava could see the urgency and intensity in his expression.

"About fifteen miles from Silver Creek," Quentin answered. "I'm turning off the interstate now. And, yeah, I know this trip isn't smart, but I want to get to Ava's place before dark."

"Don't blame Ranger Dalton," Caleb insisted. "I told him I was coming to Silver Creek one way or another. I didn't want him to call you until we were closer because I was afraid you'd convince him to turn around and take me back to Austin."

Ava shook her head but didn't press Caleb about what he thought he could do to stop a killer from coming after her. Obviously, he believed he could protect her in some way and, while that touched her, she was also worried about his safety. She was a cop. Caleb wasn't.

"I'm going to call the sheriff and see if he can spare a deputy to go out to meet you and finish escorting you here," Ava insisted.

Since there was only one road leading to Silver Creek from the interstate, she didn't have to guess which route Quentin would be taking, and she picked up her phone to make the call to Theo. Before she could press the number, she heard a sound she didn't want to hear.

Quentin cursed.

Just a single word of raw profanity, followed by something else that had her heart dropping to her knees.

The sickening boom of a car crash.

HARLEY HAD ALREADY braced himself for something bad happening, but he'd been praying that his gut was wrong. That Quentin and Caleb would be able to make it to Silver Creek without incident so that Caleb would be safe.

But that clearly wasn't the case.

There was the distinctive sound of metal crashing into metal. And, mixed with that horrible noise, were the moans that followed.

"Caleb?" Ava blurted out. There was absolute terror in her voice now. "Are you all right?"

The only answer she got were more moans, and that was enough to get Ava moving. She was already dressed, but she grabbed her holster and made the call to Theo. Since Harley knew there was no way he could talk her out of going to the scene, he strapped on his own holster and Kevlar vest. He had her put on a vest, too, before they hurried to the garage.

"Quentin?" Harley pressed, shifting the call to hands-free so he could focus on the drive.

Still nothing other than more of those moans.

"They're alive," Harley reminded Ava, "and Quentin's vehicle would have had airbags."

No need for him to spell out, though, that it wouldn't be bullet-resistant like their cruiser, meaning Caleb and Quentin could be in big trouble right now. Because the odds were this wasn't just an accident.

That sent Harley's mind spinning with all sorts of bad scenarios. Of the killer running Quentin and Caleb off the road so he could get to them. Maybe not to kill them right off, either, but to use Caleb to get to Ava.

It twisted at Harley to think it might just work.

After all, Ava and he were heading down the rural road toward the crash site. They'd have backup, or soon would anyway once Theo was on the way, but all of this could have been designed to kill Ava and him, especially if a lackey had been used to cause the crash with Caleb.

That would free up the killer to come after Ava.

Ava used her own phone to call Dispatch and request an ambulance, something Theo likely would have done, but this way the EMTs might make it there a little faster. Not as fast as Harley and her, though, not with the way he was speeding. He hit the sirens in case they did encounter any other traffic because Harley was very much afraid that every second counted right now.

"Caleb?" Ava called out when there was another moan. "Talk to me," she said. "Are you hurt?"

There were some other sounds. Not moans this time. But a soft swish followed by some quick movements. Harley tried to picture what was happening, and he had a bad thought flash in his head.

Oh, hell.

It sounded as if someone had thrown open the door of Quentin's truck. If so, it probably hadn't been Quentin or Caleb since they would have had to bat down the airbags first.

"Caleb?" Ava repeated, her voice even louder this time.

But Caleb didn't answer. And the call disconnected.

When Harley glanced at her, he saw the alarm flash through her eyes and tried to tamp down his own worry. He wanted to reassure her that something could have been bumped to accidentally end the call, but there was no reassurance for this. Ava was almost certainly thinking the same thing he was.

That the killer had done this.

Her hands were trembling a little when she tried to call Quentin back. No answer and, after four rings, it went to voice mail. Ava didn't give up. She tried again, and when she got the same results, she tried Caleb's phone.

It rang and rang and rang. Each of the sounds feeling like a punch to the gut. It was possible that both phones had been damaged in the collision, or whatever the hell had happened, but it wasn't likely. And that brought him back full circle to something he had to accept.

That the killer had Quentin and Caleb.

"Check with Theo and see how far out he is," Harley instructed Ava, and he said a quick prayer that the sheriff wasn't that far behind them. He really didn't want to go into this with Ava without some kind of backup.

While she made that call, Harley continued to put the pedal to the metal and maneuver the cruiser around the snakelike road. The sun was setting, barely a sliver now on the horizon, and the darkness sure as heck wouldn't be their friend. They were going to arrive on scene in near darkness, where anything could be waiting for them.

"Theo just passed the Wilson Ranch," Ava relayed to him after she finished her call, and she immediately tried to contact Caleb again.

Harley mentally calculated the distance and silently cursed. If the crash had happened fifteen miles from Silver Creek, then Ava and he were less than three minutes away. Theo would be a good five minutes behind them.

After he arrived on scene, Harley hoped he would be able to talk Ava into staying in the cruiser while he checked on Caleb and Quentin. If necessary, he'd play dirty and remind her of the danger to the baby. He'd do whatever it took to keep her as safe as possible and hope that backup would arrive in time. While he was hoping, he added that the backup would be enough to stop whatever had been set in motion.

"Is Theo alone?" Harley asked her.

"Yes." Her strained voice indicated this was a big concern for her. "But he's called in a reserve deputy. He'll get here as fast as he can."

Well, that was better than nothing, and a reserve deputy would probably arrive a whole lot faster than he could get a Ranger out here. A Ranger who'd have to come all the way from the San Antonio office. He was considering having Ava call Grayson or someone else from the Silver Creek Ranch, but he rounded a steep curve and had to hit the brakes.

Just ahead, he spotted a black truck. Quentin's. It was off the road and in a deep ditch. The truck had tilted to the side with the passenger's-side door pressed against the ditch. The front end appeared to be damaged only at the impact point of the passenger's side hitting the ditch. The rear end was another story. It had been bashed in, and Harley could immediately see why.

Behind the truck was another vehicle. A massive Hummer, and judging from Harley's initial take of the scene, the Hummer had rear-ended the truck with enough force to send it into the ditch.

"I don't see Caleb," Ava muttered, though, like Harley, she was frantically looking around to spot Quentin, Caleb.

Or the killer.

But Harley didn't see anyone. Worse, the driver's-side door of the truck was shut, and he was almost positive he'd heard a vehicle door open.

Harley inched the cruiser forward, but he didn't bother

to tell Ava to keep watch and be ready for an attack. She was. She had her gun gripped in her hand and had leaned in closer to the windshield.

He cut the sirens, hoping that would allow him to hear any sounds coming from outside. There was the spewing noise of a busted radiator on the Hummer, but that was it. Certainly, he couldn't hear any of those moans or anyone calling out for help.

Harley continued moving closer and stopped level with the truck. He kept the flashing cruiser lights on, though, to alert anyone who might be driving this way.

"I can't see through the truck's windows because of the heavy tint," Ava muttered.

Neither could he and he was thankful Ava hadn't gone into the panic mode and rushed out to check on Caleb.

Harley turned to her. "I'm less than two feet from the driver's door of the truck," he stated. "Just stay put a second and let me have a look inside. Please," he added when she opened her mouth, no doubt to argue. "I won't even fully get out of the cruiser. I'll just lower my window and reach over."

After a few seconds, she nodded, though she didn't look at all convinced this was a good idea. Still, like him, they had to know if Quentin or Caleb was all right.

Harley didn't waste any time. He lowered his window and, while muttering a quick prayer, he reached over to the truck, hoping that it didn't have an automatic locking system. If it did, Quentin had turned it off because Harley was able to open the door.

And he cursed.

Because it was empty.

Chapter Fifteen

The panic tore through Ava, threatening to bring her to her knees, but she fought it. Fought it hard because the panic wasn't going to help her find her son.

"Caleb?" she called out.

There was no need for her to stay silent. After all, the cruiser lights were flashing through the twilight, and if the killer was still there, he or she would know that Harley and she had arrived. Added to that, this had likely been the killer's plan all along; to use Caleb as bait and have them come here.

It had worked.

She refused to believe that Caleb or Quentin might already be dead. There'd be no reason for the killer to murder them right off the bat. Not when the two could be used to draw Harley and her out into the open.

"I don't see either of them," Ava observed as she frantically glanced around her for any sign of them.

If they'd been hurt in the crash, they wouldn't have gotten far, but they were in an area of wide-open pastures and thick woods. Plenty of places for Quentin and Caleb to have run to escape a killer. Of course, that meant there were also plenty of places for the killer to lie in wait.

Harley leaned back inside the cruiser and, while he continued to keep watch, he tried to call Quentin. Ava listened for the sound of any ringing or vibrating, but she didn't hear anything to indicate the call had gone through.

She tried Caleb's number again and got the same thing. No response of any kind, and she seriously doubted that both Quentin's and Caleb's phone had become disabled in the crash.

"Theo should be about six to eight minutes out," Harley muttered, maybe calculating if they could wait that long.

Heaven knew what the killer was doing to Caleb right now, but Ava tried to keep that out of her mind and focus.

"Close your door and move up a little further," she advised. "Maybe they're in the pasture on the other side of the truck"

Harley had already started to do just that and, as he inched past the truck and Hummer, Ava looked on both sides of the road. On the road as well, since there could be explosives there. She didn't see anything.

Not until they were about ten feet past the Hummer.

"There," Harley and she said at the same time.

It was a man lying in a crumpled heap in the pasture. That gave her another slam of adrenaline and fear, but again, she forced herself to focus, and she released a quick breath when she saw the man move. She couldn't tell if it was Caleb or Quentin, but whoever it was, he appeared to be alive.

And injured.

Had to be since he wasn't getting up and wasn't in any kind of defensive posture to protect himself.

Harley turned the cruiser, switching to the high beams so they could get a better look. It was Quentin. Ava could now see his holster. No gun though. It was empty. And she could see something else.

Blood.

Harley must have seen it, too, because he cursed. It was on the side of Quentin's head and cheek. He'd either been injured in the crash or else the killer had done this to incapacitate him.

"Stay put and cover me," Harley insisted. "I have to go out there. I'll check the Hummer first and then get to Quentin."

Ava knew what Harley had to do. This was their job, and a fellow law enforcement officer needed their help. She also didn't want Harley to be gunned down, but she wouldn't be able to provide much cover if she stayed put.

"I'll get out and use my door as cover," she told him, making sure it didn't sound like a suggestion. "I can better cover you from over the roof of the cruiser."

She didn't add the reminder that she was wearing a bulletproof vest. So was Harley. But that wouldn't stop them from being killed with a headshot.

Harley hesitated. Of course he did. She was hesitating, too. But she met his gaze and tried to assure him that she would do everything possible to protect herself and their child.

"Don't leave the cover of the cruiser," he warned her and then stunned her by pressing a kiss to her mouth.

In the same motion, he barreled out of the cruiser, leaving his door open only a fraction. That way, it'd be easier for him to dive back in if trouble started, and the partially closed door would give her more protection.

Ava got out, too, and she took aim over the top of the cruiser. She silently repeated to herself that she was a good shot, and if she saw anyone coming after Harley and Quentin, she could stop them, especially since Harley was out in the open and at huge risk.

She focused on Harley as he threw open the door of the Hummer and looked inside. "Empty," he relayed to her, and he jumped over the ditch.

Ava kept her eyes on Harley, but she also couldn't stop listening for Caleb. If the killer had him, where would he take him? She had to guess that the killer had planned on using the Hummer to escape with Caleb, to take him someplace where he could hold him and use him to bargain.

And draw her out.

But with the Hummer disabled, the killer might not have had a choice but to flee with Caleb on foot. If so, then there'd be some kinds of signs like trampled grass or even footprints. There would have to be something they could use to find him and get him to safety. Ava couldn't allow herself to believe otherwise.

The cruiser lights created an eerie effect over the pasture. Not quite the jerky effect from strobe lights, but it made Harley's movements seem disjointed, as if every second he was hitting a pause button. And then there were the shadows. Too many of them all over the pasture and the woods.

It seemed to take an eternity for Harley to reach Quentin, but she figured it was only a couple of seconds. She saw Quentin move and then say something to Harley. Something that had Harley's head whipping in the direction of the woods that were straight ahead. Ava glanced there, too, but she didn't see anything.

"Quentin's been stunned," Harley called out to let her know. "And he has a head injury."

"Where's Caleb?" she immediately asked.

"Someone took him," Harley quickly supplied. "Quentin doesn't know who, but he thinks they went that direction." Harley pointed to the woods again, and that's when Ava saw the movement.

A flash of someone wearing light-colored clothing.

She didn't let it pull her complete attention from Harley since it could be a planned diversion. One that could turn out to be deadly. So she volleyed her gaze between Harley and the movement while she kept her gun ready in case she had to fire. Her heart slammed hard against her ribs when she caught sight of the person's face.

· Caleb.

Her son was alive, and he was peering out from the trees as if hiding from someone.

Ava had to fight to stop herself from bolting from cover, and she yelled his name so he would know she was there. Something he likely already knew because of the lights. Caleb's head whipped up and he stepped out from the trees.

He didn't get far.

Someone latched onto him, dragging him back. Ava got a glimpse of the gun the person rammed against Caleb's neck before they disappeared back into the woods.

HARLEY SAW WHAT had just happened to Caleb. While he'd knelt there next to Quentin, he'd seen Caleb's attacker drag him back into the cover of the trees. And, Harley cursed, because there was nothing he could do to stop it. He certainly hadn't been able to fire his gun since he couldn't risk hitting Caleb.

"Do what you have to do," Quentin muttered, his voice slurred from the effects of the stun gun. Maybe because of the head wound, too.

So far, Quentin hadn't been able to tell him what'd happened, but it looked as if someone had bashed him on the head. He needed an ambulance, and even though one was no doubt on the way, the EMTs wouldn't be able to move in unless the scene was secure.

"Go," Quentin insisted.

This was the very definition of a rock and a hard place. There wasn't anything else he could do for Quentin, but he could try to save Caleb. Of course, that meant going into the woods with a killer, but he couldn't just wait while Caleb was clearly in danger.

Obviously, Ava felt the same way, and Harley had to curse again when he looked up and saw her making her way toward him.

"I have to help him," she said.

Harley didn't bother to spell out that this was exactly how the killer wanted her to react. No need. Ava knew the killer had set this plan in motion so she could end up being a victim.

He glanced at the woods, judging the distance, and it was about the same as it had been in Austin. The shooter had missed them with every single shot. Maybe the same thing would happen now.

"I'm a good cop," Ava added, no doubt to remind him that she wasn't just going to charge in with guns blazing.

Yeah, she was good, but Harley knew that sometimes good wasn't enough. Sometimes, the best cops got killed when trying to do the right thing.

"I'm going with you," Harley insisted.

He fired off a quick text to Theo to let him know what was happening, and then Harley started praying. First, that he could get Ava through this unharmed and then a prayer that they'd find Caleb alive and be able to take the killer into custody. Of course, that last part could be a long shot if Ava and he didn't manage to sneak up on the killer and take him or her by surprise. Hard to do, though, when the killer was no doubt keeping an eye on them.

"Backup weapon in my boot holster," Quentin managed to say.

Harley retrieved it for him, putting it into his hand. Since Quentin closed his fingers around it, the feeling was obviously returning, so at least he'd be able to defend himself if the killer circled back. Harley doubted that would happen though. If the killer had believed the Ranger would be a threat, then Quentin would already be dead.

"This way," Harley instructed. "And stay as low as you can."

He led Ava not toward the spot where they'd last seen Caleb. Instead, Harley made a beeline for the first cluster of trees. It was a huge risk. Anything was at this point. But it was better for them to have some cover, and then they could thread their way through the trees to get to Caleb.

If he was still there.

Harley had to believe he was. Though, it was entirely possible the killer'd had another vehicle waiting somewhere. Maybe up the road or on a nearby ranch trail. If that happened, if the killer managed to get Caleb out of these woods, then Harley figured Caleb's life wouldn't be worth much. The killer would likely use the young man as a bargaining tool and then murder him. After all, Quentin might not have gotten a good enough look to know the identity of the killer, but Caleb possibly would now that he'd had some up-close contact.

When Ava and he reached the cover of the trees, Harley didn't breathe any easier. Thankfully, there was a bright moon out, and his eyes had adjusted to the near darkness. He immediately looked around to see if they were about to be ambushed, since the killer could have anticipated they might do this. He didn't see anyone. Didn't hear anyone, either, but in the distance he could hear the sound of a siren. Theo, probably. That was good because they needed backup, and Theo would be able to decide if it was safe enough to allow in the EMTs to help Quentin.

Ava and he continued to move and Harley was once again thankful that she was in such good shape. He recalled her saying early on in the pregnancy that her doctor had told her that it was okay for her to keep up her exercise routine. This trek wouldn't necessarily be that strenuous, but the adrenaline and nerves had to be wreaking havoc with her head. Still, she kept up, moving fast with him as they made their way to where they would hopefully find Caleb.

Harley stopped when he thought he heard something. A footstep maybe. But it was hard to tell what with his heart-beat crashing in his ears. He forced himself to level out and listen, since he definitely didn't want the killer sneaking up on them and gunning them down.

Ava motioned toward their left, to an area even thicker with trees than where they already were. Apparently, she'd heard something, too, and like him, she was trying to pick through the darkness and the woods to see if there was a threat or if the sound they'd heard was just some animal trying to get out of their path.

They waited a few seconds. When there was nothing but the wail of the approaching siren, Ava and he started moving again. But they didn't get far. The next sound they heard sure as heck wasn't a footstep or an animal.

"Don't shoot," someone said. "It's me."

Harley cursed when he recognized that voice.

Aaron.

The man stepped out from one of the trees, and he had

his hands lifted in the air as if surrendering. Harley didn't let down his guard.

"Take aim at him," Harley told Ava. "I'll keep watch."

Ava did just that and was no doubt about to launch into some serious questions, but Aaron spoke first.

"What did you do with Caleb?" Aaron demanded. "Why the hell did you take him?"

It took Harley a moment to realize Aaron meant that for Ava. Obviously, Aaron had gotten some things twisted up.

Or maybe this was all an act to make them think he was innocent.

But if he was the killer, if he'd been the one who'd taken his own son, then where was Caleb? Harley certainly didn't see him. It was possible, though, that Aaron had gagged him and stashed him behind one of the trees.

"I didn't take Caleb," Ava stated, her voice as cold as winter. "But if you did, you'd better tell me where he is now."

"I don't know where he is," Aaron insisted.

Ava kept her gun trained on him. "Then why are you out here?"

Aaron fluttered his hand toward the road. "I got a text from Caleb. He said he was in trouble and told me to come here."

"Right," Ava muttered, the skepticism coating that one word. Harley was right there with her. That wasn't likely to have happened.

Unless the killer had forced Caleb to send that text.

But Harley immediately discounted that. Unless Aaron had already been in Silver Creek, he wouldn't have been able to make it here ahead of Ava and him.

"It's true," Aaron argued. "I can show you the text."

"Texts can be faked," she argued right back. "This place

isn't exactly on the beaten path. How could Caleb give you directions to get here?"

"He said I'd see a truck on the side of the road," Aaron answered without hesitation. He started to lower his arms, but Ava made a quick motion with the barrel of her gun for him to keep them in the air. "Caleb told me once I saw it that I was to park and wait. But then I saw you dragging him into the woods. What the hell happened, Ava? What's going on?"

If Aaron's story was anywhere near true, then the killer had to be the one who'd lured him here. But why? So Aaron could be killed, too, or was the killer looking to pin all of this on him? Of course, it was entirely possible that the story was all a pack of lies to get Ava and Harley to lower their guard so that Aaron could try to kill them.

Aaron huffed then he groaned. "I saw the truck on the road and the Hummer behind it. I saw the wreck. Was Caleb hurt? Tell me," he practically shouted when Ava didn't immediately respond.

"I don't know if Caleb is hurt, and I don't have him," she repeated. "Do you?"

She was no doubt looking for any signs that Aaron was lying. "You said you were parked just up the road?" Ava asked.

Harley cursed, and while he kept watch, he whipped out his phone to text Theo to let him know about the vehicle. He didn't want the killer using it to try to escape with Caleb.

"Yeah. Not far," Aaron verified. He groaned again. "What's going on?" This time his question was more like a plea. "Does the killer have Caleb?"

Before Ava could answer, Harley heard a sound coming from the area where they'd last seen Caleb. It was just a quick movement.

Then the bullet came right at them.

Chapter Sixteen

The bullet slammed into the tree just to Ava's right, less than a foot away. She automatically went to the ground, protecting her stomach, while she glanced over at Harley to make sure he was okay.

He was. For now anyway.

Like her, he dropped down, bringing up his gun to aim in the direction of where that shot had been fired. At first she thought it'd come from Aaron. But she could still see both of his hands, and Aaron didn't have a weapon.

"What the hell?" Aaron yelled.

He sounded genuinely shocked, but Ava knew that could be faked. Aaron could be calling the shots here, literally, since it could be his hired gun who'd just pulled the trigger.

A second shot came, this one blasting into the tree directly behind Harley and her. Aaron yelled out his question again, adding some vicious anger, and he went to the ground, scrambling to the side of the tree.

"Are the cops shooting at us?" Aaron shouted.

Ava didn't answer, but she knew it wasn't Theo or Quentin who was doing this. No way would either of them take that risk even if they had spotted Caleb with the killer. This wasn't a case of friendly fire. Just the opposite. These shots were coming from someone who wanted them dead.

"Ava?" somebody called out.

Her heart thudded when she realized it was Caleb. He was alive, but he sounded frantic. Of course he was. If he was close enough to the gunfire, this had to be terrifying for him.

She wanted to answer, but she knew she couldn't. Not when the killer might be using Caleb to try to pinpoint her exact location.

"Ava's here," Aaron shouted back. "I'm here, too. It's me… Aaron," he added, though she thought he'd been about to say *your dad*. "Where are you? We're worried sick about you."

The words had no sooner left Aaron's mouth when there were more shots. Three back-to-back blasts that tore through the woods, splintering the bark on the trees. Wood and leaves flew, and Ava sheltered her eyes and her stomach as best she could.

A sickening dread washed over her. Harley and she were in grave danger. That meant so was her precious baby. So was her son. She could lose everything right here, right now, without even knowing who was responsible for the hell they'd been going through.

So many dead women. So many ruined lives. And she still had no idea why the killer was after her.

"Aaron," Caleb responded, but this time his voice was different. Not so much frantic or terror but hesitation.

Ava tried not to think of what was being done to Caleb to make him call out to her. Maybe the killer was hurting him. Maybe killing him.

No, she couldn't go there. It would only cause her to lose

focus, and she needed every bit of her attention and cop's training if they stood a chance of getting out of this alive.

"No," Caleb said, and he seemed to be arguing with someone.

If it was the killer in on that argument, then that might account for why there hadn't been any shots fired in the last couple of seconds. Then again, it could be a ploy by the killer to draw them out, to make them believe they wouldn't be gunned down.

"Keep watch," Harley murmured to her.

He touched her arm, just a touch, but that was enough to help steady her. Well, steady her until she realized Harley was on the move. He stayed hunkered down, but he left the cover of the tree and darted to another one. Then another. He was making his way in the direction of where they'd heard Caleb.

Mercy, Harley had to stay safe. He had to come back to her. This didn't have anything to do with them having had sex. No, this was about her feelings for him. She was still in love with him and she needed the chance to tell him that.

"Caleb?" Aaron called out again. He groaned when Caleb didn't respond.

Ava silently had a much worse reaction. Terror for her son. But she continued watching, looking for the killer. She also kept an eye on Aaron, wishing that she could just frisk him to make sure he wasn't armed. He hadn't turned his back to her once so, for all she knew, he could have a gun in the waist of his jeans. He could be waiting for the perfect moment to kill her.

But if that was so, it meant he wasn't working alone.

With the explosives expert almost certainly dead, it was possible that Aaron had hired some muscle to carry out this sick plan.

"The person with Caleb had your face," Aaron muttered. "I thought it was you. I thought you'd lost it and wanted him out of the way."

Her face. That would certainly mesh with how the killer had staged his other victims. A mask of her face to carry out all those murders. And now this. The killer was using her face while doing heaven knew what to her son. Caleb would know it wasn't her, but that likely wouldn't be of much comfort now.

She thought of the other two suspects. Marnie and Duran. Thought of her father, too. If Aaron had been duped into coming here, then it was likely one of them was behind this. Not her father though. He wouldn't have dirtied his hands this way, but Duran, yes, he could absolutely be the one who'd grabbed Caleb and pulled him into the woods. Marnie, too. One of them could be out there right now, waiting to put the finishing touches on this plan of terror.

A gunshot blast cut off those thoughts and had Ava's heart dropping. *Please no, not Harley or Caleb.* She pivoted in the direction of the sound but didn't hear anything to indicate one of them had been hurt. No sharp sounds of pain, no one dropping to the ground.

She could no longer see Harley, but she believed she could hear his footsteps about fifteen yards away. Maybe he was moving so he could then circle back to Caleb and whoever was holding him. Or the footsteps could belong to the killer. If so, he didn't appear to be dragging anyone in tow. So, if that was indeed what was happening, then where was Caleb?

Since Quentin had been hit with a stun gun, the killer might not have hesitated to use it on Caleb. That would be especially true if Caleb was fighting to get free. Added to that, it hadn't worked to lure her out when Caleb had shouted for her, so the killer might have just stashed him somewhere to use her for another ploy.

"Caleb?" Aaron repeated, his voice a weak sob now.

Ava ignored the man so she could focus on Harley and the direction he was going. Even though he was no longer close to her, she could maybe still give him some kind of backup. She had to keep watch for Theo, too. It would take him a while to get out of the cruiser and then deal with Quentin, but after that, the sheriff would no doubt be making his way toward them.

Another shot came at them.

But not at her.

Ava quickly realized that when she heard Aaron howl in pain. Her gaze fired over to him and she saw that he'd been shot in his right shoulder. The blood immediately started to spread over his shirt. Not gushing, but this didn't appear to be just a graze or a flesh wound either.

Writhing in pain, Aaron fell all the way to the ground, clutching his shoulder. In all his moving around, Ava got a good look at the back of his jeans and didn't see any weapons. Then again, she doubted now that he was truly the killer unless his own henchman had shot him by mistake.

"An ambulance will be here soon," she muttered to him. Though Ava had no idea when that would happen with the gunshots being fired all around them. "Keep pressure on the wound until help gets here," she added.

Even though Aaron wasn't her priority—Caleb and Harley were—she still didn't want him to bleed out. It was possible Aaron was innocent of everything that'd happened, and even if he had actually had some part in it, Ava wanted him alive so he could fill them in on any details he might know. She wanted any and all info that could catch this killer and end the murders.

Her head whipped up when she heard the sound of running footsteps. They definitely weren't coming from the area where Harley should be. No, these were in the area where those shots had originated, and that meant the shooter was on the move. Maybe trying to escape. Maybe trying to go after Harley or Caleb.

She heard something else. Something that had every muscle tightening in Ava's body. A moan, the sound of someone in pain. She couldn't stay put, not after hearing that, and she wasn't much good to Harley or Caleb if she didn't at least try to help.

Ava bolted away from the tree and went after the killer.

HARLEY KEPT MOVING, kept looking for any signs of Caleb and the person who'd grabbed him. It was next to impossible to see drag marks, footprints or such, but he had heard something that gave him a good idea of the killer's movements.

Movements that could have gotten Ava killed.

He refused to dwell on that because just the thought of it twisted him up inside. Instead, Harley focused on doing whatever he could to put a quick end to this so he could rescue Caleb and then hurry back to Ava.

Harley had no doubts that the killer or someone working for the killer had gone to the area where he'd left Ava and Aaron. He'd had no trouble hearing the shots. Had no trouble imagining what those bullets could be doing. That's why Harley had backtracked and headed that direction, to try to take out the shooter before he or she could do any more damage.

But then the snake had gone on the move again.

Not slow, cautious steps, either, but moving fast. Harley

was pretty sure the person was heading back to the original spot where Ava and he had first seen Caleb being grabbed.

Harley didn't make a beeline in that direction. That would be too dangerous, to come at the killer head-on, so he went back to his original plan of circling around to hopefully come up from the side. That'd be his best bet for getting a clean shot to stop whatever the hell was happening right now.

He tried to avoid stepping on any fallen tree branches so he wouldn't telegraph his movements, but he was certain he was making plenty of noise. That wouldn't help with the element of surprise. However, the killer had to know that Ava and he would be doing everything possible to get Caleb out of there safely.

That would mean a confrontation with the killer.

Harley welcomed it. Welcomed the chance to stop the killer from doing any more harm. But he was going to have to make sure the SOB didn't get the chance to stop him first.

He paused when he heard yet more footsteps. Close ones. Not running ones this time, and they were getting closer to him. He held his breath, listening and waiting. Then he had to curse when he caught some movement from the corner of his eye and realized it wasn't the killer or Caleb.

It was Ava.

Harley was beyond thankful that she didn't appear to be hurt, but he wanted to demand to know what the hell she was doing there. He didn't have to wait long, though, for her to tell him.

"The shooter's moving that way," she whispered, tipping her head further to the left than he'd been heading.

If he'd continued on his path, he might have ended up having a face-to-face instead of sneaking up on him or her.

"Aaron's been shot," Ava added before Harley could wonder how she'd known that. "The shooter fired and then went in that direction." She motioned to his left again, and then her eyes met his. "I couldn't stay put."

Yeah, he'd already figured that out. In some ways, it was easier having her with him because he didn't have to imagine what terrible things might have been happening to her. But having her there was also a distraction, because Harley would do anything to protect her.

Anything.

"How bad is Aaron hurt?" Harley asked.

"A bullet to the shoulder," she supplied.

So that meant Aaron was likely out of commission. Well, unless he'd faked his injury, and Harley wouldn't put it past the man to do something like that. But if Aaron was truly injured, it meant Ava and he were about to face either Duran or Marnie. Of course, it could also be someone they'd hired. More than one, in fact.

If so, that meant Ava and he could be walking into a trap.

Harley had silenced his phone, but he felt it vibrate, and he took it out so he could glance at the screen. "It's Theo," he relayed to Ava. "He's heading into the woods now."

Keeping watch while trying to listen to their surroundings, Harley fired off a quick text to let Theo know about Aaron being shot and to give the sheriff a general idea of where they were. Hard to do that, though, when Harley wasn't sure. However, Theo would have heard the gunshots and would have an idea of where to go.

Harley put away his phone and turned to Ava, to remind her to stay behind him and let him shield her. But he already knew she would be as cautious as she possibly could be. So that's why he just settled for dropping a quick kiss on her mouth and got them moving.

He didn't move with a barreling pace, and that wasn't all for Ava's benefit. Harley wanted to be able to hear any little sound despite them trudging through the thick underbrush and weaving around the trees.

And he finally heard something.

Movement in the area right where Ava had pointed out. Harley didn't head straight there. Going with his plan of circling around, he went even further to the left, almost in a straight line while he kept watch from the corner of his eye for any glimpse of Caleb or his captor.

Each step felt like a huge risk, knowing Ava and he could be shot. But he was beyond thankful when no bullets came at them.

Harley stopped when he finally saw something. Ava must have spotted it at the same time because she quit moving and turned in the direction of a small clearing. Emphasis on *small*. There was only about a ten-foot strip where there were no trees, and the moonlight filtered in enough for Harley to see someone.

Caleb.

He was alive, and Harley knew the breath Ava dragged in was one of relief.

At first glance, it appeared that Caleb was alone and leaning against one of the trees on the far perimeter of the clearing. Maybe placed there as human bait to get Ava and him to go rushing in after the young man. But then Harley saw the gun and realized that someone dressed all in black was behind Caleb and pressing the barrel to his head.

Ava's next breath definitely wasn't one of relief because she knew her son could end up being killed right in front of her.

Harley tried to make out anything about the person who

was holding Caleb, but it was hard to do since they had hunkered down, using Caleb as a shield. That would prevent Harley or Ava from trying a head shot. Or anywhere else for that matter since they could end up shooting Caleb.

"I'm supposed to tell you something," Caleb said, his voice trembling. "A trade. Me for you, Ava. But I don't want you to do that," he blurted out.

The person holding him acted fast by ramming the barrel of the gun against his temple and tightening the chokehold around his neck.

Of course, it had come down to this. It was always about getting to Ava, and the killer knew she would want to save her son. But Caleb wasn't her only child. The daughter she was carrying had to be protected, too.

"I'll offer a trade," Harley stated, not to Caleb or Ava. But to the killer. "Me for Caleb."

Harley couldn't hear the killer's response but, judging from the way Caleb flinched, he'd just been given a reply to pass along.

"No deal." Caleb let him know and then he paused. "If I'm dead, I can't be used to—"

That was as far as Caleb got before his captor bashed the gun against his head again. This time, it drew blood that began to slide down the side of Caleb's face.

Because Ava's arm was against his, Harley sensed her tense and could practically feel the anger coming off her. It was torture watching this being done to her child.

"No, I won't," Caleb snarled, and this time, Harley was certain he was talking to the killer.

Caleb moved as if to try to break free of the chokehold, but the killer hung on. In the shuffle, though, the killer also moved. Not much. Just enough for a shot. It wouldn't be a kill shot to the head but rather to the killer's right leg that was now extended out from Caleb's body.

"I've got this," Ava muttered.

She didn't waste a second. With her hand steady, Ava took aim and fired.

AVA KNEW THIS wasn't a shot she could miss, but it was still a risk.

A huge one.

After all, she couldn't put the bullet in the killer's head so he or she could just reflexively pull the trigger and kill Caleb on the spot. Still, this was the best chance they had of getting all of them out of there alive, especially since there was no way the killer would let Caleb live even if Ava did sacrifice herself for him.

The shot sliced into the killer's leg and Ava immediately heard the cry of pain. Not a man's voice. No. A woman's.

Marnie's.

Caleb took advantage of the injury by diving to the ground. Or rather, trying to do that, but Marnie just dropped down with him, pulling him back into the chokehold and putting her gun to his head.

"You want him to die?" Marnie shouted, the pain and desperation coating her voice. Both were lethal factors here since they could lead Marnie to do something that almost certainly wasn't part of her original plan.

The woman could make sure all four of them died right here, right now.

Ava tried not to look at Caleb. Hard to do, though, but if she focused on him, it would be a huge mistake. She had to push all thoughts of him aside and try to treat this like any other hostage situation.

Marnie leaned her head out just a fraction from Caleb's,

and Ava kept her gun trained on her as Marnie ripped off her mask. Something inside Ava unclenched. The situation was still as dangerous as it got, but it sickened her that Marnie was doing all of this while wearing the image of Ava's face.

"It wasn't supposed to be like this," Marnie said, groaning in pain and cursing. "I should be gone now in the Hummer."

"Gone with Caleb?" Ava asked. She stayed behind the cover of the tree but kept watch for any chance of a clean shot. Beside her, Harley was no doubt doing the same thing.

"Of course gone with Caleb. I shouldn't have to be crawling around in the woods. You weren't supposed to die here. I wanted that to happen in front of Aaron. Where is the SOB? Did I kill him?"

Ava debated how to respond. She wanted Marnie to keep talking, but if the woman found out Aaron had only been injured and wasn't dead, that might cause her to start shooting again.

"I'm not sure if Aaron is still alive," Ava settled for saying. "He was bleeding out when I left him."

"Good," Marnie spat out. "I hope he dies a slow, painful death, and if there's any life in his worthless body when I find him, I'll show him pictures of his dead son and his ex-lover. I'll kill you both and show him what I've done."

Ava had already guessed all of this was to get back at Aaron. Marnie obviously hated the man.

"Aaron has to pay for killing my sister," Marnie went on, and this time her wail turned into a sob.

The woman was quickly losing control of herself. Again, not good. Because it would be impossible to bargain with a woman who felt she had nothing else to lose.

Harley didn't say anything, but he moved away from her, heading toward the other side of the clearing so he could no doubt try to come up from behind Marnie. Ava covered his movement by shifting her body just enough to step on some twigs and leaves beneath her boots. The sound might not fool Marnie, so Ava went with what she hoped would be a distraction.

"Your plan was organized," Ava said, making sure to sound like a cop. "Until tonight, we had no idea you were the one who murdered those women."

"Of course it was organized," Marnie snapped, groaning again. "I worked hard on the details, and it shouldn't have come down to this. You should be dead, and I shouldn't be bleeding. Hell, this hurts. I should hurt your son to make you pay."

That felt as if Marnie had punched her. There was nothing else the woman could have said to give her that jolt of fear. Oh, mercy. Her son could die.

"Caleb didn't do anything to Christina," Ava tried, hoping to give Harley time to get to Marnie. "That was all on Aaron. He gave her the drugs, didn't he?"

"Yes. He killed my beautiful baby sister." That caused Marnie to start crying. "He killed her, and I had to pretend to be friendly with him. Every time I saw him, I wanted to shoot him in the face, but that would have been too easy. I wanted him to pay."

"And then you were going to set him up for the murders," Ava finished for her.

"Oh, yeah. I chose women who'd been pregnant. I figured that'd convince the cops that Aaron's targets were to get back at you. And then he would have been arrested, convicted and paid and paid and paid by being locked up in a maximum-security prison where the inmates could make his life a living hell."

Ava didn't spell out to Marnie that her plan had also made others' lives a living hell. There were four dead women, and their families were dealing with the pain and grief Marnie had caused. In that moment, Ava wished Marnie as much pain and misery as she'd planned for Aaron.

Ava finally spotted Harley, but her chest muscles were too tight for her to feel any kind of relief. He was only about ten yards behind Marnie and Caleb, and he was inching his way toward them.

"You killed your explosives expert." Ava threw it out there. She purposely raised her voice to try to cover the sound of Harley's footsteps.

"The fool," Marnie spat out. "I hired him, and then he tried to milk more money from me. He had no idea who he was dealing with."

No, he hadn't, and it'd been a costly mistake. Marnie was capable of anything, and that was especially unsettling since she still had the gun aimed at Caleb's head.

"And I'm guessing you chose the women to kill because you knew they wouldn't put up much of a fight," Ava said, knowing that wouldn't be true.

"I'm not a coward," Marnie practically yelled. "I chose them because they were connected to you. So that the fool cops would think Aaron killed them so he could get revenge on your father."

Yes, Ava had figured that out. And it sickened her to think that it might have worked.

Since Harley would be closing in on Marnie soon, Ava went with what she hoped would be a step closer to saving Caleb's life. She made eye contact with him and then sharply cut her glance to the ground to his left. She waited, praying that Caleb understood. He did. He gave her a slight nod.

Caleb's movement caused Marnie to tighten the choke-hold, but he was still able to move. He jerked to the left.

Just as Ava stepped out from the tree.

A distraction to get Marnie's attention on her. It worked. The woman's gaze whipped toward her. So did Marnie's gun. Just as Ava darted back behind the tree.

Marnie fired.

So did Harley.

Both shots seemed to blast through the woods at the same exact second. Marnie's bullet missed, smacking into the tree right next to Ava. Harley's didn't miss. His shot went straight into Marnie's head. The woman made a sharp, strangled gasp. And then slumped to the side.

Dead.

Chapter Seventeen

Harley focused on Ava. Just Ava. With the adrenaline still slamming through him, it was next to impossible to process the details of what had just happened, so he grasped onto the most important thing.

And that was Ava.

He didn't respond to the texts he was getting. No doubt updates from anyone who was now on scene in the woods where Ava and he had been lured. He'd deal with the updates and the aftermath of the investigation later, but for now, he watched as the doctor pressed the little stethoscope wand to Ava's stomach. And Harley prayed that the baby was all right.

Ava was covered in nicks and bruises that she'd gotten when they'd made their frantic hunt through the woods so they could get to Caleb. None of her injuries looked serious, and she had insisted that she hadn't fallen or been bumped on her stomach, but she hadn't protested the trip to the Silver Creek emergency room to make sure all truly was well.

Harley felt his own cuts and bruises. All minor stuff. It was the same for Caleb, though he was undergoing his own exam in the room next door. They'd gotten damn lucky that none of them had been shot or killed.

Marnie had definitely gotten the worst of it.

And she'd deserved it.

Harley never took it lightly when he discharged his weapon, but it had been a life-and-death matter with Marnie. The woman had been hell-bent on killing to avenge her sister, and she hadn't cared one bit that she'd harmed and murdered so many innocent people. He figured there was a special place in hell for a person who'd done something like that.

"The baby's heartbeat is good," Dr. Medina said, causing both Ava and Harley to blow out breaths of relief. "There's not a scratch on your stomach," he added to Ava. "And, despite everything, your vitals are good."

Harley got another wave of relief that unclenched some of the muscles in his chest and stomach. It was somewhat of a miracle that Ava had managed to come out of this unscathed. Well, physically anyway. He knew there'd be plenty of emotional stuff for her to deal with, and he could curse Marnie for giving Ava what would likely be nightmares for life.

"How are you feeling?" the doctor asked Ava.

She opened her mouth, probably to give a rote response of "fine," but then she drew in a breath as long as the one she'd released. "I'll be a whole lot better now that the killer is dead and after I find out if Caleb is okay."

Dr. Medina gave her a gentle pat on the back. What the doctor didn't do was ask why she was so worried about Caleb, which meant he might have already heard some buzz about Ava being the young man's mother. That buzz could have easily started when the ambulance had arrived on scene and Ava had muttered for them to see to "her son." Harley hadn't even been sure that she'd known she had said it since he figured she'd been dealing with the shock of what had just happened.

"Doctor Jenkins is with Caleb now," Medina said. "I'm sure he'll be finished soon, and then you'll be able to speak to him." The doctor shifted his attention to Harley. "Now that we know Ava and your baby are all right, why don't I have a look at you?"

Harley shook his head. He wasn't sure he could stave off the adrenaline long enough to sit for an exam. Plus, it wasn't necessary. "Nothing hurts," he settled for saying.

That wasn't a lie. Harley couldn't feel anything but the slight sting from his very minor injuries. It wasn't enough to waste time with an exam, especially since he wanted to focus on Ava.

"Suit yourself," the doctor muttered, standing from the exam stool where he'd been sitting. He gave Ava another pat. "Go home, get some rest. Let Harley give you a little TLC."

Harley wondered if there'd been buzz, too, about Ava and him. Probably. Everyone would have known he'd been staying at her house during the hunt for the killer. Added to that, the doctor could probably sense the connection between them. A connection that went beyond the baby she was carrying.

Diving right into some of the TLC, Harley took hold of Ava's arm to help her off the exam table, and she looked at him. "You've been getting a lot of texts since you've been in here with me."

"Texts that can wait," he assured her, and even though the doctor was still there, Harley slipped his arm around her waist, easing her to him, and he kissed her.

Man, he needed that. Needed to hold her and have her mouth on his. It couldn't last, of course. This wasn't the time or the place for a heated kissing session, but he'd wanted her to know he was there for her in any and all ways.

She gave him a slight smile when she eased back, and

while some of the worry in her eyes had faded, there was still plenty there. That wouldn't be going away until she knew Caleb's status.

The doctor smiled, too, doled out a goodbye and headed out of the exam room. So did Ava and Harley. He kept his arm around her waist, and not only did Ava not move away from it, she also adjusted her body so she was even closer to him.

When they stepped into the waiting area, Harley was glad to see that only Theo was there, and he was reading something on his phone. Harley had thought that maybe there'd be a few gawkers or gossip hunters around, but thankfully folks had stayed away.

"Everything okay?" Theo immediately asked Ava.

She nodded and looked at the other exam room where Caleb was. The door was still closed.

"No word on Caleb yet," Theo let her know. "But I just got an update on Aaron. He's in surgery, but the initial report is that his injury isn't life-threatening."

That was good, especially since Marnie's confession made it obvious that Aaron hadn't had any involvement in the murders. "Did Aaron say anything about Marnie when he was in the ambulance?"

Not that there would have been much for the man to say, but Harley knew that Deputy Nelline Rucker had ridden in the ambulance with Aaron. Nelline would have reported anything back to Theo.

"Nelline informed Aaron that Marnie was the killer," Theo explained. "Aaron filled in the blanks, and I think it hit him pretty hard just how close Marnie came to succeeding in setting him up for the murders. Apparently, Aaron seemed grateful that she'd failed rather than gripe about us having him on the suspect list."

Harley wouldn't have cared a rat about the griping. There'd been probable cause for them to believe Aaron might be guilty. And the man was likely guilty of supplying those drugs to Christina and withholding that he'd been the one responsible. Aaron would no doubt end up paying for that, maybe even with some jail time, depending on whether or not the local DA would want to pursue it.

"What about Quentin?" Harley asked. There was probably something about that on his phone, but he didn't want to let go of Ava so he could check.

"He's fine," Theo assured him. "Once the effects of the stun gun wore off, he decided to stay at the crime scene to assist the deputies and the CSIs." He looked at Ava. "He was cursing himself, though, for not stopping Marnie when she threw open his door after ramming the Hummer into his truck. He was apparently a little disoriented, and he saw the mask Marnie was wearing."

Yeah, a mask of Ava's face. There was no way Quentin would have just fired if he'd thought it was Ava. Of course, after a split second or two, the Ranger would have realized it was a mask, but by then it would have been too late. Marnie would have hit him with the stun gun and then taken Caleb.

"Did Quentin happen to say how he made it out of the truck and into the pasture?" Ava pressed. Harley had wondered the same thing, though Quentin hadn't gone far from the collision.

"He said he crawled there after he got back some of the feeling in his legs, but then he collapsed. He was trying to go after Marnie and Caleb."

"I'm surprised Marnie didn't just kill him," Harley commented.

"Quentin was surprised, too, but I guess that wasn't part of her plan," Theo said. "Of course, judging from what you and Ava told me, it hadn't been part of Marnie's plan for the crash to disable the Hummer."

True, the woman had obviously planned on using it to escape with Caleb and then use Caleb to draw out Ava. With Aaron already on scene, he would have looked guilty. On the surface anyway. But the CSIs would have examined Quentin's truck and known that Aaron's vehicle hadn't been responsible. Marnie had likely planned a fix for that, but it was a detail they might never learn since the woman hadn't been able to carry out the finale of her sick plan.

The doors to the ER slid open and all three of them turned in that direction. Harley automatically put his hand over his gun, proof that he was still battling the adrenaline. He got another slight surge of it when he saw the two men who came rushing in.

Edgar and Duran.

Great. Just what Ava didn't need on top of everything else, and Harley geared up for his usual sparring battle with the senator. At least he now knew that Duran wasn't a killer. That didn't mean, though, that he still couldn't be a thorn in Ava's side.

"Ava," Edgar said the moment he spotted her.

Edgar made a beeline toward her, and for a moment, Harley thought the man was about to pull her into his arms. He stopped just short of her, no doubt recalling that Ava wouldn't want such a gesture from him.

"I'm not hurt," Ava said right off.

Edgar slid glances at both Harley and her, silently questioning if that was true when he obviously noticed the nicks and bruises. "Good," Edgar murmured, sounding both genuine and relived. "And Caleb?"

Ava's body tensed. "Still waiting to hear. He's in the exam room."

Edgar nodded but didn't jump to say anything. Maybe because he didn't know what he could say, considering he'd forced Ava to give up Caleb all those years ago.

"I'm hearing reports that all of this is connected to Aaron," her father said.

"All of this is connected to Marnie Dunbar," Ava corrected. "She confessed to the murders and planned to set up Aaron."

Harley glanced at Duran, expecting the man to balk about having ever been a suspect. He didn't. Maybe, like Aaron, he was just thankful he was alive and the danger was over.

Of course, things still weren't resolved on several levels.

Not with Ava and Caleb. Not with her and her father. Not with Harley. But Harley was hoping to work on that once he was able to get Ava to himself.

Edgar's attention landed on the arm Harley still had around Ava, and while his mouth didn't exactly turn into a scowl, there was the initial punch of disapproval. Much to Harley's surprise, however, that faded.

"If you had any part in keeping Ava safe," Edgar said, "then thank you."

Harley shrugged and figured that was as close to a compliment as he'd ever get from the man.

Edgar went silent again, but it was obvious there were things he wanted to say. Maybe to try to start resolving things between Ava and him. The man must have decided that was a lost cause, though, because he muttered a goodbye and turned as if to leave. He didn't get far. Edgar immediately turned back around.

"I'm sorry," he blurted. "For a lot of things." He added a glance to Harley, maybe to let him know that part of the blanket apology was for him. Edgar swallowed hard. "I'd like to see my granddaughter when she's born. If that's possible," he tacked on.

Ava took her time answering. Several long moments crawled by. "All right," she finally said. "But only if you show due respect to Harley. He is her father."

Edgar nodded, and even though Harley figured the man would have some trouble with that respect thing, he still saw this as a start in the right direction. Ava didn't need Edgar to be part of her life. Their daughter wouldn't, either, but a grandparent was good for a child to have. Added to that, it could perhaps end up mending some of the old wounds between Ava and him.

"Goodbye," Edgar muttered, but it didn't have his usual impatient snarl to it. "Keep them safe," he added to Harley.

Edgar and Duran again seemed to be on the verge of walking away, but the exam room door opened and Caleb came out. He stopped when he spotted them, giving each a glance, maybe to see if there'd been some kind of argument in progress. Obviously, he didn't see signs of that and started toward them.

"Are you okay?" Ava asked, directing her question both at Caleb and the doctor who stayed in the exam room door. The doctor gave her a thumbs-up.

"I'm fine," Caleb assured her. "How about you and Harley?"

They both echoed Caleb's response, but Ava placed her hand on Caleb's jaw, turning him so she could do her own exam. Like them, Caleb had his share of small cuts, and the bruise on his head from where Marnie had hit him with the gun, but it didn't look that serious. Harley was glad to see that someone had cleaned the blood off his neck and face. Not Caleb's, but rather the spatter from Marnie's head wound.

"Thank you," Caleb said, also extending his appreciation to both of them. "Trust me, I'm very thankful you're both good shots."

Harley was thankful for that, too. Both Ava and he had put bullets in a killer, and they'd had only small windows for those shots.

"Sir," Caleb greeted Edgar when he finally turned his attention to the man. He nodded an acknowledgment to Duran as well. There was no anger in Caleb's expression or tone, though he had to know by now the part Edgar and Duran had played in his being put up for adoption.

"Caleb," Edgar said back. "I was just telling Ava that I hoped I'd be able to see my granddaughter when she's born." He paused, cleared his throat. "Maybe you'll be there for that so I can see both of you."

Caleb looked at Ava, no doubt to get her take, and when she only nodded, Caleb smiled. "Sounds good."

That seemed to cause Edgar to relax a little and he offered Caleb his hand. Caleb shook it, and then Duran and Edgar left with Duran already muttering something about Edgar needing to schedule a press conference.

Caleb's phone dinged with a text and he glanced down at the screen. "That's Quentin. He's out front in a borrowed cruiser and said he'd give me a lift home. Is it all right if I go?" he asked Theo.

"Sure. You can give your statement tomorrow morning. If you can't come here for that, I can send Ava and Harley to Austin to take it."

Caleb smiled again. "Either way is fine. Call me and let me know what works best for you," he told Harley and Ava.

"One more thing," Ava said when Caleb started to leave. "The press will soon pick up on you being my son. There could be reporters."

Caleb made a dismissive sound. "I'll handle it," he assured her, and then the young man did something that had Harley silently cheering. Caleb hugged Ava. "See you tomorrow," he added in a whisper, and his smile widened when she brushed a kiss on his cheek.

Apparently, that was another part of Ava's life—a huge one—that just might have a happy resolution. Of course, they'd need to keep an eye on Caleb, and it was possible he'd require counseling for what he'd gone through. If so, they'd make sure he got it and anything else he needed. Caleb wasn't his bio-son, but he was a brother to Harley's daughter, and that made him kin in Harley's book.

Caleb walked toward the exit and turned back to wave at them. "I love you," Ava blurted out to him, causing Caleb to flash her an even bigger smile.

"Love you, too," Caleb said. He was still smiling as he walked out the door.

The tears immediately sprang to Ava's eyes. Happy ones. But she quickly wiped them away. No way would she want her boss to see her crying.

"I'll go have a word with Quentin," Theo muttered. "To see if he has any updates from the CSIs."

That was a ploy on Theo's part to give them some time alone, since Quentin would have already texted any updates before he'd left those woods. Harley was glad, though, that Theo had played the ploy card because he really did want time alone with Ava.

Since the ER wasn't exactly a private place, Harley took Ava by the hand and led her back into the exam room. He shut the door and pulled her into his arms. She practically melted against him, and he steeled himself in case she broke down into a full sob.

But she didn't.

When she looked up at him, he saw that her eyes were still a little misty with tears, but she didn't look anywhere on the verge of sobbing.

"Our lives have changed so much in the past forty-eight hours," she murmured.

Yeah, they had, and if Harley had his way, there'd be other changes. Good ones, he hoped. He'd intended to kiss Ava again, to get those good changes started, but she beat him to it. She slipped her arms around his neck, pulled him to her and kissed him as if there were no tomorrow.

Or better yet—as if there were plenty of tomorrows.

Mindful of her injuries, Harley tried to keep the kiss gentle, but Ava apparently wanted to go in an entirely different direction. Her mouth was hungry and hot, filled with so much need. And it released the ball of tension inside him, since that need was for him.

He kissed her back, going hungry and hot as well, until he robbed both of them of their breaths. They stopped only for some much-needed oxygen and dived right back in for a second kiss. This one fueled the heat, but it also settled the rest of their raw nerves. A good solid attraction could do that.

Love could do it even faster.

Harley probably could have chosen a better time, a better place than an exam room in the ER, but he didn't want to wait another second. He wanted the whole package with Ava, and he needed her to hear that now. Better yet, he needed her to want the same thing he did.

"I'm in love with you," he said when the second kiss broke. He stayed close to her, his forehead pressed against hers while they stayed body to body and breath to breath.

Harley waited. And waited. That tension started to coil inside him again when Ava didn't immediately respond, but then he realized she wasn't talking because she was gathering enough air so that she could speak.

"Good," she finally said. "Because I'm in love with you, too. I was worried about how you'd react when I told you."

"Worried?" He eased back now so he could meet her gaze.

She nodded. "I wasn't sure you were ready for it."

The tension vanished and Harley smiled. "Ava, I've never been more ready for anything in my entire life." He slid his hand between them and over her stomach.

Over their baby.

Oh, yeah, this life, this love, was exactly what Harley wanted.

* * * * *

TEXAS
SCANDAL

BARB HAN

All my love to Brandon, Jacob and Tori, who are the great loves of my life. To Samantha for the bright shining light that you are.

To Babe, my hero, for being my best friend, greatest love and my place to call home. I love you with everything that I am. Always and forever.

Chapter One

Tiernan Hayes stood on the steps of his back porch and whistled. Loki, his black Lab mix who was all heart and every kind of trouble, had chased after a squirrel and disappeared into the scrub brush. Since the one-year-old rescue had given chase to a rabbit yesterday and come home reeking of skunk spray, Tiernan didn't have time for a repeat performance. *Not two days in a row.*

"Loki," he shouted as he jogged across the small yard toward the wooded area on his property. He owned as far as the eye could see and then some. His decade on the rodeo circuit might've given his body every crick and groan, but it had also made him enough money to start a custom saddle business and buy his own four-acre piece of the Lone Star State. Not too bad if anyone asked him.

He listened for Loki's heavy breathing or the sound of twigs breaking as he bolted across the scrub. Something moved deeper into the trees and to the clearing. The back of his property backed up to a farm road. Even though there was little traffic, he still worried Loki would run in front of a truck. The animal was bright. That wasn't the problem. He was curious and had way too much puppy inside him to make good decisions. Any Lab owner would agree that it took about five years for them to settle down enough to become the best dog anyone could hope to own.

One down. Four to go. But who was counting?

Tiernan had a busy day ahead. Orders were stacking up. His brothers had reached out to tell him to come home to the family cattle ranch his grandfather had built from scratch. Duncan Hayes was the reason Tiernan had left Cider Creek after high school graduation. The man had been a bear. His grandfather's recent death from heat exhaustion had weighed heavy on Tiernan's heart, since his mother was left to work the multimillion-dollar operation on her own. She had requested everyone come home for an announcement. A couple of Tiernan's brothers made the trip and deemed it necessary for everyone to follow suit. If Tiernan could get ahead of his orders, he would make the trip. At this rate, he was looking at the New Year before he could wrap up all the Christmas presents on order. He didn't have it in his heart for a young rider to be disappointed at the holidays.

In fact, he'd taken on too much after a few parents begged. The money would come in handy, too. He never took for granted the fact he was building his business—a business based on his success on the circuit. He was developing a reputation by delivering high-quality custom saddles on time.

Since there was still no sign of Loki, Tiernan headed deeper into the thicket. He whistled again without any luck. This dog was determined to make Tiernan work for it today. Hells bells. The clock was ticking, and he was already pulling eighteen-hour days in the small shop he'd built behind his log-cabin-style home. Everyone had told him that he could set his own hours as an entrepreneur, and yet he worked all of them anyway.

Growing up working a cattle ranch had given him the

right skills to survive. Calving season, which ran from January to March at Hayes Cattle, had taught him how to go days without sleep.

His boot caught on a vine. He narrowly escaped a face-plant by grabbing hold of the closest tree trunk, a mesquite. Pain shot through his right shoulder with contact. When he brought his gaze up, he saw movement ahead in a small clearing. Wind gusted, sending a stench that hit Tiernan so hard it nearly doubled him over. Bile burned the back of his throat at the smell of rotting meat with a tinge of sweetness to it. He was familiar with the scent.

Loki was digging where Tiernan guessed was the source of the smell. A dead animal shouldn't be buried.

"Loki," he said in more of a commanding than casual tone. "Come."

Loki's ears perked up. He craned his neck around, locked on to Tiernan and then bolted toward him. The dog had two speeds—full-on assault as he gunned toward Tiernan and passed-out-on-the-floor mode, usually belly up.

Tiernan fished his cell phone out of his back pocket. He checked the bars to make sure he had service before calling 911.

"Fire, sheriff or ambulance?" the female voice asked on the other end of the line.

"Sheriff," he confirmed.

"What's the nature of this call?" the dispatcher asked after introducing herself as Helen.

"Based on the smell and the fact there's a fresh grave, I suspect there's a dead body buried on my property," Tiernan said. He knew better than to tamper with a site that might be considered a crime scene. He'd tracked enough dangerous poachers in his younger years and worked with enough law enforcement to know how important preserving a crime scene could be to an investigation.

Of course, he hoped like hell he was wrong about the dead body. Years of experience said he wasn't.

"What's your location, sir?" Helen asked.

A twig snapped to the left. Loki caught sight of something moving, so naturally he took off toward it.

"Loki," Tiernan scolded. It was too late. The dog had selective hearing when he locked on to a target, and he'd already disappeared into the thicket. Tiernan bit back a curse.

"Sir?" Helen said.

"Sorry." Tiernan turned to follow Loki as it occurred to him a murderer might still be on his land. Since he hadn't been expecting anything in the neighborhood of chasing down a cold-blooded killer, his Colt 45 was inside his workshop. It came in handy when there were coyotes around.

He gave his location and told Helen where a deputy could find him. Then, he stayed on the line with her until Deputy Calhoun arrived on the scene.

"I'm Tiernan Hayes," he said to the deputy before extending a hand. Calhoun gave a firm shake. "My dog caught a scent and ended up here." He motioned toward the site, wondering if he'd ever get the putrid smell out of his nose.

Calhoun walked over to the fresh grave after tying a bandana around his face to cover his nose. A small shovel extended from his left hand. Digging lasted less than two minutes before he glanced over and then nodded, confirming there was a dead body inside.

As far as thick gray clouds went, the ones slowly rolling across the Austin sky hinted at a gloom and doom kind of day. Melody Cantor walked to her sedan, light in her step despite Mother Nature's somber mood. The job interview had gone well, and an offer was promised, meaning she would be able to put in her notice at the soul-sucking job where she presently worked for one of the wealthiest men in Texas. At thirty-three, she was starting to realize how fast time flew. Wasting another day as the right hand of real estate tycoon Byron Hunter, with his endless demands and sparse compensation by comparison, wasn't worth it. Melody had drawn the line when he'd looked the other way while his firstborn son made an inappropriate pass at a Give Thanks–themed open house two weeks ago. There was nothing to be grateful for while she was trying to fight off Spence Hunter, who'd seemed determined to keep her from climbing down from the ladder she'd been on.

If luck was on her side, the offer from Community Planners would be waiting in her email inbox by the time she arrived home. The company was much larger than the family-owned operation where she currently worked.

A white slip of paper fluttered like a bird trapped in a cage on the windshield of her Camry. A parking ticket? Melody bit back a curse and denied this could be an omen.

As she neared her vehicle, which she'd wedged into what she believed was a legal spot, she realized the paper was too wide to be a ticket. A note? Was someone cursing her out for taking a spot that belonged to them?

Great. Just great.

Melody snatched the paper from her windshield and flattened the note onto the hood of her car.

Drive fifty miles west.

Right now? Was this a prank? She glanced up and down the street, unsure of exactly who or what she was looking for. Someone laughing? Someone staring? Someone paying special attention to her now that she'd read the message?

No one seemed to notice her or care, but it was impossible to see everything. Someone could be hiding.

A cold shiver raced up her spine as she reread the chicken scratch handwriting. What was fifty miles from her current location? This had to be a misunderstanding or some kind of practical joke.

Melody reached inside her handbag and located the key fob. She palmed it and then clicked the unlock button. Camrys weren't exactly rare. This note being placed on hers was probably a mistake.

She took the driver's seat and then closed the door behind her.

What if it wasn't, though? She locked the door before grabbing her cell phone to check Google Maps. From her location, fifty miles west of Austin would put her in Blanco, Johnson City or Meadowlakes. Just shy of those would put her in Marble Falls or possibly Shovel Mountain. Since she didn't know anyone who lived in any of those cities, she crumpled up the note and tossed it onto the passenger seat, determined not to let the cryptic message ruin her post-interview high.

Besides, it wasn't a ticket, which was no small miracle considering parking in Austin was almost as confusing as sitting in on her employer's meetings with his accountant at tax time.

A thought struck as Melody navigated out of the parking spot where she was sandwiched between a red Tesla and a Ducati motorcycle. Could this somehow be related to her father? After all, he was in prison awaiting trial for mail fraud. He'd convinced a whole lot of folks they'd be better off handing over their money to "get in on the ground floor" of his new business opportunity. An investigation into his business operations turned up even more charges.

The scheme he'd initially been busted for turned out to be the tip of the iceberg on his illegal dealings. But walking in on her father while he was cheating on her mother with Melody's favorite high school English teacher in her office had shattered all her beliefs about growing up in what she'd once believed was the perfect family.

When it came to Henry Cooper Cantor II, her attitude was more like, *What has he done now?* Her brother, Henry Cooper Cantor III, who went by Coop, worked for their father and claimed the man was innocent. Evidence didn't seem to agree. Melody had walked away from the family drama after catching her dad with his pants down years ago. She'd donated her trust fund to feed the hungry and never looked back. Now, she wished she had kept some so she could repay at least a portion of the money her father had taken from others. The thought of all those lavish birthday parties during her childhood that must have been funded by her father swindling other people out of their cash almost made her sick. Did it make her a target?

Fifty miles west? Was someone waiting out there for her to show up? A murderer? A rapist? Since her current line of thought had taken her to a dark place, she took in a slow, deep breath to hit the mental reset button.

The note creeped her out more than she wanted to admit.

"Call Coop's cell," she said to her phone after speaking the magic words to get its attention. Through some magic of Bluetooth technology, the call started ringing through her stereo speakers. She wondered if anyone even called them stereo speakers anymore. If not, what would the new name be? Car speakers made it simple enough.

"You okay?" Coop asked, sounding more than a little caught off guard by the random call. Granted, she could be better about keeping in touch. Since her parents' divorce, the four of them no longer spent holidays together, let alone have regular conversations. There were no more birthday parties or Sunday brunch tables for four. Her mother, Tilly, had drawn a line in the sand that said she wanted out of all activities that involved her ex. The term *coparenting* was a joke when it came to her mother's perspective on their former family. Thankfully, Melody and Coop had been old enough to take care of themselves.

"Fine," she said, realizing she sounded the opposite.

"Is it Dad?" he asked.

"No," she countered, feeling a little defensive at the abrasiveness in his tone.

"Then what?" he asked.

"Am I not allowed to call and check on my brother?" she asked, feeling every bit the hypocrite. He wasn't too far off base. Lately, neither one called the other unless there was something to do with their father's case. Usually, it was more bad news.

He didn't respond.

"Okay, you got me," she said. "I don't call just to check on you but that doesn't mean I don't care or think about you."

The truth was that she'd basically cut herself off from the family when she dumped her trust fund into Austin-area food banks. Her father had flipped out and her brother had called her delusional for thinking money grew on trees. He couldn't begin to fathom why she might not want Cantor money or wasn't bursting with pride to have the Cantor name.

Melody never once looked back after getting rid of the trust. Her brother had lost most of his betting on the stock market, thinking he could double it. So, he'd gone to work for their father to rebuild his personal wealth and she'd worked at ordinary jobs they all thumbed their noses at.

The reason for the tension in her brother's voice dawned on her. If her father was involved in illegal activity, wouldn't it stand to reason Coop had been, as well? At the very least, he had to have known about the criminal activity. The question was whether or not he was an accomplice or simply looked the other way.

"Are you doing okay, Coop?" she asked. "I mean, about everything?"

"There's no reason not to be," he countered a little too quickly. "Dad will beat this because he didn't do anything wrong. This is a witch hunt, nothing more."

"You said the exact same words the last time we spoke several weeks ago ever since Dad has been in jail," she said. As much as she wanted to believe those words, there was far too much evidence to the contrary to be that naive or blindly loyal.

"Because they're true," Coop shot back. His defensiveness was on full display, coming through loud and clear on the line.

"And you?" she asked. "You didn't answer my question about how you're doing."

"Dad is in jail," he said with an accusatory tone. "How am I supposed to feel?"

"I guess that's a fair point," she reasoned, figuring this call was a mistake. Her brother would go to his grave defending their father. He'd treated her like the enemy after she freaked out over the man cheating years ago. Coop had made it seem like she was the reason the family had broken apart and their mother resented everything about her relationship with their father. As though witnessing her father's infidelity hadn't been soul crushing enough for Melody, the backlash was somehow her fault.

"I took a few days off and headed out of town to get my head straight," he said. Coop had always lived in a fantasy world of his own making. Reality didn't seem to have a place once he'd made up his mind on a subject. Words like *facts* and *evidence* had no bearing after Coop decided on their father's innocence.

"Sounds like a good idea," she said. A piece of Melody wished she had the ability to turn a blind eye to reality. Maybe then she would be a lot happier. Knowing the truth was awful on a lot of levels when it came to realizing her father wasn't the person she'd believed he was for all those early years.

Hoping to make a quick pit stop at home to change out of her interview clothes, she saw a law enforcement vehicle on her street. What was going on?

There was a man sitting in the passenger seat of the SUV. He was better looking than anyone had a right to be. She didn't recognize him. When he made eye contact, a trill of awareness shot through her despite the ominous scene unfolding.

For a split second, she thought about ditching the clothing change idea to avoid the hassle of going inside the apartment while something was going down. Work wasn't far from here. Although, the thought of going into the office right now held no appeal. Besides, it might be better to find out what was up.

As she pulled into the spot where she usually parked at her above the garage apartment, the SUV pulled in right behind her, blocking her exit. Awareness was quickly replaced with fear as one of Austin PD's finest came walking up to the driver's side, right hand resting on the butt of the gun strapped to his hip.

"Coop, I have to go," she said before ending the call and steeling herself for whatever was about to happen.

Chapter Two

"Ma'am, is your name Melody Cantor?" Deputy Calhoun asked as Tiernan watched and listened from the front seat of the deputy's SUV. He'd been warned the stop would be recorded before the deputy turned the camera on. It was routine, he'd said. From the moment the body had been found to now, Tiernan wasn't certain if Melody Cantor was a witness or a suspect. Based on the camera being turned on to record what was happening, his mind snapped to the latter.

Tiernan couldn't get a good look at the driver from this vantage point. The glimpse he'd gotten of her as she drove past had stirred up a foreign feeling in his chest along with a jolt of attraction. She shifted and a pair of worried eyes glanced into the rearview. Hers were a deep shade of brown. Long, russet hair fell down her back in waves as she stepped out of her vehicle.

A thorough investigation would fill in the fine print of the report. But looking at her right off the bat he wondered how someone of her size and stature could have bludgeoned a young man, lifted his dead weight, and then managed to bury him. Very little blood was found on his clothing according to the deputy, and the victim been covered with a blanket.

Since part of Tiernan's property backed up to a farm road and all indications pointed toward the body entering his property from there, he acknowledged the perp wouldn't have had far to go to get to the burial site. The loss of life hit Tiernan as a gut punch.

Still, this woman didn't fit any of his preconceived notions of a murderer. Plus, hadn't he been told or read somewhere along the way women normally used poison and not brute strength to commit murder?

Deputy Calhoun didn't slap cuffs on her, so that was another good sign she was being treated as a witness for now. The lawman had balked at first when Tiernan had asked to ride along. Dropping the last name Hayes to the sheriff had given Tiernan an advantage. Under normal circumstances, he wouldn't think of using his family's stature for special treatment. As a citizen, he had a right to know what was going on. As a former rancher, he was protective of his land. As a human being, he wouldn't rest until he had answers.

There wasn't a whole lot of crime in the small town northeast of Austin where Tiernan lived. He'd chosen Mesquite Spring for its small-town feel and close proximity to the city where he had access to supplies for his business. It didn't hurt matters this location was far away from Fort Worth where his heart had been broken. He had no plans for a repeat performance anytime soon.

"A man has been murdered, ma'am," the deputy said.

"This has to be some kind of misunderstanding," the brunette said with a tinge of worry in her voice. The deputy had left the SUV windows open and it was otherwise quiet outside, so Tiernan could hear the exchange if he strained. "You're welcome to check my trunk right now." She popped the hatch open with the squeeze of her thumb. He'd heard the deputy's first question, whether or not her name was Melody. She must be the person in question because there they were talking and walking toward the back of her vehicle.

"Again, I apologize for the inconvenience and appreciate your cooperation, Ms. Cantor," Deputy Calhoun said before shining a light inside the back of her vehicle. He looked unimpressed and he cut the beam off in less than twenty seconds.

"Go ahead and look again. Search my whole car if you need to," she said on a sharp sigh, her tone a dare. She planted balled fists on her hips. "I can promise you won't find anything no matter how hard you search."

"Has anything unusual occurred recently?" he asked as he moved toward the back seat and repeated the quick look.

"Yes, as a matter of fact it has," she said. Tiernan tried not to notice the way her body curved in a lazy S pattern. Standing next to the deputy, Tiernan would guess her to be five feet seven inches, above the average height and most of it coming from long legs. "I found a note on my windshield after an interview I just had that instructed me to drive fifty miles west."

Even from this distance, Tiernan saw Calhoun's forehead wrinkle in concern with the revelation. Was she being set up or lured somewhere so she could be next?

The victim was male, so Tiernan wasn't making any easy connections. Serial killers were known to target a certain type of person. This didn't add up.

"Can I see the paper?" Calhoun asked.

"I wadded it up and tossed it onto the passenger seat, figuring someone had made a mistake," she stated. "Can I ask a question before I go get it?"

Calhoun nodded.

"What's actually going on?" The trepidation in her voice made him think she was preparing for the worst, but what did that mean? "Am I under arrest or some kind of suspect? Because I'm confused right now as to what's going on and am starting to believe that I might need to request a lawyer."

"Like I mentioned, there's been a murder, so I'm not at liberty to discuss the details of the case with you," he stated. "All I can say is that your name came up during the investigation."

Melody took a step back as though she'd experienced a physical blow. She dropped her gaze to the concrete like she might find answers there. A few seconds later, she glanced into the SUV's passenger seat and searched his face. Normally, he would smile but this wasn't the time for pleasantries. Plus, the panicked look on her face made it clear she wasn't in the mood.

"How?" she asked, folding her arms across her chest as if creating a barricade between her and the shocking news. She glanced around before quickly continuing, "Why? I mean, this doesn't make any sense. Murder? Who is dead? And where did this happen? How on earth would that be connected to me? I just got out of an interview. You can verify where I've been this morning. Unless…" Her gaze shot up and to the left, like the answers she couldn't find on the concrete might be up there somewhere. Confusion wrinkled her forehead, and his heart went out to her. He was no investigator but she looked like she'd been bowled over by a truck.

"Those are all good questions, ma'am. That's why I'm here, trying to piece together what happened and why," Deputy Calhoun said. "There are a lot of open-ended issues in this case. We're hoping you can provide some information that can close some loops."

"I'm not sure how I'm supposed to do that if you don't

tell me who was…" She clamped her mouth shut and closed her eyes.

There was a single slip of paper in the deceased person's pocket. No ID. No wallet. No money. Just a slip of paper with a name and address. Tiernan hadn't gotten a glimpse of the paper and had had to deduce this was the person they were picking up after asking if the deputy could wait while he changed out of the clothes he'd been wearing. Clothes that smelled like death. He never wanted to see those items again, so he'd tossed them in the trash can outside. The deputy had also given a helpful tip to rub a little vapor rub underneath his nose to help overpower the stench. Otherwise, he'd be smelling dead body for several hours, possibly even days. He'd come upon deceased animals before, but they'd never had the kind of impact finding a human being did.

"I'm not sure how I can be of help, but I'll do whatever you need," she finally said.

"Do you mind riding to the sheriff's office with me? We have a few more questions and you might be more comfortable answering them there," Calhoun said as Melody tensed up.

"I'll get the note first," she said before walking around to the passenger side of her vehicle. She retrieved a small piece of paper a little wider than a parking ticket. The city of Austin made their fair share of revenue from the fact parking was a joke downtown. She held the slip out to Calhoun, who asked her to wait a second. He came back to the SUV long enough to retrieve an evidence bag.

Melody dropped it inside with a shocked look on her face. There was no way she was processing everything that was going on. It was evident on her face and the way she stood there, looking lost. A primal protective instinct surged in him at the sight. One that had no business in the middle of a murder investigation. She was innocent. He didn't doubt that one bit. She would have to be one hell of an actress to pull off looking this lost and in shock.

"I have a ride-along passenger today," Calhoun said. "That puts you in back."

"I guess it's settled then," she said, but her tone told him that she wasn't thrilled with the idea.

Tiernan exited the vehicle and held the door open. "Why don't you take my seat? I don't mind riding in back." There was no rhyme or reason for his actions. From somewhere down deep, he didn't want the deputy to have the image of her riding in the cage back there. Chalk it up to Tiernan's chivalry or those pesky protective instincts, but he knew she wasn't a suspect.

"Thank you," Melody said with a grateful look in her eyes as she rounded the front of the SUV and then climbed in the seat. He shut the door behind her and took his place in back.

"Don't let him forget me back here," he said with a slight smile as Calhoun examined the outside of her vehicle, bending down long enough to get a good look at her tires.

"That's a promise," she said. The honesty and determination in those three words shouldn't cause his chest to squeeze.

Which was probably why he felt compelled to add, "No one would blame you for hiring an attorney."

He glanced up at the recording device that was pointed toward Calhoun as he performed his inspection. The audio would reveal what Tiernan had just said but he'd kept the advice generic enough. No one should get too wound up over his words and he'd done nothing wrong.

"Can I ask how you're attached to all of this?" she asked as she craned her neck around. Her heart-shaped face with those golden eyes made her even more beautiful up close.

Her kissable pink lips weren't something he should be focusing on right now, so he managed to force his gaze away.

Since the camera faced the opposite direction, he brought his index finger up to his lips as he fixed his gaze on the recording device. And then he willed her to understand what his actions meant.

MELODY GOT IT. The handsome cowboy in the back seat pointed toward some kind of ceiling-mounted recording device. He didn't want to talk because of the piece of technology spying on them. This man would be called gorgeous by most standards, but she didn't care about his looks right now even though he had the whole tall, muscled, almost intimidatingly handsome bit down to a tee. Since he'd been riding in front, she highly doubted he was a suspect. Who was he and how was he connected to any of this?

Deputy Calhoun climbed into the driver's seat, took a second to acknowledge the musical chairs and then shrugged before closing the door and pulling out of her apartment complex. The passenger in the back seat remained silent. Based on the fact neither seemed to want their conversation replayed in a courtroom someday now that she was on board with the situation, they both stayed quiet on the drive to the sheriff's office.

Melody hoped her questions about the man with cobalt blue eyes would be answered soon. He appeared to have her best interest at heart and yet she had no idea how or why. Patience wasn't exactly her strong suit. With no other choice, she sat back in her seat and recounted the day's events. She'd gotten up early to get ready for her interview and showed up fifteen minutes before her scheduled time. In her mind, not getting the job wasn't an option. She'd pulled out all her tricks in order to put her best foot forward.

Her mind snapped back to how small her problems seemed in comparison with someone being murdered. If she hadn't just spoken to Coop on the phone, she would have been beyond scared for him. He was safe. Her thoughts shifted to her mother.

"Is the person murdered one of my family members?" she asked, breaking the code of silence out of a sense of urgency.

"I don't have a name," Deputy Calhoun stated.

"Male or female?" she quickly followed up. Melody might not be close with her mother but that didn't mean she wouldn't be heartsick if something happened to Tilly Cantor.

The deputy clamped his mouth closed like he was bound by oath not to reveal the sex of the victim.

"I need to know if my mother is alive," she said quietly.

"Male," came the voice from the back seat, a voice that sent a wave of calm along with tingling sensations through her.

The deputy shot a murderous look toward the back.

"I haven't checked my m-a-i-l," the man said with a shrug, trying to cover for the fact he'd just answered a question the lawman didn't. "But I didn't mean to say that out loud."

"I hope you don't feel the need to blurt out any other details, Mr. Hayes," the deputy chastised. It didn't seem to affect the man in the back seat one way or another.

Melody recognized the last name Hayes from Hayes Cattle, one of the most successful ranches in the state. Also, one of the wealthiest families. She should know. The Cantor name used to mix and mingle with only the best. Although, her father had groaned about the Hayes sticking to themselves and not accepting invites. What had he called them? Rich rednecks? The snub had hurt his feelings more than he wanted to admit. But then her dad had always been about social standing over substance.

Given her present circumstance, she wondered if she should heed the handsome stranger's advice and stop talking without a lawyer present. The thought caused a shiver to rock her body. The note was all that much more chilling now that she knew a murder had occurred. Once again, she wondered if someone was trying to lure her out of town and away from civilization. Have her show up to a place that couldn't be traced to a text. The note could have easily been destroyed with a match. The flimsy paper would light up in a heartbeat, leaving no trace it had ever existed. It would look like she'd taken a drive and then never came back.

Would the person have done away with Melody's Camry? Sold it for parts? She'd read the car's popularity made it an easy target for thieves.

Deputy Calhoun pulled into the parking lot of the sheriff's office. There was a jail behind a small brick building. Would she end up behind bars before the day was over? Share a cell with her father?

Tamping down what she hoped was an overreaction, she hopped out of the passenger seat almost as soon as the deputy pulled into a spot. He hadn't cut off the engine before she was opening the back door.

"Tiernan Hayes," he said with a gravelly campfire voice that awakened parts of her she'd become a little too good at ignoring. As he exited the vehicle, the scent of vapor rub assaulted her. It might be December but the smell caught her off guard. Shouldn't he be wearing Axe or some chick-magnet cologne instead?

Filing the question under *to be continued*, she took the extended hand and shook. A jolt of electricity shot up her arm.

"You already know my name, but I'm Melody Cantor." She wasn't sure why she felt the need for a proper introduction, except that she did. Was it a restart?

"Good to meet you," he said before adding, "Wish it was under better circumstances."

She nodded before wrinkling her nose.

"Are you feeling okay?" she asked. Her grandmother had used swaths of vapor rub whenever Melody had the slightest cough.

"Yes. What makes you ask?" He studied her and her heart practically melted under the scrutiny. Then, he must have caught on because he leaned toward her and whispered, "Helps get rid of the smell of death."

Melody suppressed a gasp. It clicked. He must have found the body.

Chapter Three

Tiernan resisted the urge to drop his hand to the small of Melody's back as he walked her inside. She'd become too quiet after his revelation, no doubt the shock of it all catching up to her. He'd witnessed plenty of dead animals in his day growing up on the ranch, but a human was different. Awful. Tiernan Tough had been a chant from the crowd during his rodeo days. Right now, he felt anything but. The vapor rub had covered up a good part of the scent. But he'd probably never forget it.

The sheriff greeted them in the lobby. He was tall and lanky, wearing all desert brown colors except for a black Stetson, which was appropriate for this time of year. White was reserved for summer.

"Sheriff Cleve Tanner here," he said, extending a handshake to Melody first and then Tiernan, who introduced themselves in turn. "Would you mind waiting in my office while I speak to my deputy?"

Tiernan's gaze shifted to Melody, waiting for the okay. She gave a slight nod.

"Sounds good, Sheriff," Tiernan said before being led down a short hallway and then into an office that looked like a time capsule from the '70s.

"Make yourselves comfortable," Sheriff Tanner instructed, motioning toward the pair of chairs opposite his massive desk. The room was dark with wood paneling lining the walls. The windows were small. There was an American flag and a Texas flag behind and to either side of the cowhide executive chair behind the oak desk.

The sheriff closed the door as he left.

Melody immediately turned to him and grabbed his forearm. "Please tell me what is going on."

Physical contact sent a zing racing up his arm. She seemed to feel something in the same neighborhood, considering she released her grip at the exact moment the zing occurred. She stared at her hands before fisting them and dropping them to her sides.

"I don't know much," he warned, not wanting to get her hopes up too much. "There was a shallow grave on my property. My dog ran after a squirrel and then must have caught a scent. I found him digging at the site. I'd smelled dead animals before and knew the stench didn't come from one of those, so I called 911 rather than disturb the area in case it turned out to be a crime scene."

"How did you know to do all that?" she asked as an eyebrow shot up. "I probably would have trampled all over the place."

"I grew up on a cattle ranch, and have tracked poachers in the past," he said by way of explanation. "The sheriff and his deputies trained us not to disturb a possible crime scene. You'd be surprised at how much information they can get from a shoe print sometimes." His answer resonated, considering she nodded and then took the couple of steps to the pair of chairs. She perched on the nearest one, back ramrod straight. She looked ready to bolt at a moment's notice and like she needed to be as close to the door as possible.

"You already said the...*it* was...a man's body when the deputy refused to discuss the murder," she restated.

"That's right."

"When he first told me the crime was murder, I was worried that it was my mother," she said, twisting her fingers together.

"There any reason your mind went there?" he asked.

"My father is in jail, so it couldn't possibly be him," she said, like she'd just explained her father had gone out for milk.

"When was he arrested and what were the charges?" he asked, figuring this might be an open-and-shut case after all. A father in jail. A piece of paper with her name and address on it. How much danger was she in? Someone could either be trying to locate her or target her.

"Business related," she said before asking, "How are you associated with this crime?"

"The body was found on my property," he explained.

She took in a deep breath before nodding.

"He scammed a lot of people out of money," she continued. "My father, that is."

"Revenge is a good reason to go after someone. Were you somehow connected to your father's business?" he asked.

She shook her head.

"What did the note left on your car say?" he asked, remembering that she'd said something about it to Deputy Calhoun. "The one Calhoun took for evidence."

"It told me to go fifty miles west." Her face twisted in the same confusion he felt.

"That's it? There was no reason given." What were the chances those two events could be coincidental? He doubted it, even though they didn't seem connected on the surface, either. The body had been buried at least a day or two ago.

Did the murderer have a plan to get her out of town, knowing there would be heat? Wouldn't the person think to check the victim's pockets? The chances the killing was a random occurrence that was not connected to Melody in some way seemed slim to none. Unless the address was a trail the killer wanted the law to follow.

"No other words were written," she said. "If I was supposed to figure out some hidden meaning behind the message, then I failed miserably."

"We could try rearranging the letters later," he offered.

She gave him a look that said they were two strangers thrown together by circumstance and there would be no later. And then the gravity of the situation dawned on her as she bit down on her bottom lip and pleaded with her eyes.

"Your name was on a piece of paper along with an address in the dead man's front pocket," he finally explained. She deserved to know what she might be up against. The lawmen weren't showing their hand, so to speak.

"That's awful," she said, but recognition dawned. "And that's why Deputy Calhoun came to ask me questions."

"He was checking out your vehicle, as well," he pointed out.

"Which means he was assessing whether or not I was a witness, accomplice or a suspect," she surmised.

"My thoughts exactly," he confirmed. "But I'd like to add a possibility. You could have been the victim's target, and someone stopped him before he got to you."

Melody sucked in a breath.

"I'm just trying to cover all the bases," he quickly added.

She nodded but didn't speak.

"The investigation should reveal how long the victim has been…" He checked her gaze and realized she was still in shock and didn't need a recap of what had happened. "The deputy and sheriff will be able to put together a timeline. It might be a good idea for you to start thinking about how you can prove where you were and maybe think about your own safety when you leave here."

She nodded as some of the spark returned to her eyes. The truth was that she didn't have a whole lot of time to figure out her next moves if this office decided to put her on the suspect list. At this point, Tiernan couldn't say one way or another what the sheriff had up his sleeve. Catching her unaware wasn't something Tiernan could stand by and watch if he had the power to help, especially when she turned those honey-brown eyes on him like she did just now.

"Why are you helping me?" she asked with a lost quality to her voice. The sound was the equivalent of a knife stab to the chest.

"Because I can and it's the right thing to do," he admitted. It was the truth. No one would accuse him of being perfect, but he would never turn his back on someone who needed help.

"You seem to have caught on to something law enforcement hasn't put together yet. What is it?" she continued after a quick nod.

"I just don't see you dragging a body from the trunk of your car to the spot where it was buried. The victim would have had to walk there himself and then climb in the grave," he stated as honestly as he could. Plus, her vulnerability tugged at his heart. She'd seemed genuinely caught off guard when they'd cornered her in her parking spot. Ever since, she'd had that lost quality that he was unable to ignore.

"Do you recognize my last name?" she asked with a raised eyebrow.

He had to think about that one. *Cantor.*

Realization dawned. He remembered reading the reports

now. Dots were connecting as to who she was and why she might be defensive around law enforcement. Her father claimed to be innocent of all charges, but the evidence against him was significant and there was a long line of victims who'd lost their life savings.

"You do know who I am," she said with disappointment in her voice.

He confirmed with a nod.

"Is that why you believe you're being treated this way?" he asked.

"Makes sense, doesn't it?" she said without a whole lot of enthusiasm in her voice. "I'm related to Henry Cantor. Therefore, I must be bad, too."

"People aren't their families," he retorted, indignation rising up. He should know, considering he was nothing like Duncan Hayes. That was a story for a whole other time.

"Try convincing other people when their minds are made up," she said with the kind of honesty that left no room for doubt. It was true, though. A family name like theirs came with expectations. Some good, some bad. It all depended on what the others before them had done. In his case, Duncan's reputation in the community was untarnished. At home, he'd been one mean son of a bitch. Insiders knew the man cared more about keeping up appearances than taking care of his own.

"It shouldn't be true," he said on a frustrated sigh.

"But it is," she continued. She was right. The sheriff's next steps would tell them where she stood, and he feared this situation was about to go south for reasons that weren't her fault.

THE DOOR OPENED and then the sheriff walked in. He didn't give off the vibe of being the brightest bulb in the bunch, which worried her. His jaw was slack, and there was a dull quality to his eyes. Sheriff was an elected position and stellar intelligence and qualifications weren't always top of the list with voters. Sometimes, it came down to loyalty and connections to prominent families. She should know. Her father had pulled together plenty of parties over the years with elected officials.

Cleve Tanner's face was scrunched with determination as he walked with a long stride straight to his chair without glancing over. Melody took it as a bad sign. Her heart sank to her toes along with any hope things weren't about to get worse.

"Will you excuse me?" Tiernan said as the sheriff took his seat.

"Uh, I guess so," Sheriff Tanner said, looking up with surprise. Tiernan had caught the man off guard.

"Thank you, sir," Tiernan said. She took note of the formal quality to his voice. He turned to her. "Don't answer any questions until your lawyer arrives. Okay?"

Melody blinked up at Tiernan. He winked just out of view of the sheriff as if to say *trust me.* Trust was a hard sell for Melody these days. Her belief had been, *I'll trust a person about as far as I can throw them.* For so long, the saying had become ingrained in her. In this case—and mainly because her back was against the wall—she would choose to trust Tiernan.

"Got it," she said to him.

"Cooperating with us now is in your best interest, Ms. Cantor," Sheriff Tanner made a point to say. "You might be able to provide information that could keep the trail of a killer from growing cold."

A couple of responses came to mind. Melody clamped her mouth shut.

"Blame me if anything goes wrong," Tiernan said. "I'm the one advising her not to speak up on behalf of her innocence."

"Hold on there a minute, tiger," Sheriff Tanner said. The man didn't seem to realize just how condescending his tone came across. "No one said she was a suspect. This is an ongoing murder investigation. Time is of the essence."

Tiernan's blue eyes registered the slight. He stood tall and stuffed his hands inside the pockets of his jeans. "Let's be honest, Sheriff. This *is* an ongoing murder investigation, and let's get real about how I've been treated versus how Ms. Cantor has. The body was found on my property, after all. I have a vested interest in finding the real killer and not wasting valuable time and resources."

"You were the one who called it in," Sheriff Tanner pointed out. "I'm aware of the location of the crime scene."

"No one checked my trunk for signs of a struggle or drops of blood," he said. "I'm strong enough to carry dead weight from my vehicle to the spot in question. Why not consider me a suspect? Don't I make a whole lot more sense?"

"You're missing an important point. Your name wasn't found on a slip of paper inside a dead man's pocket," Sheriff Tanner pointed out.

Melody realized Tiernan's genius after the sheriff spoke. He'd just given away his position as to whether or not she was a suspect *and* handed his piece of key evidence over in the process. She had to give it to Tiernan. He was smart. And, based on the sheriff's response, she was in serious trouble. The kind of trouble that involved lawyers and court dates and the possibility of her being handcuffed.

Tiernan fished out his cell phone and held it up. Then, he stepped into the hallway, leaving the door open. From where he stood, she could hear the conversation play out. The lawyer's name he mentioned caused the sheriff to sit up a little straighter. The conversation was short and efficient. The sheriff's gaze narrowed as Tiernan returned to the room.

He held the phone out to Melody.

"All you have to do is agree to representation. John Prescott is on the line," he said to her.

There was no way she could afford to pay him, but she could figure out how to let the attorney down later. Right now, she needed to get the sheriff off her back, so she took the offering.

"Mr. Prescott, this is Melody," she said. Tiernan had already explained to him who she was.

"I'd like to take your case pro bono," Mr. Prescott said. "And, please, call me John."

Several questions popped into her mind along with the saying, *don't look a gift horse in the mouth*.

"I would very much like to be your client, John," she said, making eye contact with a dejected-looking sheriff. She had no idea why Texas's most respected criminal attorney had just offered to work with her, but she had Tiernan Hayes to thank for it. The last name had pull in this state and she would do good to remember the fact. She stopped short of comparing him to her father. Tiernan had on simple clothes—jeans and boots. His calm, polite demeanor was the opposite of her father's charismatic personality. He'd charmed plenty of people out of their money.

"Good," he said. "Would you mind handing the phone to Sheriff Tanner?"

"Not at all." She studied the sheriff. "John would like to speak to you."

"Are you sure this is the path you want to take?" Sheriff Tanner asked as he stared at the phone being offered.

"You haven't given me much of a choice, have you?" she asked.

"Okay, then," Sheriff Tanner said, reaching across the desk for the cell. He held it to his ear. "Yes, sir." There was a beat of silence. "No, sir." Another beat of silence passed. "Well, sir, there's…" John must have cut Tanner off. He brought his other hand up to rub his chin. "She's right here."

The phone came back over the massive desk as Sheriff Tanner rested his elbows on his desk in a look of defeat.

"This is Melody again," she said.

"Tanner should be telling you that he doesn't have any further questions," John said. "I'm sending a car to pick you and Tiernan up. I'd like to meet as soon as possible, and since you're closer to Tiernan's house, I thought that might be faster. Can I tell the driver to take you home with Tiernan?"

"I guess that would be okay," she said, figuring a change of clothes would have to wait. There was no way she could go back to the office today. Everything was happening fast, and she needed a minute to process. It would probably be good to have a conversation with Tiernan, considering the body had been found on his property. He'd given her a quick rundown a few minutes ago. The information was beginning to take seed and questions were taking shape. Or maybe she just needed to hear it all again, slower this time. A man was dead who had her name and address in his pocket. She wouldn't rest until she figured out who he was and why he was trying to find her.

"Good," John said. "Do you mind giving the phone back to Tiernan?"

"No, not at all," she said. "Thank you for taking this case."

"Innocent people deserve good representation," John said

with conviction that made her believe he was the best person for the job.

She thanked him again before handing the phone over to Tiernan. Their fingers grazed and she did her best to hide the sensual shiver that ran up her arm. More of that warmth exploded in her chest as their gazes locked.

Melody took in a breath, trying to calm her nerves. The vapor rub scent was a stark reminder of the real reason she was in the same room with Tiernan Hayes. A man who might have been coming after her had been murdered. And she would do whatever it took to find out why she'd just become a target.

Chapter Four

"We'll be leaving now, Sheriff," Tiernan said, as he leaned against the doorjamb after closing out the call with the hot-shot lawyer who was on board to represent Melody. "Unless you have any additional questions, in which case I'll get Prescott back on the line."

Sheriff Tanner shifted his gaze to a spot in the corner of the room where the ceiling met two walls. He picked up a pencil on his desk, broke it in half and said, "I guess we're done here. But Ms. Cantor is advised not to leave town without contacting my office first."

"Her phone works anywhere, so unless you have a reason to detain her here, she can go anywhere she pleases," Tiernan continued, not liking the sheriff's reactions.

"Free country," Tanner conceded with a frown as he tossed the splintered wooden pieces on top of his desk.

Melody walked out of the office and into the hallway, whispering a thank-you as she passed by. Tiernan held back the urge to smile. First of all, it was way too early to claim victory with the sheriff. He might not come off as the most intelligent person, but it was anyone's guess who might be behind the man, pulling the strings. The sheriff had to have connections in order to get the job in the first place, which meant he could be tied to prominent families—families who weren't too thrilled with the daughter of Henry Cantor. Greed was right up there on the list of motives for murder.

Melody stood beside him in the parking lot. She rubbed her arms to stave off the sudden chill in the air. Tiernan had to resist the urge to wrap his arm around her to keep her warm.

A dark blue SUV arrived within ten minutes at almost the same second Prescott texted the ride should be pulling up. Tiernan acknowledged the driver with a nod before opening the door to the middle row of seats. He offered a hand to help Melody climb inside. His reaction to skin on skin contact as she took the offering left him speechless. He climbed in behind her, clearing his throat to ease some of the sudden dryness. He hadn't had this type of reaction to touching someone in longer than he cared to remember.

After closing the door behind him, he turned his attention to the driver as Melody buckled in. "I'm guessing you already have my address."

"Yes, sir," he said. "We are good to go."

The ride to Tiernan's house was quiet. He didn't expect much talking in the presence of the driver, but he could also see the wheels turning in Melody's mind. Tiernan wasn't too far off from spinning out mentally, considering his thoughts kept looping back to the body found on his property. Loki was home alone, too. The Lab mix had no idea he'd uncovered a dead body—lucky him. Still, Tiernan had been away for hours. Loki needed to go out. He needed attention.

The driver stopped in front of Tiernan's porch. After thanking him for the ride home, Tiernan slipped out of his side and came around the back of the vehicle to open the door for Melody. Once again, sparks flew when she took his hand as she climbed down. She suppressed a yawn for the third time in ten minutes. All the adrenaline from the day would be wearing thin by now.

After Tiernan closed the door, the driver pulled away. Tiernan reached for Melody's hand and then linked their fingers. As soon as he unlocked the door to his home—using a key to enter was something he'd never done before—he stepped beside Melody to intercept an overenthusiastic Loki. At one year old, the rescue dog still had more puppy energy than brain development to stop his impulses. The ball of excitement and energy barreled toward them from his spot by the sliding glass doors across the room in the dining area. The main living area was open concept. He didn't need a whole lot of privacy considering he lived alone.

Tiernan dropped Melody's hand and stepped in front of her to shield her from Loki. When her hands came up to his back, her nails dug into his shoulders and she hunkered down behind him, he realized she was afraid.

"I probably should have warned you about this guy, but he doesn't have an aggressive bone in his body," he reassured as Loki put on the brakes and skidded toward them on the rug. His big paws got away from him, as usual, causing him to bowling ball slide into Tiernan's shins.

"It's fine," she said with a tone that said anything but. Tiernan had learned the hard way those two words strung together oftentimes meant the opposite.

He bent down and scratched Loki's belly. Melody backed into the corner. His heart went out to her.

"Go ahead and make yourself comfortable," he said to her before leading the Lab outside by the collar.

Loki did his business almost immediately. Accidents inside the house had been few and far between in recent months. Tiernan picked up a tennis ball from the basket on the small porch, and then threw it. He repeated the game long enough for Loki to burn off some of his energy—energy that was never in short supply with the breed.

By the time he walked inside again, Melody was perched on a bar stool at the granite island in his kitchen. Muscles corded, breathing shallow, she looked ready to jump at the slightest noise. She white-knuckled the wooden stool as Loki bolted toward her.

"Loki, sit," Tiernan said in a calm but direct voice. To his surprise, Loki did. After running out Loki's energy, it was about a fifty-fifty shot as to whether the dog would listen. "Behave."

"I got bit as a kid, so big dogs still scare me even though I know all dogs aren't like my neighbor's," Melody confessed.

"I'm sorry that happened. Loki's energy can be over the top," he responded. "But I can assure you that he would never bite, not even playfully."

She nodded, her gaze still locked on to the dog. When someone had a bad experience early on with an animal, trying to convince them not all dogs were out of control was useless. Tiernan hoped she would stick around long enough to see that Loki wasn't a threat, and maybe change her mind about animals. Or at the very least plant a seed. Loki might be a hot mess at times but Tiernan couldn't imagine his life without him.

"Give me a sec to get him squared away," he said to her as he crossed the room toward the pantry where he kept dry food.

"Do whatever you need to," she said.

Tiernan filled the dog's bowl and then topped it off with half a can of wet food. "Steak and rice today, buddy."

"How old is…*he*…right?" Melody asked. "He's a boy." There wasn't a whole mess of confidence in her tone about Loki's sex.

"Yes. He's a boy," Tiernan confirmed. Loki had already hopped up and resumed his position as Tiernan's shadow. "The shelter where Loki came from found him digging through the trash at a construction site, searching for food."

Her face twisted in a grimace. "Poor baby."

"He'd been underweight as a three-month-old, but they got him in time before he was completely malnourished," he continued.

"Do they know where he spent those early months?" she asked.

He shrugged. "It's anyone's guess according to the volunteer. There were no others like him found in the area. No lactating mother anywhere, either."

"Sounds like someone might have abandoned him after taking him away from his family," she said as some of the tension lines eased in her forehead and the corners of her mouth curled into a frown. An emotion passed behind her eyes as she glanced over at Loki, a mix of compassion and heartbreak. "I've heard of people driving out to the country to drop off puppies or dogs they no longer want."

Tiernan gritted his teeth before nodding.

"He was flea bitten and scared, but his heart was still open to learning and trusting. Many more weeks in the old environment fending for himself could easily have changed that," he explained. "Which would have been a shame because his heart is as big as the Texas sky."

"It's surprisingly easy to become so broken by life that you can't ever get back to that innocent trust again," Melody said before compressing her lips like she'd just given away more than she probably should with the statement.

"All I know is the minute those big brown eyes looked up at me from behind the plexiglass, I knew I'd found my next best friend," he said. "No more dumpster diving for this guy. Only the best. A comfortable place to lay his head down every night and someone who will make sure he never suffers again."

"He's lucky to have you," Melody said with a small crack in her voice that caused him to wonder about her background. A sound like the one she'd just made came with a backstory, one he hoped she'd stick around long enough to tell him.

LOKI MIGHT BE a tornado but his story softened Melody toward the hyped-up animal. When she really looked at him, she found the warmest pair of brown eyes. It would be impossible to be scared of the Lab after knowing what he'd been through in those formative months. Even after living with Tiernan for some time, Loki still inhaled his food. Was that because of his past? Was it something he could ever get over? Or would he always eat fast for fear the meal would be taken away?

Melody didn't grow up with dogs, so she had no idea what they thought or needed. A couple of her friends had owned tiny dogs that could fit inside a purse. Loki had to be in the seventy-five-to one-hundred-pound range. He was definitely goofy, she decided as she watched him slop water all over the floor around his bowls. When she really thought about it, he did have more of a "big kid" energy than fierce beast.

With a sigh, she decided that she actually felt sorry enough for him to be brave the next time he came barreling toward her or bolting past so fast he accidently crashed into her legs.

Tiernan walked over to the fridge, and she forced her gaze away from his muscled backside. He had the kind of broad shoulders that were far too tempting to look at for long. Her body's reaction reminded her just how long it had been since she'd had good sex…any sex. Her thoughts were bouncing all over the place. Anything to avoid thinking about the fact a person was dead and had been buried in a shallow grave on this man's property. If that wasn't horrific enough, her name was somehow connected.

It was awful.

"I have enough leftovers to feed us both," Tiernan's voice broke through. "If you don't mind pasta."

"Pasta's good," she said, figuring she wouldn't be able to eat much anyway.

"Then, I have spaghetti from a restaurant and a mean lasagna that I made on my own," he said without looking back.

"You cook?" The question came out faster and sounding more shocked than she meant it to. "Wait, that wasn't what I intended to say."

He spun around with a disgusted look on his face that almost made her laugh.

"You don't think men can cook?" he asked with more of that disdain coming through.

She put her hands up in the air, palms out, in the surrender position. "I heard how it sounded the minute it came out of my mouth. I just didn't think you would know how to make Italian food. Most guys are more on-the-grill types in my experience."

"All I can say to that is maybe you've been around the wrong people," he said as he cracked a smile. "You're taking the lasagna because now I have something to prove."

"I was going to ask for it anyway," she teased, appreciating a precious few moments of levity. She had a feeling the lawyer from the phone call would be here soon and all lightness would be sucked out of the room when they went through the details of everything they knew so far about the case.

Loki stood at the pair of sliding glass doors, looking anxious.

"Should I let him out again while you heat up food?" she asked, surprising herself with the question.

"Never hurts," he said with the kind of ease that made her feel at home.

Tiernan's hospitality was most likely ingrained in him, given his background as a Hayes, but there was something special about his calm demeanor that she reminded herself not to get used to. Pretty soon, she would be walking right out the front door and heading back to her apartment. Alone.

The thought of being by herself tonight sent an icy chill racing up her spine. She stood up and then walked over to the glass doors, first unlocking and then sliding one side open. Loki glanced up at her with those brown eyes and her heart melted a little more.

"Go on," she said for lack of anything better. She had no idea how to tell a dog to go outside.

Loki obeyed and a trill of satisfaction coursed through her. The biting incident happened when she was in kindergarten. Maybe it was time to let it go.

"Should I follow him outside?" she asked.

"He knows what to do," he said as a buzzer dinged and the smell of Italian filled the air. "Leave the door cracked and he'll come in when he's ready."

"Sounds like a plan," she said, turning around to the sight of Tiernan setting a plate down where she'd been sitting. "I doubt I can eat much."

"Try. For me," he said in a gentle way that caused her to sit down and pick up her fork. He had the kind of masculine voice that had a way of rolling over her and through her. "Besides, Prescott will be here soon and we'll go over the details of everything that happened when he arrives. For now, we have a few more moments of peace and quiet."

The dread in his voice connected on a soul level with the emotions running wild through her. It was next to impossible not to think about what had happened or who might be involved. And yet, the idea of getting a break even for a little while sounded too good to be true.

"Okay," she said on a soft sigh. When did life become so complicated? Unsure she could get down one bite despite the amazing smell of the lasagna, she surprised herself in cleaning her plate.

"I take it you approve?" Tiernan said with a smirk that caused her heart to flip.

"It wasn't awful," she teased back.

He picked up her plate and stacked it on top of his. "Good to know that I rank right up there a notch above awful." When he made eye contact, her heart skipped another beat. The man was good-looking, to say the least. The fact he could cook put him in a whole new category of great catch. So much so, she glanced around for signs of female companionship. There was no way this man was unattached. Melody bit down on her bottom lip rather than ask his relationship status. Besides, it was none of her business and she was clearly hanging on to topics that would help her avoid thinking about the tragic—and possibly dangerous—current circumstances she found herself in.

"We both know the lasagna was mouthwateringly good," she said. "I just didn't think you were the kind of person who needed the ego boost with a whole bunch of flattery."

"When it comes to cooking, my ego can use all the help it can get," he said as he ran the dishes underneath the water in the sink.

"Well, it was amazing," she reassured. "And I'm the one who should be doing the dishes since you cooked."

"Reheated," he countered. "There's a difference." He didn't miss a beat. "And thank you for the compliment."

"You cooked my meal at some point," she said with a fist on her hip. Negotiating with this man didn't seem like it was going to do her a whole lot of good.

The sound of tires pulling up the drive stopped all light conversation. It was like a heavy cloud descended over the room, the air suddenly thick. She needed to know the details of what was going on despite nothing inside her wanting to hear specifics on how a man was murdered. Then there was the lawyer who was now her defense attorney. She would be pressed to go into the whole story behind her father's incarceration.

Dredging up the past was the worst. She avoided talking about her family at all costs. Now, she had no choice. Moving to the kitchen window, she watched a polished-looking man exit his Suburban. The serious look on his face fired off warning shots as she tried to prepare for what was ahead.

Chapter Five

John Prescott was several inches shorter than Tiernan's six-foot-three-inch height. He was slim with a runner's build and someone who probably played tennis on the weekends with his wife at the country club. He'd graduated UT Law first in his class and had a national reputation for winning in court. Tiernan hoped bringing in Prescott for Melody's case was overkill, but he wouldn't take any chances considering she was being treated as a suspect instead of a witness.

Tiernan moved to the front door and then opened it before Prescott reached the small porch. "Thank you for coming and taking this case personally." The man, the legend of Texas law, wouldn't normally handle a case that wasn't highly visible but he'd come from Cider Creek, just like Tiernan, and folks from there had a way of sticking together. Their families knew each other and went way back. Prescott was a few years older than Tiernan, so the two had never been in the same grade in school.

"No question," Prescott said without hesitation. He hopped the couple of steps onto the porch, and then extended a hand. A small laptop was tucked underneath his left arm. His grayish-blue slacks were tailored, as was his steel-colored shirt. His handshake was firm and relayed a message of confidence. His gaze shifted over Tiernan's right shoulder to Melody, who was standing behind him. Tiernan could feel her presence without looking back.

"Mr. Prescott," she said. Her voice had a forced calm that said she was anything but. He could only imagine what must be going through her mind right now.

"Please, call me John," Prescott said as Tiernan stepped aside so the two could shake hands.

"Melody," she said in response.

"Come in," Tiernan urged as Loki plodded over. The full stomach helped calm his two-year-old-after-eating-a-bowl-of-candy demeanor. Night was always the best time with him after he'd played out most of his energy. He had two speeds, breakneck pace and dead stop. In the evenings, Loki would curl up on the couch next to Tiernan while he watched a game.

Tiernan led them into the kitchen as Loki loped along, straggling and bringing up the rear.

"Does anyone want coffee?" he asked.

Prescott looked to Melody. She nodded. "Make it three," he said.

"Won't take but a second," Tiernan said, moving into the kitchen and quickly putting on a pot. He'd always been one of those people who could drink a cup and still fall asleep an hour later.

"Who is this, by the way?" Prescott set his laptop down on the granite island and then took a knee beside Loki, whose tail was cranking up to a feverish wag. It was a good indicator of his energy level. The attention pushed him into hyper mode.

"That would be Loki," Tiernan said. The dog rolled over onto his back, exposing his belly in a display of complete trust. Prescott had a way with animals that impressed Tiernan.

"He's a good boy," Prescott said. Anyone who was this good with dogs couldn't be a bad person. It had become a litmus test of sorts and held true to this day. Tiernan kept an eye on anyone a good dog didn't take to.

After a few minutes of tummy scratching, mugs were filled with coffee. Tiernan brought them over and set them down as Prescott stood up then took an empty stool. He sat farthest to the left, Melody took the middle seat and Tiernan sat to her right. She pushed her chair away from the granite island far enough for everyone to be able to see each other's faces before picking up her coffee mug and rolling it around in her palms. A nervous tick?

The ease from earlier was gone. Tension so thick Tiernan could cut it with a knife filled the room as Prescott opened his laptop and booted up.

"The reason it took me a while to get here is because I drove past your house on the way," Prescott stated with a frown. He grabbed the cup by the rim and managed a sip before setting it down again. "I crossed paths with the sheriff and a deputy who were on your street."

"What? Why would they be at my home?" she asked as concern lines wrinkled her forehead. Tiernan wondered the same thing. Why?

"It's not unexpected in a murder case," Prescott said, stopping long enough to turn and make eye contact with Melody. "But it says they are looking at you as a suspect, so we need to keep our guards up at this point."

"Are they planning to arrest me?" she asked.

"Not today, they're not," he said. "I intend to keep it that way."

"How?" she asked, a slight tremor in her voice.

"By proving your innocence, for one. I have investigators on the case to make sure the law dots every *i* and crosses every *t*. They'll do their jobs correctly and find the real suspect. My people will also be searching for a killer," he continued.

Melody nodded but there was pure panic in her eyes.

"My father is…"

"I know about Henry Cantor," Prescott said with sympathy. "You aren't your father, but we will be battling against his reputation."

Melody sucked in a breath. "Just when I think I can distance myself from my father, something like this would happen, linking me with his name again and dragging me down right with him."

"I'm sorry to ask this, given what sounds like a difficult relationship with your father. I know all the information that has been in the news about him so far. What else do I need to know? I'll need you to tell me about everything."

"Can I ask why you're locking on to my father?" she asked, cocking her head to one side.

"The description of the person who was killed matched up with a missing-person's report. Nothing has been ID'd, or should I say released, about the deceased but I have someone on the inside at the coroner's office." Prescott leaned forward as he spoke. "This is unconfirmed information, so it goes without saying that it doesn't leave this room."

"Okay," Melody said with trepidation in her voice. The kind that said she realized she needed to know what was about to come out of the lawyer's mouth but wasn't all that sure she actually wanted to. Riding the fence meant she didn't fall onto either side. It meant she was still in the in-between state of not knowing the horrific and real details, and having to deal with the news. Not exactly bliss but not hell, either.

"You know I won't say anything," Tiernan reassured when Prescott's gaze shifted to him.

"The victim was bludgeoned to death with a sharp object, possibly an axe," Prescott began as Melody shuttered.

"Sorry for the directness," Prescott said.

Melody took in a slow breath. "I need to hear this. Please. Go on."

"Based on lividity, he was killed forty-eight hours ago. His name is Jason Riker," Prescott said, then not so subtly checked Melody's reaction. "Does that name ring any bells?"

"Not for me, it doesn't," she said. "I feel like it should, though."

She told him about the note she found on her vehicle after the job interview.

"Do you have an approximate time the note was left?" Prescott asked as he turned toward the small laptop and then opened a file. He made a note of the incident.

"My interview was at nine thirty sharp," she said. "I was there for about an hour. It was there when I got out."

Prescott nodded and added the time and then pulled up a map. "That would put you about…"

"Blanco, Johnson City or Meadowlakes," she said before Prescott could run his finger fifty miles west. The cities had been committed to memory. "What's going to happen at my home? What's happening right now?"

"Right. Sorry. The sheriff called on a judge to issue a search warrant, saying he has an informant," Prescott said.

"They won't find anything," she said almost immediately.

There was a scenario in which she was being set up. Tiernan had no plans to mention his theory at this point. But it meant the sheriff might actually find "evidence" linking her to the crime.

As Melody took a sip of coffee, Tiernan made eye contact with Prescott. The lawyer had the same idea, and there was something else. A piece of information that he was keeping to himself. Based on the look on his face, it was important.

"I have someone checking into any possible connections between you and the victim," Prescott said after Melody set her mug down on the hard granite.

Was that it? He'd found a link?

MELODY DIDN'T LIKE the sound of any of this. Her home was being picked through at this very moment and she'd never felt so helpless in all her life. Correction, this was the second time she'd felt completely helpless. The first happened when she caught her father, pants down, growling and grunting in a way that made her nauseous to think about to this day. She mentally shook off the image. And now this. All her private things being examined as her home was searched. This felt like a violation of the worst kind.

Tiernan reached over and took her hand in his as though he sensed she needed the reassurance. His touch brought on a lot of distracting sensations that she couldn't focus on right now.

"I apologize in advance for the next question that I have to ask," Prescott began. "Will the sheriff find anything incriminating in your home?"

Melody shook her head vigorously. "Absolutely not."

"Okay, good," Prescott said. His face was a study in calm whereas Melody was starting to freak out.

Tiernan squeezed her hand and more of that warmth spread through her, bringing her pulse down another notch.

"Tell me about your family," Prescott continued without missing a beat.

"My parents are divorced. Have been for quite some time

now," she said. It was strange focusing on the details of her family, considering she spent most of her time trying to avoid the topic altogether while distancing herself from them. "I have a brother by the name of Coop. His actual name is Henry Cooper Cantor III, but we've always called him Coop."

"How well do the two of you get along?" Prescott asked.

The answer to his question was complicated and she hated getting into the details of their family dynamic. Since her freedom might be on the line, she cleared her throat and started. "I used to look up to my brother. He's a few years older than I am and was a shining star in our family. He was athletic and popular in school. He was always nice to me. I was his kid sister. I thought we were this idyllic family. My mom was a tennis mom who had wine nights with the other moms from the small college prep school my brother and I attended."

She stopped long enough to take a sip of coffee.

"My world came crashing down when I caught my father with my English teacher," she said before compressing her lips into a frown. "My brother defended our father, saying it was just boys being boys."

"It's hard to believe jerks out there still believe that load of crap," Tiernan said low and under his breath. She couldn't agree more.

"Your brother, Coop, is in business with your father, correct?" Prescott asked.

"That's right," she confirmed.

"And yet he hasn't been arrested," Prescott continued, making notes in the computer.

"No. He hasn't," she said. "He maintains our father's innocence."

"The evidence against your father isn't exactly minute,"

Prescott said, sounding as surprised as she'd been when she'd first heard her brother defending the man.

"According to my brother, our father has done nothing wrong, not in business or in life," she said.

"What do you believe?" Prescott asked.

"He's guilty," she said without hesitation. Saying the words stung. This wasn't what she wanted to believe about her father. There was strong evidence pointing toward his guilt and she knew he cheated in his marriage. It made sense the man would be no different in his business affairs.

"Your brother has a vested interest in your father coming out of this situation with a clear record," Prescott noted. Then came exactly what she'd been thinking. "The feds could come after him next."

"Yes, and they most likely will," she said. "The way he's defending our father makes me fear Coop is covering his own tail, as well. Family loyalty is one thing. His reaction to our conversation recently made me think he might be hiding something, and I'm afraid he's going to end up going down the same path if he hasn't already."

"Your father's arrest could be a wake-up call," Tiernan spoke up. "If he is aboveboard in his dealings and honestly didn't know what your father was doing."

"It's possible our father could have been shielding Coop from what was really going on," she said, appreciating Tiernan's viewpoint. She figured everyone would write her brother off based on his association with the business. She could only hope for his sake that he wasn't up to his eyeballs in it. "My brother would believe anything our father said, take it at face value."

"For now, we'll assume innocent until evidence states

otherwise," Prescott said. "It doesn't hurt to keep a close eye on your brother." Those sobering words would keep her up at night.

"You don't think he would commit murder and then implicate me, do you?" she asked, hating to hear those words come out of her mouth. It was awful to be in a position to have to think them let alone say them out loud.

"Right now, I'm considering every possibility," Prescott said with an apologetic look.

One of the worst things about her father destroying their family by cheating was that he never once apologized for his actions.

"Is there an inheritance?" Prescott asked.

"None that I'm aware of," she said, issuing a small sigh. "And I doubt my father would give me anything anyway, after the way I treated my trust fund." The thought of what she'd done was almost enough to make her smile.

"What was that, if I may ask?" Prescott asked.

"Donated it to local-area food banks," she admitted. "It wasn't like I was trying to throw anything in my parents' faces with the gesture, even though they took it that way. My brother flipped out. It's part of the reason none of us are close. I work a regular job with a jerk of a boss, and I live in a small apartment over someone's garage. But when I put my head on the pillow every night, I sleep just fine. I wonder if others in my family can say the same thing."

A cell phone buzzed but no one made an immediate move toward one.

"That's mine," Prescott finally said when it went off again. He pulled a small, thin cell from his front pocket that she didn't even realize was there. As he read the text that had come through, he frowned.

Melody's heart sank to her toes. This news was going to be bad.

Chapter Six

Hearing about Melody donating her trust fund to feed the hungry caused Tiernan to look at her in a whole new light. From the sounds of it, she'd been through the ringer with her family and was determined to come out the other side stronger and more independent. Those were traits he admired in a person. But Prescott's phone and his expression brought Tiernan's attention back to the present problem.

"I told you that I have investigators working on the case in the background," Prescott said.

Melody nodded as Tiernan squeezed her hand. He wanted her to know she had support because she'd received precious little. The way a lightning bolt struck the center of his chest when she squeezed back made him wonder how much trouble he was in with her.

"Turns out, Jason Riker is your half-brother," Prescott said with a grim expression.

Melody sucked in a breath as a look of shock stamped her features.

"Then it's possible he was coming to meet me and not try to kill me," she surmised. He hoped she wasn't being too optimistic. Although, as far as he knew there were no weapons found on the victim. Which didn't mean there weren't any. They could have been taken or used on Jason.

"I probably shouldn't be surprised that I have a half-brother...*had*," she corrected herself, "out there somewhere all these years. Maybe the better question is whether there are more siblings."

"I'll have to see if I can get access to the accounting from your father's arrest. I might be able to gain access to the specific evidence against him. Although, it's still early. Your father has been arrested and the DA will be very careful about not giving away the specifics of his evidence," Prescott said. "Unless I can link these two cases and then the DA's office will have to hand it over while I'm in discovery."

"The thought of connecting my name to my father's during this trial isn't exactly warm and fuzzy," Melody said. "I can also probably kiss off the job I interviewed for, as well. Possibly even my job when news gets out that I'm now linked to a murder and under suspicion." She grabbed her cell phone and fired off a text to say she wasn't coming in.

"I'll do my best to suppress the news, but this will be public record," Prescott warned. "The sheriff shouldn't want information leaking about an ongoing murder investigation. I'd have more confidence in his law enforcement abilities if I felt he got the job on merit."

"I've never had occasion to meet the man before," Tiernan conceded. "My opinion after today is right on target with yours."

Melody nodded.

"Do you have any questions for me?" Prescott asked as he closed his laptop. He turned and gave his full attention to Melody, making eye contact.

"I'm sure I'll have a million by morning," she said, suppressing a yawn. "Right now, I just want to go home and put my head on the pillow in the hopes this was all a bad dream."

"Fair warning," Prescott said. "There may be reporters on your doorstep."

Melody sucked in a breath.

"Why?" She opened her mouth to ask another question and then clamped it shut almost as quickly. "Never mind."

"Is there somewhere else you can stay for a few days until all the attention dies down?" Prescott asked.

"How about here?" Tiernan asked without giving it much thought. "You're here already. You've yawned three times in the last few minutes. I have a guest room that's sitting there empty."

"It's not a bad idea," Prescott urged. "If I need to get a hold of either of you for additional questions, you'd be together."

Melody took a few moments to mull it over. She finally nodded. "If it's not too much trouble, I'd like to stay tonight."

Prescott stood and then tucked his laptop underneath his arm. "Lay low for a few days if at all possible."

"I can call in sick from work," she said. "If I still have a job."

Prescott nodded and offered a look of sympathy.

"For what it's worth, not many people would care how they got their inheritance," he said. "The fact you did and were willing to walk away from a trust fund because you felt others were defrauded out of money says a lot about your character. It's an honor to defend you."

Melody's smile didn't reach her eyes but it was easy to see she appreciated the words.

"I don't know if it was my smartest move now that I'm likely to be unemployed when I wake up tomorrow," she quipped. "But it still feels like I made the right decision a few years ago, so I wouldn't change a thing."

Prescott's smile was big enough for all three of them. "Ma'am." He nodded toward Tiernan before saying, "I can show myself out."

Tiernan followed anyway so he could lock the door. Melody sat at the granite island, her expression a little lost. Her life had been turned upside down today, and the exhaustion was beginning to show.

"If you want to shower, there are always fresh linens in the bathroom. Soap and shampoo is always stocked," he continued. "There's a bathrobe hanging on the back of the door. You're welcome to use it."

Melody nodded. She glanced around the room. "Where does Loki sleep?"

"Usually out here in the main living room. I leave my door open, and he comes in and out as he pleases," he said.

She glanced over at the couch and then at Loki's bed, where he'd gone to curl up in a ball. "Mind if I sleep out here?"

"On the couch?" he asked, thinking a bed would be far more comfortable for her. And then it dawned on him. Was she scared to sleep alone?

"IF YOU DON'T MIND, I'd rather be out here," Melody answered after a beat of silence. The couch looked comfortable enough and she had no desire to sleep in a strange bed alone. Based on the layout, in the guest room she'd be on the opposite side of the cabin, far away from Tiernan. The irrational fear someone could break in and somehow get to her crept into her thoughts. Now that it was there, it would be impossible to get rid of. Plus, even though she was tired, she wondered if she could get any real sleep anyway.

"Not a problem," Tiernan said. "I have a few things to address on the work front, so I'll be out here while you shower."

"Oh, good," she said. Having him nearby sent another wave of calm through her. She realized her concerns were probably unfounded and yet she couldn't quite shake them off, either. Knowing someone died either coming after her in order to hurt her or searching for her for some kind of answers or connection was wreaking havoc on her mind.

She excused herself after being told where to find the shower. The layout was intuitive and the furnishings comfortable. There was a masculinity to the design, with the oversize leather sofa across from a tumbled stone fireplace. The cabin had large rooms with high ceilings and looked more high-end resort on the inside than fishing cabin.

The rain shower had good pressure and the warm water was heaven on earth. If only she could wash off this day. Melody ended the shower, dried off and slipped on the white cotton robe. She cinched the belt around her waist, pulling it tight to ensure the robe stayed closed. She scooped up her business suit, wishing she had casual clothes with her. She didn't even have her car, not that it would matter. She wasn't leaving town so there were no extra clothes in the back seat. Her gym bag was at home. All she had with her was what she'd put on that morning. Morning seemed so long ago.

"Do you have anything I can put these dirty clothes in?" she asked after clearing her throat. She didn't want to surprise Tiernan as he sat there in one of his oversize leather chairs that flanked the fireplace, gaze intensely focused on the laptop.

He made an immediate move to set the tech down on the floor beside his chair and get up. "I'll take those." He cut across the living room and took the ball of clothes from her hands.

"All I need is a grocery bag or something to put these in until I can swing by my house tomorrow," she said, then realized it might not be so easy to do that if reporters and the law could be snooping around. Murder wasn't something that happened every day in small towns like Mesquite Spring. Austin was another story altogether.

"I'll throw them in the wash," he said as she let go.

"I can do it if you point me in a direction," she said. "Besides, you've already done enough for one day."

"Don't worry about it," he said, like it was nothing. "The washer and dryer are in the hallway leading to my bedroom. I have to head that way to take a shower anyway, so it's no trouble."

"If you're sure," she said.

"I'm good," he confirmed with a small smile.

"I found the toothbrush and supplies in the basket on the counter," she said. "Are you always this prepared for company?" She didn't want to go there in her mind that he had a string of women who came through a revolving front door. The lack of female touches in the home and the fact he didn't wear a gold band reassured her there didn't seem to be anyone special in his life.

He shrugged as his smile grew, revealing perfectly straight, white teeth. "I have a housekeeper who comes in once a week to take care of all those details. I'll be sure to thank her on your behalf when she comes in Monday."

"Thank you," she said. "To both of you." Her gaze dropped down to his Cupid's bow mouth where it lingered. Suddenly, she realized just how naked she was underneath the cotton covering.

Standing this close was a bad idea, so she took a step

back, thankful she didn't fall. She wasn't exactly the athletic one in the family. She left sports up to her brother, who'd played just about everything.

"I put out blankets and a pillow on the couch," Tiernan said. "There's still a few things for work that I need to handle, so I'll grab my laptop when I'm out of the shower. It'll only take me a few minutes. Are you good if I come back in the living room?"

"Of course," she said. "As tired as I am, it'll be hard to shut down my thoughts. I'm just looking forward to lying down for a little while and shutting down as much as possible. You won't bother me if you work in here. In fact, it might be nice to have company in the room."

"Okay," he said. "I'll be back in a few minutes." He exited the room. She was grateful Loki was content to stay with her.

After drinking a full glass of water, she made a bed on the sofa. Her cell was inside her purse, turned off. She'd flipped it off after the meeting with the sheriff on the ride home. As she climbed underneath the cover, she started thinking about all the stuff she needed to take care of. She'd left her boss hanging today and was afraid to check in at this point. They would manage at the office fine without her. It was a real estate development office, not a hospital. Still, work piled up on a daily basis. She could only imagine how many calls and texts were waiting on her phone, not to mention her email. The iPad in her purse was turned off, too. It was probably good for her sanity but not her livelihood. She had a little money saved. It wasn't like she spent money on anything but rent and food. She'd been needing to walk away from her bully of a boss for months. He kept her so busy she didn't have time to look for another job until today. She figured that was by design. The pay was good even though the hours were long. The last straw had been when he'd thought it was perfectly okay for his son to hit on her. The kid wasn't old enough to legally drink. Meanwhile, she was thirty-three years old. The boss had called his college son's actions "harmless." The real estate development company was small and family owned. Her HR contact was a relative of the boss. The only option was to find another job where she would be respected.

This wasn't the time to be angry with herself for not listening to her small circle of friends—friends she'd lost touch with because she'd been too busy to keep up relationships over the past three years. Too many years had been sacrificed with little time off only to end up being chased around a desk like the #metoo movement hadn't happened. Time wasn't stuck in the past, when men got away with bad behavior with a slap on a back and a cigar.

Maybe being forced to quit would end up being a good thing for her. Maybe she shouldn't let it get her down. Maybe this was exactly the push she needed to get a real fire under her backside about getting another job. As soon as the new one read about her in the news, they would rescind their offer—if there was going to be one in the first place.

Thinking about work only depressed her.

Melody shifted her thoughts to what she knew so far about the case. Someone had tried to get her far away from the area at around the time the body was found. Everyone was a suspect and she needed to keep them at arm's length at least for a few days until the news cycle shifted and attention moved to something else. There was always a new, bigger story in Texas these days. Could she outlast the interest?

She fluffed the pillow as a bare-chested Tiernan walked into the room. It dawned on her that she knew very little about the man. Since she figured sleep was about as close as rayon to silk, she decided asking a few questions couldn't hurt.

"Mind if I ask what you do for a living?" she asked, motioning toward the laptop on the floor.

He walked over and sat down as she forced her gaze away from ripples of lean muscle and droplets of water rolling down olive skin. Jeans hung low on his hips. The man was billboard-worthy hotness that had her throat drying up at the sight of him.

"I make custom saddles," he supplied.

"For horses?" she asked, realizing there weren't many other kinds. "Never mind. Stupid question."

"There are no stupid questions," he said with a warm smile that had a way of lowering her defenses while putting her at ease. A sharp contrast to butterflies going wild in her chest every time she looked into those disarmingly blue eyes of his. Dark hair and stunning eyes got her every time.

"What kinds of saddles? Like, for a major chain or feed stores?" she asked.

"Mine are custom," he said with a raised eyebrow. "You really don't know who I am, do you?"

The question got her attention but the amusement in his eyes piqued her interest even more. "Not really. Not personally, despite knowing you have a big last name. Why? Is that bad?"

He laughed. The deep timbre sent a trill of awareness skittering across her skin.

"That's a good thing in my book," he said.

"I'm afraid you're going to have to tell me if you don't want me to do a Google search later," she said.

"Don't do that," he said, like it was a major warning. She doubted there were any skeletons in his closet.

"Then you might as well tell me. That way, I'll hear your version," she said. She had no plans to discontinue this line of questioning until she got to the bottom of why she should know him. "Or would you rather the internet be the one to educate me?"

Chapter Seven

"First of all, don't believe anything you read about me on the internet." Tiernan was afraid of what Corinne Moore had printed about him in the society section of newspapers and blogs. Plus, he figured telling Melody something personal about himself might help her relax enough to get at least some sleep. She might not think she needed it or even be able to but he would do what he could to assist. "I used to be on the rodeo circuit."

"And now you have your own line of saddles?" she asked as her eyes widened. "Well, now I really am curious about your background. You must have been good at it considering sponsorships only go to the best."

"It's not a line, exactly," he said. "I have a workshop out back behind the house where I make custom saddles for individuals."

"As in one at a time?" she asked before her jaw fell slack.

"That's the deal," he said.

"They must cost a fortune," she said under her breath.

"Not exactly," he teased. "But close."

"Then, you must really be somebody for people to be willing to pay extra to have you make a saddle," she said with no hint of awe in her voice. She said the words as though she were reading the ingredients on a soup can.

That really made him laugh. He mainly dealt with rodeo folks who idolized him and treated him like something different than human. Like he didn't put his pants on one leg at a time like everybody else. Melody was a breath of fresh air.

"I did okay back in the day," he said.

"What does that mean? You aren't that old," she countered.

"I'm thirty-three," he said. "Pretty old in my world. Besides, I'm a little beat up. I decided to quit while I was still on top."

"Is that how you were able to hire John Prescott and have him show up on a moment's notice?" she asked. "Your fame?"

"Family connection helped there," he explained. "The Hayes name moves mountains in Texas despite Cider Creek being a small town."

"I'm not sure I've heard of Cider Creek," she admitted. "Is it far from Mesquite Spring?"

"It's about a thirty-minute ride from anywhere in the lower half of Texas," he said.

"That's impossible," she said in disbelief. The look on her face said she thought she was being played. "Texas is too big."

"Not by air," he said. "We have helicopters on standby near the ranch. Half an hour might be an exaggeration but it's not too far off base depending on who is holding the stick."

She gave a slight nod and he realized she must have grown up in a similar life of privilege. Tiernan may have butted heads with Duncan, but he realized how fortunate he'd been on the financial end.

"Your family has a lot of money," she hedged.

"Yes," he said. "Last I checked they did."

"Why not ride the gravy train?" she asked, and then a look of embarrassment heated her cheeks. "I'm sorry. That question was out of line. I just thought maybe you make two saddles a year and then live off your trust fund the rest of the time."

"I have no idea what's in my trust fund," he said.

"None?"

"I'm fully capable of earning a living on my own," he said with a little more ire than intended. He had to laugh at himself. As it turned out, the mention of living off a trust and not earning his own way still got him heated around the collar. Corinne, his ex, had been a Fort Worth social-ite who never understood why he needed to work given his family name. She'd been charming and flirty in the begin-ning, until the socialite went for the jugular. "I set out to prove myself when I was eighteen years old and still wet behind the ears. I guess the subject is still a sore spot with me even though I've long since proven I can make my own way in life."

"You had a very successful rodeo career from the sounds of it," she said. The respect in her voice cut through some of his indignation. His pride had taken a hit at the suggestion he lived off a trust fund and couldn't make a life for himself.

"I'm doing all right by most standards," he said.

"Your cabin is beautiful," she said, glancing around. "Don't take this the wrong way but I'm a little surprised there aren't trophies everywhere."

"I saved a few that meant a lot to me," he said. "Those are in my workshop. I always thought it was important to sepa-rate who I am from what I do, if that makes any sense at all."

"Must have been tough sometimes," she continued. "Most people let all that fame go to their heads, it seems like."

"Ranchers aren't bred that way," he said. "You wouldn't be able to tell a millionaire cattle rancher from one who struggles to make ends meet if you saw them walking down the street. Both would look you in the eye when they spoke and shake your hand."

"They must be some of the most grounded people on earth," she said. "Cider Creek sounds like a nice place to bring up a family."

"I haven't given it much thought," he admitted. "My siblings and I loved the land. Our mother is a saint for putting up with six kids."

"Six?" Melody barely got out the word. Her shock was written all over her face. "My mother had her hands full with two. Or maybe I should say it seemed difficult to juggle both us and all those glasses of wine."

He laughed at the image that popped into his thoughts. "I'm sure she did the best she could. The affair must have been hard on her."

"Not really," she said. "You think two people are in love because they're all you know until you realize your mother is more in love with a lifestyle. I think she was embarrassed more than anything else. An affair wasn't cause to leave. The first time my father had money issues was all it took for her to bolt. She used the affair as an excuse but that had happened two years earlier."

"Watching your family dissolve in front of your eyes had to have been hard on you as a kid," he said.

She nodded before turning the tables. "What about your parents?"

"Father died when I was in middle school. Parents were high school sweethearts. They danced around the kitchen after supper." A knot of emotion formed in his throat at the memory. He'd blocked all those out years ago. "They were the real deal."

"I can't imagine how wonderful that must have been," she said wistfully. "I'm sorry for your loss."

"Thank you," he said. Her words brought a surprising amount of comfort. "It was hard on all of us. We didn't talk about him all that much anymore. Looking back, our mother must have been in terrible grief over losing the love of her life."

"I'm sad for her," Melody said as her hand covered her heart.

"I don't think she ever truly recovered despite being a strong person," he said. "There were cracks afterward, but we all knew she was doing her best. When it came to our relationship with our mother, we had a lot of love."

"That would be awful for anyone. The fact she survived and continued to bring up you and your siblings showed her true strength," she said.

Those words were balm to a wounded soul. He didn't realize how good it would feel to talk about his parents and what had happened in the past. Keeping everything locked inside for so long was like carrying a boulder on his chest. Remembering how much they'd loved each other lifted some of the ache.

But then it was easy to talk to Melody.

"Tell me more about your saddle business," Melody said, pushing up to sitting. Her long waves had dried and fell down her back and around her shoulders.

"Orders have kept me working fourteen-to eighteen-hour days leading up to Christmas, which will be here before we know it," he said, going with the change in topic.

"You've been off this entire day because of me," Melody

said as she glanced at the clock on the mantel. "I should let you get back to work."

"Believe it or not, I've enjoyed getting to know you and doing something useful today," he said. "I've been at the saddles for the past couple of months straight with no break, and helping someone else brings me back to my roots. It's a rancher-like thing to do."

He could have sworn disappointment flashed in her eyes. He couldn't for the life of him figure out why.

"Are there more people like you and your family in Cider Creek?" she asked, a wistful quality to her tone.

"All ranching communities have people like us," he said.

"Somehow I doubt that," she said so low that he had to strain to hear. Before he could respond, she said, "I should try to get some real sleep. Tomorrow is going to come early."

"Do you want me to work in another room?" he asked, not liking the wall that had just shot up between them. There wasn't a whole lot he could do about it, either.

"Whatever works for you," she said before adding, "But I'm good with things the way they are right now if it's too much trouble for you to leave."

Tiernan took the hint, picking up his laptop and rebooting. He made himself comfortable in the chair. A wall might have come up, but she trusted him enough to let him keep watch over her while she at least tried to sleep.

He pulled up orders and recalculated how much time he had left to finish them before Christmas. He'd intended to have everything delivered the day before Christmas Eve. Now, he'd lost a day, so he'd be working on Christmas Eve to get everything done on time.

On Christmas Day, he could collapse if he had to pull a few all-nighters. He could personally deliver at least one of the saddles, which would give him an extra day back since he didn't have to ship. He could finagle the order in which he completed the saddles and still make this work.

People were depending on him, and he never let them down. Could he make the same promise to Melody?

MELODY OPENED HER EYES, surprised she'd been able to fall asleep at all. The dim lighting in the room made it easy for her eyes to adjust. She glanced around the room to get her bearings. Her heart skipped a beat the second her eyes landed on Tiernan. The glow from his laptop cast shadows on his face that highlighted a strong jawline and cheekbones that could crack granite. The man was carved from perfection.

Her movement caused his gaze to shift to her. For a long moment, their eyes met, and it ranked right up there with one of the most intimate moments of her life.

"Hey," he said, his voice gravelly.

"Hi," she said, feeling like she could have thought of something better. As it was, her throat was suddenly dry, and forming words became a challenge. She cleared her throat. "What time is it?"

He glanced down at the corner of the screen and then his eyes came up again. She blinked to lessen the impact, but it was a fruitless attempt at best. She had the same reaction as a few seconds ago when their gazes touched.

This time, she took in a long, slow breath.

"Quarter after nine," he said.

"That late?" she asked, surprised. "How did I sleep so long?"

"You were out like a light, so I closed all the blinds. I figured you needed as much rest as possible," he said.

It occurred to her that she was wearing nothing but a bathrobe, so she performed a quick scan as she pulled the covers up. Relief flooded her when she confirmed nothing was out that shouldn't be. The only bare skin he might have seen was her foot and a sliver of ankle. In some cultures and periods in history, that was enough to be considered scandalous.

"Can I interest you in a cup of coffee?" Tiernan asked, setting the laptop down on the coffee table. Loki snored from the other side of the room until the piece of tech tapped the wood. The dog jumped to attention before launching himself toward the living area.

"Coffee would be nice," she said, still full from the lasagna last night. "Thank you."

"Not a problem," he said.

"Have you been on that thing all night?" She motioned toward the laptop.

"On and off," he admitted.

She sat cross-legged on the couch as Loki overshot and smacked into a wood coffee table. Thankfully, both dog and furniture were fine. The thud turned out to be the scariest part of the incident. His wagging tail was a whole tornado of its own.

Melody reached over and petted him. This dog understood the fire drill phrase, *stop, drop, and roll*, because that was exactly what he did. She recognized the maneuver from last night with the lawyer. "I know what this means." Loki wanted belly scratches. The bighearted pup really was growing on her. She wasn't ready to officially declare herself unafraid of large dogs, but Loki had wormed his way into her good graces a whole lot faster than she thought possible. His owner was making headway there, too, which was exactly the reason she needed to keep her guard up around him. On a soul level, she realized how deeply a man like Tiernan Hayes could hurt her.

He brought over a fresh cup. Their fingers grazed as he handed over the mug, causing more of those sensations to rocket through her.

Something had been niggling at the back of her mind since waking up. She took a few sips of coffee in an attempt to clear the coffers. She also realized she might be overstaying her welcome.

"Did you sleep last night?" she asked.

Tiernan shook his head.

"How are you still operating?" she asked. "I wouldn't be able to form sentences without at least a couple hours of sleep under my belt."

"You'd be surprised what growing up on a cattle ranch will do for you," he said on a chuckle. "During calving season, we got used to going two to three days without sleep. I don't even want to tell you all the places I was found asleep as a teenager."

Melody couldn't help but smile at the images of him, head back with his mouth open, passed out, rolling through her thoughts.

The niggling feeling returned. This time she knew what it meant.

"My brother made a point of saying he's been out of town for a few days trying to get his head straight about our father's case," she said.

"Was he setting up an alibi?" Tiernan asked.

"There's only one way to find out," she said. "But I don't think my lawyer would approve."

Chapter Eight

After hearing Melody's idea, Tiernan had no doubts Prescott wouldn't give the go-ahead.

"If I'm in the room with my brother, it'll be easier to tell if he's lying when I ask him where he was. His voice always shifts an octave when he's being untruthful and he doesn't blink as fast," she argued. Her point was valid. He just didn't think it was a good idea to put herself at risk.

"Reporters could be camped out in front of his home or office, or both," he pointed out. "At the very least, you'd be handing yourself over to the dogs, which doesn't seem like the right play."

"It's going to happen sooner or later," she argued.

"This thing could die down," he said. The sharp look she threw his way was the equivalent of a dart. He was grasping at straws to try to keep her from following through. "Then again, it might not. News in this area is few and far between. People could be chewing on this for a while."

"The case might be more cut-and-dried if a suspect was behind bars," she said. "As it is, people will think there's a killer on the loose and they will worry they might be next. That will keep interest in the story alive, and we all know where there's interest there will be almost constant coverage."

"No arguments from me there," he said. Corinne had set out to tarnish his reputation by spreading rumors he was a player and a boozer who would end up in the tabloids someday under the heading "Tiernan Hayes Falls from Grace." Melody's problem was on a much bigger scale. The stakes were higher. Attention would be on her for a long time to come.

"Plus, let's face it. I can't stay here much longer," she continued. "You have work to do. You must be behind after yesterday."

"I figured out a plan to catch up," he said as her gaze darted toward the exit.

"Which probably doesn't include having a houseguest," she said.

"It's no trouble on my end to have you here," he said, thinking she might have someone out there worried about her. She wasn't close with her family but that didn't mean she didn't have friends she could stay with or a guy. She hadn't looked at her phone once in the short time he'd known her, which didn't gel with what he knew of her workaholic life. It also led him to believe she was doing this on her own. "Unless someone else is out there concerned you haven't checked in."

She shook her head. "There's no one special. I work all the time as right hand to the owner of the company, so the few friends I used to have gave up on me a long time ago when I declined invite after invite."

"Working on your career is important," he said, able to relate a little too much to the scenario she described. He had buddies on the circuit. There were people he could call to go out for a beer who still believed in him. The thing about having any amount of fame was that women dated him for his name. A few he'd believed were actually interested in getting to know him turned out to be snapping incognito selfies.

Then he met Corinne. She'd done a number on him, and he'd shied away from dating ever since. Head down, a year passed before he realized he hadn't been on a date. All of which brought him to his current single status.

"I had a great interview yesterday," she said on a sharp sigh. "An offer was supposed to come through either last night or today."

"You haven't checked your phone to see," he said. "How do you know it didn't?"

"I'm afraid of my cell after what happened yesterday," she admitted. "The second news gets out that I'm somehow connected to a murder, my mother will freak out. My current boss most likely blew up my phone with texts, demanding to know where I am. The man has no boundaries. Well, not actually him but someone else in the office will get that assigned task. I know that I need to check in considering the fact I have responsibilities but I just can't right now."

"I don't blame you for not rushing toward that insanity," he said.

"It would be nice to know if I got the offer, though," she said. "I'm certain to lose my job and even if I don't, I can't go back there anymore. Not to work for a guy who thinks his college son can hit on me without any consequences."

Tiernan felt his jaw muscle clench. "That is the furthest thing from being acceptable."

"Tell my old boss that," she quipped. Then, she studied his face for a long moment. "On second thought, maybe not."

"I have a temper, but I'd never use it on someone," he defended. "I learned to keep it under control years ago when I saw the aftershocks. Sure, it might feel good in the moment to get out the rage with a willing participant. In the long run, it only ever made things worse. Broke relationships to the point they could never be repaired." He stopped himself right there before waxing too poetic.

She nodded. "I was angry with my father for so long and I just held it all inside. At some point, it becomes poison and you have to let it go."

"Have you?" he asked.

"I'm a work in progress on that one," she admitted. "Since my parents' divorce, it's been easy to restrict visits to holidays. I never have to stay long because I'm always off to the other person's house." She sat there, silent, for a moment that stretched on. "It occurs to me that I had a sibling I never met or knew about. How strange is that?"

"We might be able to get some information about the young man now that we have a name," Tiernan offered, picking up his laptop.

A host of emotions played out across her face before she settled on saying, "Let's do it and see what we come up with."

He moved to sit beside her so he could share the screen. Their outer thighs touched, causing heat to rocket through him. The urge to lean into it was darn near a physical ache the size of Texas sitting square on his chest. With her background, it was nothing short of a miracle she hadn't turned out to be a manipulative woman like Corinne. She'd had daddy issues worse than anything he'd seen, and he'd seen plenty. The impact a father had on his daughter had caused Tiernan to take note. Not that he planned on having kids anytime soon. They were a "one day" possibility that always seemed pushed into the future. At thirty-three and with no desire to get mixed up with another Corinne, he figured single life wasn't so bad. Being a bachelor had its perks. There was no one around to tell him not to watch a game on Sunday afternoon in the fall. Texas and football were right up there with God and country to most folks. He couldn't say he was as obsessed with the game as most in these parts, but he liked to watch the occasional battle on the gridiron.

He typed in Jason Riker and isolated the search to Texas. An Instagram account turned up at the top of the page. He clicked on the link. The first thing he noticed was the young man's face in the circle.

"He can't be out of high school yet, can he?" Melody asked. She must be thinking the same thing. "This makes everything so much worse."

Tiernan couldn't agree more.

"I recognize this woman," she said, pointing to one of the posts of what looked like mother and son. "And, look," she commented. "Her name is Bebe."

"Okay, let's see if we can figure out his age based on his posts," Tiernan said. There weren't many, which surprised him. He'd never gotten into the whole social media craze beyond hiring someone to manage a couple of pages for him, but young people seemed to be on it all the time.

He didn't have to scroll for long considering there were only eighteen posts.

"There's no hint of the kid except art he'd posted that looked like he'd done," she said out loud as she pointed to the picture. "What about tags?"

Tiernan hit the button, and then scrolled.

"You hit the nail on the head with your guess about his age," he said. "Look at this photo from June where this kid says she missed him at graduation in a comment."

"He's practically a baby," she said low and under her breath.

Tiernan nodded.

"Looks like he played soccer at one point," he said, scrolling down to a team photo with the words *best friends* as a caption.

"He left school before graduation? I wonder why?" Emotion came over her in a thick wave, threatening to drown her. She tucked her chin to her chest and sniffed, hiding the fact a few tears had spilled down her cheeks. The urge to thumb those droplets away was too great to ignore. So he reached over, electricity be damned, and did just that. He let his thumb linger on her chin as he tilted her head toward his. Her tongue darted across her bottom lip, leaving a silky trail, and it was as though a bomb detonated inside his chest. If he sat like this much longer, instincts were sure to take over. Before he could put a little space between them, Melody shifted her position enough to kiss him.

TIERNAN'S THICK LIPS tasted like dark roast, her new favorite flavor. His spicy scent flooded her senses, awakening something deep and primal within her. Need welled up and one word came to mind...*more*. She wanted more of Tiernan. More of his muscled arms around her, holding her. More of his rough, calloused hands roaming her body, reminding her she was alive. More of his weight on top of her, pressing her into a mattress, helping her get lost even for just a little while.

In this moment, she was in a haze and all she wanted was to lean into it, into him. So, she did. Melody parted her lips and teased his tongue inside her mouth. The low, throaty groan that tore from his lips only acted as more fuel. She lifted her hands to his shoulders and braced herself by digging her nails into his skin.

In the next second, Tiernan shifted their positions until he was on top of her, covering her with his heft. He balanced most of his weight on his arms and a knee that was acting as an anchor against the leather.

Her stomach felt like she was base jumping as he brought his chest flush with her body. Melody couldn't remember the last time she felt anything near this magnitude with a guy before. Was it the circumstances?

Did it matter? She was here. He was here. And all she wanted to feel was nothing but him, surrounding her, inside her, moving to their own tempo until the building tension found sweet release.

Tiernan abruptly stopped kissing her, but he didn't move. She gripped his forearms, willing him to stay right where he was for a little while longer.

"You're beautiful," he started, and she feared the rejection that was sure to come next. "But this can't happen."

Those four words were her least favorite from now on. She wriggled out from underneath him, making certain her robe didn't open in the process and reveal more of her than she intended. At least she was covered. "You're right." Her cheeks heated. If embarrassment could kill a person, she'd be dead. The minute she thought the words *kill* and *dead*, she wished she could take them back. Her heart ached for the kid. She forced her thoughts back to the current situation as she picked up her coffee cup and then took a sip.

What was this murderer doing here? Was he really coming for her? Or did he have questions? Questions about their father? About her? About Coop? The sheriff wasn't giving up information, so they needed to figure things out on their own.

When she looked over at Tiernan, she realized he was studying her. No matter how gorgeous this man was or how tempting those Cupid's bow lips were, she didn't have to touch a stove twice to remember it burned. She got the message loud and clear. *You're great, but...*

It didn't matter what came after the last word because everything she needed to know had been said right then and there. Practically throwing herself at a stranger, no matter how drop-dead beautiful, was crossing a line that she'd never once considered doing. Then again, she'd been running on instinct and pure need, and had gotten caught up in the moment. There would be no repeat.

"I won't ask if everything is okay," he said. "I won't waste your time with a stupid question."

He was dead on the nail there. Everything was most certainly not fine.

"I'm here instead of in my own home," she said. "This is a great place, but it's not mine. I have no idea what the sheriff and his deputies have done to my personal belongings. I probably should have been there to catalog what was taken, if anything." The idea someone could have planted her address in Jason's pocket struck like a physical blow. The same person might have put something in her home to tie her to the murder, which could also explain the note on her vehicle telling her to get away for a while. "Will Prescott check out the area where I was instructed to go?"

"I'm sure he already has someone on it. Probably already did after learning about it last night," he reassured.

She nodded.

"There are so many questions, and it feels like my life is on the line," she explained. The look on Tiernan's face was the same one from the sheriff's office yesterday. It was a mix of determination and frustration on her behalf. "I'd like to find out more about Jason, too. Where did he grow up? We have the name of the high school, but did he live in a house or apartment? Was his mother married or single? Did she work two jobs or live off a trust fund? How long did she know my father?" She calculated the math on the age difference between her and Jason. "I was fifteen years old when he would have been born. That's high school. The last name Riker doesn't ring any bells but the incident happened eighteen years ago."

"Do you think it would help to visit your father?" he asked.

"In jail?"

"Captive audience," Tiernan said.

She thought about it for a minute before responding. "You do make a point. It isn't like he can go anywhere." Even so, the idea of confronting her father about another affair was as appealing as sticking a butter knife through her eye sockets. "He could refuse to talk about it with me. Or, he could ask the guard to take him away."

"How long has it been since you've visited him?" Tiernan asked.

"I haven't," she said. "We have spoken on the phone. To be honest, I didn't think I could handle seeing my father locked behind bars. He hurt people, and I'll never forgive him for what he's done. People lost their homes and their savings because of him. But at the end of the day, he is still my father. That little girl tucked deep inside of me still wants this all to be a misunderstanding. And as long as I'm wishing, I might as well go all in and ask that my father turn out to be the hero six-year-old me believed in." In real life, people were flawed and sometimes jerks, and everything she believed she knew could be turned upside down in an instant with no rhyme or reason.

"Bad things happen to good people every day," he said after a thoughtful pause. "People can be damn disappointing."

"That sounds loaded," she said, flipping the tables. "Who let you down?"

Chapter Nine

Tiernan issued a sharp sigh. He opened his mouth to speak but then clamped it shut again. "Let's just say I've learned not to take people at face value. And when someone shows you their true colors, believe them. Don't stick around and give them second or third chances because you think you know them and convince yourself the signs aren't red flags."

It was the reason he'd stopped the kiss before he fell down that rabbit hole again. Besides, Melody had been through a traumatic experience and was most likely searching for proof of life. Nothing could happen between them. Not after he'd been burned.

"Sounds like there's a story behind those words," Melody said. Her eyebrow slightly arched.

"But with your parents, blind trust is usually the case," he continued, purposely not addressing her comment. He'd said too much already.

She studied him as she tilted her head to the right. He'd seen this look before. It seemed to be her go-to while she was deciding whether to push a subject or move on. After a slow sigh, she said, "I went all in with mine. Granted, I noticed that my mother was on the shallow side and my father could be superficial, but I kept making excuses for them in my mind. Like my dad just likes nice things and my mom enjoys friends and tennis more than carpool and baking cookies. I convinced myself that not every mother asked how their children's day was. Mine volunteered at school on a regular basis. She was on the PTA and kept close tabs on my grades."

"Those are acts of caring," he said.

"Looking back, I think mine and my brother's successes were her report card to our father," she countered. "It was as though she justified spending her days at the tennis club if she volunteered a couple of times a month at our school and we were the 'perfect' children. Once the money train stopped, she was out."

Tiernan knew women like that. In fact, he'd dated one. Corinne. All sparkle and no substance. "Mothers should be there for their children, offering unconditional love and support."

"Or be like me and just don't have kids," she said.

"Not everyone is cut out to be a parent," he agreed. "But, somehow, I think you'd be different."

"How so?" she asked, her eyes widening in shock. "Why wouldn't I be exactly what my parents taught me to be? Cold and indifferent?"

"Because you're not built that way," he said. "For one, you could be living a whole lot more comfortable life but you chose to give it all away."

"In favor of earning it myself," she quickly added.

"Which speaks to your character," he pointed out.

She gave a reluctant-looking nod. "Speaking of family, I can't help but wonder if Jason's mother knew my father was married when they had an affair."

"No doubt, she is grieving the loss of her son, but I still

think we should go talk to her and get the lay of the land," he said.

"Agreed. Do you think we could stop off at my house first?" she asked. "I'd like to get clothes and check out the damage after the law searched my apartment."

"We can do that," he said. "Is there a back door, by chance?"

"No. I live in an apartment on top of a UT professor and his wife's garage," she said.

"Then, we'll have to play it straight," he said. Her expression twisted, so he added, "I'll do everything I can to protect you from reporters or bloggers. If we're lucky, they'll assume you're not coming back and take off."

"Sounds almost too good to hope for," she said.

"It probably is but we'll charge ahead anyway." A hoodie would help so she could hide as much of her long russet locks as possible. They could be tucked inside. Sunglasses would shield at least some of her face. "I have a hoodie you can wear that should swallow you whole."

"That should help hide me," she said. "What about bottoms? All I have is the skirt I wore yesterday."

"My ex was about your size," he said. "She left a few pieces of clothing that I didn't have time to donate, even though they've been sitting here six months." He stopped short of retracting the offer when he realized how much he didn't like the visual of her in Corinne's clothing. "Your undergarments are in the dryer. At least those are yours." He also didn't need the image of her silky pink panties stamped in his thoughts, especially when his mind wandered to envisioning her wearing them. The matching silk bra didn't help matters, either.

"That would be nice," she said. "I don't want to wear my interview outfit, and the baggy clothes should help me hide."

He nodded. "I'll get your things." He stood up. "Are you hungry?"

"I could probably eat," she said. "I *should* try to get something down before we head out." She stood up and then paused. "You know, rather than speak to my father first, I'd like to find Bebe Riker and hear her side of the story. My father is a master manipulator and liar, and I'd like to go in with as many of my ducks in a row as possible."

"Sure," he said. "I'll dig around on the kid's Instagram and see what I can find out about her."

"Do you think Prescott already did? Shouldn't we just ask him?"

"I'd like to stay under the radar with our actions until we find something worth sharing," he said. "Prescott will definitely do his own investigation with a small army to help. Having you follow the trail might spark something. It's possible you've seen Bebe before hanging around and it just hasn't clicked yet. The same could be said for Jason. This could be the first time he was coming to you. Maybe being around his mother or seeing some of his things will stir something. You never know."

"Will you be okay to slack off work today?" she asked. "We have a lot of plans, and it sounds like it's going to take a good chunk out of your day to follow through on all this. I don't want to take you away from your livelihood."

"I'll figure it out," he reassured. There was no way he was letting her do this alone if she was willing to accept his help. One person was dead and they had no way to narrow down possible suspects. At this point, everyone they came into contact with had to be treated like a threat.

"If you're sure," she said, doing that thing with her head while she studied him.

"Scout's honor," he promised.

"Why don't I believe you were ever a Boy Scout?" she asked.

His response came in the form of a chuckle. He clamped his mouth shut and then walked into his bedroom to grab the clothes. He needed to finish getting dressed, too. After he threw on a shirt and socks, and then located Corinne's sweatpants, he headed into the living room. "Give me five minutes to feed Loki and let him out before we grab a bite and then take off."

"It'll take me that long to get myself together," she said with a small smile before taking the offerings and heading toward the guest room.

Loki was winding up to his usual overactive self. Tiernan fed his dog while he thought about whether or not it was a good idea to bring Loki along for the day. Leaving him here alone was a recipe for disaster. Tiernan could grab a leash and water container so he could tie Loki to a tree while they visited the prison. That trip might not happen today, though, depending on how it went with the other two stops. She was right about one thing. They had an entire day planned with all the driving involved. It occurred to him they would have to check prison visitation hours since it wouldn't be a drop-in situation.

After filling his dog's bowl, he walked over to the sliding glass door and opened it. Loki was a well-oiled machine at this point when it came to bolting outside and doing his business despite the occasional squirrel chase. After what happened yesterday, Tiernan stood at the door and kept watch.

The hairs on the back of his neck pricked as he looked out onto his yard. He surveyed the land. Was someone out there? Watching?

MELODY TOOK A step into the living area and then froze. The look on Tiernan's face as he looked out onto the back-yard caused her stomach lining to braid and a knot to form in her chest. She cleared her throat so she wouldn't startle him. "Everything okay?"

The first clue he was concerned was the way he stood at the door with his hands fisted at his sides, tensed up like he was ready for a fight.

"I'm just watching Loki," he said without a glance in her direction. It was her second clue he was on guard.

"Mind if I join you?" she asked, figuring his answer would be a good gauge at how worried she should be.

"No," he said. The third clue was how quickly his answer came. His arm extended out like when a driver stepped on the brakes too hard, and their arm flew out to shield their passenger from being thrown into the dashboard. Then, he called Loki's name with the same authoritative voice as someone in law enforcement who'd walked into a hot situation.

The knot in her chest tightened as she stood rooted to her spot. She glanced around, looking for anything she could use as a weapon. Her gaze landed on a fireplace poker. If anything went down, she wanted to be prepared.

A few seconds later, the black Lab came bolting through the glass doors, but Tiernan didn't immediately shut them. Instead, he took a step to block the opening with his heft. He stood there, arms crossed over his chest and his feet apart in an athletic stance.

Rather than work herself up to full freak-out, she decided to check out the fridge to see if there was anything easy to grab. Food might prove a good distraction and there were knives in the kitchen she could use if needed.

At the moment, she was a ball of anxiety just thinking about law enforcement officers picking through her personal belongings, going through her home. The helpless feeling took her back to standing in the doorway to her English teacher's room when her father had his slacks around his ankles and her teacher bent over a desk. The grunts still echoed in her head and made her sick to this day. She'd spent years trying to block the image that had a way of popping into her thoughts every time she saw her father.

Melody tried to shake off the gross feeling. That day, the perfect family of four image had exploded like a watermelon being tossed onto a summer sidewalk. Except there'd been no way to clean up the shattered pieces.

She sighed, doing her best to force the memory out of her mind as she focused on the contents of the fridge as she opened the door. The inside was surprisingly organized for a bachelor. She'd clearly been dating the wrong guys because she was lucky to find a box of cold pizza and beer in theirs.

For a split second, her mind went to Tiernan having a woman in the background. Then, she remembered he did. A house cleaner.

Containers were neatly stacked and filled with food that looked delicious. There was a container of milk and another filled with orange juice. She searched for eggs, grated cheese and maybe some chives. After locating the items, she loaded her arms.

Turning around, she nearly plowed into Tiernan. The solid wall of a man caught her by the arms, and then held her steady until she regained composure.

"Are you okay?" he asked, dipping his head down until he found her eyes. Locking on was a big mistake on her part if she was going to keep from kissing the man again.

"Fine," she muttered, hearing the shakiness in her own voice. "Is it all good outside?" She could play off her nerves as being concerned there was an intruder on his property. Would he buy it?

"False alarm," he said, letting go of her arms. The absence of him was immediate when he took a step backward. "But I'd rather be safe than sorry."

"I couldn't agree more," she said, turning toward the counter near the stove. "Mind if I whip up some eggs?"

"Sounds good to me," he said. The only hint that he was as affected as she'd been came when his voice cracked. He coughed to cover. "I can help or do a little digging to find out more about Bebe."

"We'll get things done faster if we divide and conquer," she said. Putting distance between them seemed like a good idea right now. The temperature in the kitchen had gone from moderate to blazing hot a minute ago.

He nodded, hesitated like he was about to say something, and then shook his head as he walked off.

Melody got busy rinsing and chopping green onions. His kitchen was orderly and intuitive. What it lacked in size, it made up for in ease. Everything she needed was within reach. She remembered milk, so she grabbed the container from the fridge. After whisking all the ingredients, aside from the cheese, she turned the heat on the gas range and located a suitable pan. A loaf of bread sat next to the fridge and she'd spotted a toaster. While the eggs worked in the pan, she made toast. Finding jelly in the fridge was the equivalent of hitting the lotto.

Plates were filled in a matter of minutes. She brought

them over to the granite island and set them down near the stools. She skipped one so she wouldn't have to sit so close to Tiernan that she could smell his spicy male scent. Getting too used to it, to him, would be a fatal mistake to her heart.

Loki made a bed right next to her feet as she claimed her spot. Tiernan walked over, laptop in hand. He glanced at her and then his plate but didn't comment on the distance in between. The dog was growing on her, too.

"I found information on Bebe," Tiernan said, keeping his gaze on the screen. He positioned it so she could see. "She's the morning manager at Green Things Grocery in Lake Thickett."

"Where is that?" she asked.

"It's in between Cider Creek and Austin," he supplied.

She shot him a confused look. "You've talked about Cider Creek, but I'm still not sure where it is."

"It's northeast of Austin," he said. "GPS will give us the exact distance but it's safe to guess an hour to an hour and a half."

"And the grocery?" she continued. "I'm guessing that's in town."

He nodded before pulling up the grocer's website. "They open at 6:00 a.m. and close by eight thirty."

"I can scarcely imagine living somewhere they roll up the streets by nightfall," she said with an involuntary shift that made Tiernan chuckle.

"Not everyone is cut out for the country," he said.

"I wouldn't exactly call Austin cosmopolitan," she countered.

"True," he said as he picked up his plate. A wall had come up after the kiss even though chemistry still pinged between them. He didn't seem like the type to let himself go there again once a door closed.

It was a shame they hadn't met under different circumstances. Tiernan Hayes was the kind of person she could see herself with—*really* see herself with. It was next to impossible to erase the kiss that had been burned into her mind and body. Just thinking about it caused her lips to sizzle.

Since focusing on the sexual chemistry—sex she was certain would blow her mind—was as productive as trying to run through fire and not come out burned, she shifted. The dishes were done in a matter of minutes as Tiernan gathered supplies for Loki.

Green Things Grocery was their second stop. Surprising a grieving mother wasn't high on Melody's list of good ideas. One part of her wanted answers about the current case. Then again, a grieving mother might take off work the day after learning her son was murdered. Another part of her wanted to see what another one of her father's conquests looked like in person. The question of why their family hadn't been enough to make the man happy had haunted her since high school. Why did young people always blame themselves for everything that happened? Because she'd convinced herself that if she'd been a better student or had made him proud he would have cared more about them.

The revelation caught her off guard. She hadn't allowed herself to think in those terms, since she'd been too young to know better. Hearing it as an adult made her realize how silly it had been to hold on to that hurt for this long. It wasn't her job to make her parents happy or keep them married. She could see that so clearly now. Strangely, a weight she'd been carrying around for the better part of her adulthood was slowly lifting.

"Ready to head to your place and get the lay of the land?" Tiernan asked, pausing at the door with Loki at his side.

"As much as I'll ever be," she conceded, unsure how it

would feel to walk into her apartment or come face-to-face with her father's mistress. She was about to find out the answer about both.

Melody followed Tiernan outside and into his dual cab pickup.

The drive to her place took an hour. Tiernan circled the block. Austin had foot traffic at pretty much all hours of the day and night thanks to the University of Texas at Austin. Fifty thousand students meandering through downtown kept the area lively.

Tiernan exited the pickup after leashing Loki. The pair came around to her side and then opened the door for her. She still hadn't checked her cell phone, trying to avoid pain as long as possible.

As soon as she exited the pickup, Tiernan reached for her hand. Slipping her hand into his palm brought on a surprising wave of calm. She didn't want to think about how incredible those calloused hands would feel roaming over her exposed skin.

Between holding hands and having a dog on a leash, they were probably a convincing-looking couple to outsiders. She brought her free hand up to grip his arm while she leaned into him. In a surprising move, he dipped his head and kissed her.

"That should sell it," he said in a whisper, but his raspy voice gave away the affect the kiss had on him. The moment his lips had closed down on hers, her heart engaged in a freefall. It would be so easy to get lost in Tiernan.

They climbed the stairs outside the garage, hand in hand. The wooden stairs groaned underneath Tiernan's weight. Loki trailed behind, trying to wind through their legs. She could only imagine what her landlord must think of her right now. Thankfully, she didn't see his car in the garage.

He should be at work by now. His wife traveled during the week, so Melody wasn't worried about her showing up.

She pulled out her key ring, which had too many bobbles on it. They made it easier to find in her purse but also heavier. Plus, she'd collected them from various life events, making it difficult to throw them away. Each bobble was a reminder of a place she'd visited. Out of the corner of her eye, in the crack of wood under her foot, she saw metal glint against the sun.

Melody bent down and picked it out from between the slats. "What is this?"

Tiernan took a knee. "What the hell?"

The bloody locket was opened just enough for her to see her and Coop's pictures inside.

Chapter Ten

Tiernan didn't like the looks of this. He glanced around to see if anyone was particularly interested in the two of them. The locket was evidence they needed to turn over to Prescott. "Be careful in case a fingerprint can be lifted."

He ushered a silent Melody into the apartment after she fumbled with the keys to unlock the door. After a quick check around the living room to make sure the home was secure, he closed and locked the door behind them.

Loki must have picked up on Tiernan's mood because his ears went up on full alert. He froze except for his tail, which always had a mind of its own, wagging like crazy. Nerves kicked the swishing movement into high gear. Right now, he was in overdrive.

Melody tossed the piece of jewelry on the counter and took a step back. She'd long since dropped his hand. He missed the feel of her delicate skin against him. She would probably laugh at the description because she was one of the strongest people he knew. But her skin was like touching silk.

"I need to let Prescott know about this," he said, pulling out his phone. He snapped a picture of the "present" before shooting over a text to the lawyer. "Let's leave that alone until we get instructions on how to move forward."

"Okay," she said with a hollow quality to her voice that brought out his protective instincts. "I'll just grab an overnight bag and throw some clothes inside."

He nodded as she excused herself.

"Hold on," he said before she entered the hallway. He held out Loki's leash. "Take him with you."

A flash of relief passed behind her eyes as she took the offering. Tiernan planned to join them in a minute after he scoped out the place and made sure the area was secure. Law enforcement didn't exactly turn her apartment upside down. There were a couple of bills scattered on top of the counter. The place looked picked through but not ravaged. Throw pillows had been tossed onto the couch rather than neatly placed. A few drawers were ajar.

Tiernan walked through the living area and into the small but efficient kitchen. Her apartment had a clean but feminine look. Her furniture was in mostly neutral tones with soft throw pillows. The round marble table against one wall in the kitchen had two chairs that looked like something he'd find in one of those cool cafés. Modern? Contemporary?

Either way, he could see himself comfortable here. There were a few plants to give the place enough green. Other than that, the look was simple.

Once he'd checked in the pantry and behind doors, he moved into the hallway. There were essentially three doors. The first one on the right housed a washer and dryer. The second was a bathroom with all the essentials. The third was a reasonably sized bedroom. The decorating carried over from the living room and kitchen. The platform bed had a cloth headboard. There was an overnight bag sprawled out on top of the covers.

Loki came running toward Tiernan as he entered the room. His run was abruptly halted when the slack ran out of the leash. Rather than get her arm jerked out of its socket, Melody let go.

"Hey, buddy. Sit," Tiernan said, but this wasn't one of those times Loki could calm down enough to obey. Tiernan balled his fist and raised it to chest level. The hand signal had a better success rate once Loki hit a certain level of energy.

It worked. He plopped his butt on the wood flooring.

"Good boy," Tiernan reassured.

All the drawers in this room were closed at this point. Only the closet door was still open. He imagined Melody had gone through and straightened up the place.

"Have you noticed anything missing so far?" he asked.

She shook her head. "I keep important papers inside the nightstand. They all look to be in order."

"The law would be looking for a weapon or possibly your laptop," he said.

"Oh. Right," she said. "I guess I should have been looking around for that. The necklace freaked me out, and just seeing anything out of place like drawers still being opened when I walked in is strange. Knowing people were in here without my permission." She shuddered. It was easy to see the physical impact in her body language. The mental had to be twice as rough.

Loki heard a noise. He whirled around toward the window, giving the sound his full attention.

"It might be nothing, but we should get out of here as soon as possible," Tiernan said as he followed the dog over to the window. He kept out of view in case someone was downstairs watching, leaning his back against the wall beside the curtain.

After a few seconds ticked by with all three of them frozen, save for Loki's swishing tail, Tiernan risked a glance.

Whatever the dog heard must be gone now. For all he knew, it could have been a bird or squirrel in a nearby tree. Dogs had far more sensitive ears than humans.

"Looks okay out there," he said to Melody.

She immediately jumped into action, filling the last of the space in the overnight bag. After zipping it up, she shouldered the strap. Tiernan met her in the middle of the room and took the bag from her.

"I'll just take a quick look around," she said. "To be fair, I usually keep my laptop on my bed because I check email at night. The fact that it's not here means the sheriff's office must have confiscated it." She issued a sharp sigh. "Is that even allowed?"

"If they have a search warrant signed off on by a judge, I'm afraid they can take anything they view as evidence," he said, thinking he needed to update Prescott. Although, the lawyer most likely already assumed the worst. Lawyers were good at that in Tiernan's experience. The good ones decided everything that could go wrong on the case already had.

He followed Melody into the next room where she scanned the place. She walked over to the scattered mail, swept it up with her hand and then dropped it inside her purse.

"I don't know how I'm supposed to pay my bills without my laptop," she said on a frustrated sigh. "My accounts aren't on my phone."

"We'll sort it out back at my place if you'd like to stay over again," he promised, fully expecting her to reject the offer.

"Okay," she said with a look of relief. "Then, I won't panic about my electricity being turned off because I didn't pay the bill on time. My brain is scattered right now and I suddenly can't remember if it's due or if I paid it."

"I have to get some work done in my shop this evening," he started. "I can always lend you a laptop. You can come out there with me if you don't want to be in the house alone."

Her gaze widened and she tilted her head. "You wouldn't mind?"

"No trouble at all," he said. The relief in her eyes was all the thanks he needed. Besides, he actually liked being around her. This way, he could kill a few birds with one stone.

"At first blush, it looks like the laptop is the only major item the sheriff's office took," Melody said after giving the living room and kitchen a once-over. "If something was planted here before they showed up, that's a whole different conversation."

There was a lot about her situation that seemed orchestrated. For instance, the note on her vehicle being left the same day the body was found. Could it be a coincidence? Was someone in the know? Her brother came to mind. They were going to have to speak to Coop.

Prescott hadn't returned Tiernan's text with instructions on how to handle the locket, and Tiernan sure as hell wasn't leaving it behind. He'd watched a crime show with Corinne once where a detective placed evidence in a paper bag.

"Do you use paper or plastic?" he asked her as she stood at the door with her hand on the handle, a clear sign she was more than ready to get out of there.

"At the grocery?" she asked. "Paper."

"Where do you save the empties?" he asked.

She motioned toward the sink. "In the cabinet under there."

Tiernan retrieved a folded-up bag from the stack. Using

a paper towel, he picked up the necklace and placed it inside. "We'll have to run this by Prescott's office while we're downtown before we head over to Green Things."

"Okay," she said. Her quick, overly enthusiastic response said she dreaded facing down her father's one-time mistress. She couldn't avoid it for very long. The stop with the necklace would only add an extra twenty minutes in between here and the grocer, where he hoped to get a few answers.

MELODY SAT IN the pickup with Loki while Tiernan ran into the law office. She could see the receptionist through a wall of windows from their parking spot in front of the downtown Austin building, making it easy to keep an eye on Tiernan. There was something comforting about having him in her line of sight at all times after being in her apartment. The awful feeling of her home being violated returned, washing over her like a rogue wave threatening to suck her under and drown her.

Then there was her half-brother, Jason. Facing his mother while she was reeling from the loss of her child made Melody sick to her stomach. There was no getting around the visit. It had to happen, so she would put on her "big girl" pants and push through.

Another minute passed before Tiernan was back in the driver's seat. At least they'd handed off the locket. An involuntary shiver rocked her body. Where had it come from? Who did it belong to?

"I should have taken a picture of the locket before you turned it in," Melody said to Tiernan.

"It's on my phone," he said with a raised eyebrow as he checked to see if a car was behind them.

"Right," she said. "I forgot."

He backed out of the spot and navigated into traffic. She

should probably check her own phone at this point. She had time to kill between now and arriving at the grocer. This might be a good opportunity to get through some of her messages and voice mails. Most of them would be work related. Since she was most definitely fired after not showing up yesterday and today, she might as well face the music and get it over with.

After retrieving and turning on her cell, she took a good look at the screen. The button indicating texts showed the number fifty-seven. Her email icon showed double the number. The second wasn't a huge surprise, considering she was the communication gatekeeper for a real-estate tycoon. She would take great pleasure in being able to hand off all those to someone else. There was always a backup in case she needed to take a morning off to attend something like jury duty. Pamela Steiner was that person.

Rather than go through each email, Melody clicked the button beside every name she recognized and forwarded the lot directly to Pamela. She typed a quick note welcoming Pamela to the position. She'd made no secret of wanting the job when Melody moved on at some point. HR had been on a cross-training kick for the past two years. Looked like their efforts were about to pay off big-time.

There were half a dozen emails left from folks she didn't know. One by one, she clicked through them. Four were work related. One was spam that had gotten past her filter and managed to land in her inbox. The other contained a pointed message.

"Hey, I got something creepy in my spam folder," she said to Tiernan as she studied her cell.

"What is it?" he asked.

"'You did this and now you'll pay,'" she said as she read the screen. Ice water ran cold down her back.

"That's direct," he said. "Forward it to Prescott. He'll need to see it."

"The words aren't the worst part," she said. "It came from my mother's inbox but there's no way she sent it. For starters, it would be the first time she emailed me. I highly doubt she would start now."

"Someone could have easily phished her email," he said. "It doesn't require the most top-notch hacking skills if they can get someone to click on a link. Then, they can send a note from their 'inbox' remotely."

"My mom knows how to use her iPhone six ways past Tuesday, but I could see her falling for a scammer when it came to emails," she said. "All it would take is something happening with my brother for her to immediately click."

"Hackers have gotten good at tricking folks," he said. "I fell for it one time and got locked out of my email. That was a long time ago. I learned my lesson."

"It only takes once," she agreed. "Do you have Prescott's email handy, by the way?"

"It's in my phone," he said, fishing it out of his pocket before handing it over. "You're welcome to check my contacts."

Tiernan's gaze locked on to something or someone in the rearview as he handed over the cell.

"I need your thumb," she said, noticing the tension lines on his face as he bounced back and forth between the road in front of him and whatever he was keeping an eye on behind them.

"Just enter the code, instead—111111," he said.

She entered the numbers and then glanced over at him. "Everything okay?"

"We have a tail," he said. "What I'm trying to determine is whether it's law enforcement or someone to be worried about."

Those words weren't exactly reassuring. Going home might have been a mistake. They'd found the locket, though. It made her wonder if the person who'd dropped it had arrived after the law. Wouldn't an investigator find the piece of silver jewelry? Granted, it had been wedged in between wood slats, and the sun was just right to cause a glint that had caught her eye. The law might have been focused on getting inside her place rather than scanning the outside. And yet, wouldn't they be more thorough?

She'd read news stories of high-profile investigations where officers and deputies had mishandled evidence. There'd been other cases where key pieces of evidence had been introduced late in the game from the original crime scene or couldn't be used because it had been trampled on by an officer. It happened.

Another explanation was the sheriff had made up his mind she was guilty and went in mostly looking for her laptop to confiscate. He might have instructed his deputies to take certain items. Someone had gone through her mail. She never left it scattered around on the countertop.

It was probably good that she wasn't home when they'd searched the place. Of course, her landlord probably let them in. She would have some explaining to do once this was all over.

She located Prescott's contact information and then forwarded the email to him. There was a small sense of accomplishment that came with clearing her inbox despite the scary message. It dawned on her to check the date the message came in.

"Three days ago," she said out loud.

"The sheriff will check your phone logs and your emails,

so I don't feel a sense of responsibility to pass the message along," Tiernan said.

"Good point," she said. "Is there anything they won't touch?"

"You, as long as I'm breathing," he said so low she almost didn't hear it. The reassurance helped calm her nerves a notch below panic. Was it a promise he could keep?

Melody checked the time. The ride over to Green Things took an hour and twenty minutes. Before Melody realized it, the truck was parked in the lot and she stared at a green and white building.

"I'll crack the windows and leave Loki inside since it's chilly," Tiernan said. "Are you ready to go inside and meet Bebe Riker?"

"No," Melody said. "But I don't see how there's any other choice."

Chapter Eleven

Bebe Riker stood in the middle of the store in front of a grand Christmas display. The holiday was a couple of weeks away and she was already supervising the deconstruction of the elaborate presentation, shifting to what looked like an endcap display instead. Long black hair pulled off her face in a ponytail, she was the shell of a woman who was most likely a former beauty queen.

Melody froze the minute her eyes landed on Bebe. She reached for Tiernan's hand, most likely for reassurance. He didn't care what the reason was because linking their fingers felt good to him, like when a puzzle piece that had been lost was found and fit perfectly.

For a second, he wondered if Melody would chicken out and head right back out the door. Instead, she just stood there. Staring. There had to be half a dozen emotions playing through her mind. Facing her father's mistress—a mistress who'd had his child—had to be one of the worst things she'd ever do.

Bebe turned around and caught them watching her. She did a double take, giving away the fact she recognized Melody. A long pause where no one moved passed before Bebe issued a sharp sigh, barked orders at the pair of high-school-age boys breaking apart the exhibit and then stormed toward them.

Melody's grip tightened before she let go of Tiernan's hand altogether. She tensed, ready for the squall headed their way. Bebe stopped a couple of feet in front of them.

"My name's Tiernan," he said, trying to deflect some of the tension. He held out his hand. Bebe took it and gave a polite handshake.

"I'm Melody," she said. "But I think you already know that."

Bebe nodded, not offering her name in return. "What brings you to my part of town?" The way she said those words, then crossed her arms over her chest gave Tiernan the impression Bebe decided she was from the wrong side of the tracks when it came to the Cantors. Then again, Melody's dad might have pointed out the fact on his way out the door. The bastard.

"Your son," Melody said.

Bebe started tapping her toe against the sterile white flooring. Red-rimmed brown eyes sized them up. "Well, he's gone, so you're wasting your time." The older woman's chin quivered but no tears formed in her eyes. The toe tapped faster. "I'm only here today because I didn't know what else to do with myself."

Despite putting up a tough front, everything else about her body language said she was broken. Was Jason's death the reason? Or was his murder the straw that broke the camel's back?

"I'm sorry," Melody said with the kind of compassion that would normally melt a glacier in the dead of winter.

Tap. Tap. Tap.

The toe tapping sped up.

"He didn't deserve what happened to him," Melody continued. "I don't have children, so I won't pretend to know what you're going through."

"Then don't."

"I was hoping to talk to you, but I understand if you can't—"

"It was only a matter of time with the track he was on," Bebe said through clenched teeth. Even though her beauty had faded, remnants remained. Her hair still had a shine that made it look raven-like. Her face was heart shaped and her eyes big and brown. There was a dullness to them now but he could see where they would have been beautiful when they sparked. She was slim, but hints of curves remained. Although she was mad right now, it was easy to see that she wasn't hardened. It was more like tired. Heavy. Like she carried the weight of the world on her shoulders. There was no wedding ring or tan line where a band would have been, giving the impression she'd been a single mother. A tough road. His own mother had brought up six children on her own while living on her father-in-law's ranch. At least she had her mother to pitch in. Still, Tiernan and his siblings would qualify as a handful.

"I'm sorry I didn't know about him until now," Melody said.

"I'm not surprised," Bebe bit out. She ground her back teeth as the clank of a metal reindeer smacked against the tile behind her. "I have work to do and we're not exactly family, so..."

"Jason deserved better from my father," Melody said. "He was a bastard for treating people the way he did."

"Heard he was in jail," Bebe said with unbridled animosity in her tone. She turned before Melody could respond. "Serves him right."

Melody caught Bebe by the arm. "It does." Bebe froze

and slanted a death stare on Melody's hand. "But Jason didn't deserve what happened to him. I'd like to talk to you about it because all the women around my father are treated like throwaways, including me."

Bebe didn't meet Melody's gaze. She stood still for what seemed like minutes.

"I'm the wrong person to ask for help," she said with finality as she jerked away from Melody's grip.

Melody glanced over at Tiernan, and then they retraced their steps to the pickup where Loki sat. Tiernan opened the door, and the rambunctious pup jumped out. He ran over to a patch of grass and did his business before hauling back.

"Good boy," Tiernan said as Melody reclaimed the passenger seat.

"That was useless," Melody said. "All I did was cause that woman more pain. My family has done enough to her. I shouldn't have come here."

"Mind if I let Loki run in the field next door for a few minutes?" Tiernan asked, figuring the dog had sat inside the cab and been good long enough. His energy was ramping up and needed release before they made the trek home.

"Of course not," she said. "He's been so good. Besides, it'll give me a chance to get through some of these texts."

Tiernan called Loki after grabbing a tennis ball from the back seat. Loki came roaring over. Thankfully, the lot was empty save for two cars parked up closer to the front door. He'd intentionally parked far away in case Loki bolted when the doors opened.

As Tiernan cut across the parking lot toward the field, he saw Bebe standing at the window, hands on her hips, looking in the direction of the truck.

MELODY'S NERVES WERE on edge. Tiernan's presence had kept her calm enough to follow through with talking to Bebe, but staring into those dull brown eyes had pierced her. Knowing her father had broken more than just her family caused a knot to form, braiding her stomach lining. Even though she realized none of it was her fault, she couldn't help feeling like dirt for his actions. The man had hurt so many people. Guilt slammed into her at ever believing in him, thinking he might be a decent human being after all.

On a sigh, she glanced down at her cell phone and the number of texts she was facing with no desire to read any of them. The promise of feeling better after clearing the deck was the only reason she pushed forward.

A knock on the window startled her. A gasp escaped before she could suppress it. A woman stood next to her. Bebe.

The window was cracked but the pickup was turned off. Melody motioned for Bebe to take a step back. She complied.

"Hey," Melody said as she exited on the passenger side.

Bebe clamped her mouth shut, and for a second, Melody wondered if the grocery manager would decide coming out here had been a bad idea and bolt back into the store. Her eyes said she had something to say.

"You really didn't know about us?" Bebe asked.

"No," Melody said a little defensively. She glanced over at Tiernan in the field who was watching with interest. Having him there was nice even though it was a temporary arrangement. "I distanced myself from my father when I caught him in the act cheating on my mother with my high school English teacher."

"Ouch," Bebe said, twisting her face in discomfort as if she'd been the one to walk in on them.

"You could say it scarred me," Melody admitted, letting a little bit of her guard down with Bebe.

"I'd say," Bebe added. She twisted her fingers together. "Jason always wanted a sister."

"I wish I'd known him," Melody said as a rogue tear escaped. She apologized.

"Don't ever say you're sorry for having an emotion," Bebe said. "I wish I could cry. It might make me feel better to get some release." She shook her head. "All I get is dry eyes and a heart that feels like a thundercloud that can't rain."

Acting on pure instinct, Melody leaned in and hugged Bebe. Her body stiffened at first, but then she relaxed into it.

"Thank you for that," Bebe said when Melody let go. "I still haven't given the coroner instructions on where to send the...*him*, after they release him. I just can't believe he's gone. When I look at the front door, I expect him to come bursting through. His hair was always in need of a cut. He was a mess this year after he decided to locate the bastard who walked away from us."

"Why now? Why after all this time?" she asked, hoping the reason could give a hint as to who his real killer was. Could her father have been afraid his secret was about to get out?

"It was about six months ago," Bebe said. "Jason said he didn't want to graduate high school without knowing who his father was." She braided her fingers again. "I warned him that he would be disappointed." She flashed eyes at Melody. "Henry told me straight out that he wanted nothing to do with the kid after I told him I was pregnant."

There were so many words that came to mind at this moment. She wanted to unleash them on her father.

"Before that, he made me feel like the most beautiful person in the world," Bebe said, a wistful quality to her tone. "I was younger then. Naive, I guess. I fell hook, line and sinker. When he told me that I couldn't come to his house for dates because he was caring for an ailing mother, I didn't see that as a red flag. I think it made him look noble in my eyes."

"How old were you when the two of you got involved?" Melody asked.

"Nineteen," Bebe said. Barely older than Melody at the time. This made her sick. She'd once broken off a friendship with a girl named Leslie who said she didn't like sleeping over at Melody's house because of the way her father looked at her. Melody had jumped to his defense. Now, she wanted to give Leslie a call and apologize. How could her father be such a jerk, and Melody not see it sooner?

"That's so young," Melody said.

Bebe nodded. "He was older than me. Obviously. I believed his story that his wife and kids were killed in a boating accident on Lake Travis. It made me fall even harder for him, but then I used to bring home every stray animal, too. Turns out, I'm a sucker for a sob story."

"Good people believe others," she said. "It's a sign you were a nice person."

"I hope something good can come out of this," Bebe said. "It's been nothing but heartache since the day I found out I was pregnant." She glanced up. "Oh, don't get me wrong. I loved my kid with all my heart. And your dad, too. I never would have slept with someone without falling for them."

"You were manipulated, pure and simple," Melody pointed out. "He preyed on you because you were young, and he could. He can be convincing, too. Believe me, I know better than most. The man had me believing we were the perfect family for most of my life."

"You were a child," Bebe said. "There were so many red flags. I should have known better."

"Signs only work when we know to look for them," Melody countered.

Bebe nodded and some of the weight in her eyes lifted. "That's a real fair point." She worked her fingers. "I guess I owe you an apology for the way I treated you when you first showed up."

"Not necessary," Melody said. "But I would like to know more about Jason. We looked at his social media page. He seemed like he was thriving before he went to find my dad."

"He was a good kid." Bebe sighed and gave an exasperated look. The kind of frustration that came from a mother who couldn't quite figure out what had happened to her child. It was the same expression she'd seen from parents of teenagers after they talked about eye rolling and slamming bedroom doors that came out of seemingly nowhere.

Melody could only guess how much more difficult child-rearing could be when there was only one parent. All the hard decisions fell on one person's shoulders. No one to bounce ideas off of or take some of the heat during an argument.

"Did he quit soccer because of my dad?" Melody asked.

Bebe made a dramatic show of shrugging her shoulders. "Who knows what actually happened to make him quit sports. He came home from school one day and said that he was leaving the team. I never got the real reason out of him. All he said was that he was turning a new page in his life. He'd gotten in a couple of fights at school with his teammates. It's happened before, so I thought it would blow over like always."

"High school can be hard. All those raging hormones and kids being forced in close proximity all the time," Melody sympathized.

"You don't have kids." Bebe's eyebrow arched as she examined Melody.

"No," she admitted. "Afraid I'm not interested in having any, either." She wasn't sure why she felt the need to point that out when her mind had indicated she would consider having a family with someone like Tiernan. The thought shocked her as she forced herself to focus on Bebe. "Why do you ask?"

"You seem to understand a lot about parenting," Bebe said. "More than most single folks."

"I doubt that," she said by way of defense. This wasn't the time to go into how pitiful her personal life had become or the fact there'd been no prospects for a decent date in more months than she cared to count. Annabelle, the administrative assistant from work, would wag her finger at Melody and tell her to go do whatever young people did these days instead of sticking around the office long past closing hours. Melody defended herself by saying she was a career woman. Was that all? Or had her father's action left an indelible mark on her heart? Did he make it impossible to ever trust people, especially men?

"You're welcome to come by the house after work," Bebe said. "I get off in two hours. I wouldn't have come in at all except that I don't have anything else to do with my time now that Jason's gone." Her chin quivered. She blew out a breath. "I can show you pictures and you're welcome to go inside his room. If you want to know who he was."

"I'd like that a lot, actually," Melody said. She glanced over at Tiernan. He'd done so much for her, there was no way she was keeping him from his work the whole day. Plus, the day wasn't turning out like she'd expected. There were other stops needing to be made, too. She could swing by on her own tonight, maybe even bring Loki with her. "Any chance we could come by tonight instead? Maybe bring dinner?"

Bebe smiled but it didn't reach her eyes. "That would be nice."

"Six o'clock okay?" Melody asked.

"Six o'clock," Bebe parroted as Loki came running toward them. "I'd better get back inside. Let me give my number in case you need to get a hold of me."

Melody grabbed her cell phone and entered Bebe's number.

"It's really good to meet you," Melody said when they were finished. "And for what it's worth, I'm sorry about my father."

"He helped make you," Bebe said with a wink. "That means he couldn't have been all bad."

Melody hadn't thought about it that way. She'd put her father on a pedestal until the bubble had burst. And then she'd seen only the worst in him. No one was all bad or good. There had to be layers in between, gray area.

As Bebe walked away, Melody turned toward Tiernan, emotion welling up inside her like a squall. More than anything, she wanted to lean into his comfort and draw from his strength while the storm blew through her. Get lost in him?

For reasons she refused to examine, she walked right up to Tiernan and said, "Where do you stand on kissing?"

Chapter Twelve

Tiernan didn't need a whole lot of convincing to bring his hands up to cup Melody's cheeks and his lips down on hers. The second they touched, a full-fledged fireworks show went off inside his chest. This was the new benchmark for kissing, and he lacked the will to stop. He suspected a wildfire this raging wouldn't come along a whole lot in one lifetime. All he could do at this point was surrender. The damage was going to be vast and deep. He'd deal with the destruction later.

Loki was right beside them, his body against Tiernan's leg. The dog stayed put as Melody's hands came up to brace herself against Tiernan's chest. He dropped his own far enough to take her by the wrists and lower her hands to her sides. Looping his arms around her waist, he pulled her body flush with his. More of those rockets exploded as he splayed his hand on her lower back.

She tasted like honey as he drove his tongue inside her mouth. He wanted more but this wasn't the place for it. He couldn't stop, either. His heart pounded the inside of his ribs, and it was suddenly like he'd just run a marathon for how intense his breathing had become.

This time, Melody pulled back first. He leaned into her

and rested his forehead on hers as he caught his breath. "You're beautiful."

"So are you," she said. The comment made him crack a smile. He found her hand and then walked her over to the passenger side before opening the door. Loki immediately jumped into the back seat of the dual cab.

Tiernan closed the door after Melody claimed her seat. He took his next and she filled him in on her conversation with Bebe.

"I told her we'd be back for dinner, but I know you have work, so I can come on my own," she said.

There was no way in hell that he would stand by and let her take off on her own without him. Not with how wily the sheriff was being with the murder case. Tiernan didn't trust the man as far as he could throw him. Not to mention a killer was still on the loose. "I'll come back with you."

"Are you sure you won't have to work?" she asked. "Because I thought maybe I could bring Loki with me to keep me company on the ride."

"He would like that," he said, touched by the fact she wanted to spend time with Loki. The two had become fast friends despite her childhood bite experience. Some folks never got over a trauma like that one. The fact they were bonding warmed his heart—a heart that was opening up more and more as he spent time with Melody. "I'd feel a whole lot better if I came with you. Plus, I'd like to learn more about Jason and his mother." He was also thinking of ways he could possibly help her with taking care of her son's burial. "Sounds like she could use a few friends right now."

"I'm sure she would like having you there," Melody said. "I know it would mean a lot to me, too."

Was it a good idea to get this close to Melody? Logic argued against his heart. It wanted to see where this could go.

The thought of being away from her caused a foreign ache in his chest. It was probably nothing more than his protective instincts on overdrive.

"Then, I'll figure out the rest," he said, assuming his timelines were short, and he sure didn't want to disappoint a customer. Meeting his deadlines would take some finesse. Everything was doable with the right attitude.

They arrived home in time for a quick lunch of sandwiches and chips, deciding against making a stop to see her father in prison. Melody unpacked in the guest room while he pulled the meal together. By the time she returned, he had food on the table.

She picked up the plates. "No, sir. You don't have time for this." She motioned toward the sliding glass door. "I'll feed you while you work if I have to so you can meet your deadlines."

It had been a long time since someone had taken care of Tiernan. His independent streak was a mile long and Corinne had all but told him that his job was to tend to her. It was a nice change of pace to be with Melody. She had a similar stubborn streak but put others first instead of only thinking about her needs. The proof was in offering to come back to have dinner with Bebe. Melody must have sensed the woman didn't have anyone else. The fact she was at work the day after her only son's body was found spoke a whole lot about her loneliness. His heart went out to the woman. He couldn't imagine loving and protecting someone, from literally helpless infant to a young person full of life ahead and promise, only to have it all cut short. His chest squeezed thinking about the loss, the hurt.

"My workshop is this way," he said to Melody, grabbing keys off the ring before leading the way outside and to the building behind. His pride and joy. He didn't normally lock the door. These were different times.

The workshop was a converted barn, complete with barn doors that slid open. He'd left the metal bar on the outside for show and ambiance. It reminded him of growing up at Hayes Cattle Ranch and his family business. His grandfather might have soured him and his siblings on working there but that didn't mean his childhood on the ranch hadn't been incredible. He'd run around on the property like a wild buck, roaming free on too-hot summer days. Every last one of them worked to keep up the ranch. Duncan Hayes had hired hands once the kids grew up and took off. Now, he was gone and Tiernan was dragging his heels getting home to find out what was on his mother's mind. She'd called a family meeting. He suspected it was to figure out what to do with the business now that Duncan was gone. A conversation no one had wanted to have.

At this point, half of them had gone back. He wasn't ready. His own business had been as good excuse as any.

"This place is impressive," Melody said as her gaze roamed over the big open space after he flipped on the lights. A hydraulic press took up what used to be a stall. "You'll have to walk me through how you make one of those after you get caught up." She nodded toward the desk on the left side of the room. "Is that where I should set down our plates?"

"Sure," he said, closing the door behind them. Loki ran around the room with his usual excitement. He had a bed to one side of the room along with a few toys in a basket, not that they stayed there much. He couldn't count the number of times he'd stepped on a squeaky toy. The tile flooring made for easy cleanup when Loki knocked over food or water bowls, which happened more than Tiernan wanted to admit.

As Melody set up at the desk, he grabbed an extra stool.

"I just keep thinking about Bebe," Melody said as she sat down. Loki came rushing over, sat down next to her and looked up at her with the biggest pair of sad brown eyes.

"Don't fall for it," Tiernan warned. "Dogs have the ability to whip out their 'puppy eyes' when they want table scraps. Trust me, he goes back to being his normal self when the food is eaten or put away."

"He is looking extra cute right now," she said with a smile. "Is he allowed to have one bite or is the plate off limits?"

Tiernan would feel like a complete jerk for being the reason Loki lost out on a sliver of turkey and cheese.

Before he could respond, a clicking sound from the door area caught Loki's interest. He hopped up and bolted toward the noise. Melody's face twisted with concern as Tiernan held up a finger to indicate she should sit tight for a second while he checked it out.

A sound like a hammer splintering wood repeated several times as though someone was running around the building. Tiernan bolted toward the door and tried to slide it open. He bit back a string of curses that would make Granny blush when it wouldn't budge.

Tiernan threw his shoulder into it as Loki started running around the perimeter of the former barn. A window broke and was immediately followed by the stench of smoke.

Bottle after bottle exploded through windows as fire broke out in the shop.

MELODY JUMPED TO her feet. She'd seen a fire extinguisher attached to a support pole. "Is this thing up to code?"

"It came with the building," he said, already running toward another one. "Considering these are our best hope, we can't be too picky."

"How flammable is the barn?" she asked, wondering just how much time she had left to live as she ran toward the wall. The bottles crashing reminded her of the Molotov cocktails she'd seen in old movies.

She pulled her shirt up over her mouth and nose. At this rate, smoke would fill the room and they'd die from inhalation before the fire ever got to them. Her brain snapped to Loki, and there was no way in hell she planned to let that happen to him. She jerked the red canister off the wooden pole. "What do I do?"

"Pull the pin, aim and squeeze the trigger," he said as he did the same as he checked his gauge and cursed. He said the same word she was thinking. "Mine has no pressure."

She checked hers.

"Mine's low, but there's something here," she said. "Take it and I'll call 911."

They made the exchange but not before he tested his out. The pressure gauge was on the money. There was not enough.

She immediately grabbed his cell phone and made the call for help.

"The operator says it'll take fifteen minutes for the closest volunteer firefighter to reach us," she said, knowing full well an entire house could go up in a matter of minutes. She glanced around for anything she could use to slow the progression of the fire. There was a sink in one corner that might help if it worked. She grabbed a pair of buckets that were hanging on the wall, no doubt leftovers from the original barn.

Filling the buckets, she ran over to the left wall and threw the water in an attempt to douse the flames. Loki was going crazy at this point. The air was getting thicker by the minute.

"We can't wait to get out of here," Tiernan said. "We're going to have to break out through the wall." He ran over and grabbed the metal stool that he'd been sitting on a few minutes ago.

A few seconds later, he was using the stool like a battering ram against the wooden wall. She joined him, using a long, metal tool. She had no idea what it was and didn't care at the moment. With all her might, she pounded the wood. Between the two of them, they started making progress.

When there was enough give in the wood, Tiernan threw his shoulder into it repeatedly as both began to cough. One last burst, and the wood exploded. Tiernan went flying onto the grass outside. Loki immediately followed, but he caught sight of something or someone and tore off in a different direction.

"Loki, no!" Melody shouted but the dog was locked on to something. Tiernan had already jumped to his feet, scanning the area no doubt for something he could use to put out the blaze. A water hose would be like bringing a straw to an ocean to drain it.

"Don't let your guard down," he said to her as he ran to the house. He retrieved a pair of working fire extinguishers and handed one over as he yelled for Loki. "We won't have enough juice to put out the blaze with these but maybe we can slow the fire down enough until help arrives to be able to salvage something."

She nodded before pulling the pin. *Aim and squeeze.*

Loki was still gone when the fire truck arrived. Half the building was standing. The contents had to be ruined either by fire, extinguisher, or water damage. Tiernan looked gutted at the damage to a business he deeply cared about.

Panic gripped her at what could have happened. That wasn't just a close call. That could have been certain death. The person who set the fires knew they were inside. Had they been watching? Waiting?

The sheriff would have to believe her now. Have to take her off the suspect list. It dawned on her that she needed to call Bebe to cancel their dinner plans. Melody hated to do it but she had no other choice. They would need to stick around to give statements and find Loki.

Ice ran through her veins at the thought someone wanted her dead. Because of her, Tiernan could have been killed and Loki was missing. She had to face the fact it might not be good for Tiernan's longevity if she stuck around. The idea of anything happening to him was worse than her being murdered.

She lived alone and had very few friends. She'd distanced herself from a dysfunctional family. She wasn't close to anyone at the office. Would anyone even miss her?

The answer was sobering.

"I have to find him," Tiernan said to her, breaking through her heavy thoughts. "Can you handle things here?"

"Yes. Go," she said, praying he could find him and wishing she could go with him to hunt for the dog who'd made his way into her heart.

In a surprising move, Tiernan dipped his head down and kissed her before taking off in the direction Loki had gone.

Melody figured this was as good a time as any to reach out to Bebe. She retrieved her cell phone, which thankfully had survived along with her handbag that was wet but okay, and made the call.

"Hello?" Bebe sounded unsure if it was a good idea to answer.

"Hi, it's Melody," she said.

"Oh, Melody," Bebe repeated the name.

"Everything all right?" Melody asked. She didn't like how shaken Bebe sounded.

"Yes. Fine," Bebe said. "What's up?"

Melody didn't want to worry Bebe but she didn't want her to think they were blowing her off. "There's been an incident at Tiernan's house and we need to stay in tonight to deal with it."

"Nothing bad I hope." Bebe's tone raised with concern and a defensiveness that said she couldn't take much more bad news.

"An accident happened in the workshop," she reassured. "I'd still like to come for dinner. Maybe tomorrow night? Would that work?"

"Sure," Bebe said with a twinge of disappointment in her voice. The loneliness must be almost unbearable. Melody's heart nearly cracked in two. "Do what you need to. I'll be around."

"Is it okay if I reach out later once we get this all sorted out?" Melody asked.

"Sure is," Bebe said, a little more reassured-sounding now.

The fire didn't take long to put out with the proper equipment.

"Fire Marshal is on his way," one of the firemen said. "I'm Jerome, by the way."

"Melody," she said as he tipped his chin in acknowledgment. "What about the sheriff?"

Jerome shrugged. He wasn't nearly as tall as Tiernan. Jerome was thick. Thick hands. Thick neck. Thick arms. Stocky would be a better term to use to describe him. The two-man team had stood rooted to their spots as they'd sprayed chemicals to put out the fire.

"All I know is the marshal wants us to be careful now that the blaze is out, so we don't trample all over possible evidence. Basically, this is being treated as an arson case."

A yelp echoed through the night.

Loki.

Chapter Thirteen

Loki was in trouble. Tiernan had heard the same sound coming from his dog when he'd got himself tangled up in barbed wire on the neighbor's property. The panicked yelp cut right through Tiernan's chest. He pivoted toward the sound and pushed his legs until his thighs burned. Branches slapped him in the face as he zigzagged through the trees.

The toe of his boot caught on scrub brush, causing him to take a couple of giant steps forward and ending with him face-planting into a tree trunk. Arm out in front, he managed to minimize the impact and come up with only a couple of new scratches and—thankfully—no brain damage. Something cold and wet dripped into his eyes. His first thought was sweat. As he wiped away the moisture, he realized it was blood. Not great but not enough to stop him, either.

Calling out to the dog would be a mistake in the event the person who'd set the fire had Loki. Not a thought Tiernan was thrilled about but he had to consider the possibility. Alerting the bastard to Tiernan's presence would take away the element of surprise and put him at a severe disadvantage.

With any luck—not something Tiernan could rely on considering he'd gotten where he was today by hard work and *not* relying on chance—Loki had stepped on something and that was the cause for the distress call. There were wild boars in these parts along with other animals, predators.

Chest pounding, pulse jacked up to the sky, Tiernan tried to breathe through a burst of adrenaline. In another minute, his sensory overload would settle, and his thoughts would be crystal clear until the boost wore off.

Another yelp from Loki didn't help matters. Tiernan muttered a curse and shifted direction a little more east. He knew this property like the back of his hand, which should provide some advantage.

Loki started rapid-fire barking now, making it easier to home in on his location. Had he freed himself from something or someone? An animal?

Nearing the sound, Tiernan slowed his pace. The moon provided enough light to see now that his eyes had adjusted to the darkness—darkness that came early in the winter. The scratch on his forehead was bleeding, not exactly a sieve but not a dribble. Foreheads were bleeders. He could assess the damage once he got back to the house.

The barking stopped, and then a moment later Tiernan heard heavy breathing. The black Lab burst from behind a tree in full-on get-the-hell-out-of-Dodge mode.

"Loki, sit," Tiernan said with authority. The dog was too wound up to listen, but something might register.

Loki blasted past and then seemed to have a second thought when he looked left to right and slowed his pace.

"Loki," Tiernan repeated.

The dog made an about-face so fast he was almost a blur. Tiernan kept an eye out in the direction from which Loki came just in case something or someone followed.

Rather than wait for Loki to double back, Tiernan turned toward home and ran while urging his buddy to follow.

Sticking around out here wouldn't do either one of them any good. The sheriff and his deputies could search the property in case the arsonist tried to escape this way.

At this point, Tiernan had half a mind to nominate Loki for search and rescue. It might be a good way to put his highly sensitive sense of smell to use. Then again, working dogs had high stress and Loki deserved pampering.

Tiernan turned an ear toward the trail behind them, on alert to see if they were being followed. So far, so good. But he wouldn't take anything for granted.

MELODY PACED THE length of the cabin as she waited for the sheriff to input his report into the laptop mounted on his dashboard. She'd gone over the details of what had happened despite wishing she was out there, searching for Loki beside Tiernan. She second-guessed agreeing to stay back and deal with the law. The sheriff had taken notes. He'd nodded at all the appropriate times. So, why was she convinced that he didn't believe her?

Tiernan would corroborate her story when he returned with Loki, which was the only scenario she could allow herself to consider. Her brain couldn't accept any other outcome. Hope was all she had at this point, and she intended to hold on to it like a child's hand as she crossed a busy street.

The deputy walked around, gathering evidence and taking pictures from various angles. The evidence would fall in line with her statement. No question there. Then, it occurred to her that she should have called Prescott before giving her statement.

Melody palmed her cell, figuring better late than never. He picked up on the first ring.

"There's been an incident at the house." She went right

into it. "A fire in Tiernan's workshop while we were inside. Someone barricaded us in."

"Is the sheriff there?" Prescott immediately asked.

"Yes. I've just given a statement," she said. "I could be wrong but it didn't seem like he believed me."

"If he asks you any more questions, refer him to me," Prescott said. "Where's Tiernan?"

"He went to follow Loki after he ran off," she said, hearing the shakiness in her own voice. The thought of anything happening to either one of them gutted her.

"Has he spoken to the sheriff?" Prescott asked.

"Not yet," she said, then hesitated before asking the question that was simmering in the back of her mind. "Would it be possible for me to be placed somewhere safe while we sort all this out? I can't go home and there's no one else that I trust."

Prescott seemed like he needed a minute to process her request and all the implications that came along with it. "May I ask why?"

"Yes," she said. "I'd like to leave Tiernan out of this."

"I understand," Prescott said. "Could I offer a few thoughts?"

"Okay," she said but doubted there was anything he could say to change her mind. She needed to spend a couple of days in a safe house so she could gather her thoughts and figure out her next move. Involving Tiernan further only put him in more danger.

"Tiernan Hayes is a big boy," Prescott started. "He wouldn't be here if he didn't want to be."

"Understood," she said. Before she could come up with an argument, the lawyer continued.

"He is already involved," he said. "The person who set the fire was going after Tiernan, as well. This has now become personal for him since the perp brought the fight to his doorstep, twice now."

She bit her bottom lip rather than mount another argument.

"You can leave him but that doesn't make him safer, because he'll go after the perp full throttle," Prescott said. His logic made more sense than she wanted it to. "If you stay put, it'll help me contain him so he doesn't end up in real trouble. As long as you're there, he won't take unnecessary risks."

"You make it sound like he would go rogue and do something stupid," she said. "If there's one thing I know about Tiernan it's that he's smart."

"I'm not suggesting otherwise," Prescott said. "But he could turn reckless in his pursuit of the perp, and everyone involved will be a lot better off if he lets me do my job."

Before Melody could respond, Prescott redirected the conversation. "The handwriting on the note found on your vehicle and the one in the victim's pocket match. They have a handwriting expert taking a look at the evidence."

"It's creepy but maybe this will help move the investigation in a better direction," she said.

"We can hope, but I wouldn't relax just yet," Prescott warned. "The sheriff is requesting a handwriting sample from you."

"To clear my name?" she asked.

"Or to prove his case," Prescott said.

There was no way that would happen because she didn't write either note.

Melody issued a sharp sigh as a dark figure emerged from the trees. Correction, *two* figures were running full force. Her heart would sing if it could hold a note.

"He's here. Loki's fine. I'll call you back," she said to

Prescott as she cut across the lawn, running toward them. As Loki neared, she dropped down to her knees while tears streaked her cheeks.

The Lab bowled her over. She collapsed onto her side as Loki dropped his head down in dog pose. The sight of Tiernan must be what people meant when they described what heaven on earth looked like. Her heart nearly exploded in her chest as the tension she didn't realize she'd been holding released as though a dam broke and floodgates opened.

By the time Tiernan reached her, she was sitting up and hugging Loki. His fur was slick with—she checked her hands—blood.

Sheer panic replaced calm as Tiernan reached her. A gash on his forehead was pulsing blood. Their gazes locked for a couple of seconds as he took a knee. The worry in his beautiful eyes for Loki while Tiernan was clearly in need of medical assistance himself tugged at her heartstrings.

"What happened?" she asked, studying his gash. "You're hurt."

"I'm not worried about me right now," he said. "It's probably just a scratch."

She bit her tongue because Tiernan wouldn't listen, not right now, not while he was intent on making sure Loki would be okay.

It took a few minutes, but Tiernan was finally able to calm Loki down enough to run his hand over the dog's head and torso. Loki whimpered when Tiernan's hand reached his right hindquarter.

"I think I just found the problem," Tiernan said. In the next few seconds, his T-shirt was off and he was using it to stem Loki's bleeding while offering quiet reassurances that were working.

Panting on his side, Loki lay flat against the grass. As

Tiernan calmed him, Melody found the fireman from a little while ago and asked if he had an emergency medical kit.

"Yes, ma'am," Jerome said before jogging over to his truck. He followed her over to Tiernan. "That's a big cut on your forehead, sir. Mind if I take a look?"

Before Tiernan could dismiss the offer, Melody said, "I'll watch Loki." She sat near the Lab's head and stroked him behind the ears.

Jerome hollered at someone to bring a bowl of water for Loki before going to work patching up Tiernan's forehead. By the time Jerome had cleaned the wound and put antibiotic ointment on it, Loki was lapping up bottled water being poured into another one of the firemen's hands.

"You're going to be all right, little buddy," the fireman said. There was something special about dog lovers. The way they all pitched in to care for strays or dogs belonging to others. She'd seen people stop traffic to help out a lost dog. Restaurants in downtown Austin put bowls in front of their establishments with fresh water for passersby. Dog lovers were a community unto their own.

Before she could give Tiernan an update, an all-black sporty Mercedes-Benz wheeled into the drive, kicking up a dust storm in the process. Through the cloud emerged Prescott, wearing jeans and a hand-tailored black button-down shirt. He walked with purpose straight to the sheriff's vehicle.

"Our job here is done when the lawyers show up," Jerome said on a chuckle.

"Thank you for everything," Melody said, stopping short of giving the man a hug out of gratitude.

"All in a day's work," Jerome said before he and his buddy headed back toward their vehicle, stopping off at the sheriff's SUV first.

Looking at Tiernan now, she realized Prescott was right. If she took off now, Tiernan wouldn't stop until he found the person or persons responsible for the fire and for hurting his beloved Loki. Her leaving would only make matters worse. Tiernan might take more risks, as the lawyer had pointed out.

Seeing how protective his nature was didn't help her keep an emotional distance from the man. She would have to try harder or risk losing her heart.

Prescott finished with the sheriff, then headed straight toward them. Tiernan reached for her hand but she moved it in time to avoid contact. The less their skin touched, the better as far as she was concerned.

The hurt look on his face almost gutted her. The serious expression on the lawyer's face said bad news was coming their way.

Chapter Fourteen

"The sheriff is off his rocker," Prescott started in while Tiernan double-checked Loki's wound. The bleeding had stopped. A good sign. Still, he needed to get to the vet as soon as possible.

"What does that mean exactly?" Tiernan asked. Melody's rejection from a minute ago had bruised his ego. He told himself it was for the best. As it was, he was falling down a slippery slope when it came to how he felt about her. The wall she'd put up between them was a good reminder not to get too close.

"This is clearly an arson case," Prescott said. "There's no way either of you would do this on purpose to detract attention from Melody as a possible murder suspect."

"He said that?" Tiernan asked, furious. "Because that means he's questioning my honor."

"Not in exactly those words," Prescott stated. "I told him that I expect a copy of his report on my desk by morning or that I'd be calling in experts to review the evidence on my own."

"What did he say to that?" Melody chimed in.

"That I wasn't allowed to tamper with his crime scene," Prescott said.

"What right does he have to insinuate something like that?" she continued.

"None," Prescott said. "But this is a small town and he probably has Sunday night poker with the local judge. Which is why I'd file for a change in venue for a trial if he does a stupid thing and arrests you."

Melody gasped and her eyes widened.

"They'd have to take me in, too," Tiernan said, meaning every word.

"I think he's prepared to do that if he goes down that route," Prescott said. "Make arrangements for Loki just in case. Okay?"

Tiernan nodded.

"Does that mean I'd spend time in jail?" Melody asked, clearly mortified.

"Not more than a couple of hours," Prescott said. "I would immediately file a motion to relocate the case to Austin where you'd get a fair jury pull and trial. If the sheriff is making a move like this with me, his confidence tells me something. He must think he has this thing in the bag."

"That doesn't sound good," Melody continued, staring up at the vast evening sky. There was a chill in the air and she'd started shivering. His shirt was bloody or he'd hand it over.

"Can we move this inside?" he asked Prescott. "Loki will do better indoors. Plus, your client is cold."

Prescott nodded. "Of course. My apologies."

Tiernan scooped up the seventy-five-pound Lab and carried him to his bed on the floor in the dining room. "I need to get a vet over here now. Mind if I make a quick call?"

"Go right ahead," Prescott said. He palmed his cell phone and started firing off a bunch of texts, no doubt to the investigators he'd already hired to look into the case.

"I'll put on coffee," Melody said, looking like she needed something to do more so than a caffeine boost. Her hands already trembled. Then again, she might want the warmth.

While on the call to his vet, Tiernan retrieved one of his jackets from the closet and brought it over to her as she stood at the coffee machine. He draped it around her shoulders.

She thanked him without making eye contact. The shivering stopped, though, so he'd take the win.

Prescott tucked his phone inside his pocket as he joined them in the kitchen. "Is there another place you can stay besides here?"

"My apartment is a terrible idea," Melody said. Her ringtone sounded. She fished her cell out of her back pocket. "My mother?"

Tiernan knew the two weren't close. The call seemed to catch her off guard.

"Do you mind if I take this?" she asked, looking at Prescott.

"Go ahead," he said. "Tiernan can bring you up to date if you miss anything."

"Hello?" Melody answered after a quick nod. Nervous tension pulled her shoulders taut. Concern lines scored her forehead. She rolled her head around like she was trying to ease some of the knots.

He turned to Prescott with an ear toward Melody.

"Coffee?" he asked the lawyer.

"Yes, please," Prescott said. The move also stalled for time since he wanted to hear at least Melody's side of the conversation with her mother. He grabbed mugs and began pouring, hearing a few starts and stops coming from Melody as she kept getting cut off.

"So, you're worried about Coop and that's the reason for the call?" Melody asked, indignant. She muttered a few words that he couldn't make out as Prescott took one of the mugs on the counter.

Tiernan motioned toward the dining table where he brought the other two.

"I'm sorry you don't think I'm 'there' enough for you and Coop, but you two aren't the only ones going through this and…" Melody must have gotten cut off. She issued a sigh. "What? When?"

The concern in her voice drew the lawyer's attention, as well.

"What was stolen?" she asked. A few beats of silence passed as Melody chewed on her bottom lip. He liked the look of his jacket around her shoulders more than he wanted to admit. But he was concerned about the conversation. "What else?" The blood drained from Melody's face, turning it bleached-sheet white. She glanced over at him and mouthed, *a locket*.

Tiernan cursed. Prescott nodded. He got it. The locket that had been dropped off at his office belonged to Melody's mother.

"The blood on the locket is a match to Jason's," Prescott informed. "My guess is that someone intended to plant it at your home."

Melody brought her hand up to cover a gasp, muting the mic. "It would tie me to Jason's murder."

"The sheriff said he had an informant who pointed the finger at you," Prescott said. "But he didn't produce a name."

"Because he doesn't have one?" she asked.

"That's my guess," Prescott stated. "The sheriff is stalling."

"How did the person break in?" Melody asked after rejoining the conversation with her mother. She was quiet for a long moment. "I'm sorry this happened to you." She paused.

"I'm sure Coop is out of his mind with worry. Is he going to stay with you?" Another beat passed. "I'm sure he's too busy." Silence. "No. I didn't mean anything by it. Coop is a busy person." The unspoken words were *unlike me*. "I'm sure he is doing everything he can." More of that silence came. "I'll check on you, Mom. Don't worry about me. I'm good." The words had a slight chill to them. "Talk to you later."

Her mother didn't ask how her daughter was doing?

Melody ended the call and then joined them at the table. "Sorry about that."

"No need to apologize," he said quickly. "Sounds like we solved the mystery of where the locket came from."

"My mother's house was broken into five days ago, but she didn't discover the break-in or the missing locket until yesterday," Melody supplied. "Her housekeeper figured it out and put a timeline together."

"Your mom doesn't have any camera security?" Prescott asked.

Melody shook her head. "She decided the government is keeping an eye on everyone through their own security devices. She's paranoid about being watched and doesn't want to make it any easier on them than it already is. She went on a rant about how we're all giving up way too much information about ourselves with all these devices."

Tiernan didn't use much more than a cell and a laptop. His social media was nonexistent except for his business account. For him, it was less about privacy and more about being too busy to fiddle with it. Plus, the last thing he wanted to do was stare at a screen all day. Speaking of his business, he needed to make a whole lot of phone calls to let customers know their orders were no longer possible by Christmas.

Prescott was making notes in his phone.

"Do you have a key to your mother's place?" he asked.

"No," she said after a thoughtful pause. "Not since she moved out of our family home."

"Where did the break-in occur?" Prescott asked.

Tiernan knew exactly where the lawyer was going with this line of questioning. He was assessing the risk of the sheriff accusing Melody of the crime.

MELODY GRIPPED THE warm mug, rolling it between her palms. Someone broke into her mother's place and stole a locket. "Kitchen window is where he got it. Don't you think this makes it look like someone bent on revenge is behind the crime?"

"It's a possibility," Tiernan said quickly.

"Jason was an illegitimate son who didn't get his due after contacting my father," she reasoned out loud. "There could be others out there."

"True," Prescott said. "Your father had a history of infidelity."

It was an honest statement.

"That's right," Melody said, ignoring the pain in her chest at the admission. She might know who and what her father was, but that didn't make it sting any less every time the subject came up. "We have no idea if he had more children."

"There was you, your brother and the victim," Prescott said.

"The setup makes it look like Jason was jealous and that's the reason he was coming for you," Tiernan said.

"It doesn't quite scan for me, though," Melody said.

"I tend to agree," Tiernan stated.

"Going over to Bebe's place for dinner tonight would

most likely help us get a better sense of the kid," she continued. "His bedroom will reveal a lot about him and his character."

Prescott raised an eyebrow, so she explained the trip they'd made to the grocer earlier. He frowned two seconds into the account.

"No more visiting potential witnesses," Prescott said sternly. "Understood?"

"Melody had questions about her half-brother," Tiernan defended.

"Maybe so," Prescott said. "And they weren't out of line except that we have a serious case on our hands and the sheriff is rooting around in the wrong direction. I just don't need him tying anything else back to you. It doesn't seem to matter how loose the tether is, he is looking for ways to implicate you."

Melody nodded as a liquid fireball shot through her veins. "What is it with this guy? Why is he locking on to me?"

"Good questions," Prescott said. "I suspect you're an easy target and the guy isn't exactly good at his job."

"What if it's more?" Tiernan cut in. "What if he has a thing against women?"

"My guess is the guy figures everyone in the Cantor family is a criminal at this point," Prescott said. "The law enforcement axiom, 'The easy answer is usually the right one,' applies in this case. Her being jealous of an illegitimate brother who might be stepping in to try and take away inheritance could be a motive for murder. She could be protecting her father if the kid threatened to call the media and claim his birthright."

"Wouldn't it make more sense for my brother to be the one to have…" She couldn't say the words *killed Jason*. They were too heinous, and she didn't want to believe there was even the slightest possibility her brother could be capable of murder.

"Yes," Prescott said. "Keep in mind, he has an ironclad alibi."

"Right, the trip," she said. "He wouldn't have been in town at the time of Jason's death."

"And this has been verified six ways past Tuesday?" Tiernan asked.

"As much as possible," Prescott said.

"What about the break-in?" Melody asked. "My father has a lot of enemies, and there is a strong possibility that someone might be targeting my family."

"The sheriff doesn't want to see it that way," Prescott said. "This case could turn political in a heartbeat." It dawned on her this could be the reason Prescott had taken the case in the first place. A man of his stature wouldn't normally take on a small-time client, even with a recommendation from a family as powerful as Tiernan's. Prescott saw two steps down the road and the potential for a political hotbed. Otherwise, he probably would have handed this off to a junior associate in his firm.

"I have what I need for now," Prescott said as he closed his small laptop. "If the sheriff contacts you or, heaven forbid, goes for an arrest, call me immediately."

"Will do," Tiernan said as Melody tried to process this reality. The one involving her being locked behind bars.

Tiernan walked Prescott to the front door, then locked it behind him before checking his cell phone after a message came in. "We'll figure this out before it comes to being arrested."

"I sure hope so." Melody needed to speak to her brother in person in order to judge whether or not Coop could possibly have any involvement, and the conversation couldn't wait.

Chapter Fifteen

"I need to go see Coop right now." The stern quality to Melody's voice told Tiernan she wouldn't be talked out of the idea easily.

"The sheriff might be there right now," he pointed out. "The last thing we need is to run into him."

Melody crossed her arms over her chest, ready to defend her argument. "I will be able to tell if my brother is lying. They won't."

Tiernan glanced at the clock. "It's getting late. We need to grab a bite to eat and turn in early. The vet got sidetracked but he'll be here in a few minutes. Why not take a shower while I make sure Loki is fine?"

Her gaze swung over to the sleeping dog.

"Loki," she said under her breath. "I got so wrapped up in my own problem that I forgot how much he must be suffering." The disgust in her voice was misguided at best. She didn't need to be so hard on herself.

"He's resting, which is an encouraging sign," he reassured. "Believe me, if I thought he was in bad shape, he'd already be at an animal hospital and not resting in his own bed. At this point, the vet visit is just to make sure he doesn't end up with a secondary infection and to dot every *i* and cross every *t*. I don't take chances where his health is concerned."

She nodded and gave a look of respect and appreciation that melted some of Tiernan's resolve to keep her at arm's length. He didn't need a whole lot of encouragement to go there with her.

"I could use a shower," she said after a thoughtful pause. She knelt down beside Loki and stroked his neck. "You're going to be just fine." She said the words quietly. "You are such a brave boy."

"Go get cleaned up," Tiernan urged, figuring he hadn't met a day so awful that a good shower couldn't wash it off. Watching her there with Loki put an unfamiliar ache in his chest. The twinge had him thinking about marriage and children, despite the promises he'd made to himself not to fall for anyone again after Corinne. His judgment had been so far off with her that he'd missed the target altogether. How could he trust that he wasn't falling into the same trap here? He'd known Melody Cantor all of a couple of days. Not enough time to really get to know someone. He'd rushed into a relationship with Corinne. Look how that had turned out. She'd tried to break his reputation and destroy him.

Still, when Melody looked up at him with eyes that resembled spun gold, all he could think of was figuring out how to claim those pink lips of hers and walk away with his heart intact.

He moved closer and offered a hand up, ignoring the electricity charging the air when he got within two feet of Melody. At this point, he was getting used to it. Welcoming it?

"The vet is on his way. Take your time in the shower. Once you're done, I'll heat food and we'll be set for the night," he said, doing his level best not to give in to the urge to kiss her. A place he usually kept locked up. Corinne hadn't come anywhere close, and he'd foolishly believed he was in love with her at one point in time.

Melody let go of his hand, excused herself and walked toward the guest room as his cell phone buzzed. He walked over to the counter where he'd left it and checked the screen. Outside, he could hear tires on gravel. Dr. Paul Macy was here.

Tiernan headed toward the front door. The vet had the good sense to text rather than ring a doorbell or knock, knowing an injured dog would still likely run to the door and bark at the noise. Tiernan opened the door and waited for Dr. Paul.

"How is he?" Dr. Paul asked after parking near the front porch and exiting his F-150. He had a medical bag in his left hand.

"I don't think he's as badly injured as I initially believed," Tiernan said. "I'd still like you to give him a good once-over just to make sure."

Loki limped up to Tiernan and the vet.

"Hey, Loki," Dr. Paul said, bending down to eye level with the black Lab. He reached into his pocket and pulled out a stinky treat. The man always smelled like liver bits, which was probably the reason dogs loved him. "Let's go inside and have a look at you."

Tiernan took a step back and held out his hand for the vet to enter. "Where do you want him?"

"Anywhere he will be comfortable is fine," Dr. Paul said, leading the way to Loki's bed in the dining room.

"I appreciate you coming on such short notice," Tiernan said.

Dr. Paul gave a smile and a nod. "What happened to your workshop?"

The burnt smell was still in the air outside, Tiernan had noticed after opening the front door.

"Arson," Tiernan answered honestly.

"I'm sorry to hear it," Dr. Paul said as he set down his bag and then made himself comfortable on the floor. Loki complied with lying down, considering there was another treat involved. "Was Loki around when it happened?"

"He was inside the building with us," Tiernan said, motioning toward the guest room so Dr. Paul wasn't caught off guard when Melody came out if he was still around. Chances were that he would be. Tiernan hadn't had anyone over in a long time.

"I'll check his lungs," Dr. Paul said with a frown. "It might be a good idea for me to take him into the clinic overnight so I can give him oxygen just to be safe."

"Whatever you need to do," Tiernan said.

"He's young and strong," Dr. Paul reassured. He must have heard the slight note of panic in Tiernan's voice. "His cuts aren't very deep, so that's good. Although, I do need to deal with them. Wouldn't want to risk infection."

"He's been to your clinic before," Tiernan said. "He'll be comfortable there."

"I'll stay with him overnight to make certain," Dr. Paul promised.

There were no words for the appreciation Tiernan felt for Dr. Paul and his quality of care. He offered a handshake as the vet stood.

"What do you need help with?" Tiernan asked.

"I'll grab the stretcher from the truck," he said before heading out the front. He returned a few moments later with stretcher in hand.

With Tiernan's help, Loki was inside the truck curled in a ball within a couple of minutes. A knot lodged in Tiernan's throat as Dr. Paul pulled away. The thought of something bad happening to his own kids someday nearly gutted him.

The walk to the living room was slow. He needed to get on his laptop after dinner so he could update his clients on the status of their orders. Like it or not, Christmas was coming with the speed of a roaring freight train. If someone had told him that he would be in the thick of a murder investigation right now he wouldn't have believed them.

Tiernan moved into the kitchen and heated a couple of plates of food before setting them on the granite island. As he turned around, he stepped on one of Loki's squeaky toys. Tiernan wasn't big on displays of emotion, but the reminder caused a squall to rise up in his chest. His ribs squeezed around his heart to the point he had to take a couple of slow, deep breaths to right himself again.

"Everything okay?" Melody asked as she walked into the room. He'd seen her out of the corner of his eye. She glanced around the room and her face dropped. "Where's Loki?"

MELODY'S HEART WENT out to Tiernan the second she saw the look on his face when she entered the living area. There was an indescribable emptiness in the space now, which was strange considering she'd never owned a pet. She could barely keep a plant alive. It was good to know herself. No innocent lives died due to her neglect.

"Dr. Paul took him to his clinic," Tiernan said, his voice rough. He cleared his throat, no doubt trying to cover.

"Why?" she asked.

He gave the quick rundown.

"Sounds like it's better to be safe than sorry," she said, trying to offer some reassurance.

He motioned toward their plates that were filled with rib eye steaks, spinach and baked potatoes. At home, Melody usually ate a TV dinner before bed. Eating here reminded her of everything she was missing in homemade meals. Granted, the ready-made ones were decently edible. This was on another level.

Melody took her seat and then started eating. Tiernan grabbed his laptop.

"There are two plates here," she said, hoping he would join her.

He nodded.

"You forced me to shower a little bit ago and it made a huge difference," she said. "I hope you'll let me return the favor by pressuring you to eat."

Tiernan stared at her for a long moment, indecision written all over his features.

"Please," she said.

Her plea worked because he walked over and sat down next to her. She reached over and touched his forearm.

"For what it's worth, I'm sorry," she said.

Tiernan's muscles tensed. "It's not your fault."

"It feels like it might be," she said. "I came into your life and look what's happened."

"Don't do that to yourself," he countered. "Don't blame yourself for things outside your control. You didn't ask for any of this, either. Bad things happen to good people."

He was making sense. And yet, guilt still slammed into her at the thought Loki was in a clinic tonight rather than home in his bed. If she'd left last night, would the fire have happened?

"Still," she said.

"The body was found on my property," Tiernan said after finishing a bite. "That couldn't possibly be your fault. You've been dragged into this as much as I have. Neither of us is to blame for the events unfolding."

"Tell the sheriff that," she quipped.

"He's a jerk and clearly not qualified to lead an investigation," Tiernan said.

Melody finished another bite. "No argument there."

The rest of the meal was spent in companionable silence. When the plates were cleared and cleaned, Melody poured two glasses of water. She held one up for Tiernan, who took the offering. He downed the contents in a matter of seconds.

"I think I'm going to grab a shower before I reach out to my clients," he said. The image of him naked wasn't something she needed stuck in her thoughts.

She glanced around, realizing she would be alone in the room. He must have picked up on her hesitation because he grabbed her by the hand and then linked their fingers as he walked them into the primary bedroom.

The room was a good size. A king bed was anchored against one wall. The headboard looked hand carved from oak. It was beautiful. There was a dresser along with a pair of coordinating nightstands. Blinds covered the windows— windows she was certain looked onto the backyard and now burned-down workshop. Her heart still hurt that he'd lost everything he'd worked so hard for. She did realize insurance would cover the cost to rebuild. But what about all that lost revenue from clients?

"I'll leave the door cracked in case you need to shout for me," he said as he walked her over to his bed. The mattress was set high, so she practically had to climb to sit on it. "What can I get you to make you more comfortable?"

"Honestly, I'm good," she said. "Okay if I lean back and rest my eyes?"

"Go for it," he said before disappearing into the adjacent bathroom. As promised, he left the door cracked enough to keep her pulse from racing. She didn't realize how much she'd come to depend on having another living being in the room until now. Having Loki around was nice. Maybe when this ordeal was over, she would get a pet. Cats were supposed to be low maintenance. Melody also needed to get a job once she got past this case. She *would* get beyond this. Right? The thought of being sent to prison was enough to send an icy chill racing down her spine. Not to mention being locked up for a crime she didn't commit. Her thoughts shifted to Bebe. No mother should have to endure losing a child, least of all one so young. It was unimaginable. Melody shook her head at the carnage her father had left behind. How did she ever love the man?

Innocence, she thought. She'd been someone who believed in family and loved her father blindly. Melody issued a sharp sigh. The worst part was not wanting to hate her father. There were times when she wished she could go back to her young and naive self. The one who believed the world was made up of rainbows and butterflies.

Then again, maybe going into a situation with eyes wide open was a good thing. Plus, she would never allow anyone close enough to hurt her again. Her own family had proved those closest had the power to cut the deepest.

Melody propped up a couple of pillows on the massive bed. This had to be bigger than a king. Custom order? Tiernan was a big guy, tall with lean muscles—muscles she didn't want to think about while she was lying on top of his bed and breathing in his spicy scent from the pillows.

It would be so easy to lean in to her attraction to him. And then what? She was facing possible jail time for a crime she didn't commit. Could she use a friend right now? The answer was a hard yes. She was still racking her brain trying to figure out who could have robbed her mother, stolen the locket and then placed it on her doorstep. What about the blood? Her skin crawled just thinking about it belonging to a half-brother she never got the chance to meet.

Her mother's call from earlier was eating away at Melody, too. Her mother might not know the situation Melody was in, but the woman didn't ask questions. She never once asked if Melody was all right or if she needed anything. Her mother called to have someone to complain to or fish for pity, sometimes both. And, plus, why was Melody just now being told about the break-in?

Melody's head hurt thinking about all this. And so did her heart.

Chapter Sixteen

Tiernan showered, dried off and threw on boxers, and then stepped into his room to find Melody asleep on his bed. His chest tightened at the sleeping image of her. Long russet locks splayed on his pillow. She was curled on her side, half sitting up. This whole scenario looked a little too right.

He moved into the kitchen to retrieve his laptop. Since she didn't want to be alone, he returned to the bedroom and set the device on the chair next to the bed.

Gingerly, he wrangled the covers out from underneath her. She repositioned until she was lying down flat and he could pull the covers up around her before returning to the chair. He needed to send out a dozen emails explaining the situation.

The work only took half an hour. Tiredness was starting to kick in as he finished up the last message. Before turning off his laptop, he checked the vet camera. Loki was sleeping in a kennel, looking happy as a lark. Tiernan could get a few hours of shut-eye now, knowing Loki was fine and would be coming home tomorrow.

For a split second, he debated his next actions. Melody had been clear that she didn't want to be alone. He wasn't sure she intended to sleep in the same bed. Since he couldn't ask her, he took the chair instead, cutting the lights down on the dimmer switch. His room could be pitch-black if he turned everything off, which could scare Melody when she woke up. He could sleep under pretty much any conditions after growing up on a ranch during calving season.

Leaning back, chin to chest, he nodded off inside of two minutes.

"Hey." A familiar voice, Melody's voice, stirred him from sleep.

He blinked a couple of times to find Melody standing next to the chair. Her hand rested on his before tugging at him to stand up. He did, bringing his other hand up to wipe the sleep from his eyes.

"Don't wake up," she said before adding, "Come to bed with me where you'll be more comfortable."

Tiernan wasn't one to argue with a beautiful and intelligent woman asking him to go to bed. Besides, he could barely think through the tired fog. So, he did exactly as she asked, throwing the sheets and comforter up and climbing into bed after her. Certain body parts woke up when she curled her lean arms and legs around him.

She smelled like the air after a spring rain. Breathing in her scent wasn't helping him fall back asleep. It didn't take long for her steady, even breathing to indicate she'd drifted off. He didn't dare move since she didn't get much in the way of sleep last night. Her hair tickled his chest as she shifted, burrowing deeper into the crook of his arm.

This was as close to heaven as Tiernan figured he'd ever get.

It took another half hour but he finally found sleep again. Morning showed too quickly. The next time he opened his eyes it was half past six. Melody had rolled onto her other side, taking him with her. His leg was over one of hers and the sheets were in a tangle around them. If he stayed here much longer, he would never get out of bed.

Reluctantly, he untangled their arms and legs and then slipped out of the covers. He rubbed his eyes again before checking his laptop. The responses were starting to roll in and, thankfully, most everyone understood and wished him well. Said they'd be waiting for the saddles however long it took, and they would wrap the rendering of the saddles he'd provided instead. He truly had the best customers in Texas.

One of his emails came from his baby sister, Reese. Apparently, there was a storm brewing back home in Cider Creek. She didn't want to go home any more than he did based on her message, which essentially asked him to help her get out of it. He fired off a response, telling her that he would be home as soon as possible, and she needed to make up her own mind about returning. There was no way he was leaving Melody to deal with the sheriff alone.

His next move was to check on Loki. The dog was still sleeping, curled up with a stuffed sloth in his paws. It was darned near the most heartwarming scene he'd ever laid eyes on. As much as he missed his dog, it was probably for the best he was at the vet's and not running around with Tiernan and Melody, like they planned to do as soon as she was awake.

Tiernan stood up and stretched. Melody rolled over and blinked her eyes open.

"Hey," she said in a raspy, sleepy voice that tugged at what was left of his heartstrings.

"Good morning," he said, moving to the side of the bed where he sat down. "How did you sleep?"

"Better than I have in a long time," she admitted, then her cheeks turned three shades of red. "Comfortable bed."

He nodded and smirked. Comfortable bed his backside.

With her, he'd slept deeper than he wanted to admit, too. They were at a standstill when it came to admitting the reason, which was fine with him. He'd faced down stubborn bulls before on the circuit. He could dig his heels in just as much.

"Have you heard from the vet about Loki?" she asked, pushing up to sitting. The blanket fell down to her full hips. She had just enough curves to be sexy, and they'd been imprinted on his body in the short time they were together last night. In fact, getting out of bed this morning had been difficult.

"There's a camera if you'd like to see him for yourself," he said, motioning toward the laptop.

"I'd like that a lot, actually," she said. "I had a dream that he was running around, causing trouble."

"He will be soon enough," Tiernan said on a chuckle. Her dream warmed his heart a couple more degrees. It was on low burn with her right now, and a spark was all it would take to start a raging wildfire inside him. He pulled up the vet's camera and pointed to Loki's kennel.

"Aww," she said. "Is he seriously hugging a stuffed animal?"

"Yes, he is," Tiernan confirmed.

"That is the sweetest thing I'll probably ever see," she said as she tilted her head to one side and clasped her hands together.

"How about your clients?" she asked as she situated a pillow behind her to lean back against. He didn't want to think about the thin cotton material of her shirt being the only barrier between his hands and her creamy skin. Or the fact she was in his bed and that made him feel like she belonged to him on a primal level.

"So far, so good," he said. "They've been understanding of the situation. At least the ones I've heard from so far."

"I'm sure the rest will be, too," she said. "The fire wasn't exactly your fault."

"Not yours, either," he quickly added before she could get too inside her head and blame herself again. He studied her for a long moment and decided she already had. "Do you always do that?"

"What?"

"Take responsibility for the world?" he asked in all sincerity. "There are a whole lot of things none of us have control over and never will." Growing up on a ranch dealing with livestock, weather conditions and Mother Nature had taught him the lesson well. Half the time, they were going on a wing and a prayer, hoping for the best.

She threw off the covers and climbed out of bed. "Speaking of which, we should get dressed and go see Coop before the vet calls to pick up Loki."

A serious wall had just come up between them. He took note of the fact she didn't want to hear his advice. Wasn't ready to accept it? From the looks of it, he'd struck a nerve.

MELODY HEADED FOR the bathroom. She realized midway that her stuff was in the guest bath, so she rerouted. Halfway there, she heard Tiernan rummaging around in the kitchen behind her as she crossed the room.

She splashed water on her face after brushing her teeth in the guest suite, then changed her clothing. A pair of jeans and a light green sweater would keep the chill off now that the temperature was dipping. Having so little material between her and Tiernan last night hadn't been the best of ideas. She'd neglected to tell him the dream she'd had about him. Suffice it to say, she woke up knowing full well if the two of them had sex the fireworks would light the sky from Texas to Tokyo.

The man had hit the nail on the head about her taking responsibility for the world, but she wasn't ready to hear those words from him or anyone else. She'd been doing just fine without someone poking around in her thoughts, no matter how devastatingly handsome the guy might be. His ability to read her was a little unsettling, too.

Besides, she needed to speak to her brother. She needed to look into Coop's eyes and ask about the note telling her to drive away from Austin. She needed to study his features when she asked if he knew anything about their half-brother. And she needed to see for herself if the muscle underneath his left eye twitched when she asked him about the break-in at their mother's place.

What lengths would Coop go to in order to protect their father? Would he be willing to throw his own sister under the bus? They hadn't been close in years. Granted, they didn't exactly call to check on each other or spend holidays together since she'd dumped her inheritance. Plus, she normally worked, which had been a great excuse to check out of a normal life. Burying herself in her job was one way to keep everyone at arm's length—a job she no longer had to worry about since she was out. The thought of doing nothing for a month or two until she figured out her next step would have scared old Melody. Staring down the possibility of prison time showed her there were far bigger problems to be faced than unemployment. Since she rarely ever went out or spent money on big ticket items, she had a decent amount in savings. Not enough to live off of for years, but she could get through a few months with her emergency fund if she was careful. There were family heirlooms that she'd been hanging on to. She could sell those if times got tight.

If her brother was willing to kill to protect the Cantor name, would he even consider how damning the evidence might be that was stacking against her? Or did he assume she wouldn't even be considered a slight possibility as a suspect? Would that have been the reason for the note being placed on her car? To cast suspicion somewhere else? Protect her from arrest?

Tiernan made good points early on in the investigation when he brought up the size issue, as well. She wouldn't be strong enough to lift an eighteen-year-old male, let alone carry him away from a vehicle with no signs of the body being dragged across the dirt and scrub.

The sheriff was locked on to her, though. Did he have other evidence? He wouldn't have to disclose everything to her attorney. Surely, he had something in his back pocket that he was hiding to keep circling him back to her. Did he believe Tiernan was in on it, too? The two of them were somehow in league with each other? Wouldn't it be easy enough to prove they'd never met before he'd volunteered to take the back seat of the deputy's SUV?

It was an angle the law might be looking into now that she really thought about it. Why would they be willing to be seen together now, though? Wouldn't that go against a secret affair? Or a business arrangement? The sheriff hadn't been too keen on Tiernan stepping in to help her when they were in his office. Was he trying to make a case against the both of them? She wished she could be a fly on the wall of his office to see what he was up to.

Heading back to the kitchen, she switched gears to caffeine and breakfast. She'd slept better last night than she could remember, but she wasn't ready to concede it was because Tiernan was in bed with her. His bed was far more comfortable than the couch she'd volunteered to sleep on the night before.

The smell of dark roast was enough to wake her up as she walked into the room. Seeing Tiernan standing in the kitchen, a lean hip against the counter, sent her heart racing, making the caffeine boost a little less necessary. Her throat suddenly dried up as she walked toward him. He held up a second mug.

"Thank you," she said. Clearing her throat didn't help as much as she wanted it to. Taking a sip after blowing on the top of the coffee was better.

He mumbled something she couldn't quite scan and probably didn't need to hear. His presence in the room already had her body keenly aware of him. The fact he wasn't wearing a shirt didn't help matters much in the attraction department.

"We can grab breakfast on the road if you want to get going soon," she said.

He answered with a slight nod. The man's carved-from-granite face and intense eyes made for one helluva package. The word *perfection* came to mind, even though he'd laugh at the description. "Might as well head out since the vet wants to keep Loki a few more hours." He started toward the bedroom. "I'll throw on a shirt."

Melody had no comment even though a few protests came to mind. She finished her coffee and put on her shoes. She still hadn't checked all her phone messages but had made a dent. Fifty-seven texts. Melody had forgotten how bad it was with all that had happened since she'd last checked her phone.

The threatening email came back to mind. Would the sheriff explain that away as her trying to make herself seem innocent? Would he suspect either her or Tiernan of doing that to throw off suspicion?

The man needed to have his head checked out because there were some serious deficiencies in his logic. She tucked her cell inside her purse and walked over to the door.

Tiernan returned, looking better than any man had a right to in a black long-sleeve cotton shirt that fit him to a tee. He finished off his coffee before setting the mug inside the sink and heading toward her.

She checked the time. "We should get to my brother's before he leaves for work. It'll probably be best to surprise him at home anyway."

Tiernan nodded. He started to say something but stopped himself. What was that about?

"He has a few 'tells,' so I should be able to read him better in person than on the phone," she said in more of a defensive tone than intended. She shook her head as though she could somehow shake off the giveaway that she was nervous about the visit.

Tiernan held the door open for her but he held his tongue. He also didn't comment on her statement, which spoke volumes.

Could she get answers from Coop? Did she really want to know if her brother was capable of murder? Because she had an ominous feeling she was about to find out.

Chapter Seventeen

The ride to Melody's brother's house north of Austin was quiet. The quick stop for fast-food breakfast sandwiches and coffee refills was the only interruption in the hour-and-a-half drive. The houses in this subdivision were new and looked like mini mansions. They also all looked alike with their brick facades and castle-like features.

"His SUV is parked out front," Melody said. It was a top-of-the-line Lincoln Navigator in shiny gold. There was a red Porsche beside it. The house and the vehicles said flashy money, a stark contrast to Melody, who drove a small sedan and wore jeans. They hugged every single curve to perfection, but she wasn't exactly dripping in jewels. Nor did she care, which was an even bigger point. "And his secondary car is here, too."

Melody and her brother couldn't be more opposite on the surface.

"What about a wife and kids?" he asked as he circled the block.

"He's married but no children yet," she said. "I think they were trying before our father's arrest and then put it on hold."

"Will his wife be home?" he asked.

"She travels a lot for work, so my guess is no," she said. "When she is home, I think she parks inside the garage."

"Who corroborated your brother's alibi?" Tiernan asked.

"I'd have to ask the lawyer or the sheriff," she said. "The law must have been by to interview my brother by now, along with my mother."

"Did she mention a visit?" he asked.

"As a matter of fact, all she talked about was the break-in and how much stress she was under because of it and the stuff going on with my father," she responded. "She expressed concern for Coop and the way the case was affecting her reputation."

His grip tightened on the steering wheel at the reminder. He'd heard Melody's side of the conversation and had wanted to shake her mother. The woman had an amazing daughter but only seemed concerned about her son. He was proud of Melody for calling her mother out on it even though it didn't seem to come easy for her.

"I'm sorry," he said.

She reached over and touched his forearm as he parked at the house across the street from her brother's. "You didn't do anything wrong."

"Doesn't mean I'm not sorry someone else didn't treat you the way you deserve to be treated," he said with sincerity. "Your mother is lucky to have a daughter as kind and considerate as you are. Not to mention the fact you already hold the world on your shoulders. What does your brother do that's so special?"

"He's Coop," she said with a shrug. "He's always been the golden boy of the family."

"Idiots," Tiernan said before adding, "I shouldn't insult your parents like that, but hell…"

"Believe me, you're not hurting my feelings," she said.

"My only ties come out of a sense of obligation." She issued a sharp sigh. "Honestly, they were a lot nicer to me before I ditched my trust fund. I think that was the ultimate slap in the face. Like I wasn't part of them any longer. I didn't blindly accept my father's behavior, and money wasn't the be-all and end-all in my life. I highly doubt they understand me."

Tiernan leaned across the divider and pressed a kiss to her lips. "You're a very special person and you should know it."

The red blush that crawled up her neck and settled on her cheeks was sexier than lacy lingerie. Not that he would mind that, either. When she showed her emotions—which he'd noticed was rare—her vulnerability made her darn near irresistible.

"I have a feeling arguing with you would be the equivalent of trying to negotiate with a bull," she said with a smile. "So, I won't even try. I will say thank you, though, and leave it at that."

"Fair enough."

Tiernan exited his side of the truck and rounded the front to open her door for her. She took the hand he offered and kept hold as they made their way toward the house after closing the door. He took a detour to touch the hood of the Lincoln. It was warm. By the time they reached the oversize wooden front door, she had a death grip. Before moving any farther, he stopped her at a point where the Navigator would block them from view.

He rounded on her and brought his free hand up to run his thumb along her jawline. The pull toward kissing her was the force of a tornado moments after touchdown. When his thumb grazed her bottom lip, the urge doubled down.

"I can take the lead with him if you're not feeling it," he said to her, locking on to those incredible golden-brown eyes.

For a minute, the world shrank to the two of them. She slicked her tongue across her lip, leaving a silky trail, and nearly obliterating his willpower in the process.

"He's my brother," she said. "I can handle him." She paused for a few beats. "I'm just afraid of what I'm about to see in his eyes."

She didn't say the word *murderer*, but he knew exactly what she meant.

Tiernan tilted his chin toward the house. "I hope you get the answers you want."

"So do I," she said, then took in a deep breath like people did when they were about to jump off a cliff. "Let's do this."

He stepped aside to let her lead the way. She immediately reached back for his hand and then linked their fingers. Ready or not, they were about to face her brother.

MELODY RANG THE doorbell and waited. She had half a mind to call her brother to make certain he answered, figuring no one actually came to the door anymore. Except Coop did after another round of church bell sounds.

"Hey," he said, his gaze bouncing from her to Tiernan and back. "Everything okay?"

The top two buttons of her brother's crisp white shirt were unbuttoned. His tie was loose around his neck.

She tightened her grip on Tiernan's hand. "I just wanted to stop by and ask a few questions. This is my friend Tiernan."

"Nice to meet you," Coop said, after sizing up her companion. Her brother wasn't exactly being subtle. The way his face muscles tensed gave away his disdain for her companion.

Tiernan, on the other hand, offered a polite smile and a handshake.

"Can we come inside?" she asked.

Coop's gaze skimmed the area like he half expected law enforcement to jump out of the bushes. She could think of plenty of reasons her brother might be jumpy and none of them had to do with being overcaffeinated.

"Sure," Coop conceded after checking his Rolex. "I have a couple of minutes before I need to head out for work."

"We won't be long," Melody said. "We have an important package to pick up soon."

Tiernan followed her inside the entryway of her brother's palatial home. Coop had darker hair. His muddy-brown eyes were cradled by dark circles. As much as Melody didn't want to read too much into her brother's nervous disposition, it was hard not to under the circumstances. Melody reminded herself that Coop had been stepping in at work to take their father's place while the business was under investigation, and also while maintaining the man's innocence in corporate affairs.

Coop took exactly five steps into the two-story foyer, stopped and then spun around on them. "What can I help you with today?" Up close, his complexion was ruddy and stress cracks were permanently etched around his eyes and mouth. All signs of the carefree, life-comes-easy brother from years ago were gone. The one who made the family proud on the sports field, oftentimes being carried on his teammates' shoulders after a game-winning play, was no longer the person standing in front of her. Instead, she stared into bloodshot mud orbs.

"Did you hear about the break-in at Mom's?" she asked, tilting her head to one side as she examined Coop.

He threw his hands in the air. "I'm just glad she wasn't home at the time. Who knows what might have happened then."

"Interesting to note not much was taken," she continued

with a nod of acknowledgment. "And, yes, I'm relieved our mother is fine."

"I'm guessing the person was casing the place," Coop said a little too enthusiastically. Besides, when did he use terms like "casing" during normal conversation? Was he watching cop shows all of a sudden?

"Could have been," Melody said. "I'm sure the law will conduct a thorough investigation and nail the bastard responsible."

She caught a two-second flash of emotion pass behind his eyes. Again, she was scrutinizing her brother and it might not be warranted. Everyone in the family had been through a lot since their father's arrest. Coop had taken it the hardest since he worked most closely with their dad.

"Yes," he said. "That's the hope."

"Do you think we should hire our own investigators?" she asked, reaching for something to catch him off guard with. "Just in case the police aren't as thorough as we would like them to be?"

"It's an idea," Coop said, his voice unchanged. "We can talk it over." He folded his arms. "It might be spending money unnecessarily, though. With Dad's legal troubles, money isn't as free-flowing as it used to be."

"The expenses must be racking up," Melody said. "I'd help if I could."

"Your inheritance is gone," Coop said quickly. A little too quickly? She must have shot a look because he added, "You gave it away a long time ago and divorced yourself from the family financially. No one expects you to pick up now and suddenly start contributing."

"Speaking of family," Melody said. "Where's Janice?"

"Dubai," he said. "She's been there all month with her charity league."

Melody nodded before redirecting the subject. "Have the police been here lately?"

Coop's eyes widened to saucers, and he didn't blink. "No. Why?"

"Just curious," she said. "With the theft at Mom's place, I thought maybe they'd stopped by to question you."

"I was the first one Mom called when this happened," Coop said. "They talked to me at Mom's place since I went over immediately."

"Oh, really," she said. His normal "tell" signs conflicted with each other. "I only just found out about it."

"I told Mom not to call and worry you," he said.

"Why would you do that?" she questioned. What reason on earth could he have for wanting to keep something as important as their mother's home being broken into from her?

"Because you have enough on your plate with the job search," he said.

Since when did her brother start keeping such close tabs on her? Melody wanted to believe this was all out of good will, but her gut instincts were picking up on red flags. Coop was hiding something.

"Where were you that night when Mom called?" she asked.

"I was at a Longhorn game and stayed at the family cabin," he said. She must have shot quite the look because he immediately said, "Do you want to see the receipts?"

Given he was so quick to offer, she declined. Coop loved his alma mater and was involved as an alumnus.

Before she became too defensive about their mother not making any secret out of favoring Coop over Melody, she said, "I'm glad you were there for her. She didn't quite sound herself on the phone."

"The whole event shook her up," he said.

"I can only imagine how awful and violated she must have felt to have her personal space invaded like that," Melody said, thinking about the parallel to Tiernan's workshop—a workshop he'd obviously lovingly built and took great pride in. Frustration settled over her along with a weighty feeling of helplessness that had no business on her shoulders.

"I'm just glad I wasn't too far. I got to her pretty fast," he said by way of explanation.

Melody's mom had remarried and then divorced. Although she enjoyed living alone, her mother had never acquired a taste for solitary life. Melody wouldn't be surprised if the woman wasn't already scouting her next husband despite the divorce being less than a year old.

"You guys don't have to protect me from everything," Melody said. "I would have liked to have known sooner."

"You're my little sis," Coop said, pulling emotional strings that took her back to their childhood. "I'm always going to look out for a Cantor."

The warm and fuzzy feeling Melody had experienced faded when her brother added the last bit. Because the look in his eyes said he was dead serious.

"Could I ask a question, if it's not too much trouble?" Tiernan interrupted. He squeezed her hand slightly. She took the gesture to mean she should trust him.

Coop didn't look thrilled. Then again, her brother hadn't been real excited to see either one of them since he opened the front door to find them standing there. "Depends on what it is."

Her brother's response caught her off guard. He'd been in defensive mode the whole conversation. The visit she'd hoped would answer some of her questions, and hopefully clear her brother, had backfired.

"I'll take that to mean I can go forward," Tiernan said. "Have you been home all morning?"

Chapter Eighteen

"Yes. I'm about to leave, though," Coop said. Tiernan knew he was lying.

"We don't want to hold you up," Tiernan said, tugging at Melody's hand. They'd gotten all they were going to from her brother. There would be no confessions coming from this guy. He was too busy covering his tracks. His attitude was as prickly as a startled porcupine. He was guilty as sin for something, but Tiernan didn't want to condemn the man without proof.

Melody followed Tiernan's lead, walking outside beside him.

"Take care of yourself, Coop," she said to her brother. "You look tired, like you haven't slept in days."

"I'll be fine," Coop said. The man was a brick wall when it came to having any tender feelings toward his family. Despite their differences, Tiernan never once doubted any one of his family members would have his back with one phone call. It shouldn't be a rare quality among siblings, but he was beginning to realize just how much it was. He was also starting to think he needed to head home, if only to reconnect with his brothers and sisters. Looking back now, he was embarrassed at how much he'd neglected his relationship with his mother and grandmother. Duncan Hayes should never have been granted that power—power they'd all handed over to the man who'd seemed larger than life when they were kids.

"I mean it," Melody said to her brother. She let go of Tiernan's hand before walking toward Coop and hugging him. "Let me know if you need help with anything."

"Have you been to see Dad?" Coop asked after the brief hug that he'd returned more out of a sense of obligation than anything else, based on the man's expression.

"No," she admitted. "We've talked on the phone, though. He told me not to come."

"Probably doesn't want his children to see him locked behind bars like some kind of animal," Coop said with disdain.

"People have to suffer the consequences of their actions, Coop," Melody said with compassion.

Her brother bristled. "Only when they do something wrong. Our father is innocent." The insistence with which he spoke those words came across more like trying to wish something into reality as opposed to believing it to be true. It reeked of desperation that caused Tiernan to have doubts. Some folks believed if they said something over and over again, it would eventually become the truth. That sounded like the case here.

"I know you want to believe that, Coop," Melody said. "So do I. But the evidence says otherwise." She stared at her brother for a long moment. "Do you have a good attorney?"

"The same one Dad has, but I won't need him," Coop said with more defensiveness in his tone.

"You should get a lawyer separate from the company and definitely different than Dad's," she said. "I'm no expert on the law, but it seems like a good idea to have someone who can differentiate your case from our dad's."

Coop's gaze narrowed and his lips thinned. His sister was looking out for him but his response to her was to be angry. Granted, the man didn't appear to want to hear anything that might be considered contrary to his own opinion. Tiernan had stared down bulls with less of a stubborn streak. Coop had decided he was right and had no plans to alter his opinions despite a mountain of evidence pointing toward his father's guilt.

"I'm fine," Coop said with impatience. He was like a teapot just shy of boiling over.

"Of course you are," Melody soothed. She was trying to bring a sense of calm to a situation that had gone south from the minute Coop laid eyes on them.

"I've already thought through it all," Coop continued. He might be listening, but the man wasn't truly hearing a word coming out of Melody's mouth. His brain was already clicking ahead to whatever defense he might need to mount next. "Hey, sis, I appreciate your concern."

The about-face caught Melody off guard, based on her expression and lack of an immediate response. Coop was good at manipulation. Was he capable of murder?

Sizing him up, Coop was sturdy enough to carry an eighteen-year-old. Melody mentioned something about her brother having been a college athlete, so there was that. He appeared to keep up some kind of workout, based on his general muscle tone. He was decently tall—over six feet tall. He'd proven willing to go to great lengths to protect the family name. His loyalty to their father didn't come across as sincere. It was more like self-preservation. Prescott would have investigators dig into the Cantor family business records to make sure Coop didn't have any involvement in the crimes. Based on Tiernan's understanding, the family had their hands in a few pies. Some of the revenue was from legitimate sources. The illegal income came from their father. *Alleged* illegal income.

"Be careful, Coop," Melody said, not budging from in front of her brother. "I don't just mean legally."

"I'm fine," came the response.

"One more question before we go," Melody said before taking a step back and reaching for Tiernan's hand. He had a premonition that she was about to drop a bomb.

"Shoot," Coop said.

"What do you know about Jason Riker?" she asked.

Coop's mouth fell open before it snapped shut. "Pretty much everything everyone else knows. A kid was murdered in a nearby county and there aren't obvious signs as to the reason."

"Really?" Melody's disappointment in her brother was apparent by the expression on her face and tone in her voice.

"What?" Coop asked, trying to play innocent when he clearly knew more. "Should I know more about him?"

"Other than the fact he's our half-brother?" Melody asked.

"No way," Coop said. "The only people who belong in our family have the last name Cantor."

"It wasn't his fault that he didn't," she countered, much to Coop's disgust. And *disgust* was the only word to describe the look on his face.

"How could you betray us and claim this kid as a relative?" Coop asked.

"Are you kidding me right now?" she asked, fist on her left hip. Tiernan squeezed her right hand. It was time to go. The conversation was getting heated and that wouldn't go anywhere useful. They had the information they needed to move forward. Anything more than this was going to be pure frustration, like beating a dead horse. But Tiernan had no plans to interfere with family matters. He squeezed

Melody's hand again in an attempt to ground her. A look passed behind her eyes that told him she understood.

Rather than debate her side, Melody held a hand up to stop her brother from responding. "Look, I didn't mean to offend you. I agree that the Cantor name is special and worth protecting. Our dad shouldn't be in jail if he's innocent. You'll get one hundred percent agreement with me on that point. And, Coop, I truly hope that he is innocent. I can scarcely think about another outcome. I *want* everything to work out the same as you do. So, I'll leave it at that."

Coop nodded. The man was going to great lengths to protect his family's legacy. Was Duncan Hayes any different? Probably not. And it was the main reason Tiernan was unable to respect Coop. He'd experienced firsthand a person who cared more about image than substance. Tiernan would take a hard pass on believing in someone like them. He and Melody got what they came for. Now he needed to get her out of there.

THERE WERE SO many thoughts running through Melody's head right now it was like a pinball machine on full tilt. The only tether to reality was Tiernan. The way he squeezed her hand said it was time to go. She listened. They walked away. *Disappointment* wasn't nearly a big enough word to describe how she felt about her brother right now. Why was she so surprised, though? Coop acted exactly as she'd feared he would. Sketchy.

The way he'd initially pretended not to know who Jason was sickened her.

Melody walked away with Tiernan after a quick goodbye to Coop. Disappointment sat heavy on her chest because she also realized her brother was hiding something.

Once she was settled inside the truck, she stared over at

her brother. He was hastily moving to his SUV while having a conversation on his cell phone. She had no doubt he was covering his tracks.

"What do you think of Coop?" she asked Tiernan as he drove away. Her brother's house quickly filled the rearview.

"Probably the same as you," Tiernan said honestly. She appreciated him for it.

"He's guilty as sin," she said, hating that she had to say those words about her own brother. Facing things head-on had been an acquired taste for her, having grown up in a family famous for sweeping everything under the rug, including her father's infidelity.

"I know," Tiernan confirmed. "He lied about not being gone this morning. His Lincoln was hot to the touch. There's only one reason for that."

Melody gasped. "He was driving it before we even got there."

"That's right," Tiernan confirmed with a frown. He clearly didn't enjoy bringing her bad news about her family member. In fact, based on his expression, he didn't think it was his place at all. Except that he must realize she deserved to know what was going on and that her brother was trying to pull the wool over her eyes.

"I had a bad feeling the whole time we were talking that he was lying to me or hiding something. I couldn't quite put my finger on it," she confirmed. "You're right to tell me your observations, by the way."

"It's not what I wanted to see, if that makes a difference," he said.

"Actually, it does," she said. "I've never been all that close to Coop. He's always been the older brother who was more into his friends than staying at home on a weekend night to be with me. However, I did idolize him for a long time and I felt that instinct kicking in."

"He made no secret about trying to play that card with you," he continued. "For instance, the whole 'little sis' bit was contrived." He glanced over at her as he navigated onto the highway. "I'm sorry."

"No. Don't be," she argued. "I need to hear it because I'm always going to have a soft spot for my brother. We grew up together. He's my family."

"Funny how family can manipulate us," he said with the kind of wistfulness that said there was a story behind those words. Since she needed a distraction from her own family drama, she decided to ask about Tiernan's.

"What happened in yours, if you don't mind my asking?"

"My father died when I was in elementary school," he started. "My grandfather stepped in to be 'the man' of the family and destroyed it instead."

"I'm sorry to hear that, Tiernan," she said. "Is that why you don't live on your family's ranch?"

"It's a big part of it," he said. "We all jumped ship the minute we turned eighteen."

"What about your mother? Are the two of you close?" she asked.

"Looking back now, I was a jerk to take off the way I did," he said. "She did her best to mediate. I think she just wanted us to have something from our dad and that was the reason she put up with her father-in-law."

"You were barely out of high school when you left," she said. "We all thought we had life figured out back then, didn't we?"

He chuckled, and it was the first break in tension this morning. "I can't speak for you but I was an arrogant little twit. More testosterone than common sense."

"I read somewhere our brains aren't fully developed until we're twenty, so there's that," she said.

"Explains a lot of my bad choices early in life," he said. "Not the ones I made later, I'm afraid."

Tiernan was finally opening up about his personal life, so she decided to capitalize on the moment.

"A story like that always begins with a romance," she said, ignoring the flush she felt along with the twinge of jealousy.

"I recently made a bad decision there, too," he said. "Guess I can't blame youth, hormones and inexperience on that one."

"People can slip past the radar," she said. "Doesn't mean we're stupid. Just means we actually trusted someone who took advantage of us."

His self-deprecating laugh probably shouldn't charm her. "When you put it like that, I don't feel like as much of an idiot."

"You're not," she said. "Believe me. We've all been there at one time or another."

"Explain," he urged.

"I was engaged after college," she admitted. Before he could accuse her of baiting him to get his secrets, she added, "Looking back, he would have turned out just like my father and brother. We were the 'perfect' couple on the outside. Both came from politically climbing families. My father approved very much, despite the fact Brently Fox would have cheated behind my back and never truly loved me. Between that and my father's behavior in general, I stopped trusting everyone a very long time ago."

Tiernan studied the stretch of road in front of him for a long moment. "Sounds like a lonesome way to live."

"When you put it like that, it is," she conceded. "I never

get hurt, though." To say she had daddy issues was a lot like saying brown was a color. But she was just beginning to realize how deep those scars were.

"Never take a risk. Never get burned," he agreed, nodding. Then his tone changed. "I rode broncos when I was younger and there were rides that scared the hell out of me deep down. I never let those fears take the wheel. Fear is good. It's built in us to keep us alive. Sure doesn't make us happy, though. Some of the highlights of my career came because I stared those fears in the eyes and dared them to do their best."

"I can't imagine how scary your job must have been," she said, not quite ready to run toward the unknown or what scared her. "I've always taken a safe route there, too." Looking over her life so far, she'd never pushed out of her comfort zone until recently. And despite the dangerous circumstances, she'd never felt more alive.

Could she face down her fear enough to ask Tiernan what she wanted? One night of distraction. One night of getting lost with him. One night of what would be the best sex of her life?

She opened her mouth to speak, then clamped it shut when his cell started buzzing.

Chapter Nineteen

"Where the hell are you?" Prescott asked. He'd never been one to lose his composure, so Tiernan was taken aback. This wasn't a good sign considering they were in the middle of a murder investigation and the sheriff had blinders on when it came to other suspects.

"Anywhere you want us to be," he responded, hoping this new development wasn't as bad as he feared it might be. "Why?"

"How fast can you get home?" Prescott continued.

"Half an hour," he responded. He'd have to push the speed limit. "Do we get to know why?"

"I'll tell you when you get there," Prescott said before ending the call.

"I should probably call Bebe and let her know we can't come tonight for dinner," she said. "I hated having to cancel last night, especially since she sounded so disappointed."

A half dozen thoughts slammed into Tiernan's mind. None he liked. "Go ahead and do that. In the meantime, I'll see about how fast I can get us back to my place."

Melody dug in her purse for her cell, producing it a few seconds later. She made the call and waited. "Rolled into voice mail." She paused for a few seconds. "She might be at work right now, so hopefully she'll reach out."

He nodded. His thoughts bounced from the interaction with Coop to what on earth could be waiting for them back at his place. His next thought was Loki. He hated the thought of leaving him at the vet any longer than necessary. It didn't seem like they had enough time to swing by and pick him up.

"You're worried, aren't you?" Melody asked. "You get these deep grooves in your forehead that give you away."

"Remind me never to play poker with you," he conceded. "I guess I never noticed since I rarely check the mirror."

"How bad is it?" she asked. "In your mind, at least."

"I have half a mind not to show," he admitted.

"But?"

"That would be like admitting guilt to whatever we're about to be accused of," he said.

"You don't think good evidence might have surfaced that we need to be told about in person?" she continued.

"We'll know soon enough." He didn't intend for those words to come out like the world was ending. Hearing how they sounded, he needed to clarify. "At least Prescott is asking us to come home. I'm thinking in a worst-case scenario, he would tell me to drive to the sheriff's office where he would meet us."

A sigh of relief filled the space between them.

"I didn't mean to worry you," he clarified. She must've assumed the sheriff could come to arrest her any minute with the way the case had been moving so far.

"It's not your fault," she said. It was, in a sense, because he could have been choosing his words more carefully. "I've never been in this position before and the sheriff seems locked on to figuring out how I'm responsible. I'm still scratching my head as to why. If anyone in my family was guilty, it would have to be my brother."

"His alibi checks out," Tiernan said. "He said he had receipts if you're talking about the break-in at your mother's place."

"I'm not surprised he would be at a Longhorn sporting event," she said. "It's the trip I'm more concerned about. How do we know he went anywhere?"

"There wouldn't be hotel receipts," he said, thinking out loud.

"That's right—he has a cabin, so there's not really a good way to track him there," she said. "Actually, it belongs to the family. I just never go since I cut myself off financially. Plus, how could I enjoy staying anywhere that was potentially bought with other people's retirement income that had been stolen from them?"

"Do you still have a key to the place?" he asked. A quick trip out there might answer a few questions about her brother's alibi.

"Yes," she said. "I've been too lazy to return it."

Somehow, he doubted she'd be too lazy to do anything. He would believe her more if she blamed the slip on an overly busy schedule. She'd already admitted to working all the time to the point of sacrificing a social life. Then again, since Corinne, he could be accused of doing the same. "It might be time to visit the family cabin."

"After we face the music with Prescott," she said. The visit must've been weighing heavily on her mind, considering the fact she'd been tapping her index finger on the door handle for several minutes now. The tempo picked up with her stress levels. He had a tell when he was concerned and so did she.

Since they were almost there at this point, he didn't answer. They could swing by the house and find out what bomb her lawyer was about to drop. Next, they could drop by the vet's office for Loki. After, they could head toward her family cabin to poke around and see what they could find. On their way back, they could take time to visit with Bebe. It was a full schedule. Since he didn't have any work to do, he could spare the time. Besides, something was niggling at the back of his mind since the visit with Coop, and he couldn't quite put his finger on it.

Tiernan pulled onto his gravel drive and headed down the lane leading to his cabin. Back at Hayes Cattle Ranch, there was security twenty-four seven. This place was home and, until yesterday, wasn't in need of protecting like a livestock business worth millions of dollars. His small business was successful by most standards. It brought in enough for him to live comfortably and never have to touch his inheritance. He, like Melody, didn't care about the money in the way most folks did. As long as he had a decent roof over his head and plenty of food on the table, he considered himself well-off. His banker would classify him as a millionaire, but a million dollars didn't go as far these days. Now, the big deals were billionaires. Tiernan had no interest in reaching that stratosphere of wealth. He did just fine on what he made.

Prescott's SUV was parked in front of the cabin. The lawyer's arms were crossed as he leaned against his vehicle. He must have been standing there for quite some time.

Pulling up alongside him, Tiernan parked and exited the truck. He made an immediate cut around the front end of his vehicle in order to open Melody's door for her. Prescott followed. As soon as she exited the passenger side, he started with the news.

"The sheriff was on his way to bring Melody in for questioning," Prescott started, his tone heated. "I told him that I'd do the honors and that, as her attorney, I had a right to speak to her first anyway. I don't, by the way. But the sheriff didn't seem ready to push my buttons."

"Why would he want me to come in all of a sudden?" Melody asked, confusion drawing her eyebrows together. "All we did was sleep last night."

"Where have you been?" Prescott whirled around on them mid-pace.

"Out for breakfast," Tiernan cut in, not wanting Melody to have to answer. It was a partial truth. They technically had eaten food on the way down to Austin.

Prescott threw his hands up in the air. "I can't help you unless you trust me one hundred percent with the truth."

Melody shot a glance at Tiernan. One he recognized as her wanting to come clean. So, he gave a slight nod.

"I asked Tiernan if we could visit my brother this morning before we picked up Loki from the vet," she started.

Prescott looked ready to blow. "Why would you do that?" He paced the length of the truck. "Don't you trust me to handle this case? Because these day trips are hurting us more than you realize."

"What's that supposed to mean?" Tiernan asked, doing his level best to contain anger that was raging toward the surface.

Prescott stopped, dug his heels in the gravel and said, "Bebe Riker is dead and the last person on her cell phone records is Melody."

She gasped, immediately bringing her hand up to cover her mouth.

"We visited her and then you phoned her. We had plans," Tiernan said.

"I just called her again in the truck on the way over here,"

Melody admitted. "We were supposed to go over last night for dinner and—"

"I know," Prescott interrupted. "One of her employees overheard you making plans."

"How on earth? We were in the parking lot when we had that conversation and there was no one else around," Melody quipped.

"This is a reminder you both need to hear. Someone is always around either watching or listening. You were the last one in contact with Bebe on her cell and you had plans. Any district attorney worth his or her salt would come after you for the murder, building more of a case against you," Prescott said, his voice toned down a few notches at this point. Tiernan couldn't fault the lawyer for being frustrated with them. They probably shouldn't have gone out on their own without consulting him or at least dropping a text after the fact. Those last words, though, resonated.

Tiernan sat on the information while Prescott continued.

"As your attorney, I need to know what moves you're making that might make my job even more difficult," he said.

Melody sat down right there on the gravel, cross-legged, a mix of emotions flashing behind her eyes. Anger. Sadness. Guilt. Regret. Tiernan had an overwhelming urge to give her a hand up and then bring her into an embrace.

"Give us a minute," he practically growled to the lawyer. From the corner of his eye, he saw Prescott's jaw nearly drop to the ground when he'd pulled Melody against his chest and then looped his arms around her waist.

Prescott disappeared inside his own vehicle a second later. He had questions about their relationship. The sheriff had insinuated they'd pulled this off as a couple. Being a couple would damage both of their defenses. So being a couple wasn't something Tiernan could afford to want. It wouldn't be good for Melody. *For Melody's case*, he corrected.

MELODY PULLED AWAY from Tiernan and forced her chin up. Two lives were lost…and for what? The senseless loss was staggering. The fire was clearly an attempt on her and Tiernan's lives. If they hadn't escaped, there would be four people dead. And to what end? Three of those people were tied together by one man… Henry Cooper Cantor II.

What about her brother, Coop? Why was he safe? Or was he? Was someone knocking down the Cantor children one at a time?

"I'm okay," she finally said to Tiernan. His face twisted and she immediately knew he could tell she was fudging the truth. "I'll *be* okay." She needed a minute to breathe and process what was happening so she could decide her next steps.

"Take your time," Tiernan said, ever the sea of calm. She had no idea what she would've done without him over the past couple of days. She'd grown to depend on his steady nature even though he caused butterflies to release in her chest. Trust wasn't something she was used to giving freely, so she was walking in foreign territory. He hadn't given her a reason not to believe he would be there as much as she needed him to be. Not only had he volunteered to help her see this through, but he was also following through on the commitment. Until he showed her otherwise, she would risk believing in him.

Melody took a couple of laps around the truck to work off some of her stress. She returned to speak to Tiernan, who gave a nod for Prescott to join them. The lawyer did and the three of them resumed their conversation.

"I suggested we go speak to my brother because I believe

in my heart that I would be able to see right through him if he lied to me," she said by way of apology. "If you want to point a finger at someone, blame me."

"I'm trying to keep you out of prison," Prescott said in a far calmer voice now. "And I'm trying to keep others from accusing you of a crime you didn't commit."

She nodded and thanked him.

"Was he lying?" Prescott asked.

"Yes," she admitted. As much as she didn't want to deliver the news, it was the honest truth.

"His vehicle was warm, even though he denied leaving home this morning," Tiernan interjected. "He also said he could produce tickets to the Longhorn game he was at during the break-in and theft at their mother's home." He paused long enough to clench his back teeth. "Something you said a few minutes ago resonated with me. There's surveillance everywhere, so we should be able to track down whether or not he was actually at the game."

Prescott was nodding and taking notes on his cell phone.

"We felt bad for Jason's mother," Melody said. "It's the main reason we went to see her. My father rejected his own child. The kid was doing well until he tracked down his biological father. Then, he spiraled." She didn't speak the words that having any contact with her father was toxic. They hung in the air anyway. "We were planning to have dinner with her last night when the fire broke out and changed our plans."

"Speaking of cameras," Prescott started. "What about here?"

"I didn't lock my doors before this situation occurred," Tiernan admitted. "Why would I think I had a need for watching a deer cross my lawn?"

"Fair point. This area is considered one of the safest," Prescott agreed.

"Not much else beats it except for my hometown of Cider Creek," Tiernan added. She would like to go there someday. Possibly even meet his family. His mother had been through hell and back, but she must be a remarkable person if she brought up six children after losing the love of her life. The woman got brownie points for surviving a loss of that magnitude and being able to march ahead. It didn't sound like she'd remarried, either. Instead, she'd stayed on at a ranch to be near the man she loved. Tiernan hadn't said those exact words but it wasn't hard to put two and two together.

"The paper from the note on Melody's vehicle and the one in Jason's pocket matched," Prescott said, confirming they most likely came from the same source.

"My brother said he took a trip to our family cabin." Melody hopped back in the conversation. "Tiernan and I were planning to pick up Loki on our way to check it out. There would be signs if he'd visited recently."

Prescott nodded. "Would you be considered trespassing?"

"I know where the spare key is," she said a little too defensively.

"Be careful," Prescott instructed, not that he needed to. Melody had no plans to let her guard down.

"We will," Tiernan promised.

"Let me know whatever you find, if anything," Prescott further requested. "Take pictures and treat the place like a crime scene."

"Got it," Tiernan said. He'd talked about growing up on a cattle ranch. She intended to ask him why he was so good at investigations.

Prescott tucked his cell phone away. "I'll see what I can do about getting footage from the Longhorn game on the night of the break-in. I suspect a ticket was bought but never used. And I'll work it out with the sheriff so you don't have to go to his office. He can go through me for information for the time being."

"Speaking of which, information is a two-way street, right?" Tiernan asked the lawyer, who nodded. They exchanged quick goodbyes before Prescott headed out. The lawyer's vehicle kicked up dust from the gravel, causing it to disappear.

"Can we pick up Loki now?" Melody asked, waving her hand in the air, missing the black Lab who was a bundle of energy and unconditional love. He had convinced her that she needed a dog in her life.

"Let's go," Tiernan said, motioning toward the truck.

Loki was the easy part. It was a no-brainer to see him. The cabin? Not so much after what had happened during her last visit.

Chapter Twenty

Loki was a sight for sore eyes as Dr. Paul brought him out to the parking lot. Tiernan took a knee as the energetic Lab came bolting toward him. Impact nearly knocked Tiernan over so he put a hand down behind him for balance.

"He did great last night," Dr. Paul said as Melody dropped down next to Tiernan. He didn't hate having her by his side. Loki bounced from him to her and back in a heartbeat, taking all the affection he could get out of them.

It did the heart good to see him in such great shape.

"Everything checks out?" Tiernan asked.

"He's fit as a fiddle," Dr. Paul said. "Already had a hearty breakfast and a few extra treats for being such a good patient."

Loki ran over to the grassy area in the empty lot and took care of business. Tiernan stood and went through the motions of checking his empty pockets for a bag.

"Ralph will take care of that," Dr. Paul said. He and his partner had gone into business together years ago instead of having children.

"Thank you," Tiernan said. "And thank you for everything you did for Loki."

Dr. Paul's smile was ear to ear. The pride he took in his

work showed in times like these. Melody surprised both of them by walking over and giving Dr. Paul a quick hug.

"This guy has become very important to all of us it seems," she said, motioning toward the black Lab that had bounded over to her side. If that didn't twist Tiernan's insides, he didn't know what would. Hearing her say those words stirred more of the feelings he'd been trying to avoid since Corinne. When he really thought about it, he'd never felt this kind of connection to his ex. Melody was the new bar for future relationships.

"Loki is special," Dr. Paul said before adding, "There are no follow-up instructions. He doesn't need any medication and can go on living his normal spoiled life."

"Will do," Tiernan said before walking over to his truck with Loki in tow. Tiernan opened the door and the Lab jumped right inside. Melody followed after taking the hand he'd offered, reclaiming the passenger seat. By the time she'd clicked on her seat belt, Tiernan had exchanged a handshake with Dr. Paul.

Sliding into the driver's seat, he was struck at how suddenly Melody had shown up in his world. But then life was full of surprises. He needed to take note of that fact the next time storm clouds covered the sun and his world darkened.

She gave him the address to the family cabin, which he immediately plugged into the GPS. They had a little more than an hour to kill. Longer if they stopped off for food.

Traffic wasn't bad. The burritos were even better. The cabin took ten extra minutes to reach after the stop at the largest gas station/convenience store in the state. They needed a Buc-ee's in Cider Creek. The promise of clean bathrooms along with more fuel pumps, food options, and road snacks than anyone could imagine made pit stops here a destination. Then again, he hadn't been home in so long there might already be one there and he wasn't any the wiser. On the rare times he'd called his mother, she never mentioned anything had changed. Buc-ee's would be a topic of conversation. Guilt slammed into him for the neglect he showed his family. Duncan Hayes was gone. As much as Tiernan didn't wish anyone harm, he couldn't muster a tear for his dear old grandfather, either.

The Cantor cabin was more like a lake house. It was an A-frame made from wood. There was a porch and a second-story balcony of almost equal size. The place was all windows and views.

"I thought you said this was a cabin in the woods," he said to Melody as he parked.

Her forehead creased as she shot him a look. "I haven't been here in so long. It seems smaller to me now."

"I get that you didn't want to use this place given its purchase history," he said, but he'd also picked up on something else in her tone when she mentioned it before.

"There's more to it," she said. "How about I tell you later?"

"We don't even have to talk about it if the subject makes you uncomfortable," he said. There was no need unless she felt like telling him what the tone in her voice was about. He'd picked up on the subtle sadness.

"I want to talk," she quickly countered. "Not with everyone. But I don't mind telling you. I actually haven't told anyone so much about my family and our relationship in such a long time." She paused for a second. Long enough to bite down on her bottom lip—lips that were in the shape of Cupid's bow and darn kissable. "Actually, I never discuss my family with anyone else. You're the first person to hear my side of the story."

He smiled at her before heading out of the truck. The

fact she wanted to share her secrets with him caused more of that stirring in his chest that he'd been trying and succeeding in avoiding for many years up until now. He was clearly failing when it came to Melody. She was a rogue storm that blew into his life unexpectedly and without all the damage left behind. She was the good kind with lightning that cut across a velvet sky and thunder that caused the walls to rattle.

Then again, they would have to part ways at some point. The thought darn near gutted him. But what did he plan to do about it? Right now? Nothing.

Tiernan opened her door and then refocused on the cabin. The place was nice. There was a tire swing hanging from a large oak tree. He suspected there was a lake or some kind of water source nearby. He'd better keep an eye on Loki since he loved gunning straight for just such places, coming back drenched, muddy and happy as a lark. Or sprayed by a skunk. Tiernan never knew what he was going to get with his oversize pup but he could bank on trouble following.

"Watch out for tracks leading up to the house," he said to Melody. At this point it was later in the afternoon. The sun was out today, warming his skin. There was a chill in the air like nobody's business. His thoughts wandered to his own family and how they were doing. Seeing what Melody was going through with her family reminded him to be a better son. Other than Duncan, his family was loving. They were good people who cared about one another. Why was it so much easier to hate a jerk than to focus on the good people in his life?

"Okay," Melody said, checking the ground as she walked toward the A-frame. She spun around. "Do you think we should hide the fact we're here?"

"What did you have in mind?" he asked.

"Parking a little bit away from the house," she clarified. "I mean, I doubt my brother would show up here but he might send someone. My mother could show up at some point. I don't come here any longer and haven't for years so I have no idea what anyone's habits are."

"Good idea," Tiernan said. "Can you keep Loki with you?"

Loki had other ideas. He followed Tiernan back to the truck.

"Never mind," Tiernan said. "I'll take him with me instead." He paused at the door to his truck. "Do you want to come with us?"

"You'll only be a minute, right?" she asked.

"All I intend to do is park outside of view. Just up the lane a little bit," he said. "You should be fine until I get back."

"I grew up coming here," she said. "I still know this place like the back of my hand. Go on. I'm good here."

Tiernan climbed into the driver's seat after allowing Loki passage. The night at the vet's office did him good. The Lab had more energy than Tiernan had seen in a while, which was saying something.

There was a spot to pull off not too far from the A-frame that should keep the truck blocked from view. The good thing was that no one knew what Tiernan's truck looked like. Correction—Melody's brother would know if he'd been paying attention this morning. Coop had looked stressed out, so those details might have escaped him. The guy had been cagey, and Tiernan didn't pick up on one single warm vibe toward Melody. Would it be the same with his siblings when he visited home again? He couldn't imagine a world where the Hayes kids, grown as they might be, would turn against each other. Self-interest was the only vibe Tiernan had received from Coop. The guy could be a younger, more deviant version of Duncan, which probably didn't help much.

Tiernan was predisposed to not liking the guy based on the association with his grandfather. Was it fair to put them both in the same bucket? Maybe not. Tiernan hadn't spent enough time around Coop to decide one hundred percent if his instincts about the guy were correct. But then, initial impressions were usually right.

Hiking back to the A-frame, Loki bolted. Not unusual for the pup, but the move was unsettling to Tiernan in this situation. His radar was already on high alert as it was. The last thing he needed was another reason to be stressed.

Rather than shout for his dog, he kept a low profile. If Loki took off too far, he would be bringing home ticks at the very least. The dog had a way of finding trouble, Tiernan was learning. So, he headed in the direction his dog had taken off to instead of the A-frame.

"Loki," he whispered.

When no dog came tearing through the woods, Tiernan whistled. Still nothing. He bit back a few curse words that would make Granny blush. Thinking about home earlier made him miss all the important people in his life. Or maybe it was the fact he seemed to be surrounded by death—death had a way of reminding people to live.

MELODY CHECKED THE ground for footprints leading up to the front door. This time of year, wind whipped the dirt around so she didn't expect to find any. Her assumption was correct. She wasn't sure exactly what to look for other than obvious signs, like a light being left on. Her brother hadn't washed a load of laundry in his life. There would most likely be dirty clothes in the master bathroom in a hamper. What else?

The front door was locked, which wasn't unusual. The planter still held the key. Sun reflected off the windows, making it impossible to see inside. Being back at this house after decades away, she had no idea what the place looked like any longer.

Walking inside was like stepping into a time capsule. Between the pair of long, white couches facing each other in the living room and the antler chandelier over a massive dining table next to the kitchen, not much had changed. The lamps even looked the same as she remembered. A white marble coffee table sat in the middle of the room. Two benches opposite each other along with the couches formed a loose box around the coffee table in the living room. The place was set up for entertaining. The dining table seated twelve. Happy memories from her childhood and teenage years came flooding back. Granted, they were pleasant because she had no idea what her family truly was at the time…a house of cards ready to be blown away by the first strong wind.

Brently's family had come here, too. This room at sunset had housed their engagement party. Even then, during the height of her obliviousness to how bad her father truly was, there'd been a little voice in the back of her mind asking if Brently was *the one*. Was he comfort? Familiarity? The known?

Looking back, her heart never raced in the way it did when Tiernan was nearby. No one made her feel so out of control in a way that was exciting and comforting instead of scary. He'd been right by her side during this whole ordeal—an ordeal that needed to end with justice carried out.

Starting in the living room, there weren't any lights left on. The room was bright from the sun, so she methodically checked each bulb and light switch to be sure. Blankets had been tossed onto the sofas and not straightened, but that didn't exactly mean anything. There was a small, local cleaning service that used to come before and after family trips here. Did the pair of sisters still clean the house?

Moving into the dining room, nothing seemed out of place. There wasn't much inside this area except for a curio cabinet that housed dishes and a couple of decorative vases along with the large table and chairs. There were no signs of the room being disrupted in any way.

In the kitchen, there were no dishes in the sink. She checked the dishwasher. None inside there, either. Of course, it stood to reason the cleaning ladies might have come and gone. Coop would never make the call himself, but Janice might. She'd probably stepped into the role of Melody's mother after the divorce. There was so much she didn't know about her own family now that she'd severed ties for the most part. It was an odd feeling. Mother, Coop, her sister-in-law, even her father were essentially strangers to her now.

The bathroom hamper was empty. Then, it dawned on her to check the fridge. The cleaners never threw out food if it hadn't expired. Melody made the trek back into the kitchen to check.

Halfway through the living room, a noise outside startled her.

"Tiernan?" she asked as she moved toward the sound. The front door was cracked open, and an uneasy feeling someone was watching her pricked the tiny hairs on the back of her neck.

Chapter Twenty-One

Tiernan trudged through the scrub toward the sound of Loki panting and twigs breaking. The dog was trouble times ten. It was a good thing Tiernan had an almost endless well of patience with animals. People, not so much. Except when it came to Melody. She was the exception to pretty much every rule he'd ever made and tried to enforce.

"Loki, come," Tiernan said with authority as Loki blew by.

The dog did an about-face and bolted back to Tiernan's side. He darn near fist-pumped the victory. Since he was turned around, he headed back toward where he believed the road to be, found it and then walked to the A-frame. By now Melody might have some sense of whether or not her brother had, in fact, visited like he'd said or if that was another in a growing list of deceptions.

The front door was cracked open, so he walked inside and glanced around.

"Melody," he called out.

There was no response. Tiernan's pulse jacked through the slanted roof. He probably should have brought his shotgun from home for protection but hadn't thought of it. Tiernan bit back a curse. Since he could see straight into the kitchen, he headed there for a weapon as Loki tore through the downstairs at almost full speed. All the rest he'd gotten at the vet's last night was causing him to bounce off the walls at this point. Tiernan wished he'd had time to throw the tennis ball to work off some of that puppy energy.

After locating a cleaver, Tiernan took the steps two at a time, doing his level best to be quiet. There was a small landing with several oversize beanbag chairs, and a pair of bedrooms with what looked like a Jack-and-Jill bathroom in between.

An animal-like grunt came from the room on the left. Tiernan bolted toward it with Loki jumping in front. Loki stopped. His ears came up, his hackles raised, and a low, throaty growl tore from his throat.

Tiernan moved to the side of the door frame before having a look inside. Melody sat on the bed. She had tape over her mouth, her hands and ankles were bound, and she was rope-tied to the bedpost. Every muscle in Tiernan's body corded. He had to suppress the instinct to run to her because whoever did this to her was nowhere in sight.

The second her eyes met his, she tried to warn him. She motioned toward the closet and then shook her head. Her wide fearful eyes were knife stabs. The coil in his chest tightened to the point of pain.

But it was the snick of a bullet being lodged in a chamber that came from behind him that demanded his immediate attention. He turned sideways so he could keep an eye on Melody.

"Hands up," came the sheriff's voice. Cleve Tanner stood on the landing.

Startled by the voice and the noise, Loki turned and barked. He didn't seem to know which way to fix his attention, committing to neither side.

Tanner had on jeans and a sweatshirt along with his boots. There wasn't a hint of law enforcement employment on anything he wore, which said a whole lot about his intentions.

Considering there was a gun pointed at him, Tiernan complied with the request. The second the sheriff saw the knife, he zeroed in on the center of Tiernan's chest with the barrel of his gun.

"Set the knife down on the carpet, along with your cell phone," Tanner instructed. "Make a move that I don't like and all three of you are dead. Guess who'll go first?" He shifted the barrel to point at Loki.

Tiernan pulled on every ounce of self-discipline to refrain from charging at the sheriff to tackle him at the knees. Right now, Cleve Tanner had the upper hand. The lawman knew it, too. Once again, Tiernan complied, but he clamped his jaw so tightly that he feared his back teeth might crack. To hell with it.

He fished his cell from his pocket, and then slowly dropped down.

"Kick them toward me when you're done," the sheriff instructed.

"I don't know how you expect me to do that with a knife," Tiernan said, rolling his cell in the man's direction.

"Toss it," the sheriff said. "But if it hits me, your dog is the first to die."

Carefully, Tiernan chucked the knife. Fighting the urge to lunge at the sheriff, Tiernan slowly stood up.

"You're okay," he reassured Loki in as calm a tone as he could muster. A not-so-silent rage was boiling to the surface inside him. He was no match for a gun. This situation must have caught the sheriff off guard because there was no silencer. Tiernan put his hands in the air. "What next,

Sheriff? What do you plan to do? You couldn't kill us in my workshop."

"That wasn't me," the lawman said before seeming to catch himself.

Melody was going crazy in the next room, trying to communicate something. Loki's nerves were fried. The unpredictable pup was causing near cardiac arrest for Tiernan.

"Tie him up," the sheriff said as Loki looked on. His growl was enough to put fear in an MMA fighter. "And tell the woman to be still or I'll shoot you next."

Why the sheriff hadn't fired already dawned on Tiernan. An investigation could tie this place to the crime. There would be blood spatter everywhere. Too much to fully clean it all. The sheriff knew all the ins and outs. His DNA could be linked to the scene. It was amazing what forensics could do with a small hair sample in this day and age. Threats were one thing. Discharging the weapon was a different ballgame. So, Tiernan would have a little leeway.

The fire in the sheriff's eyes said he'd do it if that was the only way.

"I'm going to take a knee to calm my dog down," Tiernan said as he slowly lowered himself. This had the added benefit of making him a smaller target. Besides, if the sheriff shot at Loki, Tiernan had no qualms about taking the bullet instead. He held on to his dog by the collar. The move worked. Loki's tail was going a mile a minute but he stopped the rapid-fire barking.

"Shut her up now," the sheriff demanded.

"It's going to be okay, Melody," Tiernan reassured. He turned to her and winked to communicate he understood what she was trying to tell him. Someone else was there. The person hadn't made themselves known. Tiernan couldn't figure out the sheriff's involvement. What did he have to gain by implicating Melody? Why wasn't he investigating Coop?

"What's the endgame here, Sheriff?" Tiernan asked. By his count, the sheriff was outnumbered. Then again, Melody had indicated someone else was around. Was the person in the closet the mastermind behind this all? To what end? What was there to gain?

Tiernan's cell buzzed. The sheriff's muscles tensed. The screen was visible. John Prescott.

"You had to get other people involved," the sheriff said. "You couldn't leave well enough alone."

"He's on to you," Tiernan hedged. "And he's heading this way." The little white lie might force the sheriff's hand. "If I don't pick up, he'll be suspicious."

"How stupid do you think I am?" the sheriff asked, shaking his head. "You answer and you'll give him some type of signal behind my back. I'm not stupid, Hayes."

"Speaking of last names," Tiernan continued. He saw how rattled the sheriff had become and how much he was trying to cover. It was the little things giving him away now. The twitch just below his left eye. The way his chest moved up and down a little faster because his breathing was shallow. A shot of adrenaline would do that to a person. "Mine is well known in this state. Do you think my family will accept my disappearance? My murder? Because I know they would move heaven and earth to find the person responsible for my death."

The sheriff needed to know the field he was playing in.

"Aren't you an elected official?" Tiernan asked. "You can kiss that job goodbye. But then, you'll be living in a cell anyway. Do you know what inmates do to former law enforcement officers?"

He still couldn't piece together why the sheriff would be

involved in any of this. Cleve Tanner didn't strike Tiernan as being exceptionally bright.

"You'd better get out here, Mr. Cantor," the sheriff finally called out after a long pause. "This one is causing trouble, and you have to make a call as to what to do next. This is more than I'm getting paid for." The secret was out now. The sheriff was being bought off to set Melody up for murder. Getting rid of Melody would have made it impossible for her to defend herself in court. Murders that Coop Cantor had committed with a possible assist from a lawman.

Coop Cantor came flying out of the closet. "What the hell?"

Loki went crazy, lunging toward him. Coop backed up a couple of steps until his back was against the window.

"Call the dog off," Coop demanded. Sweat dripped from his forehead. His armpits were stained.

"Are you seriously planning to kill your own sister?" Tiernan asked as he stayed crouched low. "Because you'll never get away with it."

Coop shot a look that said he had the law on his side, and it was standing behind Tiernan with a gun aimed at his back.

"Have you ever killed someone?" Tiernan asked. "Because I have. It was an accident, but I still have nightmares. I still see Mary Jane's face when I close my eyes. Watch her drown all over again as I stood there frozen on the pool deck thinking that she was being silly and not taking her last breaths." The made-up story rolled off his tongue and seemed to be having the right effect. Coop shifted his weight as he white-knuckled the windowsill behind him.

"This situation is complicated," the sheriff said. "I didn't sign up for this. I did my part and you were supposed to handle the rest."

Tiernan wished he had his cell phone so he could record

this conversation. It was too far away to reach. Any sudden movement would backfire. He had, however, managed to unclip Loki's collar. The studs on it could do serious damage wrapped around his fist as he delivered a punch. Get him close and he could take down the sheriff. Coop was strong and athletic. Not as fit as Tiernan, though.

The numbers were off. It was two against one since Melody was tied to the bed. One of them had a gun.

This tension in the room ratcheted up a few more notches with Loki going wild. Tiernan called his dog, noticing Loki had positioned himself in between Coop and Melody. Did the Lab mix have a protective instinct that Tiernan hadn't witnessed before?

"Shut the dog up," Coop demanded, his voice rising in panic. Panic wasn't a good thing except that it could serve as a distraction. The sheriff took a step closer to Tiernan. The man was almost near enough to spring toward and disarm.

Out of the corner of his eye, he saw that Melody had just freed her hands from the bedpost. Her movements were subtle and the chaos with Loki drew attention away from her.

In a flash, their gazes locked. Tiernan knew exactly what to do.

MELODY JUMPED UP, hopped a couple of steps, and threw herself at Coop. She'd worked her wrists free from the ties, ignoring the burn. A bullet split the air. There was no time to check for injuries or see if it hit a target. The window broke from the sheer force of his weight, and her brother fell backward with a shocked look on his face. He was half in, half out and trying to grab hold to keep from falling.

She might not know her family any longer but the same was true of them. They had no idea who she was or what she was capable of doing. She grabbed her brother by the legs. He tried to buck her off, but he nearly lost his grip and plunged to the ground. A fall like this one probably wouldn't kill him unless he landed wrong.

"What the hell, sis?" Coop asked. The last word came across like fingernails on a chalkboard after what he'd tried to do to her.

Since he was bigger, stronger and more athletic, she had to make a difficult decision. She picked up his legs and pushed as hard as she could.

"Are you trying to kill me?" Coop asked, surprise in his voice. And a little panic, too. One hand was gripping the frame while the other dangled outside.

With no time to waste, she leaned forward and bit his fingers. One last shove and her brother dropped like a hundred-and-eighty-five-pound bowling ball. Despite the bastard Coop had become, her heart hurt as she heard him scream out in pain at the landing. She risked a glance and saw that a bone had come through the leg of one of his trousers. He was alive, though.

Melody immediately turned in time to see Tiernan on top of the sheriff, squeezing him with his powerful thighs. The sound of a vehicle pulling onto the gravel drive twisted her stomach in a knot.

Chapter Twenty-Two

"We have company," Melody said while Tiernan squeezed his thighs harder as he pinned down the sheriff. Between Tiernan and Melody, they'd done well. They made a good team. One Tiernan wasn't quite ready to walk away from. They had company outside and he feared this fight was just beginning.

"Do you know how to shoot a gun?" he asked her. He could hold the sheriff if she could handle whatever walked up those stairs.

"No," she admitted. "I'm guessing it isn't that difficult."

"I can walk you through everything you need to know," he said, motioning toward where the Glock had flown after knocking it out of the sheriff's hand.

Loki bolted toward the open-concept stairwell. At least they would be able to see whoever walked through the door from this vantage point. The dog might offer a distraction, a moment of hesitation that could give Melody a clear shot.

"Go over there," Tiernan said, motioning toward the opposite side of the landing. "Pop up, aim and shoot."

Melody nodded. Her hands trembled and there were red marks on her wrists. There were fifteen rounds in a Glock

19. One had been fired as Tiernan had wrestled for control of the weapon.

The sheriff tried to buck Tiernan off. He fired off a punch that sent blood shooting from the sheriff's nose. Sitting on top of a lawman while Melody had the guy's gun didn't look good. Of course, Tiernan wasn't expecting a deputy to walk through the door.

"Knock, knock." Prescott's voice was a welcomed relief coming from the front door.

"Don't shoot," Tiernan whispered.

Melody set the gun down and backed away from it. "We're in here and we're alive."

From their vantage point at the top of the stairs, they watched as the front door opened and the lawyer walked in.

"There's a mess up here," Tiernan immediately said.

"There's another one outside, too," Prescott said as Loki practically bowled him over.

"The sheriff is dirty," Tiernan explained as Melody kept far enough away to stay free of any wild arms or feet should any break loose. "And he's trying to knock the daylights out of me right now."

Prescott held up his cell phone. "Help is on the way. I already called for law enforcement and an ambulance."

"How did you know to come here?" Tiernan asked.

Prescott held up his cell phone. "Easy to track the sheriff's location with tech nowadays after attaching a small device onto his service vehicle. Couldn't figure out why on earth he would follow you guys here."

"Did he plant those notes, too?" she asked.

"My guess is they were going to tie back to you at some point, so, it's likely," Prescott confirmed.

Melody dropped to her knees and put her face in her hands. "It's over. It's really over."

All he wanted to do right now was haul her against his chest and be her comfort, claim those lips as his. Right now, she deserved answers.

The lawyer crested the top of the stairs with his cell phone in his hand. "I'm going to get a recording of this." He tapped the screen. "What you're seeing here is my client being victimized by law enforcement." He looked to Tiernan. "As a witness who had to subdue the sheriff, can you offer a statement as to what happened here?"

Tiernan gave a quick and dirty rundown of the events. Prescott asked Melody to do the same. She provided her side and her encounter with her brother. Prescott walked around the upstairs and the bedroom where the events took place.

"Sheriff, you're going away for a long time unless you start talking," Prescott said. "I can't guarantee that you won't anyway, but your cooperation will go a long way toward a more lenient sentence. Then again, you already know how this works, don't you?"

"I didn't kill anyone," the sheriff conceded. "I got paid to make sure the evidence led back to Melody Cantor."

"Why?" Prescott asked as Melody excused herself, no doubt to check on her brother. "What did Coop have to gain? There wasn't any family money, was there?"

"All I know is that he needed to get rid of anyone who could come after the family money. There were trust funds set up and he would get all the money if his half-brother and sister were gone. He didn't want to kill Melody at first. If she was a felon he wouldn't have to. Her inheritance would fall to him," the sheriff explained. "Then, everything started getting complicated when Tiernan got involved. Coop said she was going to be an easy target because she had no one to turn to."

"To be clear, you were paid off to look the other way for

two murders, two attempted murders, *and* you were supposed to make sure the evidence for Jason's murder led back to Melody Cantor," Prescott surmised.

"Yes, sir. That sounds right," the sheriff admitted. This piece of human garbage needed to be locked up for the rest of his life. "The fire in the workshop was me."

"Your boot prints would have already been all over the area," Prescott deduced.

The sheriff nodded.

"Thank you," Prescott said as the sounds of sirens filled the air. He excused himself to meet law enforcement so he could explain the situation.

It took every ounce of willpower inside Tiernan to refrain from hammering the sheriff for the life he'd tried to destroy, the life of the woman Tiernan had fallen for. Greed was a disease in some folks. The sheriff must have seen Melody as his ticket to pad his retirement illegally.

A deputy came up the stairs within minutes. He took over for Tiernan, zip-cuffing the sheriff as another deputy removed the weapons and placed them in evidence bags.

"Why my land?" Tiernan asked, referring to burying Jason's body.

"It was a mistake to get you involved," the sheriff stated with remorse. Not for a life lost but most likely because he got caught. "It was remote, and I rarely saw anyone on the road behind your property."

The miscalculation was responsible for the sheriff's arrest.

Tiernan glanced up at the deputy, who nodded and then took over. The second Tiernan was freed of his duty to sit on the sheriff, he bolted downstairs. The scene in front of him as he stepped outside made him fall in love with Melody all the more. She sat on the edge of the porch, her arm around Loki, comforting him.

"Hey," Tiernan said, not wanting to startle her. "How do you feel about having company?" He could only imagine how awful it must be to learn her own flesh and blood had set her up for murder.

"Hey," she said back. She had a surprising amount of composure under the circumstances. "Sure, come on and sit down."

He joined them, sitting beside her.

"I don't have words to say how sorry I am your own brother was willing to hurt you in such a horrible way," he started, wishing he could take away her pain.

"Remember this morning when you realized my brother's truck hood was warm and he denied going anywhere?" she asked. He took note she didn't address his comment.

"I do," he said.

"He'd dropped my sister-in-law off at the airport along with their bags," she said, staring out onto the lawn as, one by one, the emergency vehicles pulled away. "I'm guessing the only reason we caught him at home was because he had to go into the office like everything was normal. Janice was never in Dubai. She was headed to Brazil. Coop was probably waiting for word of my arrest after stealing a bracelet my mother gave me when I turned eighteen and planting it."

"The bastard deserves the prison sentence he'll get for orchestrating this," Tiernan said. He would give an arm if it could take away a fraction of the sadness in her voice right now. This might not be the time to tell her how he felt about her. Not while she was still reeling from losing the last tether to her family. "I don't know who used the ticket for the Longhorn game, but it couldn't have been him."

"Or the sheriff just planned to cover that up, too," she said with disgust.

Prescott, who had been sitting in his vehicle and taking notes, exited and walked toward them. He held his cell out in front of him. "There's someone on the line who would like to speak to you."

Melody blinked a couple of times but didn't respond or reach for the phone.

"It's your father," Prescott said. "Maybe hear him out."

Melody took in a deep breath before Tiernan looped his arm around her waist. She leaned into him, causing all kinds of fireworks to go off inside his chest.

"Dad," Melody said after taking the offering.

"I'm sorry, Mellie," her dad said, reminding her of the nickname he'd called her most of her life before she walked away from the family.

"It was Coop," she clarified.

"I'm not talking about the ordeal you've just been through," he said. "I'm sorry for that, too. I owe you an apology for so much."

"Water under the bridge now," she said, not sure where this was going. "We don't have to rehash the past."

"I let you down and swore I would never do it again," he continued, unfazed. There was a kindness to his tone that she didn't recall ever being there. "I've had a lot of time to think recently, and all I can say is that I should have been the father you deserved. I wanted to be the person you looked up to when you were a little girl, Mellie."

Tears pricked the backs of her eyes at the admission.

"You stopped talking to us, to me, and I thought giving you space was for the best," he said. "But that wasn't fair to you, either. What I'm trying to say is that I'd like to become the person I saw in your eight-year-old eyes, and I'm just hoping I'm not too late."

A few rogue tears fell. She tucked her chin to her chest to hide the emotions spilling out of her eyes.

"It's hard, Dad," she said. "I want to believe you're different but I can tell you that I can't go back. You'd have to be honest with your dealings with me and everyone else before I could even consider it."

"I'll make the commitment right now if you'll promise to let me make this up to you," her father said.

She'd wanted to hear those words for so long. Could she trust him?

Tiernan's words came back to her. Without trust, she could never let anyone in, which sounded lonely. It was. It had been. And it was time for second chances.

"Okay," she said. "I'll try if you will."

"You've made me a happy father, Mellie," he said. She could hear the emotion welling up in his throat. "I have to go now. We'll talk soon."

"Sounds good, Dad," she said, betting there were hundreds if not thousands of grown women out there wishing they could have one more conversation with their father. Melody wouldn't waste this chance to let him make things right between them.

She ended the call and handed the cell phone back to Prescott.

"Your father asked me not to tell you this, but I refused because there's something you should know," Prescott said.

Melody cocked an eyebrow. "That is?"

"He's covering for your brother's actions. Coop was the one taking the money. Your father blindly signed off on the paperwork making him liable, and he refused to give his son up to the law. Said Coop was young and didn't belong behind bars for the rest of his life," Prescott said.

"Wait. What?" Melody couldn't hide her shock.

"I'm in the process of talking him into changing his plea. Now that he knows what Coop was doing with his freedom, your father is more inclined to come clean," Prescott informed. "Anyway, just thought you should know." He excused himself and disappeared first into his vehicle and then down the road.

Most people lived in a place somewhere between right and wrong. The gray area. Her father wasn't faithful in his marriage and that made the business dealings that much easier to believe. She figured Coop was responsible for Jason's murder, too. Had he even made a visit to their father? Or had Coop interceded?

There had to be some good in her brother, too. It was lost. Buried underneath layers of ice. But, someday, she hoped the casing would melt and he would find himself again. In the meantime, he was going to have a lot of time to think.

And then there was the man sitting beside her. She couldn't let another minute pass without speaking her mind.

She turned into him and got comfortable in the crook of his arm. She couldn't look into his eyes when she said the next words in case he didn't feel the same.

"Tiernan Hayes, I've never met anyone like you," she began. "I could live a whole lifetime and not meet another one like you." Suddenly, her mouth dried up. She pushed through the nerves and the awkwardness that came with not being able to say the words perfectly to express her feelings. "What I'm trying to tell you is that I've fallen in love with you, and it's okay if you don't feel the same way. I just thought you should know and..."

That was as far as she could go. It was like running out of gas, and she couldn't force another word out of her mouth.

Tiernan brought his hand around to her chin. He lifted her face so that she was looking directly into his eyes. "I've met a lot of folks in my life, but it wouldn't matter if I hadn't. There was something in my heart that recognized you almost from the minute I first met you. Like lightning striking. It's taken a minute to seed because I kept trying to convince myself that I didn't know you. But somewhere deep down, my soul recognized yours. I'm in love with you, Melody. I don't want this to end. Ever. Does that scare you?"

"Those six words are music to my soul," she said. "Because I can't imagine being with anyone but you."

"I'd like to take you to meet my family," he said. "It's time for me to go home and make things right. Will you go with me? Stay with me? Be with me?"

"Forever," was all she said, all she had to say for him to lean in and kiss her so tenderly it robbed her of breath. He pulled back just enough, his lips still gently pressed to hers.

"That's a good place to start," he said, his mouth moving against hers.

For the first time in Melody's life she was right where she belonged, with Loki and Tiernan. She'd found her man, her dog and her home. And there was no other place she wanted to be than right here in Tiernan's arms.

* * * * *

COMING SOON!

We really hope you enjoyed reading this book. If you're looking for more romance be sure to head to the shops when new books are available on

Thursday 12th October

MILLS & BOON
MODERN
Power and Passion

Prepare to be swept off your feet by sophisticated, sexy and seductive heroes, in some of the world's most glamourous and romantic locations, where power and passion collide.